7

ARMOUR-BEAKER

Mark Morgan

Bible
Tales
www.BibleTales.online

Published in Australia by Bible Tales Online.
www.BibleTales.online

The King's Armour-bearer

ISBN (eBook): 978-1-925587-34-0
ISBN (Paperback): 978-1-925587-33-3
ISBN (Hardcover): 978-1-925587-35-7

Cover picture: "Knight at the Crossroads"
by Viktor Mikhailovich Vasnetsov (1882).

Free Download

Paul in Snippets

A 109-page PDF novelette by Mark Morgan.

The life of Paul painted from the Acts of the Apostles.

Get your free copy of *Paul in Snippets* when you sign up for the Bible Tales mailing list. As well as the eBook, you will receive a weekly email newsletter with micro tales, informative articles and special offers.

Visit **https://www.BibleTales.online/free-pins**

www.BibleTales.online

To my ever-patient wife, Ruth.

THE KING'S ARMOUR BEARER

Contents

Foreword

This story began in the pressure-cooker atmosphere of NaNoWriMo[1] during November 2019. To "win" one must write a 50,000 word novel in a month and, as usual, there was far too much else in life to concentrate on. It was the third time that I had taken the NaNoWriMo challenge, so you might expect that I would have gained some skills of planning and making steady progress. But no, once again the last week of the month was a desperate attempt to make up the writing time that had been committed elsewhere earlier in the month. Nevertheless, desperation begets its own determination and the 50,000 word target was reached with *more than 3 hours to spare!* For some time, the manuscript stopped there, as other vital areas of life caught up, and it wasn't until February 2020 that I picked up the story again, reviewed the existing content and fleshed it out further. In 2021, I began a weekly eBook serial that provided the impetus I needed to finish the story which had grown to more than twice its NaNoWriMo-based beginnings.

This story differs from other novels I've written in that there is not much in the Bible about the time of King Jehoshaphat, and nothing at all about the protagonist I had chosen. In some ways, this gave me more freedom, but it also seemed to bring with it a greater responsibility to get things right! I can't really explain it, but I felt the need to make Ben-hail a true representative of a genuine warrior in Judah when King Jehoshaphat was leading his kingdom. I pray that my efforts in this have been at least partly successful.

Particular thanks go to Ruth, my wife, who helped me find time to write, patiently read what I wrote, and humoured me when I spent inordinate amounts of time on research into minute details.

No manuscript is ever without errors, but early readers have helped eliminate many typos, bad grammar and uncomfortable usage. Cathy, my oldest daughter, has tirelessly undertaken the thankless task of proof reading the entire manuscript more than once. Thanks, Cathy.

---

[1] www.nanowrimo.org

I have a request to make of you, dear reader: if you find any errors; typos, spelling errors, poor grammar, unkempt use of vocabulary, or, most importantly, errors of fact where the story misrepresents the Bible, please let me know. I can't correct printed books, but electronic versions and any new printed editions can be fixed.

Mark Morgan
September 2021

Resources

Jehoshaphat's family tree

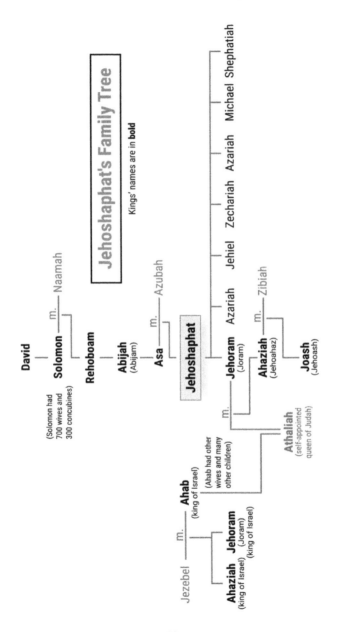

Ben-hail's family tree

Ben-hail's family tree is not found in the Bible and is made up for this story. However, some of the names included in his family tree are found in the Bible and they are shown in **bold**.

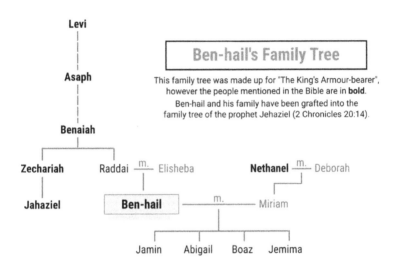

Judah

About 850BC

10 0 10 20 30 40 50   75   100
SCALE OF KILOMETRES

10   0   10   20   30   40   50
SCALE OF MILES

PHOENICIA

LEBANON

Mt. Hermon
(Sirion)

SYRIA
(ARAM)

MEDITERRANEAN SEA

MT CARMEL

Sea of
Galilee

BASHAN

Plain of
Megiddo

V. of Jezreel

Jezreel

Ramoth-
gilead

ISRAEL

Samaria

THE ARABAH

River Jordan

GILEAD

River Jabbok

HILL COUNTRY OF EPHRAIM

Bethel

Mizpah
Kiriath-   Ramah
jearim   Gibeon   Jericho

Rabbah

AMMON

Heshbon

Ekron

Jerusalem

PHILISTIA

Aijalon

Bethlehem

Tekoa

Wilderness
of Jeruel

Ascent
of Ziz

DEAD SEA

Mountains
of Abarim

The Shephelah (Lowland)

Hebron

Engedi

R. Arnon

MOAB

Gaza

JUDAH

Beersheba

Kir-hareseth

THE NEGEB

Approximate border of Judah

AMALEK

EDOM

Bozrah

- 12 -

Timeline of Jehoshaphat's life

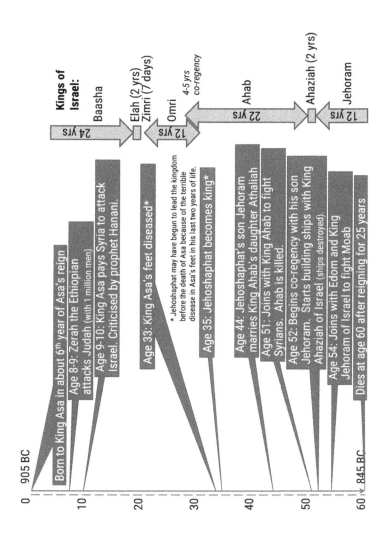

Kings of Israel:

Baasha — 24 yrs

Elah (2 yrs)
Zimri (7 days)
Omri — 12 yrs

4-5 yrs co-regency

Ahab — 22 yrs

Ahaziah (2 yrs)

Jehoram — 12 yrs

Born to King Asa in about 6th year of Asa's reign

Age 8-9: Zerah the Ethiopian attacks Judah (with 1 million men)

Age 9-10: King Asa pays Syria to attack Israel. Criticised by prophet Hanani.

Age 33: King Asa's feet diseased*

* Jehoshaphat may have begun to lead the kingdom before the death of Asa because of the terrible disease in Asa's feet in his last two years of life.

Age 35: Jehoshaphat becomes king*

Age 44: Jehoshaphat's son Jehoram marries King Ahab's daughter Athaliah

Age 51: Joins with King Ahab to fight Syrians. Ahab is killed.

Age 52: Begins co-regency with his son Jehoram. Starts building ships with King Ahaziah of Israel (ships destroyed).

Age 54: Joins with Edom and King Jehoram of Israel to fight Moab

Dies at age 60 after reigning for 25 years

905 BC

845 BC

0
10
20
30
40
50
60

Chapter 1

ABIEL'S ACADEMY

The upswing of the sword seemed effortless, but it was terrifyingly swift. Frantically, and only just in time, the heavy shield swung across, nudging the blow away so that the speeding blade passed harmlessly through air instead of tearing through flesh and sinew.

Smoothly the young attacker took advantage of his older opponent's unbalanced movement; a small turn of his supple wrist and the sword was now raised, angled to begin another lightning attack.

Fear made the defender's movements ungainly as he jumped desperately back.

"Enough, Ben-hail! Enough!"[2]

Ben-hail smiled suddenly and quickly lowered the point of his glittering sword until it touched the ground. It was as if his companion had interrupted some harmless teenage sport, not the deadly game of swordsmanship played out with naked blades.

"Sorry, Abiel," he said, breathing hard. "I was concentrating."

"You certainly weren't taking any hints," said Abiel. His voice shook a little, and his chest was heaving.

"I've been trying to speed up my attacks, sir. You told me that if you hurry your adversary they're more likely to make mistakes."

"I suppose I did. But I didn't expect you to use it against me!"

"I was trying as hard as I could against you because it's safe – you're so much better than I am with a sword that I know you'll never be in any danger, even if I get everything right at the same time."

"Ah, I see," said Abiel thoughtfully. It was true that he was a master of swordsmanship, and that he always encouraged his students to try their hardest against him. The fear he had felt in the last few moments was unprecedented. Ben-hail was growing up fast, he thought ruefully, and showed an astonishing aptitude for sword-fighting.

---

[2] Ben-hail was an official of King Jehoshaphat named in 2 Chronicles 17:7.

"Did you like my last upper thrust, Abiel? I tried to make it as powerful as possible without putting myself in danger of losing my balance when you parried it."

"It was very well directed, Ben-hail, and your transition was faster than anything you've used against me before." In truth, it was faster than anything he had ever seen before from *anyone*, either in training or in battle.

"Thanks, Abiel. It felt good. But I wasn't so happy with my defence earlier. It felt too slow. Do you have any other suggestions as to how I can speed up more?"

The older man wiped his hand across his brow and shook his head slowly. At first, he couldn't remember any moment in their bout in which Ben-hail had moved with anything less than frightening speed. For the first time, Abiel realised that if he had to fight to the death with his protégé, he would have no hope of victory. Putting the thought out of his mind, he tried to relax and think back over every move Ben-hail had made; to assess the bout impartially. He had to acknowledge that all of the young man's moves had been the actions of a master, yet even so, with the removal of the threat of that naked blade, Abiel's expert eye could discern room for improvement. For a moment he struggled to overcome his pride, then took a deep breath and offered the advice that would surely enable his pupil to further outstrip him in swordsmanship.

Ben-hail listened carefully to the expert advice, then applied the new ideas as the two of them faced each other again. He was a quick learner, and after half-an-hour of practice, the new arts had been explored, mastered and seamlessly added to his already breathtaking array of skills.

As they continued to fence, Abiel was on his guard, doing his best to prevent Ben-hail from slipping into that state of complete concentration where all his movements became as smooth and swift as those of a striking snake. It was not easy; for with Ben-hail, that concentration was his normal state of being when handling a sword.

The training bout finally finished after a testing hour, and Abiel was glad to have it done. The session had been an eye-opener to him. After just two years of training, this stripling had clearly eclipsed his teacher. Yet Abiel was not just *any* teacher: he was acknowledged as the best fighter with sword and shield in all Judah. It was tempting for him to suggest to himself that age was catching up with him, but he knew that it wasn't true. It was not his own greater age that made his opponent so difficult to fight: it was that Ben-hail had an easy freedom of movement that made even the most complex of athletic manoeuvres seem simple. What was more, the athleticism was blended with an efficiency that made his every move achieve twice as much as it would with anybody else. With newly-opened eyes, Abiel had seen the truth: Ben-hail made him look – and feel – old and awkward.

Abiel sent Ben-hail away to join the roster of students preparing the evening meal, and immediately called his second-best student, Beker, from a nearby practice area. Abiel wanted to test his skills; he needed to prove to himself that he wasn't too old to fight.

For the next half-hour, Beker fought valiantly, using all of his considerable skill in both defence and attack, but Abiel was like a circling hornet, always out of reach until he attacked with delicate precision and lightning speed. His opponent looked lost in the face of the onslaught, and a trickle of blood on his arm showed where Abiel had effortlessly threaded his sword through Beker's defence and gleefully touched his arm. Were it not for Abiel's great skill in stopping the thrust, Beker would have been badly injured, but even so, the instructor was not pleased with himself – he had allowed his self-satisfaction to overcome his professionalism.

The session went well for Abiel and he felt much better at the end of it. His technical skill had not been challenged and his ability to predict exactly what his student would do next had carried him through without danger. He could almost excuse the pinking of his student in the joy of knowing that his skill had not deserted him.

His work finished for the day, he walked away from the practice area, pleased, but marvelling more than ever at the consummate skill of his master student.

With a sword in his hand, Ben-hail was certainly something to marvel at.

$$\infty$$

Since the days of King David, and probably longer, the army of Israel had made a practice of gathering together soldiers who stood out from the rest of the army because of their courage and excellence. Stories were still told of David's mighty men and their amazing achievements[3] – though some soldiers now followed modern, disparaging ideas and said with knowing smiles that the stories were mere exaggerations and overstatements. Not surprisingly, they weren't the sort of soldier who ended up in the king's elite troops! No, King Asa's mighty men were those who believed in the heroes of the past, and were confident that men could still achieve amazing deeds.

Ben-hail was the most convinced of them all. The death of his father had left his mother a widow, and Ben-hail was her only son. Four days after his seventeenth birthday, he had left home and joined the army of

---

[3] 2 Samuel 23:8-39; 1 Chronicles 11:11-47

Judah. He had his own reasons for this – reasons which he never discussed with anyone, not even his mother.

By then he was already a strapping young man, and such men were needed to defend the kingdom. He joined as a volunteer, but always with the intention of winning a place in the regular army – a feat that volunteers could achieve through displays of skill and courage. Ben-hail quickly showed both, and was subsequently invited to attend one of the training academies dotted about the kingdom, where promising young volunteers were given training to equip them for permanent work in the army of Judah. Ben-hail had been fortunate enough to be assigned to the country's foremost academy, run by Abiel, a leader amongst Asa's mighty men. Abiel was a superb swordsman and an acknowledged expert at training soldiers. His successful training methods included some new ideas that concentrated on developing both physical fitness and technical skill. Under his guidance, Asa's army had become much more professional.

Even in his early training, Ben-hail stood out. He was outstandingly athletic, and his tutors were convinced that he only needed a little guidance to achieve amazing results as a fighter – and possibly as a leader, too.

Over the two years that had followed, many of their expectations had been fulfilled. Ben-hail's physical presence was intimidating: his shoulders grew ever wider and his steadily increasing height left him towering over the smaller students. His powerful arms could bend and loose a bow with both ease and accuracy, and his stamina was the envy of many another student. Even after using a sword for several hours, he seemed to lose none of his speed or accuracy of movement. In short, he was the ideal student, and many of his tutors began to wonder if this young man might be the one to win the coveted Grand Prize.

But at the moment, the Grand Prize was taking a back seat. The nation's need for champions was greater than any mere prize. Judah was surrounded by enemies and the army was under pressure. Not only so, but activities on the border made many wonder if there were also enemies within.

Chapter 2

KING ASA

King Asa sat on the roof of his palace in the late afternoon sun. He felt old: the responsibilities of rulership weighed him down.

He should be busy with some of the never-ending tasks of leadership, judgement and decision that he had shouldered for almost 40 years. But he was too tired, and the pain in his foot seemed to be getting worse every day.[4] He must see a doctor about it again.[5]

He was never completely alone, but at that moment, only his personal attendant was with him on the roof, and even he was discreetly out of sight. He had sent away his bodyguard – although he was sure that they wouldn't be far away. They never were. No doubt, if he called, they would be on the roof within moments.

But he wanted peace and quiet. He wanted time to think, and the freedom to make up his own mind, just for once, without the endless advice that everyone gave him.

His son Jehoshaphat was old enough to be king.

He, Asa, felt too old to be king.

He had reigned for 38 years – successfully, it seemed – and yet now the kingdom was in trouble. Israel, ever the domineering big brother, took any opportunity to poke at Judah's defences, to sneer at any difficulties they faced. Syria, Judah's ally against Israel only a few years earlier, had switched sides again and was now attacking the few remaining areas that Judah still controlled across the Jordan River. The Philistines were like irate hornets, stinging Judah at every opportunity. Edom and Moab were causing even more trouble than usual, and the Ammonites had made attacks across the river that had touched Judah's pride.

If only his foot didn't hurt so much, he would lead out his army and teach their enemies a lesson. What had happened to the peace he deserved? He had done his best as king: done his best to lead his kingdom

---

[4] 1 Kings 15:23
[5] 2 Chronicles 16:12

back to Yahweh.

Of course, there had been that incident with Hanani[6] – but there was no point in thinking about that any more. He'd said that he was sorry about it, and it was too late to change anything now. Anyway, it hadn't really been his fault. Just another person trying to tell him what to do when it wasn't their place.

The sunshine was warm and comfortable, and having his foot up on a stool eased the pain somewhat. Was it time to bring Jehoshaphat into his confidence more? Perhaps even time to transfer some of the tasks of the kingship? If his foot didn't improve, he might have no choice anyway.

Why would God let him suffer so much? He wasn't perfect, but no-one is. Hadn't he done God's will and obeyed his commands? His father Abijah had followed Yahweh,[7] but he, Asa, had been closer to God and more dedicated in his worship than his father had. As for his grandfather Rehoboam, he had been no great leader of faith. Even his great-grandfather Solomon the Wise had strayed from his faith in Yahweh when he reached old age.[8] Asa reflected comfortably that *he* hadn't done anything like that. Surely God owed him the blessings that were promised to those who served God? But instead, he had this problem with his foot.

It was hurting more again, and he kept moving it gently, trying to ease the pain. At the moment, it was more pleasant to think about the past than the present. He leaned back, remembering the day when he had been crowned king. His father had died unexpectedly after ruling for only three years, and Asa, as the oldest son, had been made king.

Taking over as king so unexpectedly had been almost overwhelming. Abijah had been healthy and well until one morning he began to feel pain under a tooth. The pain had quickly become excruciating, and his face, particularly the lower jaw, swelled up badly. Within two days he was confined to bed; within a week he was dead.[9]

Asa now understood that it might have been the best way for things to happen, as it had allowed no time for the preparation of rebellion and no opportunity for others to press their claims to the kingship. On the very day that his father died, he had been anointed king – at 21 years of age.[10] Jehoshaphat was now 35 years old. He had been trained to administer the kingdom, given plenty of preparation for his future career as king.

---

[6] 2 Chronicles 16:7-10

[7] See 2 Chronicles 13:3-18 for the positive and 1 Kings 15:3-4 for the negative.

[8] 1 Kings 11:4

[9] We know no details of Abijah's death except that it occurred after he had reigned only three years (1 Kings 15:1-2; 2 Chronicles 13:1-2).

[10] We don't know Asa's age when he became king. This is a guess.

Of course, actually being king was quite different from doing the same work while someone else carried the unbearable load of kingship. Still, he felt no doubt that Jehoshaphat was old enough and experienced enough to be much better prepared to be king than he had been himself.

A gentle breeze was cooling the late afternoon air and it was almost time to return to the rat-race of ruling a country. Solomon had said that it was not wise to ask why the older days were better than now,[11] but he couldn't help feeling that the problems he faced now were much greater than those in his past – and wondering why.

The rat-race could wait just a little longer.

King Asa allowed his thoughts to drift nostalgically over the earlier parts of his reign. The Ten Years of Peace[12] that marked the start of his reign had been a return to the times of peace enjoyed by King Solomon. No enemy had entered the land of Judah at all. They were ten comfortable years in which Asa had been eased gently into the demands of kingship. Asa had used those years to concentrate on the worship of Yahweh. How his faith had grown in that period! The temple had then been a place of refuge from the heavy load of ruling a kingdom and God had seemed his friend. Righteousness had felt worthwhile and rewarding.

Then Zerah the king of Ethiopia had attacked with a million men![13] Asa could remember his utter disbelief when he heard the news. On that day, too, he had been looking out from the roof of his palace – gazing south-west. The advisor who brought the news had spelled out what it meant. The terror that had gripped him then was still fresh in his mind, along with the pictures he had conjured up in his mind: hordes of black-skinned soldiers surrounding Jerusalem, scaling the walls, slaughtering his people by the thousands. He could laugh about it now, but it was a shaky laugh, and the fear was quick to return. That campaign was a major triumph for Judah. In fact, it had been his greatest victory. Would he be remembered for it? A million men, defeated by an army little more than half the size![14] Yet it had been the hand of Yahweh that had delivered the victory, not Asa's army, and he remembered his great love for Yahweh, his faith and happy confidence at that time.

But faith was so hard to maintain.

People relied on him to lead the kingdom and guide them by his faith, but they also wanted him to satisfy their own preferences. Everyone wanted someone else to make the big decisions, but they wanted all the decisions to go their way.

He felt worn down by the oppressive task.

---

[11] Ecclesiastes 7:10
[12] 2 Chronicles 14:1
[13] 2 Chronicles 14:9
[14] 2 Chronicles 14:8-9

Yes, it was time to hand the kingdom over to Jehoshaphat – but maybe it was best to do it in stages.

Or was he just doing what he complained about in others: wanting someone else to take responsibility, but making sure that he kept control?

Well, he could start by including Jehoshaphat in all decision-making. Put another throne next to his in the throne-room. Choose some areas of government that he could take over completely; particularly things that involved walking or travelling, he thought wryly, flexing his foot again.

How about defence? The army? Yes, that would be a good starting place. After all, Jehoshaphat had been trained for battle from an early age and was a good leader – if a little soft.

The commanders of the army were always pestering him: they wanted more money, more men, more weapons, more uniforms, more chariots, more engineers. More everything – except enemies! Maybe they would leave him alone if Jehoshaphat took up the task.

"Zur," he said quietly.

The servant came quickly from behind and said, "Yes, my lord?"

"Send for Prince Jehoshaphat."

"Yes, sire."

Zur hurried to the stairs and disappeared from sight.

Now that he had made a decision, Asa was feeling better. Jehoshaphat could take over the problems of defence – he had a faith in Yahweh that might help with the current problems. Asa had always been pleased with Jehoshaphat's spirituality. In the back of his mind he wondered whether his son had more faith than he did himself.

Faith, thought Asa, was quite different from belief, just as confidence is different from hope. Asa had always rejected the gods of Canaan and the surrounding nations. For him, there was one God and only one: Yahweh, the God of Israel.[15] Yet it wasn't easy to make everyone feel that way! He was king, but he knew that many of his subjects followed other gods. Baal was popular, Dagon had a following too, and Chemosh had many adherents. Why, even his own grandmother had made an image to Asherah![16] As a young and enthusiastic devotee of Yahweh, he had happily taken action against idols, forbidding the horrible forms of worship that people seemed to delight in. Nevertheless, it hadn't been easy giving the rebels a stark choice: change their behaviour or leave Judah.

---

[15] 1 Kings 15:14

[16] See 1 Kings 15:13 and 2 Chronicles 15:16. Note that both of these passages say "mother" and so does 1 Kings 15:10. However, 1 Kings 15:2 and 2 Chronicles 11:20-22 name Maacah as Asa's grandmother while 2 Chronicles 13:2 names his grandmother as Micaiah. Overall, it is hard to be sure of the names of Abijah's and Asa's mothers.

Only 21 years old! It was amazing what he'd achieved back then! But the idols had made a comeback over the years of peace, and he'd never managed to get rid of them from the areas of Israel that he had taken over. Altars had been built secretly in many places, and many high places throughout the land were consecrated to other gods. He had often wondered whether his grandmother had replaced that Asherah pole. Not long before she died, when he repeated to her the importance of the exclusive worship of Yahweh in the kingdom, he had felt that something was wrong. She'd had a smug look, and he had wondered why. Should he have challenged her? She was so old, and it seemed cruel to punish her all over again. And, of course, he wasn't sure...

Idolatry was so much more determined than pure religion. For many, religion was so much more attractive when immorality was mixed in – much more so than holiness and innocence.

He sighed and wondered if he should purge the land of idolatry one more time. He knew that many of his people were not committed to the pure worship of Yahweh, but it was so hard to keep everything under control for so long.

And, of course, his own behaviour hadn't been above reproach, which made it hard to insist that others obey him. He was ashamed when he thought about some of the things he had done, but he wasn't willing to think about them in detail. They weren't all his fault anyway. He pursed his lips and looked down at his leg as it gave another twinge. There was nothing wrong with it on the outside, but inside, the pain was often terrible. Why had God afflicted him like this? He would call his doctor as soon as he had sorted things out with Jehoshaphat.

"Prince Jehoshaphat is here, sir," said Zur, interrupting his reverie.

Asa looked up and smiled at his oldest son, who was waiting to be invited to approach. He was a respectful young man, but confident too, and Asa was proud of him.

"Come here, my son," said Asa, "I need to speak to you."

Jehoshaphat approached and bowed before his father, who waved him to a nearby couch.

"Jehoshaphat, I am pleased with you." Asa smiled as he spoke. "As my oldest son, your attitude to me, your brothers, the kingdom and our God do you honour. In short, you are responsible and godly, and, I think, ready to take over some of the rule of the kingdom of Judah." In this short speech, Asa had heaped more praise on his son than ever before, and he felt that Jehoshaphat looked a little surprised. "What do you think of that?" he asked.

Jehoshaphat's response was still quiet and respectful. "Thank you, sir. I value your trust in me and hope that I can work to your satisfaction."

Such formality between a man and his oldest son, thought Asa ruefully. If only I could get to know him better as a man. After all, he will take over my kingdom, and I don't really know him well enough to be sure what he will do. Still, what I do know of him is good – a lot like his mother.

"Your mother is proud of you too, and will be very pleased when she hears this news."

"Shall I tell her, sire?"

"Yes. She has wanted me to take this step for several years, but she has never tried to push me into it. Oh, that all queens were so amenable! Anyway, first, I want you to take responsibility for the army. You know how the army works from within, but now you must learn to direct it. You know the commanders and their attitudes. Now you must learn when to listen to their advice and when to direct them in your own way."

Jehoshaphat looked thoughtful and nodded slowly.

"I will inform the commanders tomorrow," said Asa, wincing as a sudden shaft of pain shot through his foot. He waited until the pain subsided, then continued, "From now on, you will be involved in all decisions that could have an impact on the army or the defence of the nation. You will be included in my councils and you will join me whenever I meet any visiting dignitaries."

"Very well, father. Can we speak sometime about your aims and aspirations for the army, and the kingdom itself, my lord?"

"By all means," said Asa, pleased that he had made the right decision. Jehoshaphat was taking this job seriously, and his attitude would go down well with the army leaders. "I believe that you have a good knowledge of the army and its structure, but we can talk together privately once you have spoken to the commanders. I have some ideas, and if you have any questions, we can discuss them too. From then on, you will be responsible for the defence and development of the kingdom."

"Thank you, sir. I will do my best – with God's help."

"I have great confidence in you, Jehoshaphat. This will give me more time to concentrate on getting this foot treated."

Chapter 3

A Morning Run

"Morning's here," shouted the commander of 50. The unbroken darkness that shrouded the tents gave the lie to his statement, although a faint glow in the eastern sky suggested that possibly he was merely exaggerating. "Out of your beds, you lazy loafers! Sandals on."

Ben-hail groaned, rolled sleepily out of bed and stood up in the cold blackness, adjusting his cloak and tightening his leather belt. "Where are my sandals?" he asked, of no-one in particular. Two of the other three occupants of the tent were also stirring, rubbing the sleep from their eyes and beginning to get ready for the new day, but the third continued to snore noisily.

"Ah, found them," said Ben-hail. He stooped and prodded the snorer with one of the sandals. "Hey Kilion, wake up. It's time for a run."

Kilion jerked and swallowed his snore. "What's that...?" He stopped and yawned, then continued, "What's up?"

"You're going to be in trouble if you don't get up for a run, that's what," said Ben-hail.

"A run?" grumbled Kilion. "In the middle of the night? Why don't they let us sleep?"

"This is the army," said Ben-hail. "If you want sleep, try another profession. Besides, at least it's cooler running in the early morning." He tied his sandal thongs by feel. "And if you don't get up now, you'll have to run in the heat of the day as well."

"Anyway, how could anyone sleep with that snoring?" said Darda, as he rolled up his bedding and laid it near the tent wall. Regulations must be observed. Inside the tent there was still utter darkness, but outside a faint grey light was beginning to spread across the sky.

"Better get up, Kilion," said Darda.

"I'm too cold."

"You'll be colder soon if you don't hurry," warned Ben-hail.

"Ready, Eliam?" asked Darda.

Had there been any light in the tent, Eliam would have stood out from the others because of his great size. He truly was a giant, but in the darkness, his habitual silence left him unobserved. He grunted in reply and the three left the tent together, leaving Kilion to overcome his lethargy on his own.

Outside the tent, there was plenty of movement – and plenty of noise as well. One thing there wasn't plenty of was light, and many of the young men hurrying from their tents collided with others doing the same.

For students at Abiel's Academy, the day normally started with an early morning run, and it was worth hurrying to the starting line: Abiel rewarded early risers with the more pleasant job assignments for the day. Late arrivals not only received the less pleasant chores, but were also given an extra midday run when the scorching sun of Judah made the hills seem twice as steep – twice as insurmountable.

Ben-hail and his tent-mates made their way beyond the cluster of tents to the assembly area where Abiel stood waiting near a solid tree stump that had once been a spreading terebinth. All of the branches and much of the stump had been used to fuel the academy's cooking fires, but the remainder doubled as a rough lampstand, holding a torch that burned vigorously in the cold morning breeze. Winter was coming on and the early mornings were steadily becoming colder.

The camp held two groups of 50 young men, who were undergoing training as potential permanent soldiers in King Asa's army. In those days, the majority of the army were volunteers with little specific training. Whenever a breakdown in international relationships demanded it, they were called away from their farming or other trade and learned their soldiering in the terrifying atmosphere of battle. Survivors who had shown coolness in battle and an aptitude for soldiering might later be given a chance to join the core of professionals that formed Asa's permanent army. This select group was always ready for action, and most were deployed near the borders to protect the kingdom. The rest were stationed near the king, to protect the king and his capital city, Jerusalem.

King Asa and his commanders believed that, all other things being equal, a well-trained army would always beat a bunch of terrified amateurs. In the early, peaceful years of Asa's reign, the academies dotted around the kingdom had turned out enough well-trained soldiers every year to replace those who retired or fell in battle, but in recent times the number of casualties had been rising – worryingly so. More professional soldiers were needed, so the student intake was increased and some new academies were opened. Yet the commanders were convinced that just trying to train more students would inevitably lower the standards – unless the training methods could be improved. With this goal in mind, a trial had begun two years before where the training program in some of the existing academies had been changed to see if a higher percentage of students could achieve the necessary standards. Abiel's Academy was included in the trial and its commander had been earnestly applying – and further refining – the new methods. Some students whose entire training had been within the new regime were now approaching graduation, and the commanders of the army were looking for answers. Were the new training methods successful, or was more drastic action needed to strengthen the army?

Ben-hail and his companions had been selected two years before after several scuffles with Israel, and were being trained in the foremost training academy in Judah. Coveted positions in the army awaited those who satisfied the exacting requirements of Abiel and his two commanders. But Abiel and his methods were also on trial, and the results of the upcoming Great Tournament would be more important than ever.

"This is the day that Yahweh has made,"[17] shouted Abiel, "and we're celebrating it with a little run. Keep up with me. Don't forget what happened to Asahel[18] – even a mighty man is at a disadvantage if he is chasing. Always work hard to be at the front."

They had heard it all before. Abiel was a seasoned warrior and believed fitness was necessary for a good soldier. He also believed that faith was essential to turn a good soldier into a great soldier – a truly mighty man. His goal was to deliver mighty men to the commanders of the army; men who could turn a battle for Judah, not on their own, but with Yahweh's help.

Ben-hail was standing in one of the two lines of cold, sleepy men who faced Abiel in the grey dawn. The commanders of 50 were now visible in the quickly growing light as they scanned their charges, checking their alertness and tidiness. Any failure in tidiness attracted unwelcome attention in the form of extra duties around the camp, and sleepy-looking soldiers often found themselves doing extra exercises to wake them up. Each company of fifty was made up of five squads of ten men, each with an appointed leader. The commanders of 50 knew their 50 men were all present if the five leaders of ten were there. If any leader was missing, it meant he was busy fetching slow soldiers. Ben-hail's leader was missing, and he guessed that Kilion must be the reason. Late risers were dragged unceremoniously from their beds, or driven from them by the liberal application of jugs of ice-cold water. In winter, it was

---

[17] Psalm 118:24
[18] Asahel – one of David's mighty men – died when Abner, King Saul's army commander, struck him with the butt-end of his spear as Asahel chased him (2 Samuel 2:19-23).

sometimes difficult to get bedding dry before the next night fell.

As Abiel began to give them directions for the morning's run, Kilion arrived panting and stood next to Ben-hail, shivering. His hair was wet.

"Ah, Kilion," said Abiel, breaking off his instructions when he saw him, "Kind of you to get up at last and join the rest of us. You look cold. Come to see me at midday and I'll give you some exercises to get you warm, with a nice long run to finish off. This is the third time you've been late this month, so once you've finished your extra run, I'll give you some extra training too."

"Extra training" meant time spent with Abiel in the sword-fighting arena. Kilion could look forward to an exhausting day, probably with some minor scratches to remind him of the need to rise and shine quickly, even when the morning was cold. Ben-hail felt some sympathy for Kilion and wondered if his friend would ever succeed in his goal to join Asa's elite special forces.

Abiel finished shouting his instructions, then led the two groups of 50 out of the camp and north along the road, as he always did. The run would take the companies up and down the nearby hills for an hour or so, leaving the road after a while to turn east before working southwest and finally approaching the camp from the south. In ordinary circumstances, Abiel led all the way and the line of men gradually stretched out further and further behind him.

It was almost a point of honour in the company that none of the students should ever overtake their leader, but precious few could ever have done so anyway: Abiel had always been a very fast runner, and although he was now 35 years old, he was still remarkably fit. In fact, some compared him to Asahel, who was said to have been as fleet of foot as a gazelle.[19] It was a coveted achievement for any trainee to return to camp within two or three metres[20] of the camp commander. Kilion was a runner who could achieve such glory. When he was running well, he could stay close on Abiel's heels from start to end. But he was moody, and events like that morning's summary discipline for lateness always left him sullen and uncooperative. Ben-hail frequently did his best to jolly him out of his sulkiness, but all too often it was an impossible task.

By the time they had covered about half of the distance on this cool morning, Kilion and Ben-hail were well back in the column of runners. As they reached the top of one hill and began to run slowly down the other side, they could see Abiel starting up the side of the next hill.

"Let's go faster down the hill," panted Ben-hail, who chafed at being towards the back of the line. "We can do better than this – he's almost an old man, yet he's leaving us behind."

---

[19] 2 Samuel 2:18
[20] 4-6 cubits; 2 or 3 yards. All units have been converted to metric.

"Who cares?" said Kilion sulkily. "It doesn't matter what I do, they all keep picking on me."

"Are you giving up? If you are, you might as well quit the academy completely."

"Maybe I should. They never give me a chance anyway."

"You chose to stay in bed. Have you given up?"

"Not entirely, but there's no point in trying hard today."

"If you won't try hard today, you might as well leave the academy this afternoon. You know that the commanders won't pass anyone who doesn't try hard. Consistently. That's why they make the training tough. They don't want quitters." Or sulkers, he added silently to himself.

"I could still beat him back to camp if I wanted," said Kilion belligerently.

"Oh, sure," said Ben-hail sarcastically. "Why don't you prove it?"

"I don't need to. After all, he'd just find some way to pick on me some more."

"Well, I'm going faster anyway," panted Ben-hail, frustrated by his friend's stubbornness and short of breath from talking as they ran. "You can come last if you want to, but I've got to do better than this. I don't believe you could beat him anyway!"

He hurried his step and lengthened his stride. By that time, they were halfway down the hill, while Abiel had extended his lead still further and was approaching the crest of the next. Within moments, Ben-hail was well ahead of Kilion, determined to do what he could to reduce the distance between himself and Abiel. The stony ground made it easy to slip in sandalled feet, but at least there was no problem with the light by that time. Ben-hail reached the bottom of the valley and was leaping from stone to stone across the bed of a seasonal stream flushed with autumn rains, when he heard footsteps close behind.

"I *am* going to catch him," called Kilion as he reached the stream and began to cross with light, swift jumps. "In fact, I'm gonna beat him!"

"Oh, yeah?" said Ben-hail. "I'll believe that when I see it. He's got too much of a start."

"I can do it. And you can too if you're willing to try." Kilion was still puffing, but the timbre of his voice had changed completely. Confidence and determination now filled it – exactly as Ben-hail had hoped.

What had caused the change?

Together, they started up the hill, and now the pace was faster. Before they reached the top, Ben-hail was gasping for breath, but they had already passed five of their comrades. He couldn't help wishing that Kilion had made this sudden decision earlier! Now it was Ben-hail who was in danger of being left behind.

It was quite some time before they saw Abiel again. The hills at that stage of the course were uneven, and the company was running along a twisting valley that led them towards a series of steep hills as they approached the camp from the south.

The valley swung westward and it was time to leave it and climb the steepest and roughest hills on the way back to camp. Abiel was nowhere to be seen, and they had to climb to the top of the first hill before they caught another glimpse of him, climbing out of the next valley below. They ran down the hill as fast as they could, and it was clear that they were gaining. When they reached the bottom, they could still see him working his way upwards, and they had passed another eight runners.

But breathing was getting harder and harder, and Ben-hail felt as if his legs and his lungs were on fire.

"Come on, Ben-hail," came Kilion's voice from in front as they began the climb.

Ben-hail didn't reply – he couldn't – but he did his best to keep up.

By the time they reached the crest of the hill, they had left more runners behind, and Ben-hail himself was lagging behind Kilion. Should he give up? After all, it wasn't his fault that they were so far behind in the first place! But determination was as much a part of Ben-hail as athleticism, and the pain in his legs could not stop him. His breathing was ragged; each desperate effort to bring enough air into his chest felt as if it must be the last. He had to rest – but he couldn't. He couldn't let Kilion leave him behind, couldn't let him win after that sulky stubbornness! Ben-hail was determined to be there with him at the finish, whatever the cost – if only he could.

"Look," cried Kilion excitedly, "there he is!"

Abiel was only half-way down the hill, although still running smoothly and easily – at least 20 metres[21] ahead of his nearest follower.

"And there's the camp, too," gasped Ben-hail, forlornly.

On the far side of the deep valley before them, a steep ascent led to the shoulder on which a road skirted the hill. They could also see the tents and enclosures of their camp, which sat on the same shoulder. Yet before they could begin the stiff climb to the finish, they must first relinquish their hard-won height and descend again into a valley.

"We can do it!" said Kilion and surged ahead, leaping down the hill at a frenetic pace.

For a moment, Ben-hail almost gave up. He could not breathe and his legs felt like lead, refusing to obey his wishes. It was all he could do to continue running at all. The hill sloped down in front of him and Kilion seemed to be running almost effortlessly – leaving him further

---

[21] about 22 yards.

behind with every stride. Somehow, Ben-hail kept running, and slowly, as he bounded down the hill, the air that burned in his chest seemed to come just a fraction more easily, and the agony in his legs eased a little. With a great effort of will, he lengthened his stride again and hurried after Kilion. Students in front heard their heavy footfalls as they thundered down the hill and increased their own speed to avoid being overtaken.

Ben-hail felt exhaustion creeping over him again as he leapt to one side to avoid another runner who was determined to remain in front. He landed on a boulder and immediately leapt again to reach the bottom of the valley. Another runner was left behind.

Glancing up, Ben-hail realised with amazement that Kilion was only just in front of him – somehow he had *reduced* the distance between them during that frantic descent. Kilion half-turned and Ben-hail saw him raise his right fist in joy and triumph as he pointed ahead with his left hand.

Ben-hail looked and saw Abiel climbing towards the shoulder of the hill, about 50 metres[22] ahead of them. His stride was still methodical and his progress steady. To Ben-hail, it was utterly discouraging. Abiel was running easily up towards the camp and the inevitable result. The task seemed insurmountable, the distance impossible.

"We can do it!" shouted Kilion. "Don't give up now!" And he continued to run, seemingly with renewed energy.

It was so tempting to give up, but.... Ben-hail saw a runner just ten metres[23] in front and decided that he could at least keep running until he caught up with him. Then he would see whether he could continue or not. The runner he had chosen to catch was failing fast, and within 20 metres, Ben-hail had caught up and passed him. This was the spur that lit the fire of final desperation in Ben-hail – he could not give up now! Once more, the breath rasping in his lungs hurt a little less, and the agony in his legs receded as he pounded up the hill following Kilion, now just a few steps ahead. Abiel was about 40 metres ahead. They would catch him.

Ben-hail leapt up the hill like a startled deer until he was neck and neck with Kilion, who whooped again with enthusiasm. This struggle had gained a life of its own, and neither Kilion nor Ben-hail could let it go. Yet still, the remaining task was enormous – Abiel's outstanding stamina and the untiring strength of his legs had brought him to the very edge of the shoulder on which the run would end. The last hundred metres into the camp were an easy run on a flat and even surface: a gentle, relaxing finish for a consummate runner like Abiel. But maybe he

---

[22] 55 yards.
[23] about 11 yards.

would ease up a little, slacken his pace – and Kilion and Ben-hail were now only fifteen metres behind. Abiel was still unaware of their presence as he scrambled up the last few metres onto level ground.

Calling on their last reserves of strength, Kilion and Ben-hail ran as they had never run before, thinking they saw an opportunity to catch Abiel before the first tent was reached. But they had not counted on their commander's commitment to excellence. He practised what he taught, and refused to take things easy. As the pair reached the level ground themselves, Abiel dropped from his relaxed, rhythmic lope into a final leg-straining sprint.

It would have been so easy for the two students to ease off, to finish the race a respectful distance behind their leader – but they had come too far to give up then.

Kilion lengthened his stride, while Ben-hail forced his legs to move more quickly than ever. They covered the ground like a pair of ostriches fleeing before horses, and swiftly they caught up with Abiel.

A few of the camp staff watched as the unthinkable happened: Kilion drew alongside Abiel and then, suddenly, passed him, while they were still a short distance from the tents. Ben-hail, determined not to be left out, also achieved parity with Abiel – just as his teacher reached the first tent.

All three runners dropped immediately to a walk, their chests heaving. Abiel was clearly tired from a good, honest, steady effort, but he looked in surprise at the sweat that was pouring off the two younger runners. Theirs had been a race of two parts and the second part had taken all they had to give.

"What's up, boys?" asked Abiel in surprise, his breath coming in short gasps. Ben-hail collapsed onto the ground next to the tent and lay on his back panting for breath. He couldn't answer, and felt as if it would be some time before he could.

Kilion was in a better state and was able to answer, although in an uneven voice, "Excuse me sir, I beat you."

Abiel smiled before bending over and resting his hands on his knees. He looked up. "Yes, you did," he said. "Do you know how many people have done that before?"

"I think so, sir."

"Nobody."

"Yes, sir."

"And most of them couldn't." It was not said boastfully. Abiel took another deep breath. "The others were too polite to do so."

"Yes sir. Sorry sir."

"So why did you do it?"

"Ben-hail convinced me to try, and then I decided that I really wanted to beat you. To say sorry, sir."

Abiel laughed. "How is that saying sorry?"

"I wasn't doing well earlier this morning, sir. I wanted to say sorry for being in a bad mood, and I thought the best way to do that would be to stop being grumpy and really try."

"You did well. I'm pleased. And you can forget the extra run at noon. You don't need it."

"Oh, thank you, sir. I didn't expect that."

"Will you try from now on when we go running?"

"Yes, sir."

"Will you beat me every time?" The question was a challenge, but it held a touch of sadness.

"Should I, sir?"

"I guess that you should. And if you ever don't," he said with asperity, "maybe you *will* need an extra run at noon!"

"I'll do my best, sir. Thank you, sir."

By this time, Ben-hail's breathing was beginning to return to normal, and he climbed to his feet again.

Abiel looked at him and shook his head. It was difficult for a man like Abiel to admit that he was no longer the young champion he had been – a talent without equal. The previous day had forced him to admit that he had met his master in swordsmanship, and today he had met his match in running – the two areas that he counted most his own. And Ben-hail had been central to both. Abiel was convinced that he would never have been able to beat the swordsman Ben-hail was quickly becoming, but in running he wondered if it really was old age that was creeping up on him.

"I didn't know you were a runner, Ben-hail," he said.

"No, sir, I'm not. But Kilion challenged me and I was too stubborn to give up."

"But you've never even finished in the top ten before."

"No sir." He stopped and looked down at the ground. "Maybe I haven't been trying hard enough." For Ben-hail, not trying was something to be ashamed of.

"Maybe. Well, let's see how you go from now on. I'll certainly be expecting more. Long distance running helps with stamina in battle, particularly with sword fighting." Abiel never missed an opportunity to encourage or inspire his charges. He knew that swordsmanship was Ben-hail's greatest interest and was not afraid to use that interest to stimulate him to improve in other areas.

"Really, sir?"

"If you're ever in a long battle, you'll understand what I mean. If you aren't fit enough, your sword will become a dead weight in your hand and your legs will cramp badly. The fitter a man is, the better he will be able to help his mates, and the more likely he is to survive."

By this time, almost half of the company had straggled into the camp and were gathered around Abiel, Ben-hail and Kilion. Word had already passed around the camp servants that not one but *two* students had finished in front of the commander. The runners heard of the shocking event as soon as they arrived. Everyone was curious to see what the outcome would be: Abiel was a stickler for discipline, but he was also known for praising those who complemented their natural ability with effort.

"God gives you talent," he was wont to say, "but it's up to you to use it." Everyone who entered his academy had talent – only talented students were allowed to enter – but only those with determination graduated successfully. Another of his favourite sayings was, "There's no such thing as a lazy champion." He believed this implicitly, and did his best to inspire every student to work hard. He had a good eye for spotting laziness, and if he couldn't help a man get rid of it, he could at least make sure that such men did not make their way into Asa's army through *his* academy.

"Alright, everyone," shouted Abiel. "Why are you all standing around staring? Kilion and Ben-hail have shown great determination and skill in beating me in today's run. They've set you all a good example. We'll have to see if they can do it again tomorrow morning. In the meantime, go and get ready for breakfast."

Chapter 4

HEAD OF THE ARMY

Jehoshaphat talked to several commanders and administrators of the army, most of whom he already knew. He confirmed the number of soldiers in the permanent army and the estimated number of volunteer soldiers available if they were needed. Happily, Judah's success in battle during Asa's long reign meant that getting volunteers for the army was not as difficult as it had been at other times in history.

Yet despite these positive conditions, the kingdom was still under threat, and Jehoshaphat was determined to find out why. Why were Judah's neighbours still willing to attack when their assaults had achieved such poor results over so many years? And how were Judah's enemies able to get information about where units of the army were located so that they could attack somewhere else with impunity? The commanders of the army felt sure that there were traitors around – enough to cause trouble for the kingdom – yet when Jehoshaphat asked why, nobody would give him a straight answer. Even so, Jehoshaphat was convinced that they were right and continued to probe.

Gershom, who was over the army, was an open and blunt man – sometimes to the point of rudeness – but when Jehoshaphat asked him why there were traitors among the people, he smiled gently and looked away.

"Why won't you answer me?" Jehoshaphat persisted, irritated.

"Look, sir, people do what they do for their own reasons. And sometimes people have very good reasons."

"What do you mean?"

"Well, sir, what would make you stop being loyal to Judah?"

"Nothing!"

"With all due respect, sir, I think that if you say that, you haven't thought about it hard enough. But that is all I can say, because I *am* loyal to the king."

Jehoshaphat went away puzzled. If the army commanders knew but wouldn't give him the answers he needed, then who *would* tell him? Did his father know? His intuition warned him that it would not be wise to ask.

Maybe one of the priests or Levites could tell him, he thought. He knew the old priest Jehoiada quite well and had learned much from him over the years as a tutor. Yes, he would ask Jehoiada.

The next day, he made his way to the temple and found Jehoiada teaching some young Levites the requirements for preparing burnt offerings.

"Can I talk to you, Jehoiada?" he asked.

"Of course, my lord. Do you want to talk now?"

"Yes, but if you want to finish what you are teaching, I wouldn't mind listening anyway."

"I'll just wrap it up for now and keep going later," said Jehoiada. He turned to his students and spoke warmly, "Look, lads, it's going to take some time to cover the details of what we need to look for to make sure a lamb has no blemishes. We can't keep the prince waiting for that long – his time is more valuable to the country than mine or yours. Go to the library and read over the requirements for offerings again. Remember, start with God's rules as they are written in the books of Moses, then move on to the written explanations that have been added over the years by various priests and Levites. And while you read the latter, lads, make sure they match the former and let me know if you don't think they do. Off you go."

"Should I read those instructions about offerings, Jehoiada?" asked Jehoshaphat as the students left. "I know that a king has to know the Book of the Law,[24] but what about the rest of the scriptures?"

"My lord, I don't think a king can know too much about God's commands, do you?"

"I suppose not, but if they're just instructions for the priests and Levites, is it worth the time I would spend? After all," he laughed, "surely it's not my place to tell the priests how to do their job!"

"I can only answer with a 'What if?' example, sir."

"What if *what*, then?"

"What if the priests aren't doing what they should be doing? What if they stop reading the instructions, or if the collected explanations that I was mentioning to those young Levites begin to build on *each other* instead of starting from God's word?"

"Is it a king's job to straighten out the priests then?"

"It is a king's job to lead his nation, based on the law of God."

---

[24] Deuteronomy 17:18-19

"But does that include telling the Levites how to search for blemishes on a sacrifice? Surely a king can't be telling everybody how to tie their sandals?"

Jehoiada smiled and shook his head, "No, you don't have to do that. But you do have to know enough of God's law to be able to make sure that the priests are on the right path. That is why a king is told to read God's law every day. King David wrote that he loved God's law and that it was his meditation every day.[25] He took God's instructions seriously. I don't want to criticise your ancestors, my lord, but unfortunately your great-great-grandfather Solomon the Wise didn't take them so seriously later in his life.[26] I was only eight years old when he died and the Great Division took place, but I think you know that the division happened because the king didn't take the worship of Yahweh seriously enough."

"If I end up king by God's blessing, I will *have* to do better. I want to be more like my father, anyway."

Jehoshaphat noticed Jehoiada studying him closely for a moment and thought he saw some doubt in the look. He was about to ask why, when suddenly he remembered the question he had come to ask.

"Jehoiada," he said, "I've been talking to Gershom about some of the problems we're having around the frontiers. We seem to have traitors betraying the location of our troops to our enemies. I asked him why and he said they could have certain reasons that he didn't want to talk about. He didn't quite say so, but I got the impression that he thought some of the reasons could be good reasons, too. I thought about asking my father, but decided to ask you first, because you have lived longer than most people I know, and have seen all the changes in the kingdom since king Solomon died. What reasons could people have for being traitors against Judah – good reasons, I mean, not those who are willing to betray their nation for silver?"

"Ah, well, my lord," answered Jehoiada, speaking slowly as if he was trying to buy some time in which to choose his words carefully, "I, that is to say, my lord, I really, ah, I don't think that I can help you. I am a loyal subject of the king."

"That's what Gershom said, too."

"It's the truth, and there are some subjects that are not very safe."

"What do you mean? How could they not be safe? If you are loyal to my father, how can this be dangerous for anyone?"

"Maybe it would be best to talk to your father about it – but if you do, be very careful how you introduce the subject and what you say. And please, don't mention Gershom or me!"

---

[25] Psalm 119:97; see also Psalm 1:2. Some traditions suggest that David wrote Psalm 119, but we do not know for sure.
[26] 1 Kings 11:4-13

Jehoshaphat looked thoughtful. "You and Gershom both obviously think that my father has given people reason to be disloyal."

"I wouldn't say that, my lord. I would say that certain things happened that upset some people greatly."

"Were you upset by them?"

"As a servant of Yahweh, yes, I was upset."

"And yet you say that you aren't disloyal to my father."

"That's right. He is Yahweh's anointed."

"So when did these things happen?"

"The problem began more than 20 years ago, but related situations have bubbled up again from time to time since. You wouldn't have been more than 10 or 11 years old when it started."

"Was it connected with my father's religious reforms?"

"No, sir, it wasn't, and I don't want to tell you any more. As Solomon said, a little bird can carry news to the king,[27] and I am his loyal subject. If he wants you to know these things he will tell you, although you may have to ask first."

"I will think about it. It is all very puzzling. Thank you, Jehoiada."

"You are welcome, my lord."

As Jehoshaphat walked away, he wondered what he should do. Gershom and Jehoiada were not cowards, and he was convinced that they were loyal to his father, so why were they afraid to discuss the subject? He had always had a great admiration for his father, and while this had been coupled with a healthy fear of his discipline – yes, and of his temper too at times! – his father had always been fair. Jehoiada had warned him to be careful: should he be afraid of what his father might do to him if he started asking questions?

Did he *need* to know the answers?

He had no doubt that it would help him in his understanding of the difficulties that faced the kingdom, and, after all, he *was* meant to be in control of the defence of the realm. The army was to be under his hand very soon – he couldn't ignore threats to the safety of the kingdom that his chief officers would not discuss with him!

He must speak to his father.

---

[27] Ecclesiastes 10:20

Chapter 5

ANOTHER MORNING RUN

Ben-hail was as good as his word. Ever since the day when Kilion and he had outrun Abiel so amazingly, Ben-hail had finished in the top ten runners. Morning runs were now important to him, and his running was steadily improving.

He also began to see the benefit Abiel had promised him: increased fitness *had* improved his swordsmanship. Within two weeks, his extra endurance meant that he no longer reached the stage in a bout where his sword began to feel so heavy that it slowed his movements. Not only so, but he could strive for even more speed without becoming exhausted.

Abiel noticed it and commented. His fellow students noted it also, and complained. If his movements had been uncomfortably fast for his opponents before, now they were like lightning.

Kilion also took his commitment to Abiel seriously. He had a lighter build than Ben-hail and running was his forte. Since joining the academy, his main limitation had always been his attitude – a tendency to sulk. There were still times when his friends recognised his characteristic narrowing of the eyes and pursing of the lips that signalled a lapse into brooding over perceived wrongs. But he really was trying to overcome the habit, and often they could jolly him out of his moodiness.

He had not beaten the commander every day, for Abiel had increased his effort too. Abiel admitted to himself that he was getting older, and decided to see if more exercise would increase his fitness and help him run faster. It did, and so Kilion had to work even harder to overtake him. The increased competition also encouraged others to see what they could do to improve their own times, and there was no doubt that the first few runners were returning to camp sooner. For those already used to being at the tail of the field, however, there was little motivation to improve, and the distance between first and last increased considerably.

Kilion and Ben-hail still ran together at the start, but each day there came a time when Kilion gave his friend a quick wave and slowly began to pull away in front, stepping up his pace so that he could catch up with Abiel before that final hill. Nevertheless, Ben-hail was not being left far behind, and his speed was consistently increasing. At times, Kilion wondered where Ben-hail's improvement might end.

Winter had arrived in the hills of Judah and the days were short and cold. Frequent rain turned the dust to mud and swelled the streams into rivers. Occasionally, snow would blanket the land, and on such days the students dreaded the early morning run, where every step was treacherous.

But the day that changed the direction of Ben-hail's life was not a snowy day.

It started with a slippery rock.

Rain had fallen during the night and threatened to start again at any time. The ground was slippery and the stones on the hillsides and valleys were treacherous.

Abiel had led the way as usual and Ben-hail and Kilion were some distance behind – it suited their running styles. They ran quickly but carefully down a hill until they reached the river that flowed along the valley. The river was dotted with large stones that enabled runners to cross without having to splash through the water. Kilion, a little in front, leapt nimbly from rock to rock until he reached the opposite bank. Ben-hail was following close behind, but suddenly his right sandal slipped on a rock in the middle of the river. He tried to recover his balance, stretching toward another stone with his left foot, but it was too late. Both feet slipped into the river and he fell headfirst towards another large rock. Ben-hail was dimly aware of a sharp pain in his left leg even as he put out his hands to avoid hitting his head. There was a sudden stab of agony from his right hand as it arrested his fall, and he landed with a splash in the ice-cold water. A cloud of spray obscured his landing and his toes were jammed into the jumble of rocks that formed the bed of the river. He finally came to a halt when his right knee struck a rock painfully.

Kilion heard the splash and the cry of pain and turned back. He saw Ben-hail floundering in the swift-flowing water and quickly ran to help.

"Here, let me help you up," he said, reaching out his hand.

"I can't," gasped Ben-hail. "My foot is caught between some stones."

"Well, can I pull you out? Give me your hand."

"No, I've hurt my hand, too."

"Then I'll have to see if I can get your foot unstuck." Kilion stepped down into the muddy water and slid his hands down Ben-hail's right shin until he could feel where the sandal was caught between two large rocks firmly embedded in the river bottom. He tried to twist the sandal sideways and ease it out, but it would not move. After several attempts, he changed tack, pushing the sandal further down towards a slightly wider gap where he could twist the sandal enough to free it, and Ben-hail's leg with it.

As he did so, his friend flinched and said, "Take it easy! That hurts."

"Well, you should be able to pull it up easily now."

Ben-hail gingerly lifted his right leg out of the water and together they examined it. Blood oozed from several long scratches, but, overall, the damage didn't look too bad.

"How does it feel?" asked Kilion.

"It hurts, but it's not as bad as the other foot – or my right hand, for that matter. How could I hurt myself so badly so easily?"

"Can you climb up onto this rock? At least then you'll be out of this freezing water."

Ben-hail put his right foot back into the water and lifted himself onto the rock Kilion had suggested. It was good to have most of him out of the water, and slowly he pulled his legs up onto the rock, examining the left leg closely. There was nothing visibly wrong with it, but the pain made it clear that something was wrong inside.

"Your left leg looks alright," said Kilion. "How does it feel?"

"Painful," said Ben-hail. "It's much worse than the other foot, but really, my right hand is the worst of all. I landed on it and something seemed to twang inside."

"Oh-oh, that doesn't sound good."

"No. Now it just feels sort of numb, but it still hurts a lot."

A group of three students reached the river, one of whom was Darda, their tent-mate. Seeing that Ben-hail was injured, they stopped and Darda asked if there was anything he could do to help.

"I don't think so," said Kilion, "except for telling Abiel that we'll probably need a stretcher to get Ben-hail back to camp."

"No," said Ben-hail, definitely. "I'll be able to walk."

"I doubt it," said his friend. "With both feet damaged and a hand that hurts more than either of them, I don't think you'll be walking much for a while."

"Then I'd better get back to camp as quickly as possible and fetch Abiel," said Darda. "I'll tell him where you are and that you need a stretcher."

"I'll just sit here for a few minutes and then I'll be alright," protested Ben-hail.

"Oh, and now it's started raining again," said Kilion.

The rain decided the other runners, who crossed the river carefully and ran off up the hill with Darda in the lead.

"You should keep running too, Kilion," said Ben-hail. "I wasn't thinking of how much I've been holding you up."

"That doesn't matter. I think it's better if I stay with you. You'll need help."

Kilion sat down on a rock near Ben-hail, trying to keep his feet out of the river – even after only a short time in the icy water, his feet and shins were numb.

More runners continued to arrive at the crossing, many of whom offered to help, but without a stretcher there was little anyone could do. Ben-hail was in no hurry to move any more than he had to.

"Are you ready to get out of the river yet?" Kilion asked, after a while.

"I suppose it's not going to get any better in a hurry, so I might as well go now."

"Can you stand up?"

"I think so," said Ben-hail, reluctantly putting his feet back into the rushing water. Watching closely, Kilion saw that the pain was great, but slowly Ben-hail struggled to his feet. "What now?" he asked.

"Try to walk across to the far bank, it's closer. Give me your left hand and you can hold on to me."

Kilion did his best to help, but Ben-hail was heavier than he, and on more than one occasion they narrowly avoided both slipping into the river again. The rain, already heavy, was still increasing, and Kilion was sure that the water level was rising.

"What's that noise?" he asked with concern.

"Maybe it's just the rain getting heavier."

Visibility was worsening as the last few runners approached down the hill. They had seen Kilion and Ben-hail and were shouting to them, gesticulating urgently to where the river rounded a bend upstream.

Kilion heard their faint cries, looked anxiously where they indicated and saw a surge of water coming around the bend. A large wave was coming down the river, roiling and turbulent. Within moments, the river would become a raging torrent, much wider and deeper than before.

"Hurry!" urged Kilion, but Ben-hail wasn't able to move any faster.

The runners approached, but all save one stopped a safe distance away, high above the river crossing. That one, however, lumbered on, and Kilion gave a sudden cry. "Eliam – just the man we need! Help!"

It was their tent-mate, and although he was not a fast runner, his impressive size did inspire confidence.

Through the rain they saw him begin to cross the river toward them, jumping from rock to rock. Kilion and Ben-hail continued their hurried attempts to escape and managed to climb onto the river bank just as the wave arrived.

It struck Eliam first, in the middle of the river, where it flowed most quickly. He was immediately knocked off his feet and tumbled along by the turbulent flood. It seemed as if his brave attempt to help would end in tragedy, but the watching students hoped that his great strength could still save him. As he was swept along, the water pushed him towards a huge rock around which the flood must part. It seemed almost effortless as he stretched out his legs in front of him and braced them against the rock. The water thundered past around him, but he held himself in position and reached up to a low branch of a huge overhanging tree that grew with its trunk on the bank and its branches spreading out across the river. Once again, it seemed just too easy as he pulled himself up onto the branch and shook his head, shaking the water wildly from his hair. Quickly he slid along the branch towards the trunk of the tree, which was about to be engulfed in water.

Even when the water struck Eliam, Kilion could still have reached safety himself by leaving Ben-hail, but instead he supported his friend and together they staggered as quickly as Ben-hail could manage towards higher ground. The malevolent wave seemed to pursue them as it surged hungrily over the river bank and swept them off their feet. Downstream towards the massive tree they tumbled just as Eliam was reaching for its branch in the middle of the river. Ben-hail was flung backwards against the trunk, with no chance to cushion the blow, but was at least able then to turn around and brace himself against the tree, avoiding being swept away immediately. Kilion grabbed desperately at a low branch and held on for dear life as the water tried to drag him away.

Up in the tree, Eliam continued sliding along the tree branch until he reached the trunk. He stood up and put an arm around the trunk, then crouched and leaned down towards Ben-hail. He had to shout to get his attention: "Ben-hail! Look up!"

Pinned against the trunk by the water, Ben-hail felt as if he was drowning in a sea of pain. Pain forbade the use of his right arm; pain filled both of his legs; pain radiated across his back from the brutal impact of the tree trunk; pain almost overcame him with every desperate breath he dragged into his chest.

Pain would surely take him away soon, he thought. Then he heard an indistinct voice from above and looked up.

"Your arm," said Eliam, reaching down towards him.

Ben-hail looked back at him blankly.

"Your arm!" shouted Eliam, reaching down further. "Give me your arm!"

Suddenly Ben-hail understood what was happening, just as he felt himself slipping sideways on the trunk. Quickly, he reached up with his uninjured left hand towards the massive hand that Eliam was offering him. He felt his hand swallowed in a grip of iron and was lifted effortlessly out of the water. Eliam deposited him carefully on the branch, then climbed around the trunk and sat down on the branch that Kilion was dangling from. Kilion was further out from the trunk, still holding on with a strong grip – but it seemed to Eliam, watching as the water tore at him with icy fingers, that he wouldn't be able to hang on for long.

"Can you move towards me, Kilion?" shouted Eliam.

"Don't know. I'll try." He relaxed his grip a little and tried to slide his hand towards the trunk, but progress was slow and difficult. After a while he called, "The current is getting stronger near the trunk. I can't go any further – it will pull me off."

"Then try to climb up onto the branch."

Kilion tried hard to lift his feet out of the water and swing them up onto the branch above his head, but exhaustion and the numbing cold made it impossible.

"I'm coming," said Eliam. He began to inch his way out along the branch. He had nothing to hang onto except for the branch itself, and it was swaying and dipping further towards the water as he went along. If he reached Kilion safely, could he pull him up onto the branch without causing both of them to fall into the torrent? There would be no second chance.

He reached his friend's hand and was about to take hold of his wrist when he slipped and almost lost his balance. Taking a deep breath, he sat back for a moment and wondered what to do. If he fell on top of Kilion, they would both be washed away. What should he do next?

"What's up?" came a voice, shouting above the roar of the water. It was Abiel, and he was accompanied by Darda and a group of six other students, two of whom were carrying a litter.

"First Ben-hail hurt himself crossing the river," called Kilion, "and then there was a sudden massive wave. We got caught."

"It's amazing they're still there at all," shouted a voice from the other side of the river. "Just amazing."

The three friends looked across at the students who had stayed up the hill, out of the flood: in the urgency of the moment, they had completely forgotten them.

"We have strong ropes with us," said Abiel, taking control of the situation. "Kilion, can you move hand over hand back down the branch towards us? Then we can give you a rope and help you the rest of the way."

Eliam retreated to the trunk, and he and Ben-hail waited while Kilion did what Abiel suggested. The turbulent water continued to tug at him, but as he moved along the branch away from the trunk, the force of the water gradually lessened. Finally, however, he reached a place where the thinning branch was bending too much, and he stopped.

By that time, Abiel had dispatched Darda a little way downstream where he hurried into the water with a rope around his waist that was held by two other students, ready to do his best to catch Kilion if necessary. Realistically, Abiel knew that if Kilion could not grasp the rope he was about to throw, there was little hope that Darda would be able to rescue him, but it might be their last chance.

"I'll throw the rope upstream of you," called Abiel urgently. "I'll try to make it wrap around your chest, and then you can let go of the branch and hold the rope instead. All clear?"

"Yes, sir," answered Kilion, breathlessly. Even if Abiel's aim was flawless, it would still be a difficult task. He would have to let go of the branch and turn around to grab at the rope. There would be only one chance to get it right.

"I'm throwing it now," shouted Abiel. It was a perfect toss, and the end of the rope flew through the air, to land in the water just behind Kilion, the current wrapping it around his chest in a moment.

Immediately, the rope began to twist and sink in the turbid water. Kilion let go of the branch with one hand and clutched at the rope. His fingers touched the rope, but it was writhing like a snake in the flood and escaped his grip. Desperately, he fixed his eyes on the sinking rope and relaxed his grip on the branch. Spinning around as he fell, he reached out to grasp the twisting rope. The watching men saw the rushing water seize him, upend him, and snatch him from sight. Within moments, the rope was jerked dangerously tight and Abiel and his students had to strain to take the load as the water did its best to carry its quarry away downstream. At first, it was all they could do to avoid being carried away themselves, but then, slowly they were able to haul in the rope, hand over hand, until Kilion appeared again, close enough to the shore that he could stand in the water and begin to scramble towards them. Then, at last, the waiting Darda was able to help him, but never once did Kilion's strong fingers let go of the rope – not until he had fought his way completely out of the torrent and onto the shore. There he collapsed on the ground for a few moments, breathing heavily.

By this time, the rain had stopped and everybody felt that the worst was over. However, it was quite some time before Ben-hail and Eliam were safely out of the tree and away from the torrent. In fact, the friends had to wait until the sudden rush of water had begun to recede, and the danger with it, before they could be helped carefully across to dry ground.

Eventually, around noon, six stretcher-bearers were able to wade through the remaining water to the tree and help Eliam lower Ben-hail onto the litter.

"Now that we don't have all the noise of the water, tell me what's wrong," said Abiel as they carried Ben-hail onto the narrow path that led up the hill.

"He slipped crossing the river and got badly hurt," replied Kilion, "and then the river rose suddenly and threw him against the tree. I wouldn't be surprised if he has something broken inside."

"Oh, come on," said Ben-hail weakly. "It's not that bad."

"What hurts?" asked Abiel.

"My right wrist and both my feet. I can walk slowly, but it sure hurts."

"What about your back?" asked Kilion. "Didn't you hit the tree with your back?"

"Yes, but it's not as bad as the rest."

"I also had to lift him up into the tree by the other arm, sir, so he might have damaged that one too."

"No, that arm's fine," said Ben-hail. "It's the other..."

"You mean, you picked him up by one arm, Eliam?" asked Abiel with wonder in his voice.

"Yes, sir," said Eliam. "I had to. There wasn't enough time for anything else, and I had to hang on with my other arm so that I didn't fall out of the tree myself."

"But Ben-hail isn't just a small man that you can pick up like a ragdoll."

"He's not really that heavy, sir. And it had to be done."

Abiel frowned and asked, "What is it in that tent that turns you into heroes? Ben-hail is the best swordsman in the academy, Kilion is the best runner, and now it seems that you are the strongest man." He looked across at Darda, who was helping to carry the litter. "What's special about you, Darda? I haven't heard anything about you yet!"

Darda didn't answer, Eliam looked sober as usual, and Ben-hail exchanged a knowing smile with Kilion – but none of the four friends answered the commander. If Abiel hadn't noticed anything special about Darda yet, they would leave him to find out.

"Let's go then, lads," said Abiel, and the carriers began to walk up the hill. "Take it easy, and try to keep it smooth."

They hadn't gone far before it became clear that carrying a large man like Ben-hail on a litter along a narrow path was not going to be easy. Only the men on one side of the litter could walk on the path, while those on the other side struggled to keep their footing on the slippery hillside. Poor Ben-hail was having a rough ride.

"Stop," said Eliam, a man of few words even in such a situation, "I'll carry him."

"I'm not light," warned Ben-hail.

Eliam didn't answer. He put one arm around Ben-hail's back and the other behind his knees. "Tell me if it hurts too much," he said, and picked up his tent-mate with no apparent effort. He walked easily up the hill, choosing his path carefully to make the journey as comfortable as possible for his friend.

Ben-hail was able to lean back against him and adjust his limbs to minimise the pain. His right foot looked the worst, partly because it had been knocked while he was on the stretcher and was bleeding again. However, it was his right wrist that hurt the most, and he cradled it in his lap to ease the pain.

They were still quite a distance from the camp, and none of the party could imagine how anyone could single-handedly carry Ben-hail up the first hill, let alone the rest of the way to the camp.

"Can I help?" asked Kilion, not sure that he could do anything anyway, but willing to try in the face of something that seemed impossible.

Eliam just grunted a negative and kept walking. He didn't walk quickly, but he wasn't slow either. As the party reached the top of the first hill, Ben-hail asked for a rest. Though it was clear that Eliam was carrying him as gently as he could, the movement was still painful.

It took Eliam almost an hour to convey Ben-hail back to camp, and everyone else in the party felt rather useless along the way. In places the path was flat and using the litter might have been easier, but Ben-hail asked for Eliam to continue if he could. He could. It was a strange procession that entered the camp after ascending the last hill – a giant of a man carefully but easily cradling in his arms a large man whose face was grey with pain, while about a dozen other men walked alongside bringing an empty litter or doing nothing in particular.

Ben-hail was lying in his tent that afternoon when Abiel came to check on him.

"How are you feeling now?" he asked.

"Everything seems to hurt," said Ben-hail.

"From the sound of it, you've done a lot of damage to yourself. If it looks like it's going to take you a long time to recover, maybe you should go home."

Ben-hail shut his eyes, troubled. Go home? Was Abiel trying to warn him gently that he might not be able to graduate from the academy?

After a while, Ben-hail opened his eyes again and looked at the commander. "I don't think this will stop me doing ordinary things for long, sir."

"We'll see," said Abiel, doubtfully. "Anyway, I think you're lucky to be alive, and the physician says that none of your bones seem to be broken. I think Yahweh must've been looking after you. You're a Levite, aren't you? God must have work for you to do, young man."

"Hmm," said Ben-hail, and shut his eyes again.

Abiel looked at him with sympathy. The non-committal response showed him just how much pain Ben-hail must be suffering.

Chapter 6

LOOKING FOR ANSWERS

"Father, can I talk to you?" asked Jehoshaphat.

"I suppose so," said King Asa unenthusiastically. He was seated on the magnificent throne of his great-grandfather King Solomon,[28] one foot resting on a stool. His diseased foot was getting worse, so he always sat with a stool in front of him – and often with a doctor standing beside him. The pain increased by the day, and concentrating on any of the work of government was getting harder and harder. He was growing increasingly frustrated with the doctors: they didn't seem to be able to work out what was wrong, and none of their suggestions helped.

"Could we speak in private?"

"Is it really necessary?"

"Yes, sir, I think so."

"Well, I'm not walking anywhere, so, Zur, clear the room. I wish to speak to my son in private."

Advisors and guards were all expelled from the throne room. Even the doctor, waiting to apply the latest potion, was forced to leave.

"They've all gone now. What did you want to talk about? Is it to do with the army?"

"Yes, my lord, it is. From my enquiries about the difficulties faced by the army, particularly around the frontiers, it seems that we have a significant problem with traitors. People who tell our enemies about the movements of our army units and the number of troops in various areas."

"Traitors, hey?" Asa sat forward and looked as if he would like to have stood up, but instead he screwed up his face in pain and put his hands on his leg. After a while, his face relaxed a little and he returned

---

[28] 1 Kings 10:18-20; 2 Chronicles 9:17-19. Shishak, king of Egypt, may have taken away this entire enormous throne when he attacked Jerusalem in 1 Kings 14:25-26, but more likely he took only the gold that covered it. This is what he seems to have done with the gold lining the temple. See also 1 Kings 6:31-35 with 2 Kings 18:16.

to the topic. "What efforts have been made to track down these rebels? Oh, how could anyone fight against God's kingdom in Judah?"

"That's what I came to ask about. Do you have any answer to that question? Are you aware of anything that could have turned some of your people against you?"

"How should I know what makes people work against their own nation? Could it be money? Family loyalties? Or could it be…" his voice trailed off.

"Could it be what, my lord?"

"A long time ago, my son, back when you were a young lad…." He stopped and Jehoshaphat guessed that he was choosing his words carefully. What was it about this question that made everyone so careful with their words? After a few moments, Asa must have worked out what to say, for he continued, "I won some amazing victories through faith. Military victories over enemies outside and religious victories over those of Judah who wanted to serve other gods and worship them. What a wonderful time it was! A time of defeat for our enemies and joy and happiness for those who served God."

"So do you think these traitors could be people who wanted to worship other gods and were upset by your religious reforms?"

Asa looked a little doubtful, but then nodded and said, "That could be it."

"You don't seem very sure, my lord."

"Well, how am I meant to understand the mind of a traitor?" There was irritation in Asa's voice.

"Do you think that these could be people who want to worship the golden calves that Jeroboam set up?"

"That could be it," said King Asa.

Jehoshaphat felt that the answer was deliberately evasive. What was his father hiding and how could he get at the truth? Was it something his father was too embarrassed to talk about?

Persistence was all very well in its place, but sometimes it was best to ease off for a while. Maybe he could approach the subject from a different direction. The answers were hidden in history, so perhaps nostalgia could be the key.

"Can you tell me more about those great military victories, father? I've heard the stories before, but I'd like to hear them again, especially as I'm taking charge of the army. How did you feel when the Ethiopians attacked? One million men on your doorstep and your army being only half that size. Was it easy to trust that God would deliver you, or were you sure that you had a better army and a better knowledge of the area?"

"I trusted God," said Asa simply. "It wasn't hard at that time. Faith is such a difficult thing to describe, and so hard to maintain. It's elusive and ephemeral. Sometimes it's easy, to be sure, but the longer you have to mull something over, the harder it is to have faith.

"We had complete peace for the first ten years of my reign.[29] And even after that, our only real problem during the next five years was Baasha, the king of Israel. He kept building up his army and looking for trouble. He was an itching sore – and a brute of a man. He wouldn't worship Yahweh himself, and he wouldn't allow his people to either. He followed Jeroboam the son of Nebat in all the worst ways.[30] He was never willing to make peace with me.[31] The only good thing he ever did was to kill Nadab and the rest of the family of Jeroboam, the one who caused the Great Division and split one people into two nations."[32]

Asa grimaced and lifted his leg with both hands, trying to ease it into a more comfortable position. He turned and looked at Jehoshaphat. "My grandfather, King Rehoboam,[33] and my father, King Abijah,[34] tried to join the two kingdoms together again, but it didn't work. I don't think that the division can be fixed now. However, if you want my advice, my son, when you are running the kingdom, try to keep the peace with your nearest neighbours. Otherwise it's like lying on the ground above an ants' nest. You keep getting bitten from every direction. Try to make peace with Israel if you get the chance."

"I'll do my best, sir. I think it's important."

"Good. Anyway, where were we? Yes, apart from Baasha, everything was going well in the kingdom before Zerah attacked. Compared with what has followed, it was comfortable and easy. I was completely convinced that Yahweh our God was looking after us."

King Asa sat back and closed his eyes for a few moments and Jehoshaphat wondered whether he had missed his chance to find answers. Then his father opened his eyes and continued with a smile.

"In some ways it was a bit like I had a deal with God," he said. "I led the kingdom towards him and he paid us back with peace."

The smile left his face and he looked weary as he went on, "But when you have peace, people find things to do in their spare time, and they aren't always good things." He shook his head. "It's ridiculous, but the worship of other gods flourished during that time. Altars, high places, idols, shrines – all sorts of things were popping up everywhere. Whatever I did, I couldn't seem to stop it. From that point of view, it was actually a relief to have Zerah attacking because everyone had to concentrate on

---

[29] 2 Chronicles 14:1 reports a ten-year period of peace during Asa's reign but not when it occurred. A few pointers suggest that it was at the start of his reign.
[30] 1 Kings 15:33-34
[31] 1 Kings 15:16
[32] 1 Kings 15:29
[33] 1 Kings 12:21-24
[34] 2 Chronicles 13:2-20

that for a while. And when we won that battle despite being outnumbered almost two-to-one,[35] I could confidently announce to the whole nation that God had given us the victory. After all, two-to-one is pretty bad odds. I had the best of both sides of life: faith and proof."

Asa sat back and seemed to forget about the pain in his foot for a time. His eyes had a faraway look in them and a gentle smile softened his appearance.

"You know," he continued, "we won that victory with very little effort." He laughed quietly. "In fact, most of the effort was chasing them as they ran away. It was definitely God's victory, not ours."[36]

"I've heard many of the details before, father, but not all. How did the battle start?"

"It was what happened just before the battle started that was important, my son. Our army was in a better position than theirs, further up the valley and with more room to manoeuvre than they had. But still, being outnumbered two-to-one was frightening. I've never seen such a vast crowd of men. I can't really describe what it looked like. Men everywhere, filling the entire valley."[37] Once again he closed his eyes, and Jehoshaphat tried to picture the scene as his father described it, tried to imagine what it would be like to be king in such a situation.

Asa's eyes remained closed as he continued. "Just men everywhere. Faces contorted with anger and fear, hatred and violence. Arms and weapons waving. Shouts echoing towards us."

He paused, as if picturing again a sea of men pouring up the valley like a wave rolling irresistibly onto the beach.

"It was then that I did the most faithful thing I've ever done in my life. I waited and prayed.[38] Everyone was waiting for me to give the order to attack, but instead I stood on a small rise so that as many in the army as possible could see me, and then I knelt down and prayed. Solomon the Wise prayed at the dedication of the temple, and it was that prayer which inspired me. I had been thinking about prayer and what to pray, so I suppose you could say that I was prepared to some extent, but mostly it was just what I felt. I felt so close to God at that time. I needed him, that's true, but I also *wanted* him. I loved him. I depended completely on him. Some of the words were written down later, and I still remember the rest pretty well: 'O Lord, there is none like you to help, between the mighty and the weak. Help us, O Lord our God, for we rely on you, and in your name we have come against this multitude. O Lord, you are our God; let not man prevail against you.'[39]

---

[35] 2 Chronicles 14:8-9 tells us that Asa had 580,000 men to fight against Zerah's 1,000,000.
[36] 2 Chronicles 14:12-13
[37] 2 Chronicles 14:10
[38] 2 Chronicles 14:11
[39] 2 Chronicles 14:11

"And man didn't prevail – God did. As I finished my prayer and stood up, I gave the signal to attack. It was the company of mighty men who attacked first. They were all men of faith and true heroes in battle. Just a few, really. But if you can picture the effect a few flies can have on a horse, that's what it was like. The Ethiopian army sort of melted away in front of them. Twitching to get out of the way! It wasn't long before their whole army was twitching and dodging, and soon they were all running away. I know it's hard to believe, but there really wasn't much fighting that day."

Jehoshaphat loved the stories of God's work with his people, but this story was all about a great victory, and it wasn't likely to be success that turned loyal subjects into traitors. He must probe more deeply.

"I suppose everybody was rejoicing after that amazing victory."

"Yes, everybody was... I don't know how to put it to get the full feeling. Everybody was ecstatic, joyful, incredulous, astonished, amazed, thankful. You couldn't find anyone in the country who didn't have a smile on his face. Even those who had no interest in Yahweh couldn't deny us the joy of victory and the certainty of his presence."

Once again a smile had spread across the face of the old king, but it was cut short by a spasm of pain from his foot. He screwed up his face and tried to turn his leg a little sideways to ease the pain, but nothing he did seemed to help. Nothing was said for a while, as Asa wrestled with his pain and Jehoshaphat wondered what to do. His father wouldn't let anyone but his flock of doctors near that foot.[40]

"Father, should I go and talk to the priests and ask them to come and see your foot, or to pray for you?"

"No!" The harsh word seemed to erupt from the king's lips, full of pain and anger. He took a deep breath and tried to calm himself. "God is not interested in my small suffering. Yahweh is God of the nations, ruler over the peoples. He gave us the ability to think and learn so that we can look after ourselves and not pester him all the time with personal trivialities. That's why we have doctors who understand things like the disease in my foot and can help with comfort and curing. Above all, God expects us to learn to cope!"

Jehoshaphat wasn't surprised by what he heard, but it did disturb him. Yes, he was confident that Yahweh worked with nations, but that was not all: he was sure that Yahweh cared about individual people too. Jehoshaphat thought of what he had learned from the priests about a man called Enoch[41] who lived many years before Abraham, even before the Deluge. He was not a king, and nothing special hung on his success

---

[40] 2 Chronicles 16:12
[41] Genesis 5:21-24

or otherwise, yet God had chosen to look after him specially. As an individual. Surely Yahweh cared about his father as a person?

"I really think that the priests could…"

"Be silent!" said Asa, his face dark with anger. He appeared to be about to say more, but then closed his mouth tightly and compressed his lips. After a few moments, he began to look a little less angry, but the expression on his face was still forbidding. "My son," he said slowly, "do not try to tell me what to do. I am king and I don't need anyone to instruct me or try to push me into their own ways. People have done that before and…." He stopped and looked down into his lap. "Enough," he said, looking up again. "My suffering is my own and my decisions are my own. At the same time, I am king, and my nation depends on me to provide leadership. But my life as an individual is only important because I am king."

"My father, you have been a good leader of the nation. Your faith saved the nation when it was under threat from an impossible enemy. And it was your *personal* faith, not just the faith of a king. I admire you for that faith."

"A king always has appointed advisors, my son. I was not the only one with faith. There were also priests who taught me about Yahweh and his ways."

"But you listened to them. You didn't have to. You chose to."

"I'm not the hero you are painting me as, Jehoshaphat. There are various things in my life that I do not want to remember," he finished, looking at his son with a warning in his eyes; "or talk about!"

And they're probably exactly the things I'm trying to find out, thought Jehoshaphat to himself, wondering whether the information was important enough to be worth the risk of further antagonising his father. His father's obvious anger at Jehoshaphat's suggestion that he should ask the priests about his leg might be a warning. However, the security of the nation, not to mention his own future reign, could be in jeopardy if he did not understand the veiled suggestions of Gershom and Jehoiada.

"Can we go back to the aftermath of the victory over Zerah the Ethiopian and his million men? Surely such a victory made the worship of Yahweh easier in the kingdom?"

"Yes, of course it did. But God does not give without expecting a return. How can I express it? When Yahweh hides himself, he still expects us to follow him and obey his commands. But when he shows his power so that only a fool could argue with it, he expects more. After our unlikely victory, God wanted more from us. He wanted revival, he wanted direction, dedication. If you like, we had taken the first step, and that was all well and good, but God wanted more. After all, we had started from a position nowhere near where he wanted his people to be. As a nation, we had slipped a long way away from God and he wanted us back, walking with him through knowledge, through love, through fear of his holiness.

"There was a prophet sent by Yahweh: Azariah, the son of Oded. He explained it all to us, making it clear that we needed to move closer to God and that if we did, he would be with us. He told me as king that I must be brave and never weak. My work would be rewarded, he said.[42]

"My son, the task of being king is onerous. A king must lead his people. At times, he must drive his people, but my grandfather Rehoboam showed that he must also obey the people at times.[43]

"When to command and enforce; when to lead by example; when to give in to the demands of your people: these are the imponderable problems that make up the crushing load of kingship. Do you want it, my son? Are you ready for it? I was only 21 when I became king,[44] and now you are already over 30. Maybe I would have been a better king if I had been your age when I became king. Our ancestor, King David, was 30 years old,[45] and King Solomon a little younger. Grandfather Rehoboam was 41 years old,[46] and my father Abijah was 38 at his coronation.[47] I was the baby of them all and Yahweh gave me ten years of peace to start with – maybe he was giving me time to grow up!"

"Maybe it was because your attitude was righteous and he wanted to work with you."

"I didn't know much about being a king back then, but I did want to do a good job."

"It sounds as if you succeeded, too. So when you were told to make sure that the nation followed God, what did you do?"

"I got to work again: got rid of lots of those detestable idols from all over Judah and Benjamin, and even from the cities that we had taken in the hill country of Ephraim back when God was destroying the family of Jeroboam.[48] Israel was weak back then, and I thought it was a good opportunity to get back some of the areas of Israel that Grandfather Rehoboam had lost. Of course, most of them are gone now, but we still control a few.[49] I also repaired the altar of the Lord that was at the front of the temple.

---

[42] 2 Chronicles 15:1-7
[43] 1 Kings 12:1-20
[44] We don't know how old Asa was when he became king, but 21 years old seems reasonable. His son Jehoshaphat was 35 years old when he became king 41 years later (1 Kings 22:42; 2 Chronicles 20:31).
[45] 2 Samuel 5:3-4
[46] 1 Kings 14:21; 2 Chronicles 12:13
[47] We don't know Abijah's age at any stage.
[48] 2 Chronicles 15:8
[49] 2 Chronicles 17:2

"Then we had a great celebration of the victory over Zerah. People came from all over Judah and Benjamin, as you would expect, but we also had many from Ephraim, Manasseh and Simeon, people who moved into the kingdom of Judah because they saw that we worshipped Yahweh and that he was with us.[50] By that time, Baasha was king of Israel, and he didn't like it at all. Oh, no. But at the time, he couldn't do much about it – not openly anyway. Who is going to openly confront a nation that has just annihilated an army of a million men with almost no casualties of their own?"

Asa paused for a while as a sour look spread over his face. "I've got to point this out, Jehoshaphat," he said. "Pay attention to what your neighbours are doing. Don't assume that you are safe from them just because they aren't turning up on your border with an army. Watch them carefully. Baasha didn't attack us, he just quietly built up his army, and worked against us on several diplomatic fronts. Yes, he was working hard alright, behind our backs....

"Anyway, we had peace to gather for worship. We sacrificed lots of the animals that we had taken from the Ethiopians, too.[51]

"I can't express how amazing it was at that time. While we were all gathered here in Jerusalem, we all entered into a covenant to seek Yahweh, the God of our ancestors. We promised to be faithful to Yahweh, and only Yahweh. We promised to be genuine in our worship, with no cheating with other gods. Everybody agreed to it, even up to popular suggestions that anyone who wouldn't worship God should be put to death."[52]

"Whoa! That seems a bit extreme! Although I suppose the Law of Moses does say that, doesn't it?[53] But nowadays? Did everyone really agree to that?"

"They certainly did. You have to remember that most of those so-called gods don't demand exclusive worship themselves, so if you demand that everyone worships Yahweh, there aren't many people who won't agree to do so. Even the ones who love other gods are willing to hide their preferences and worship Yahweh for a while, particularly if the alternative is death. I don't think we found anyone who refused, but if we had, I'm sure everyone would have agreed to execute them: men or women, young or old.[54] In fact, I had to be careful in dealing with my own grandmother, but I think you know about that.[55] We all swore an

---

[50] 2 Chronicles 15:9-10

[51] 2 Chronicles 15:11

[52] 2 Chronicles 15:12-13

[53] Exodus 22:20; Deuteronomy 13:6-15; 17:2-5

[54] 2 Chronicles 15:13

[55] See 1 Kings 15:13; 2 Chronicles 15:16. Note that 'mother' can also mean grandmother, and seems to do so in this case (1 Kings 15:2; 2 Chronicles 11:20-22).

oath to the Lord. A massive crowd was there, and everyone was shouting out their promises and blowing trumpets and horns." Asa's eyes were glowing with the happy memories and a smile had driven away his earlier anger.

"It sounds like it was a wonderful time."

"Yes, it was. I have never known such a time. Happiness was everywhere and faith in Yahweh was never easier. Everyone was rejoicing over their commitment. They really were determined, and we all found that God was close to us because we had got closer to him. Ah, those were days to remember. Those are the times when it is good to be a king."

"What about Israel? You had some people come from there, but what about everyone else?"

"Baasha was my enemy from start to end. He wasn't always willing to fight me, but he always hated me."[56]

"If only we could have peace with Israel as you were saying. Maybe it could even lead to friendship and fellowship. We could go back to having all twelve tribes worshipping God in Jerusalem again. Did you ever see any opportunities for that?"

"No," said his father. "None at all. Maybe the best we can hope for is that they will start fighting amongst themselves again and tear each other to pieces. But King Omri and his son Ahab seem to have put a stop to that for the time being at least."

"Who knows what the future might bring? Maybe there will be an opportunity sometime. What happened next then?"

"God gave us peace. I know it seems obvious, but it really did work: we committed ourselves to God and he gave us rest all around. For more than a year, there were not even suggestions of any enemies coming against us. But Baasha hated everything that we stood for. I believe he even hated Yahweh, and he definitely hated the idea that crowds of his subjects had come to Judah because we were successful and worshipped God." Asa chuckled, "I'm not sure which of the two he liked less."

Once again, the smile was suddenly wiped off his face by a spasm of pain in his diseased foot. His shoulders slumped and the remembered joy of unreserved worship of Yahweh slipped away.

"After that year or so, though, things went downhill quickly." Asa sighed, then continued, "I suppose that I could have done a better job keeping the nation on the straight path. I wanted to, but it's hard to hold the path of brave, confident action for God. As I said, faith is hard to maintain. You would think that making one stand should make it easier to make another stand, but it doesn't always work that way. I felt that I

---

[56] 1 Kings 15:16, 32

had already pushed my people as far as I could. God was demanding more of me, but I didn't pass it on. I tried to keep the people happy – as I saw it."

"I know it sounds a bit idealistic," said Jehoshaphat, "but our history seems to show that people are happiest when they are close to God. Don't you agree?"

"Yes, it is true, my son," sighed Asa again. "But I was losing my own grip on faith, too. Looking back, it was almost as if I felt that I had used up all the help I could count on – all that I deserved – from Yahweh."

"I think that I understand," said Jehoshaphat. "I can see that it must be hard when you are the king. Faith is not something you can really force on anyone else, and I can see that that could make it hard to keep insisting for many years that people obey."

"I found it hard, that's all I can say. Anyway, Baasha started attacking us wherever he could. We were driven out of the towns we had taken in the hill country of Ephraim and driven all the way back to the border that was established in the time of Jeroboam and Rehoboam. I even started to worry that I was going to be the king who lost the kingdom altogether. And the attacks didn't stop there. Baasha not only kept driving us backwards himself, he also tried to convince the other nations around to close their borders to us.

"He was trying to strangle the kingdom of Judah, and there was nothing we could do. Our army did their best, but Israel is made up of nine tribes and we are only two tribes plus the Levites and a few others who have moved out of Israel because the worship of Yahweh was very important to them.

"Every day brought fresh bad news. Every week brought our front line closer and closer to Jerusalem. I was desperate and eventually did the only thing that I could think of – I sent messengers to Aram and offered them money if they would break their agreement with Israel and help us instead.[57] It cost us a fortune – well, several fortunes actually – but they finally agreed to help us. And did we ever need it! Baasha was building up Ramah as a big fortress and border inspection point.[58] He was stopping any travellers from coming into Judah or going out of Judah.[59] Imagine what it was like with no traders being able to come in or go out! There were shortages of everything we import, and lots of foodstuffs that we normally export to other places were just sitting around going rotten because Baasha's men were stopping our traders from entering or passing through Israel.

---

[57] 1 Kings 15:18-19; 2 Chronicles 16:2-3
[58] 1 Kings 15:17
[59] 2 Chronicles 16:1

"Getting the Arameans on our side worked, though. They started attacking Israel from the north, so Baasha had to take his troops up there to defend his own borders.[60] We were off the hook. So I ordered everyone to help dismantle Ramah.[61] There was so much spare building material that we were able to build two towns with it![62] In fact, we ended up better defended than we had been before Baasha attacked."

Asa stopped, leaned back on his throne, spread out his hands and put the tips of his fingers together. He had obviously come to the end of the story as he intended to tell it.

Jehoshaphat, however, suspected that there was still something missing from the story, and wondered if it was the missing piece of the puzzle. If it was, he thought, he would have to be very careful with what he said next.

"Were there any complications with the Arameans? Paying people to break earlier agreements seems like a dangerous game. What if Israel was willing to pay even more?"

"No, there weren't any problems like that," said Asa shortly.

"That all happened when I was... ah, ten years old, didn't it? I remember some of the things that happened, but I didn't understand them. I just remember lots of people being angry. Is my memory right?"

"Yes, there was a lot of anger then, but it doesn't help anyone to dwell on events that happened more than 20 years ago."

"I suppose not, but was there peace for a while after that?"

"No," said Asa, with obvious reluctance, "there were more problems. There always are, really."

Yet again, his father was hedging, thought Jehoshaphat, and this attempt to find out the truth was looking more and more risky! He decided to try one last time, choosing his words very carefully.

"Were there any celebrations and sacrifices in Jerusalem after that successful strategy?"

"Oh, why do you keep on asking all these pointless questions? No, there were no celebrations. All I heard were complaints," said Asa, his voice rising in anger. "People telling me what to do and acting as if they should be king!

"A prophet, Hanani, came to me all het up about how I had paid the king of Aram to break his agreement with Baasha.[63] Up until then, I had believed him to be a genuine prophet of Yahweh, but his carry-on changed my mind about that." Asa was shouting now, and his fist pounded on the arm of his throne as he continued, "This worthless seer

---

[60] 1 Kings 15:20; 2 Chronicles 16:4
[61] 1 Kings 15:22
[62] 2 Chronicles 16:6
[63] 2 Chronicles 16:7-9

came to me and spoke as if he was my instructor! He had no right to say any of what he said, and I haven't thought any more about it since."

Jehoshaphat was convinced that *this* was the information he had been looking for, but he suspected there was still more to the story. A quick glance observed a brooding scowl on his father's face: probing any further could risk his position as crown prince. Were just a few extra words going too far? He decided to chance it.

"I can tell that you were very angry then, father. What did you say to Hanani?"

"I was furious, and in the heat of the moment, I very nearly had him executed. Instead, I controlled myself and had him thrown into prison and locked up in the stocks.[64] I told them to leave him there until he learned how to speak to the king properly. Still, if that had been all, I probably would've got over my temper in a day or two and let him go, but people kept sending delegations demanding clemency, *ordering* me to let him go. In fact, some even went so far as to suggest that *I* should apologise!"

The king's face looked cruel, and Jehoshaphat wondered at this side of his father that he had never seen before.

"I can tell that you have more questions to ask," said Asa, "but none of this is any of your business." Despite the harshness of his words, the threatening look on the king's face was already receding.

"My father, none of these things are my business if you don't want them to be, but I did have my reasons for asking, as I mentioned."

"Yes, and this event may be what you were enquiring about, although you didn't know it. You must be wondering why I did what I did, but Hanani had *no right* to criticise me like that. And for others to demand that I – the king! – should free him or even worse? No-one can speak to God's anointed king that way."

"As you said, though, that was more than 20 years ago. Surely the problem went away fairly quickly?"

"I'm sure it would have if I had just let it go with Hanani, but when people take it on themselves to criticise the king, that starts to sound like rebellion and revolution, so I took appropriate action."[65] He held up a hand as Jehoshaphat began to ask another question. "No, Jehoshaphat, I don't want to talk about it any more. And I don't want to hear any more about it either. I suppose that I could have handled it differently, but what's past is past and nothing can change it now."

---

[64] 2 Chronicles 16:10
[65] 2 Chronicles 16:10

Chapter 7

HANDICAPPED

Ben-hail's recovery from his slip in the river was slow and painful.

His right foot was badly bruised where it had slipped down between the rocks of the riverbed, and it sported many of the colours of the rainbow as it gradually recovered. Yet although it was the most obvious injury, it healed the most quickly and caused him the least pain.

Ben-hail began to worry about being judged lazy. For two whole weeks, he had been lying down or sitting around doing *nothing*. But while the scratches on his feet were almost healed and the most vivid bruises in various parts of his body had lost their brightness, he still could not use his right wrist at all – the pain was too great. And his left leg refused to carry his weight.

How long would it be before Abiel came to him and gave him the bad news that he must leave the academy?

What would his neighbours think if he was expelled from the army?

He spoke of it to nobody, but he was determined to get back to training as soon as it was physically possible. His background had accustomed him to hard work, and enforced inaction was hard for him to bear. His mother had worked hard to support her son and herself throughout his childhood. Life as a widow was difficult, and Ben-hail had learned early that honest toil was a worthy lifestyle. But now he could not use his right hand, the hand he had always favoured.

Exactly two weeks after his accident, while the other students were away on an early morning run, Ben-hail sat in his tent, alone and discouraged. His internal injuries didn't seem to be healing and he was beginning to have doubts about his future. Would he ever regain full use of his right hand? – or of his left leg, for that matter? Would his ageing mother be able to survive if he could not work? Abiel had been encouraging him to rest and recuperate, but Ben-hail felt that he had seemed less enthusiastic at their last couple of meetings.

Handicapped

He decided to make a determined effort to do *something*. If he could not use his right hand, he must practise using his left hand. If he could not stand because of his left foot, he must learn to use his right foot alone to get around. Otherwise, he would find himself out of a job, with no skills for anything but soldiering. His mother still needed his support and he could not abandon his other plans for the future.

Immediately, he rose from his bed, helping himself up with his left arm and standing on his right foot. They had brought him a crutch soon after his accident, but he had not been able to use it because of the pain. Well, he must learn now. He bent over and picked it up, then straightened and tried to walk with it. It was very awkward – there was no way to take all the load off his left leg, and he had to lean awkwardly over the crutch to reduce the load as much as possible.

He struggled out of the tent and decided to walk towards the far end of the camp, where the training area was located. As he approached, he saw that two of the instructors were practising their swordsmanship, so he limped over to watch.

The swords were practice swords: the points and edges were blunt. An undefended stab or slash would cause injury, but would not be likely to kill.

One of the instructors was left-handed and a skilled swordsman. Ben-hail had always found him more difficult to fight than others because his sword approached from an unexpected angle. He had also noticed that others seemed to find it difficult too. At that moment, he wished that he was left-handed and still had the use of his preferred hand – but then, he supposed that if he'd actually been left-handed, he would have used his left hand to stop himself and injured that instead.

After a while, the swordsmen stopped for a break and turned to Ben-hail.

"Recovering, Ben-hail?" asked Hadoram, the left-hander.

"No, sir, not really."

"We've been missing you and your sword here," said Ziba. "Abiel planned to get you to teach swordsmanship after Ira was called back to his company. But then you went and hurt yourself."

"Well, I can't use my right hand. I can't even hold the sword properly with it."

"You should have been left-handed," laughed Hadoram. "In fact, everyone should be left-handed, but most people aren't good enough to be left-handed. We left-handers have gifts that others only dream about."

"Oh, yes," said Ziba. "You're always telling us that, but you won't ever be the commander's right-hand man, will you? That'll be me, and you'll be left out."

"All right, all right," said Hadoram, laughing, and then he turned to Ben-hail again. "But I am serious about one thing: since you can't use your right hand to hold a sword, you should try using your left. You never know when it might come in useful."

It might be useful right now, thought Ben-hail. What if my arm never gets properly better? "But what about my feet?" he asked. "I can't stand properly either."

"That might be good for us," said Ziba smiling. "You're too dangerous with two hands and two legs working properly. Maybe I could actually beat you now with you using your left hand!"

He was only joking, but Ben-hail decided to take up the challenge anyway. "Can I borrow that sword?" he asked Hadoram.

"Oh, sure," said Hadoram, holding the blunt point and offering the hilt to Ben-hail.

"You won't be able to hold your crutch as well as the sword," said Ziba. "I hope you have good balance. This should be an easy fight for me if I can just ignore what might happen to you if you fall over. Are you sure you can do this?"

"I can try." He dropped the crutch and took the sword in his left hand, feeling its weight and balance. It wasn't the first time he had held a sword in his left hand, but it was the first time he had ever done so with the intention of using it that way. It felt strange, almost as strange as holding a quill in his left hand to write. Ben-hail was used to his sword being a weapon that he could use with fine control and a light touch. Yet in his left hand it felt heavy, awkward and ungainly.

Ziba took his position and said, "Start when you're ready."

Ben-hail hopped into position and then said, "Now."

"Can't you hold a shield at all?"

"No, my right arm is too weak and painful at the moment. I'll just have to do without one."

"I wouldn't want to do it myself, but if you want to, I'll try to remember that you aren't protected."

"I don't really have a choice, so thanks for looking after me."

Ziba moved forward with a slow and gentle push. Ben-hail brought his sword across and pushed the probing sword away. Ziba changed his line of attack and thrust with his point towards his opponent. It was not an aggressive assault, but Ben-hail was amazed how terrifying it was to see a sword-point – even a blunt one – coming towards him when he had no shield to parry it. His innate sense of timing took over and he brought his sword across, making clanging contact with Ziba's sword and deflecting it to one side. Immediately, he saw the opportunity to attack while his opponent was reaching towards him and a little off balance. With no shield, he knew that he still needed to be careful in case Ziba should recover and use the edge of his sword to attack, but his momentum had been redirected by Ben-hail's parry and it was unlikely that he would be able to realign his blade so quickly.

With a smooth transition from defence to attack, Ben-hail thrust the sword towards Ziba, who saw the danger immediately, but could not react quickly enough. He was wearing a breastplate, but even so, he was glad that Ben-hail's sword point was blunt.

"How did you do *that*?" he asked incredulously.

"I'm not sure," replied Ben-hail, "but you left an opening and I took it. At that moment it wasn't as hard as I expected."

"Well, that should teach me not to be so confident! Let's start again."

The two continued their bout for several minutes, with Ben-hail hitting Ziba occasionally, but more often receiving gentle touches or acknowledging Ziba's restraint as he pulled up short where in battle he would not have.

By the end of the exchange, Ben-hail's left hand was so exhausted that he could barely hold up his sword. It was clear that he had a long way to go before he would be a competent swordsman with his left hand.

He had also fought the entire bout without a shield and wanted to think more about what that meant. Was it possible to fight effectively – and safely – without a shield? Could it have advantages? Shields did provide protection, but they were also heavy and cumbersome; they slowed a swordsman's movements, just when he needed the greatest speed and balance.

Still, a shield could deflect a thrusting sword, and he wasn't sure just how effectively he could keep away a sword without a shield. On several occasions, he had been able to push Ziba's sword away, but on others he had lacked the strength in his wrist to divert the thrusts. His limited mobility had also made him an easy target at times.

Ben-hail left the practice area with his head full of thoughts and plans for the future. If he wanted to be able to use his sword with his left hand, he knew that he had plenty of work to do. First, he must strengthen his left wrist, but that was not all. He must find ways to improve his balance. Running had helped with his swordsmanship, and he was sure that improving his balance would as well.

As he hobbled along with his crutch, he resolved to become the best swordsman in the company with right or left hand, with or without a shield. That way no-one could accuse him of laziness. He was still concerned that his recovery was taking a long time, much longer than he had expected. Maybe the damage was permanent – but he wouldn't allow himself to dwell on that possibility.

Back in his tent, he collapsed exhausted onto the bed and began to plot a course of action. Eliam was extremely strong, and he had said before that consistently lifting heavy things helped. Ben-hail's left hand had always been weaker than his right, but maybe that was just because he used it less. He should be trying to strengthen it through use. But swordsmanship also required fine control – in that way it was more like writing than many other things. He shied away from the idea, but perhaps even learning to write well with his left hand would help to make him a more expert soldier. And anyway, what if his injured hand didn't get better?

Being able to use his left hand would also give him the advantage of surprise at times. Ehud had killed Eglon the king of Moab and escaped safely because nobody expected him to use his left hand.[66] If Ben-hail could develop his skill with his left hand, maybe he would be able to achieve…. His mouth tightened as he thought of the possibilities, and those who knew him best would have been surprised by the harsh look in his eyes.

With the enthusiasm of youth, yet tempered by some pessimism about his injuries, Ben-hail made plans. Even as a child, he had been able to look at himself impartially, see opportunities for improvement, and take them. His mother said that he inherited this ability from his father, along with his determination and power of concentration. Be that as it may, Ben-hail had always found his mother rather determined, and she was the one who had always insisted that he must concentrate on whatever he was doing!

When his tent-mates returned, Ben-hail was holding a stick in his left hand like a pen, but he dropped it hurriedly as they approached.

"Ben-hail!" called Kilion excitedly. "You should have been there. I just beat Abiel by the greatest distance ever. My running felt so smooth, it was amazing."

"Was Abiel happy with that?"

"I think he was a little bit upset, but he still beat the next man by a long way, so he was willing to accept that it wasn't just that he's getting old."

"I'm not sure that I could feel like that," said Ben-hail.

"I hadn't thought of that," said Kilion meditatively. "Now that you mention it, I don't think that I could respond like he did either. He's got real character, hasn't he?"

Ben-hail told his friends what he had been doing during their run and tentatively reported his decisions.

"Can you help me to get my left arm stronger, Eliam?" he asked.

---

[66] Judges 3:15-30

"Mmm," said Eliam, loquacious as usual. He looked thoughtful and immediately left the tent.

"Do you really think that you can learn to write left-handed?" asked Darda.

"I can't see why not," said Ben-hail.

"I remember a scribe once telling me that you're either born left-handed or you're not."

"That doesn't stop me *improving* how well I can do things with my left hand. I've already done it many times with my right hand. After all, I had to learn to write in the first place – I just found it easier to do with my right hand than with my left."

"That scribe said that he had tried to learn to write with his left hand and couldn't do it."

"Maybe not – but perhaps I can."

It wasn't arrogance or conceit: Ben-hail had always found that he could learn to do things with his hands more easily than most people. From an early age, his excellent coordination and athleticism had enabled him to reach high levels of skill in physical pursuits very quickly. His determination helped.

"So when do you start?" asked Darda.

"I started using my left hand for the sword while you were out running," said Ben-hail.

"What, standing on one leg?" asked Kilion, incredulously, "or did someone hold you up while you waved the sword around?"

"I stood on both feet, but I didn't put much weight on my left foot."

"And a shield?"

"No shield."

"But how do you stop a sword thrust with no shield?" asked Darda.

"Well, yes, that's the difficult part," agreed Ben-hail, seriously, "but I'm thinking that maybe I can learn to do that too. Just think about it – if someone thrusts a sword towards you, you can push it away with your own sword."

"Wow, you wouldn't want to miss their sword!"

Ben-hail smiled and nodded.

"I suppose it's just practice anyway – you wouldn't ever fight like that normally," said Darda.

"I'll see how it goes. I think it's all about strength and timing."

His mention of strength was good timing indeed. As he spoke, Eliam re-entered the tent carrying six stones he had found on the hillside near the camp. They were of varying size, but all were chosen so that they could be easily held in one hand. Eliam laid them out in a line in front of Ben-hail, with the smallest at one end and the heaviest at the other end.

"Start with the smallest and move to the bigger ones as you can. Here's what to do," said Eliam. He picked up the smallest stone and began to repetitively lift it above his head and lower it to his waist. After a few such exercises, he put his hand down by his side and then lifted the stone up to shoulder level while keeping his arm straight. This he also repeated several times before showing Ben-hail some other movements as well.

"Do you often do things like that?" asked Kilion.

"Yes," said Eliam, simply.

"Then maybe I should try it too," said Kilion. "I could do with some more strength in my arms."

"So could I," said Darda. "I remember a commander once saying that that sort of practice was very helpful, but everybody else seemed to ridicule the idea."

Ben-hail picked up the smallest stone and tried to imitate Eliam's movements. He found some of the exercises easy, while others were much harder. "It's harder than it looks," he said, "particularly with my left hand."

"Don't push yourself too hard," warned Eliam, "just do it often. At least twice each day, do each movement a few times."

"I feel a bit silly sitting here waving a rock around, but somehow it feels like it really is going to help. And after that bout this morning, I'm sure I need help. My hand has never felt so tired."

Kilion picked up the lightest stone and began to copy what Eliam and Ben-hail had been doing, but some of the movements he tried without success. "Wow, you could have chosen a lighter stone, Eliam. It's alright for you people who are all muscle and no brain, but for sensitive people like me, it's too heavy!"

Ben-hail laughed, saying, "Maybe you need to build up your strength too, Kilion. If there's a 'sensitive' runner like you in the Great Tournament who's also lifted heavy stones and made himself stronger than you, I reckon he'll have a good chance of beating you."

Darda also took the stone and tried to copy Eliam's movements. He could perform them all, but he obviously found some of them difficult. Ben-hail might have complained about the lack of strength in his left hand, but it was obvious that neither Kilion nor Darda could match that strength, even with their right hands. As for Eliam, he made no comment, but he had carried all six stones with no apparent difficulty, although he had demonstrated with only the lightest one.

"Hey, Eliam," asked Ben-hail, "can you do the same things with the heavier stones?"

Eliam picked up the heaviest stone and repeated his earlier movements effortlessly.

Ben-hail raised his eyebrows and shook his head slightly. "Hmm," he said. "I think that I've got some way to go!"

∞

From that day on, time passed more quickly for Ben-hail. By the end of the first day, he had repeated the movements Eliam had shown him three times. The unaccustomed use left his undamaged limbs utterly exhausted, while his injured arm and leg hurt more than usual because he couldn't help occasionally using them by accident.

Yet despite the resulting pain, he felt better.

Within three days, Ben-hail had moved on to a heavier stone, and already his left hand and arm felt stronger. He had also tried writing with his left hand several times, but given up each time in disgust. He could not make his writing look like anything but a child's scribble!

Swordsmanship, however, was his main interest, and three days of fighting left-handed had already made a big difference. It was still much harder than using his right hand and he felt hopelessly awkward – but since he couldn't use his right hand anyway, what did it matter? Anything was better than nothing. He was pleased that he no longer felt the same helpless panic when his opponent thrust a sword at him. Instead, he was learning to react with the same coolness he showed when carrying a shield in his left hand and wielding a sword with his right. In some ways, he felt that his overall swordsmanship had already improved. He had learned to watch his opponent's sword more carefully, and not to change his focus once he judged that he could safely parry a thrust with his shield. Now he watched every instant until his own sword met the attacking sword successfully, his gaze never leaving his opponent's sword and his amazing concentration never relaxing for a moment.

Abiel heard about Ben-hail's determination to learn left-handed swordsmanship and was pleased. His plans to use Ben-hail as a tutor would have to wait, but such a clear sign of resolve and tenacity piqued the commander's interest. He had planned to use the task of training other students in swordsmanship to help prepare Ben-hail for the Great Tournament and graduation, but this might be even better. A perceptive leader, Abiel wondered if this could mesh with his intention of improving the standard of swordsmanship not only in his academy, but in the army generally.

He wanted to see how Ben-hail was progressing after three days of effort. That afternoon was devoted to weapons training for the students, particularly the use of swords, spears and slings. Abiel was present for this training as often as possible – whenever he could avoid the administrative burdens that made his job so tedious at times. That afternoon he walked out of the officers' tent leaving a large pile of papers for his subordinate to handle. He knew that it would cost him extra work by lamplight that evening: though diligent, the man lacked his boss's sharp mind and often failed to spot the complexities of administration that needed special attention. Never mind, he thought. This was more important. He found Ben-hail sitting on the ground near the long open area where students were throwing spears at a collection of targets, all distant, but some further away than others. Most of the students were not able to reach the furthest target, and the instructor was giving hints for increasing the length of throw. Ben-hail had tried, but the throwing action, even when throwing with his left hand, caused great pain in his right hand and the instructor had told him to stop.

"Ben-hail," said Abiel, "how is that right arm going?"

"I think it's getting better slowly. At least, I hope it is."

"Mmm. And your other injuries from that accident?"

"My right foot is completely healed. My left foot is still very sore and I can't put my full weight on it yet."

"How is the left-handed swordsmanship progressing? Ziba says that you're getting harder to fight against."

"I've never been much good at anything with my left hand, sir, but it is starting to get easier. I still find at times that I move my hand in the opposite direction from what I mean to, though."

"Interesting. I've never tried doing what you're doing, but I'd like to see how it's going. Let's have a bout now. I'll just tell your instructor that we're leaving."

He did so and the two of them moved – Abiel striding freely and Ben-hail still hobbling – towards the sword-fighting area which was fenced into smaller squares in which students developed their skills with instructors and other students. Most of the students there were dressed in breastplates and helmets, with greaves on their legs, either engaged in a bout or awaiting their turn.

"You don't have your armour on," said Abiel. "Is it in your tent?"

"Yes," said Ben-hail.

Abiel called a servant and sent him to fetch the armour, then led Ben-hail to the square nearest the spear-throwing area. Two students, Beker and Mattaniah, were in the middle of a bout.

"We'll need this area soon," called Abiel, "but you can keep going while we get ready."

He was already wearing his own breastplate with its quilted undergarment that helped to soften any blows that were struck. The metal plate usually kept out cutting edges or sharp points, but a heavy blow could still cause bad bruising and occasionally even broken bones, unless there was something underneath to cushion the blow. In summer, soldiers in full armour tired quickly under the merciless sun, but this was still winter, and there were times when the students were glad to be wearing their heavy padding, and the armour too.

As they waited, Abiel and Ben-hail watched the swordplay. Beker was the second-best swordsman in the academy, and Mattaniah was also amongst the best. However, their fighting styles were quite different: Beker depended on his speed and skill, while Mattaniah tended to use his bulk to try to dominate the smaller man. Sometimes it worked, but often Beker was able to use his greater speed to touch his larger opponent with his sword – enough to decide a bout in the early stages of the Great Tournament – and it was clear that Mattaniah was finding it difficult to control his temper as those gentle touches kept repeating. Ben-hail noticed that Mattaniah's swordsmanship deteriorated as his anger rose.

The servant hurried back with Ben-hail's equipment. Ben-hail leaned his crutch against the fence and put on the undergarment, then fitted his armour on top, keeping his balance with difficulty. Abiel had his own training sword with him and picked up another from a rack that stood at the junction where four squares met, offering it to Ben-hail, who took it with his left hand.

Once Ben-hail was ready, Abiel turned to the two students, who were still engrossed in their bout.

"Beker and Mattaniah," said Abiel, "I need to do some special practice here with Ben-hail now. Due to his injury, he's had to come up with some novel fighting methods, and I need to go over them with him."

Beker nodded and stopped immediately, but Mattaniah scowled and glared at Ben-hail. As he left the enclosure he muttered something under his breath, before stumping away. Beker watched Mattaniah's retreating back for a moment and shook his head slightly, then leaned against the fence, eager to watch the coming bout.

"When you're ready," said Abiel.

Ben-hail stood with most of his weight on his right leg, and his legs spread a little more than shoulder-width apart. He was still not comfortable putting much weight on his left leg, but having his feet further apart allowed him to move around as much as possible given his limitations.

"I'm ready," he said, "but don't think that I'm going to jump forward to attack, sir. You will have to lead off."

Abiel moved his right foot smoothly forward and thrust his sword towards Ben-hail's chest. He was clearly ready to stop the thrust if no defence was offered, but Ben-hail swept his sword upwards so that the edge of his sword, just short of the point, engaged the edge of Abiel's sword and pushed it aside effortlessly, the blades screeching together as the threat was safely averted.

Ben-hail allowed his sword to continue its arc until he was in position to thrust towards Abiel. The movements were smooth, almost beautiful, to watch, and if Abiel had been fully committed to his thrust, he might have had difficulty recovering in time. As it was, he was able to parry the thrust with ease and step back.

"Very nice," he said, impressed. "Had you really never used a sword with your left hand until just a few days ago?"

"No sir. Why would I ever choose to use my left hand when I am so awkward with it? I still feel as if I'm about to drop the sword sometimes, and my wristwork is slow compared with what I want to achieve."

"I hear that Eliam has been getting you to work on the strength in your left hand."

"Yes, he has. It's amazing how quickly it works, too. You saw my parry just then, sir. I was able to make contact with the blade right up near the point and still have enough strength to force your blade away. Just three days ago, I couldn't have done that."

"Hmm," said Abiel thoughtfully. "If you aren't too tired, let's keep going and you can show me your defence – but don't try any retaliation, I won't be in the right place for it. I want to see how you cope without a shield."

Ben-hail spent the next several minutes defending grimly, using his newly-developed skills to protect himself against everything from horizontal slashes to terrifying thrusts towards his face. In many cases, his defence was flawless and in an ordinary bout, he would have taken the opportunity to counter-attack. In some situations, however, he made basic errors and would have suffered badly had not his teacher been an expert.

"Well, lad," said Abiel, when he had finished his testing, "you have progressed amazingly." He smiled, and asked, "But how are your left arm and wrist feeling after that?"

"They're very tired, sir. I've never done so much defending before!" He lowered the point of his sword to the ground and transferred the hilt gingerly to his right hand, then slowly flexed the fingers of his left hand, grimacing as he did so. "It's hard work!"

Abiel lowered his point to the ground likewise and began to give Ben-hail some advice. "Let's make sure you understand the advantages you'll have when fighting right-handers with the sword in your left hand. When both fighters hold their swords in the same hand, they are used to the sword coming towards them across their body. Their eyes have some angle to work with, and that makes it easier to judge exactly where the sword is: how far away it is and how fast it is travelling. When the arm, hand and sword are all coming straight towards you in one line, it's much harder to judge. That's why left-handers are often harder to fight against than right-handers. Of course, left-handers have to face that against right-handers all of the time – but they meet it so often that they get used to it. You can too. And it's easier to get used to it and counteract it effectively if you understand why it is so difficult.

"The hardest attack to defend against from a left-hander is the thrust towards the face. Obviously having a sword coming straight towards your eyes is terrifying enough, but there often won't be enough time to get your shield up and across properly, and pushing the blade aside with your sword takes consummate skill."

They began again, this time with Abiel instructing Ben-hail to concentrate on attack and not to bother with defence at all. "But," he warned, "if I hold up my hand, stop your attack as quickly as you can." He gave a crooked smile and added, "Yes, even with your left hand, you are still a dangerous swordsman."

"Am I really?" asked Ben-hail in surprise.

"Yes. Let's begin again."

The session continued for an hour, and by the end of it, Ben-hail's left hand and arm burned with fatigue. Abiel had shown him many things that he must now learn to put into practice, but still, the most important requirement seemed to be for him to increase the strength of his left hand, wrist and arm. He also admitted that he needed to develop his fine control further. When using his right hand, he could direct his sword with minute accuracy, but with his left it felt at times as if he might as well be waving a snake around by the tail for all the accuracy he could achieve! Reluctantly, he decided that he would have to undertake more left-handed writing – the action he was finding the most difficult of all.

Over the next few days, his left leg continued to improve slowly, so that by the end of the week, it was able to bear his full weight – with care – and he began to move his feet at times during bouts. He had also dispensed with the crutch and could walk without too much trouble.

However, his right hand remained painful – too painful to allow him to carry anything with it. Strengthening his left hand was one of his first priorities, and in his exercises, he had advanced to using the third of the six stones Eliam had chosen for him. His determination to improve the fine control of his recalcitrant left hand drove him to practise writing with his left hand regularly – he even wrote a few letters to his mother. He hoped that she could read them!

His left-handed swordsmanship continued to improve in leaps and bounds. Abiel would not let him fight with any of the other students, but he spent many hours in bouts with Abiel and the other instructors.

The truth was that Abiel was concerned about the absence of a shield. It seemed obvious to him that fighting without a shield was a good way to get oneself killed. After all, shields hadn't been invented for nothing! Over time, though, Ben-hail's progress in defence was gradually convincing him that fighting without a shield was actually possible, as long as the swordsman was skilled enough.

Nevertheless, he would be glad when Ben-hail's right arm was fully healed. Having his master swordsman unable to hold a sword properly was worrying: it would be far too easy for him to get badly injured.

Chapter 8

DANGER

"Stop him!"

The shout arose as a young man twisted smoothly past a guard and sprinted towards the king riding on his donkey. Several more guards stood between him and the king, but they were all facing the other way, eyes glued to an old man singing a song of praise to God as the king rode past. It was a well-known Psalm, but the old man's mellow voice gave it an irresistible beauty.

The response of the distracted guards was a little sluggish, and by the time they turned, the young man was already upon them, waving his knife threateningly.

The first guard he dodged easily, the man's desperate grab too wide and too slow. The second guard saw the knife and reached for his sword, but a hand planted in the middle of his chest caused him to stumble and fall backwards. The other three guards were doing their best to defend themselves against the sudden attack, but they couldn't move fast enough. The young assailant leapt over the fallen man and swung his knife towards the closest remaining guard. The blade would surely have been buried deep in his chest, had he not stumbled and fallen to his knees as he tried to turn around. As it was, the blade struck his helmet and slid screeching off, knocking him to the ground as well. The other two guards were caught behind him, unable to defend their king. Shouts filled the air, but shouts could not stop the unfolding attack.

No-one now stood between the fast-moving attacker and his target, the king. No-one, that is, except Prince Jehoshaphat. Another four steps and the would-be assassin would be upon him, and no bodyguards could possibly intervene.

One step, and Jehoshaphat had turned around.

Two steps, and the knife was thrust out in front of the attacker, ready to be plunged into the prince's heart. Guards from behind the king were responding at last, but what could they do?

Three steps, and a look of shock and fear filled Jehoshaphat's face as the sprinting assailant was now almost close enough to touch. He began to take a hopeless step backwards.

Four steps and the knife was thrust viciously at the prince's chest, slicing through his coat and squealing against the metal breastplate that he wore underneath. Jehoshaphat was knocked backwards and fell to the ground, his helmet striking the ground with a clang. Realising that his attack had not hurt the prince, the attacker slid to a stop, eager to redeem his failure, but his momentum had carried him several steps past, leaving him just a few metres[67] from King Asa.

Indecision was written across his face: should he return and finish off the prince, or proceed to attack the king?

Indecision breeds delay, and delay squanders opportunity. Asa's guards used the precious instants to regroup, and now the advantage was on their side. Standing halfway between his targets, the would-be assassin could no longer reach either. Within moments, he was surrounded by a circle of irate guards who surged to the attack.

"Drop your knife," shouted a guard, and the young man wisely did so immediately.

"We've got you," said the leader of the king's bodyguard as the young attacker was grabbed from behind and thrown roughly to the ground. A forest of spears encircled him and the time of danger had passed – for the king and his son, anyway. The assailant lay still, breathing heavily, just a few metres from where Prince Jehoshaphat was being helped to his feet by an attendant. He had taken off his helmet and was rubbing the back of his head.

"I'm glad I was wearing that breastplate under my coat," he said, fingering the hole in his coat and looking at the young man surrounded by guards. "What was all *that* about?"

King Asa's donkey had stopped and the king was climbing down with obvious difficulty.

"Are you alright, my son?"

"Yes, I'm fine. But why was someone trying to assassinate you?"

"I don't know, but we'll find out who it is," said Asa, grimly, "and why." He tried to walk across to Jehoshaphat, but it was obvious that his foot was causing him a lot of trouble. "Curse this foot," he said, and signalled to another attendant to bring him something to sit on. A small chair was produced from somewhere, and Asa sat down near his donkey. "Bring the man here," he said.

The leader of the guard looked concerned and said, "My lord, don't you think it would be better if we took him straight to the dungeons? It

---

[67] A few yards.

would be best to get your majesty and the prince to safety in the palace. There may be other attackers."

"You have many guards here, and now they are ready," said the king, wryly. "Bring the man here."

The young man was brought to the king. He refused to walk, so he was dragged by enough guards to make sure that he was under complete control. When he was close enough, Asa lifted a finger and the guards forced the man to kneel, with a guard holding each arm and more guards behind him with spears at the ready.

"Who are you?"

The young man didn't answer, and King Asa gave a signal to the chief guard, who struck the man on the face. "Answer the king," he demanded.

"My name is Uriel," he said.

"Where are you from?" continued the chief.

"Gibeon."

"Why did you try to kill the king and his son?"

"He deserves it. They both deserve it."

The chief guard struck the man again. "Show respect to the king," he said, mildly. "Try again."

"The king arrested my father, took away his livelihood, and stole our ancestral land."

"What did your father do wrong?" asked Asa.

"Nothing *wrong*. He just tried to do what you tell us we should do."

"What do you mean?"

"He wanted to honour Yahweh..." the young man paused and glared at the puzzled king with a challenge in his eyes; "... and his prophet," he finished quietly.

Anger suffused King Asa's face and he snapped, "Take him away. Put him in the traitors' dungeons. Feed him bread and water, but not much. I'll deal with his case some time." He looked deliberately at the young man and smiled cruelly. "There's no hurry." He turned and walked back to his donkey, and his attendant helped him mount. It was a slow process.

Jehoshaphat had been standing behind King Asa throughout the interview. As his father walked away, he pursed his lips and stroked his beard. He had even more to think about. What had the young man meant about honouring God's prophet? And why had the king reacted with such obvious anger?

☙

King Asa sent for Jehoshaphat the next day. He was led into the throne room[68] and bowed before his father. The king's foot was resting on a stool and a man was fussing around it. Jehoshaphat assumed that it was a doctor and felt sympathy for his father. If only he would allow a priest to examine the foot – maybe there was some treatment under the law that would help to cure him. However, after his father's angry response, he was not going to make the suggestion again.

He waited for his father to speak, but the king was busy looking at the dressing the doctor was applying to his foot. It looked like a hot poultice and the king didn't look comfortable with having it on his foot. Nevertheless, he bore it stoically, shutting his eyes for a while as he tried to cope with the pain. The pain in his foot seemed to be demanding more and more of his attention each day, and Jehoshaphat wondered where it would end.

When Asa was finally able to give his attention to Jehoshaphat, he asked him how he was after yesterday's excitement.

"I'm fine, thank you, my lord. My chest feels a little bruised, but it's nothing important."

"I'm glad you had that breastplate on, and I'm very glad it wasn't visible. If that young man had seen it, he would probably have attacked in a different way that would have left more than just bruises! How dare he try to do such a thing? As far as I'm concerned, he can sit and rot in prison until my foot gets better. Then I'll deal with him. Oh yes, I'll deal with him."

"Are you going to find out who his father is, or do you already know?"

"I don't know, but yes, I will find out. But there isn't any hurry. And once I know who he is, I might deal with the rest of his family too."

"Father, he said his father was just trying to honour God and his prophet. I don't understand. What did he mean?"

"Remember how I said that people had tried to tell me that I should apologise for how I spoke to Hanani? Well, I locked up the people who criticised me like that. My subjects are not my advisors, my teachers, my instructors or my supervisors."

"No, father, you are king, but..."

"My son, I am not going to discuss this subject with you any more. I am not angry with you, but I have made up my mind. What I want you to do instead is to talk to Gershom, the commander of the army. Tell him that I have instructed you to go to him and ask him about what happened in the matter of Hanani and what followed. He is to tell you the truth." Asa looked at his son shrewdly. "I wouldn't be surprised if

---

[68] 1 Kings 7:7

it was his comments that put you onto asking all of these questions anyway."

Jehoshaphat gave a slow smile but neither confirmed nor denied his father's suggestion.

"I'm feeling like an old man, my son, and my foot hurts so much that I can't concentrate enough to explain everything that has happened. Maybe I haven't always been as godly as I should have been. I know my temper has got the better of me at times."

"I shall talk to Gershom, then, my father. I think that this will help me to answer my questions about our problems on the borders, too. Thank you, my lord."

"Good. Now, yesterday's incident has worried me a little. As you know, I have bodyguards always with me. You, however, have only a few attendants. I don't think that they are even special soldiers, are they?"

"No, sir. They are there to help me more than to protect me. Of course, some of them are armed, but they're not what you would call expert bodyguards."

"We should do something about that. If people are going to attack us both, we need to make sure that you are kept safe as well."

"If I need protecting, then you need a better group of guards too, father. You would've been killed in that attack if I hadn't been in the way."

"Maybe – and you would've been killed except for some very good luck."

"I'd describe it as God's good care, father."

"Yes, you're right. But now we must show our thankfulness by doing our part. Our previous efforts obviously weren't good enough, so let's do better."

"I suppose so."

"The Great Tournament should be beginning soon, shouldn't it?"

"Yes, in four months' time."

"The last tournament was cancelled for security reasons, and this time my foot has distracted me from making sure the arrangements are progressing. It is a good boost to the morale of our soldiers and very popular with the rest of the people, so we need to get on with it."

"Well, I have heard that many units of the army and various academies have been preparing for the competitions."

"Good. Now, when you are in charge of the army, you should have an armour-bearer and a group of several men as your bodyguard. Some mighty men always turn up in the tournament: we could use some of those to form your bodyguard."

"I'm looking forward to the competitions. Some men with amazing ability always show up, and the best of them always seem to have amazing faith as well."

"Yes, they often do."

"David's mighty men had amazing faith, and they achieved incredible things."

"True," said Asa, absently. Suddenly, he leaned forward and continued, "I suggest that we bring the tournament forward. Arrange it for two months' time instead of four."

"Is two months long enough to get everything organised?"

"I think it should be. And you need that extra protection sooner rather than later."

"Are there really others like that young man around?"

"We don't know, but we need to be careful. As you know, the Great Tournament is always held at one of the army academies, and the commander takes charge of the organisation. Abiel is the best commander of them all. If anyone can arrange the tournament successfully in only two months, he can."

"I've heard of him – they say that his academy produces the best graduates."

"Yes. And he is one of the mighty men with faith that you referred to before."

"That's good."

"He's an amazing swordsman and a phenomenal runner. Some people suggest that he must even be faster than Asahel was. Hmm. I hadn't thought of that."

"Of what, my lord?"

"None of the staff of the academy at which the tournament is held are allowed to enter the competition."

"Why?"

"It avoids the temptation for officials to fix the results. Anyway, the point is that Abiel was expected to win the last tournament, two years ago, and be named the King's Swordsman, but then we had to cancel it. And two years before that, he missed entering because his mother was dying during the tournament. Throughout his career, there have always been reasons why he could never enter the competition and take the title, even though everyone acknowledges that he is the best swordsman in the land."

"Surely his mother would have excused him from her bedside to give him the opportunity to become the King's Swordsman."

"Oh, yes. In fact, she tried to convince him to leave her, but he wouldn't go. He said that with his father already dead, his mother was his responsibility."

"Amazing. But how do you know so much about him?"

"Some things stick in your memory, and that willingness to honour his father and mother seemed admirable to me. After that, I spoke to Gershom to see what could be done, and he made Abiel the commander of what's now called Abiel's Academy. Apparently he had always wanted to train soldiers, and it seemed to me that he would set the students a good example – teach my soldiers the sorts of morals I wanted them to learn."

Jehoshaphat looked at his father admiringly, yet wondering at the contradictions he seemed to present.

"Abiel is getting older," said Asa. "He's about your age, and for a soldier, that's getting a bit old. This might have been his last chance to become the King's Swordsman. Or maybe it's already too late."

"It seems a pity for him to miss out. Couldn't we appoint another commander to arrange the Great Tournament? That would give him one more chance."

"Abiel will make sure the tournament is organised in time – and organised well. No-one else will do it so well. After yesterday, I feel that we need to do something earlier than we had planned."

"Very well."

"Speak to Gershom about getting a few more personal guards for the time being, but I want you to have the very best. The best soldiers in the land. The winners of the tournament."

"I shall speak to Gershom about this immediately, sir."

The ageing king looked down at his hands and said, "Good. And about that other matter we were talking about, you could ask Jehoiada the priest as well. You may go."

Jehoshaphat looked thoughtfully at his father and left.

Chapter 9

PLANNING AND QUESTIONS

Jehoshaphat was quick to visit Gershom again. When Jehoshaphat entered, the ageing commander was sitting at a table, reviewing the available troop numbers in the north. A scroll was in front of him and he was sharpening a quill with a pen-knife.

After greeting the prince with genuine friendliness, he waved at a chair and Jehoshaphat sat down.

"Is this something to do with yesterday's attempted assassination?" asked Gershom.

"Not directly. The king wants the Great Tournament to be held two months early," said Jehoshaphat.

"*Early?* But we haven't begun any preparations yet – normally it wouldn't occur until the middle of summer at the end of the fourth or fifth month."

"I know. It seems that everyone has been hoping the king would recover from his disease enough to get things moving, and I think he might have been waiting for everyone else to initiate things."

"Last time the king cancelled it. And that was after we had already started organising it."

"Yes, but he doesn't want to do that again."

"Well..." said Gershom, breathing out slowly, "I suppose we can fall back on the arrangements we had made last time. We can hold the tournament at Vophsi's Academy."

"No. The king says it is to be held at Abiel's Academy."

"Oh!" Gershom paused and shook his head. "Vophsi won't take that well, I can tell you. Why does the king want it that way?"

"He says that if anyone can organise it two months early, Abiel can."

"That's true, I suppose. But I'll say it again, sir: Vophsi won't like it."

"I don't know Vophsi at all. Why will he care and why does it matter?"

"He's a real stickler for protocol, is Vophsi. Very quick to take offence too, if he thinks he has been slighted. I'm sure that he'll take this as an insult. Everyone knows that he was to host the Great Tournament two years ago, and that it was cancelled at least partly because of unrest in his area and some questionable behaviour by a couple of senior soldiers who had come from his academy. He'll see this as a direct slap in the face, I'm sure."

"I see. I hadn't heard of any of this. Maybe it would be best to have the tournament at Vophsi's Academy after all."

"No, sir. If King Asa says to have it at Abiel's Academy, that's what we'll do. And if the king says to have it two months early, well, we'll do that, too."

"The king wants the tournament early because he wants to get some more bodyguards and an armour-bearer for me."

Gershom snorted and shook his head. "If we can't immediately find men from our army to do that work, the kingdom's done for."

"You're probably right, but 'If King Asa says it, that's what we'll do'."

Gershom smiled and raised no more objections. The two men continued to discuss what must be done. Gershom would ride north the very next day to tell Abiel personally of the honour he had been accorded by the king.

"He might be upset, too," mused Gershom. "This tournament would probably have been his last chance to be named the King's Swordsman, and now he won't even be able to enter."

"My father said the same thing. Maybe we can do something for him anyway, or even make some sort of exemption to keep him happy. From the sound of it, he deserves it."

"I'm sorry, sir, but exemptions are out of the question. Just think if we were to make an exception and he were to win. People know why the rules were made – what would they think if a man was allowed to go outside the rules and won?"

"I hadn't thought of that."

"Sometimes we have to be cruel to be kind, sir. Abiel is respected by everyone, and that's how it should stay. Now, your father specified years ago that the tournament was to be the fourth or fifth months."

"Counting back two months from the fifth month would give Abiel the most time to arrange things."

"That means the third month. But that could be near the Feast of Weeks."[69]

---

[69] A harvest festival, also known as the Feast of First Fruits and later as Pentecost. One of the three annual feasts that all Israelite males must attend. See Exodus 23:16-17; Leviticus

"Yes, and you know my father would never allow us to interrupt that."

"Then I think it would be best to have the tournament immediately after the feast."

"I guessed that was what you'd say," said Jehoshaphat, "so I had a quick chat with Jehoiada the priest. He said that, based on the current reports of the barley crop, the feast will probably be sometime in the first or second week of the third month."[70]

Gershom looked at him with a hint of admiration. "You've done your preparation well, sir," he said.

"Thanks. Are we agreed on the timing then? For the moment, we'll assume the tournament will start in the third week of the third month, and the priests will confirm the date of the Feast of Weeks as soon as they can."

"That sounds good. And you'll explain all of this to your father?"

"Yes. I'd also like to talk to you more about the matters that may have led to the assassination attempt."

Jehoshaphat recounted some of his earlier discussion with King Asa. Gershom listened impassively to Jehoshaphat's words, but began to tap the pen-knife on the table when Asa's instructions were repeated.

"He told you to ask me, did he? How would he know that I could tell you? I have served your father for many years, but he still surprises me occasionally. He sees more than you might think. Well, sir, at his direction I will tell you what happened and what the results have been. Did he tell you to talk to anyone else, or are you to hear only my bias?"

"He said that I might want to talk to Jehoiada later."

"He really does see more than I thought! I thought we had kept our opinions secret, but he obviously knows them. Well, here goes.

"As you know, sir, King Asa had paid the Arameans to break their agreement with King Baasha of Israel. Now, logic alone says that if someone can be paid to break one agreement, the new agreement will only last until someone offers even more money. That's obvious, but it wasn't the only thing which made King Asa's choice, ah... unwise. Faith was always one of his strongest points. I was in command when we met one million men with an army of little more than half that number. But that time, King Asa believed that we would win and convinced us all that he was right. He was, too. Faith won that battle – we hardly had to do anything. So some of us were very surprised when he decided to buy off the Syrians instead of trusting God to defeat the armies of Israel and Syria.

23:9-14; Numbers 28:26-30; Deuteronomy 16:9-12

[70] The Feast of Weeks was a moveable feast held seven weeks from the day when the harvest began (Deuteronomy 16:9-10).

"Anyway, Syria attacked Israel for us as requested, and once Israel's army had left, we pulled down the walls of Ramah that Baasha had been building and used them to fortify several other towns. However, when we returned to Jerusalem, Hanani the prophet was waiting for us with a message from God. He probably thought that he was reasonably safe even though his message was criticising the king – after all, Asa was a faithful king and a great proponent of the worship and power of Yahweh. I think Hanani expected the king to listen to God's rebuke and say that he was sorry, just as King David did, or so we're told.

"But no, when Hanani gave the king that straight-talking message from God, the king almost had him executed on the spot. He was lucky to only get locked up, really.

"Now, up to this point, I'm sure you know the details. After that, we get to the part that no-one talks about openly – because no-one dares to.

"You see, Hanani was a well-known prophet. He had friends among the priests, the nobles, and the common people. When the king locked him up in prison and left him there, people started to complain. Honestly, at first nobody could really believe that the king would do something that was so much at odds with how he had lived for all of the rest of his life. But then it got worse. He started arresting anyone who complained and beating them, locking them up, confiscating their land, and so on.[71] Some of it was really brutal, and those of us who were loyal to the king found it very hard to watch. Naturally, every man who was locked up had a family, so the king was making enemies left, right and centre. And what was worse was that the people he was making enemies of were the best sort of people in the kingdom. They were the ones who had called him "Asa the Faithful". Yet righteous people who loved God's prophets were being locked up. Priests, Levites, lay people, even some soldiers. That's where *I* had a real problem.

"Some of the families of those people have become enemies of the king as a result. They say that he is fighting against God and that God is judging him through the nations that are attacking us now.

"Who is in the right, my lord? I have stuck with the king because of his faith over many years and because I have promised to serve him, but I can understand why other people – including some more righteous than I am – have decided to fight against him. Some have even chosen to pass on information to our enemies. I am almost certain that the young man who tried to assassinate the king yesterday is one of this group. I don't know what happened to his family, particularly his father."

"How many people were caught up in this purge?" asked Jehoshaphat.

---

[71] 2 Chronicles 16:10 tells us that Asa inflicted cruelties on some of the people at the same time but gives no details.

"I don't really know, sir. Your father didn't tell anyone all of the things he was doing. I knew about some of the people he locked up, and some of those whom he punished in other ways. I heard of some who were driven away from their homes and others who were possibly sold as slaves. I hate to admit it, but I even helped the king in some of these atrocities. But other... wrongdoing... was arranged by different people and I didn't hear about it until afterwards – and then only as rumours or vague stories."

"How long did this last?"

"It's still going on, sir – at least, it was until very recently. Maybe the disease in the king's foot has stopped it, I don't know."

"What happened to Hanani?"

"He is still in prison, sir."

"*Still?* After more than 20 years?"

"Yes, sir."

Jehoshaphat closed his eyes and shook his head. Was this the father he knew? The God-fearing man who worshipped so often in the temple?

"And what about the others?" he asked.

"Some are still in prison, but some were freed fairly quickly and others several years later. Others died in prison."

"No wonder there are people who are willing to rebel against or kill my father, and maybe even kill me too."

"Yes, sir. Most in the kingdom are still faithful to your father – though many don't care whether things are fair or not as long as they aren't hurt themselves."

"I need time to think about this. It is terrible, shocking, horrific! And this is *my father's work.* Did any of your family or close friends get caught up in this? After all, how would you feel if your father had been treated like that young man's father was?"

"No, sir, no-one close to me was affected. Maybe I would have more problems with my loyalty if it had been my father. I don't know, sir. But I do know that if Hanani hadn't told off the king, none of this would have happened. Prophets may think that they are doing God's work, but they are taking a big risk when they attack a king, however godly!"

ॐ

Although Gershom didn't know it, the Great Tournament was already uppermost in Abiel's mind as the commander of the army rode northwards the next morning.

Abiel had been far too young to have any part in the victorious army that had rejoiced when Zerah and his men had fled, or to have been much help with the dismantling of Ramah, although his father had taken him there on several occasions as the fortress walls built by Baasha had been taken apart, stone by stone. Yet those events had driven him to join King Asa's army as a volunteer soldier at an early age, where he had quickly stood out for his courage, self-discipline and faith.

King Asa's training academies took in new students whenever commanders recommended particularly promising volunteer soldiers for the training that would turn them into professional soldiers. Committed to Vophsi's Academy, Abiel's light, wiry frame was quickly seen at the forefront of every competition that required speed and fitness. His speed of movement fostered a skill in swordsmanship that quickly outstripped his fellow students – and most of his instructors.

Students normally remained in an academy for three years, being taught a range of skills and hardened for work as professional soldiers. Occasionally, a student would be rejected after a short time, normally when the academy commanders found "unacceptable characteristics" in them. Cowardice, cruelty and brutality, gross insubordination and laziness were the most common. The army could tolerate many character defects, but these defects were like flags that King Asa did not want waving over the army of Judah.

Abiel, however, worked hard in the academy and graduated quickly, finding his way into the king's elite forces in near record time. Since then, his career had been outstanding, and he was acknowledged by most as one of the best swordsmen the kingdom had ever seen.

Yet not everyone had followed his progress with pleasure.

Vophsi, his academy commander, was, as Gershom had suggested, a stickler for protocol. When Abiel's speed and dexterity had caught the eye of the judges in some of the warm-up rounds of the Great Tournament early in his first year in the academy, Vophsi had been displeased. For Vophsi, everything should be done in the right order: young men should wait until their elders gave them permission to excel.

Students had to be chosen by their commander before they could enter the student sections of the Great Tournament. Vophsi only ever selected students who were in their final year at the academy. Abiel sat on the sidelines without complaining, but his friends were furious – and vocal.

Vophsi heard the complaints indirectly and assumed that they came from Abiel, so Abiel missed out again when the Great Tournament came around again early in his third year as a student. Upstarts needed to be put in their place, argued Vophsi, and so did those who complained about discipline.

So Vophsi could prevent Abiel from competing, but he was unable to hide his student's skill, and his actions were viewed by many as vengeful and foolish. Once more, Abiel was included in some warm-up rounds, and this time he left no-one in any doubt not only that he could have taken out the award for Swordsman of the Academies, but also that he might well have won the open competition had students been allowed to enter it.

Such was Abiel's experience with Vophsi, and that experience had caused him to take a radically different approach to both soldiering and the training of soldiers. While Vophsi stuck slavishly to rules and precedents, Abiel acknowledged that rules and precedents were valid guides to follow: starting points from which to determine policy, but not policy in and of themselves.

Abiel was not a bitter man, but he saw Vophsi's attitude as that of a vengeful and lazy man worthy of little respect. When Abiel was later appointed to the position of Academy Commander by Asa, he had been determined to avoid the precedents he had seen in his own training. He felt that it was important to assess each student individually to see what they could offer the kingdom. Hard-working and worthwhile students would graduate from his academy with his blessing, but nobody would graduate just because they had completed three years of training.

So nowadays, Abiel ran a particularly well-organised training academy. For those who wanted to learn soldiering, it was probably the best in the kingdom, and Abiel had high standards that his graduates must satisfy. For Abiel, one of the cardinal failures was laziness. Idleness, indolence, slothfulness and slackness were all prime reasons for expulsion from his academy: Abiel was never lazy himself and he simply *would not tolerate* laziness in his graduates.

King Asa had great confidence in Abiel and respect for his ability to produce top-quality graduates who would maintain the standards of bravery and faith that the king wanted in Judah's army.

Now, Abiel was to be rewarded with the difficult honour of having to arrange and host the Great Tournament at very short notice. No-one was better suited to the task.

In fact, several days earlier, shortly before the king had made his unexpected plans for the Great Tournament, Abiel had decided that something had to be done. If the Great Tournament was to take place this year, his students must begin preparing immediately. If the tournament had been cancelled again, he was going to arrange similar competitions for his own academy anyway. As it happened, dedicated training in Abiel's Academy was scheduled to begin the very day Gershom rode north.

Chapter 10

SERENDIPITY

"Morning's here," came the familiar call, though it was almost drowned on this occasion by the rain falling on the tents. The night had been unusually cold, and a frosty morning had only been avoided when clouds had rolled in during the fourth watch of the night – unfortunately bringing with them a cold, soaking rain.

"Out of your beds, you lazy loafers! Spring's almost here. Sandals on. It's time for a run."

In Ben-hail's tent, Darda rolled over first, followed by Eliam, the silent giant. Ben-hail lay for a few moments longer, slowly flexing his left foot, which seemed to set almost solid each night and needed a gentle reintroduction to moving each morning. The injury still prevented him from joining in the morning run, but he kept himself busy with exercises for building strength and dexterity in his left hand. Abiel's training staff were all involved in Ben-hail's recovery and he was a favourite with them. His willingness to try new and difficult things was helping them to develop new ideas for treating such injuries.

No-one was looking forward to a run in the rain, but there was a certain camaraderie in silent shared endurance. However, Kilion was slow to rise as usual, and when he eventually forced himself to roll over, he was anything but silent, complaining bitterly about the cold, the rain, the darkness and the expected run.

Bed-rolls were stacked and the foursome left the tent for the windswept chill of the assembly area. News was sometimes given at this time, so Ben-hail attended before beginning his own exercises when the rest of the students left on the run.

Abiel was waiting in the cold, but today, rather than making any announcements, said that the news he had could wait until a shortened morning run was finished. He led the students away into the darkness, everyone placing their feet carefully, wishing for the light and longing for the rain to stop.

Ben-hail remained at the assembly area. Although he could walk without a stick, running was still out of the question – let alone running in the darkness and rain. Nevertheless, he was determined to be involved in the camp activities as much as possible, so he attended the assembly area with the rest of the students whenever he could. His sense of fairness and honour also insisted that if everyone else was to run in the rain, he should be out in the rain too, even though the exercises he undertook were still working on the strength of his left arm and could easily have been performed in his tent.

The supervising trainers appreciated his behaviour and helped him as much as they could. Most of the students admired him, although many felt that they themselves would have taken the opportunity to avoid the rain if they had had the chance.

Ben-hail had now worked his way up to the fifth of the six stones that Eliam had selected for him. Given the increasing ease with which he handled it, it seemed like it might be time to start using the largest stone. At times, he wondered if the constant exercise had now developed greater strength in his left hand than in his slowly recovering right hand. As soon as he could, he would begin working with his right hand in the same way.

Why was his recovery taking so long? Surely it was only a matter of time before Abiel started some form of training for the many competitions that would be held as part of the Great Tournament. Some said that the tournament would never happen again, because the ageing king was too preoccupied with his diseased foot, but Ben-hail couldn't accept that. A detached logic told him that the tournament was too important for army morale and traditions, but for him personally, the truth was that he had built so many of his hopes and plans on the Great Tournament that he couldn't let them go.

With his left hand, he picked up the sixth stone, which had become a symbol of recovery to him. From the start of his recuperation – when he wasn't feeling utterly miserable and frustrated – he had always felt sure, somehow, that his right hand and left foot would have healed by the time he had mastered that sixth, heaviest stone. Was he finally ready to begin working with it? He lifted the stone above his head, feeling its weight, then lowered his arm until he was holding it parallel to the ground. He repeated the now-familiar exercises that Eliam had shown him, realising with surprise that they were easier now, even with this heaviest weight, than they had been with the lightest when he had first begun his effort to develop the strength in his left hand.

Despite the continuing rain, his mood lightened with the success, and by the time full daylight had arrived, he had completed his exercises without too much difficulty. His mind was contentedly turning over the hopes, plans and dreams that had driven him from an early age when

Kilion led the runners back. It had been a shortened run, and Abiel was a closer second than he had achieved in any recent run. Others followed, with the stragglers finally making their way back into camp just as the rain petered out.

The stragglers found the assembly area filled with students and academy staff, waiting eagerly for Abiel to tell them all the news he had promised. As the last student entered, he began.

"For many years, the Great Tournament of Judah has found and rewarded the fastest, strongest and most accurate of our soldiers and students. This tournament normally occurs every two years, but was cancelled two years ago due to the difficult security situation at the time. Since the situation of the kingdom is not much improved, the tournament may not take place this year either. At the moment, we don't know. However, this academy intends to prepare for the tournament anyway. We begin practising for the tournament today, and every one of you – every student in this academy – will be included in the qualifying rounds and preparation. Even if the national tournament is cancelled, we will still hold our own competitions. You should all benefit from the competitions in various different fields of soldiering. They will help you to become better soldiers, and those who excel will be rewarded as they deserve.

"As you know, your supervisors and trainers are permanent soldiers, generally selected because of their ability in particular fields, and you will often be competing against them. They have all been directed to give no quarter, so don't expect them to take it easy against you when competing."

Winter was almost past and spring was nearly there: plans for the Great Tournament would normally have been announced already. Abiel had done his calculations and decided that the tournament might well be a casualty of the king's sore foot.

However, he believed in the value of competition in developing the skills the army needed and wanted to make sure that his students were prepared whether the national tournament took place or not. And he was not willing to wait any longer.

"Since most of you have never been involved in the Great Tournament," continued Abiel, shouting to make sure everyone could hear, "I will explain how our training will work and what the goal of the competitions is.

"We want to find the best swordsman; the strongest man; the fastest runner; the most accurate man with a spear, sling or arrow; the man who can hurl a spear, stone or arrow the furthest.

"We want to find the individuals who excel in these individual skills, but we also want to find the man who achieves the best results in all of these skills."

If the Great Tournament did take place, Abiel was eager to have his students prominent among the champions, and preparation was the best way to achieve this.

He began to explain the individual competitions, particularly for those who had joined the academy since the cancellation of the last Great Tournament and thus missed out on the initial training that had been so abruptly cancelled.

"Running is in two different distances: short and long. The short run is held on level ground, while the long run involves running a fixed distance across the countryside, in a way that is very similar to the runs we do most mornings. The three fastest runners in each competition would normally be sent to the Great Tournament, which may still proceed, but even if it doesn't, we may still be able to have combined competitions with some of the other academies.

"In the same way, we will find our three strongest men based on who can lift the heaviest things. In the Great Tournament, the strongest men from each academy and various divisions of the army compete for the position of the army's strongest man.

"We have two main competitions each for archery, spear-throwing and slinging: one measuring distance and the other concentrating on accuracy. Archery and slinging also each have a competition rewarding speed.

"Prince Jonathan, the son of King Saul, once climbed a cliff to attack the Philistines,[72] and our climbing competition will test you in similar conditions.

"Sword-fighting starts with some group rounds, then pits individuals against each other. In later rounds, each man left in the competition fights every other man. The most successful fighters then fight each other again, and the final bout decides the winner.

"Today, we will begin the process of selecting the students who stand out in each area of skill. If you can run very fast over short distances, we will choose you for the short distance race. If you can also run quickly over longer distances, we will choose you for that as well. If you can also fight well with a sword, you will be chosen for sword fighting too. There is no limit to the number of competitions you can be chosen for; in fact, the Great Tournament includes a special prize for the best performer overall.

"Right now, we will start with running – which is why we only had a short warm-up run this morning. Everyone will take part in this short race. The distance is only 135 metres,[73] and at first we will run in groups of ten. Our intention over the next week or two is to choose the fastest runners in the company, but we will also be aiming to include people

---

[72] 1 Samuel 14:12-13
[73] 300 cubits; 150 yards.

who are good at many different activities. Individual prizes are very good, but the all-rounder's prize will be our main aim. As a result, we may include some people who are not the best in particular competitions, but are excellent in others; such men have an opportunity to excel in the combined prize.

"Now, all students are to move to the throwing area where we have arranged an area for our races." Soon the students were gathered at the far end of the camp where targets were normally set up for spear and javelin throwing. The companies divided into their tens and the races began.

CR

Some students were quickly eliminated from the trials because, although they were good, brave soldiers, they were slow.

It was immediately after the conclusion of one race that a guard made his way to Abiel, who was supervising the record-keeping.

"Excuse me, sir," he said, a little breathlessly, "you are wanted in the administration tent, sir."

"Look, I'm busy at the moment. Is it urgent?"

"Yes, sir. It's Gershom, sir. The head of the army." The soldier's eyes were open wide – the chief of the army was the most important man he had ever met. "And he wants to see you, sir!" The soldier's expression showed his certainty that such a visit from the army commander must mean that Abiel was somehow in trouble.

"Gershom? Here? That's unusual," said Abiel, not noticing the soldier's sympathetic tone. "I'll come straight away."

As he strode towards the administration tent, Abiel wondered what business had brought the head of the army to his academy. It could easily be trouble, he decided; possibly an attack by Israel or some other neighbouring country.

Abiel was so deep in thought when he rounded the end of the line of sleeping tents that he almost ran into the commander.

Gershom did not always do what was expected of him. His short wait had decided him that his time would be better spent in taking a look around to see for himself what was going on in Abiel's Academy.

"Ah, Abiel," he said. "I need to talk to you, but since I've started to look around, first tell me what's happening in your academy."

"Yes, sir. Well, just this morning, we've begun selection trials and training in preparation for the competitions we would normally have before the Great Tournament."

"Why?" asked Gershom, his weather-beaten face serious. That one word would have frightened many of his subordinates, who would have read disapproval in it. Abiel took it as a genuine question.

"I believe that these competitions are valuable for the students, sir, and I didn't want to leave them any longer."

"Why not?"

"It's two years now since the last Great Tournament was cancelled, and that means two-thirds of my students have never had the advantage of such competitions."

"Show me what you are doing."

Abiel retraced his steps to the assembly area and explained to Gershom what was happening.

When he finished, Gershom smiled a slow smile and said, "Once again, the king knows what he is doing."

Abiel looked at him quizzically, but asked no questions.

"Let's go back to that tent," said Gershom. "I have news for you."

Back in the administration tent, Gershom explained his visit. "The king has decided that the Great Tournament will be held this year."

Abiel smiled enthusiastically. "That's good news, sir."

"And he wants you to host it here in your academy."

Abiel's brow creased. "The cancelled tournament was due to be held at Vophsi's Academy."

"The king has decided that it should be held here."

"Very well," said Abiel slowly, "if that is the king's wish."

"The king has also decided that the tournament is to be held earlier than usual."

"Has a date been set?"

"The date of the Feast of Weeks is not yet known, since it depends on when the first of the crop is ready, but the Great Tournament will begin when the feast concludes. Probably in the second or third week of the third month."

"That doesn't give much time for organisation, sir."

"No. That's why the king wanted you to arrange it, Abiel."

"Did the king say that?"

"He said the tournament was to be held at your academy."

"That's flattering."

"He was also aware that this might be a problem for you because it would take away your opportunity to become the King's Swordsman."

"I don't think that I could honestly take that title now anyway, sir."

"What do you mean?"

"I have a student here who can defeat me easily. It doesn't seem reasonable to become the King's Swordsman when I know that I am not the best swordsman."

"Tell me more about this student."

"His name is Ben-hail, the son of Raddai."

"But he is a student here?"

"Yes."

"Well, students can't enter the open competition, can they?"

"No."

"You are too noble, Abiel. He won't be in the same competition as you. You can honestly beat all the men in the open competition and be called the King's Swordsman. Where is the problem with that?"

"I have to live with myself, sir."

"Surely he has many years before him to win the title anyway?"

"Probably – but I know that I am not the best swordsman now, and that's what matters. I'm not the best now, and that's with Ben-hail injured!"

"How can this be? You have been the best swordsman in the kingdom for more than 10 years, despite what the records say about the King's Swordsmen. How can an injured student beat you?"

"He is amazingly gifted, and very dedicated to his chosen profession."

"Will he have recovered by the time the Great Tournament begins?"

"I don't know. I hope so. His injuries have been hampering him for several months now. He fights with his left hand and stands on one leg much of the time. Even so, I doubt that any could beat him."

"So he's left-handed – interesting. I know that left-handers can be hard to fight."

"No, sir. He isn't left-handed. But he fights with his left hand now because his right hand is injured."

"The son of Raddai, you say?"

"Yes. A Levite."

"Raddai, a Levite... now why does that name seem familiar?"

"His father has been dead for many years, I believe."

"Imagine another mighty man from Levi, like Benaiah the son of Jehoiada. We need heroes like that. Does he have leadership potential?"

"Possibly. He is popular, but a little quiet."

Gershom and Abiel discussed the arrangements necessary to organise the Great Tournament in such limited time. As commander of the academy hosting the tournament, Abiel would also have temporary authority over all of the other academies, should additional resources be required for the task.

"You'll need to get back to the arrangements for your own students," said Gershom as he prepared to return to Jerusalem. "Don't concentrate so much on organising the tournament that your own students don't get the training they need."

He paused, then added, "And Abiel, handle Vophsi gently if you can, but don't forget that you have the king's support."

Chapter 11

Joining the Council

As Gershom rode to Abiel's Academy, Jehoshaphat climbed the steps from the palace and entered the temple through the king's entrance. Content that he had discharged his first duty in the organisation of the Great Tournament, Jehoshaphat was now determined to pursue extra information about the fate of Hanani the prophet.

Once again, he found Jehoiada surrounded by young students, but this time Jehoshaphat insisted that he would wait until the lesson was finished. Jehoiada was teaching his charges about the Psalms and how King David had specified they should be used in worship.[74] In the future, some of these students would probably be part of Levite choirs and would need an understanding of these requirements.

Jehoshaphat listened with interest, hearing for the first time some fine details of the intimate involvement his grandfather's great-grandfather had had in national worship. New avenues of opportunity and responsibility opened up in his mind: a king could set the direction of his nation for generations.

For the first time, the dream of a re-united nation crystallised in his mind. Perhaps this could be his contribution to the kingdom! His father was sure it was impossible; that Israel's idolatry made unity – even friendship – an impossible dream. Yet they were all descendants of Jacob, weren't they? Surely God would never abandon them? David had forged a wide-ranging peace with the surrounding nations through victorious warfare, and Solomon had extended that peace through diplomacy and negotiation – and marriage agreements! Perhaps he, Jehoshaphat, could be the king who brought peace to the warring halves of Israel. It was a worthy goal, he thought. Surely God would bless it, as he had blessed the work of David and Solomon.

"That's all, lads," said Jehoiada, concluding his lesson and bringing Jehoshaphat back to the present. "After noon we'll look at more of David's

---

[74] 1 Chronicles 16:4-7, 37-42; 23:2-6, 30

contributions to worship. In the meantime, I must talk to the prince."

Jehoiada led Jehoshaphat to his personal chamber within the temple. As they entered, he asked, "Do we need the door shut, my lord?"

Jehoshaphat nodded.

Once the door was shut, Jehoshaphat began, "I need more information about what my father did to Hanani the prophet."

"When we discussed this earlier, sir, I recommended that you talk to your father. What did he say?"

"He gave me some information, then said that he didn't want to talk about it any more. He told me to talk to you and Gershom instead."

"Interesting. My lord, your father has ruled as a righteous king over Judah for many years. Yet he has not always lived up to his own expectations, and I think that must be why he wants you to talk to us. Obviously, he feels confident of what we think, even though I have never spoken to the king about what he should or should not have done about Hanani. However, he does know that we have never joined the group of people who want to rebel."

"He obviously trusts you."

"Have you talked more to Gershom?"

"Yes."

"Well, sir, I'll start with how it all began, the day your father returned from Ramah. He had been supervising the work of pulling down Ramah's defences. As he rode into Jerusalem, a crowd gathered to welcome him. Everyone was pleased that the threat to Judah had been averted. Some of us felt a bit uncomfortable with the method, but nobody could question the results achieved – not then. I heard the cheering from inside the temple and went to join the crowd near the Benjamin Gate. Hanani was waiting for the king at the Benjamin Gate of the temple, so I was quite close when he went across to your father. At that time, I didn't know who he was, and I don't think the king did either. He stood in front of your father and gave it to him straight:

" 'Because you relied on the king of Syria, and did not rely on the Lord your God, the army of the king of Syria has escaped you.'[75]

"Now at that time, your father hadn't been able to defeat *Israel*, and I don't think the idea of defeating Syria had even occurred to him as a possibility. It's sad, but even in that short time, he had lost his confidence. It was only a year since he had confidently attacked the Ethiopians, but Baasha had sapped his confidence in just a few months. There was no big confrontation, just a series of niggling attacks almost every week. Israel slowly pushed our troops back, and your father seemed to lose his way. Hanani told him off for it:

---

[75] 2 Chronicles 16:7

" 'Were not the Ethiopians and the Libyans a huge army with very many chariots and horsemen? Yet because you relied on the Lord, he gave them into your hand. For the eyes of the Lord run to and fro throughout the whole earth, to give strong support to those whose heart is blameless toward him.'[76]

"By that time, your father was looking furious, and most of the rest of us were just standing there aghast. The cheering had all died away and there was silence in the square except for the sound of Hanani berating the king.

"He finished his attack with the harshest words of all:

" 'You have done foolishly in this, for from now on you will have wars.'[77]

"Everyone in the crowd heard this condemnation of the king, and it was obvious that your father was furious. Maybe if Hanani had spoken to him in private, your father's response wouldn't have been so brutal, but he had been criticised in public and he responded in public. He told the guards to take Hanani away and put him in the stocks. Some people cheered, but mostly there was a stunned silence as the king's guards grabbed Hanani and dragged him away to prison.

"I was stunned myself, sir, and didn't know what to do."

"Did you think that Hanani's message was really from God?"

"Yes, sir. I also made some enquiries later and found that Hanani had been a prophet of Yahweh for years, even though I had never met him. I'm convinced that God was speaking through Hanani to tell your father that he had done the wrong thing."

"Then why haven't you joined the criticism of my father?"

"I am not a prophet and I did not feel that I was in a position to judge Yahweh's anointed. It took me a while to discover Hanani's background and by the time I did, I was convinced that it wasn't my place to tell the king how he should run the kingdom. If I were the High Priest or had been given a command by God then I would feel that I should talk to the king, but I am not in any such position. Maybe I am making excuses to avoid a confrontation, but I was, and still am, just a priest – even though I will probably become High Priest at some time when my father dies. My father, the High Priest, made the decision to continue to support the king, even though he accepted that Hanani's words were from God. I accepted his decision and am loyal to the king."

"I'm glad to hear it. My father probably needed support."

"However, I need to make one more point. You asked about why the kingdom was having problems and we've talked about who might be

---

[76] 2 Chronicles 16:8-9
[77] 2 Chronicles 16:9

working against your father, but that doesn't address the underlying problem. I believe that Hanani's final words are the key: 'from now on you will have wars'. You can do your best to locate all the internal enemies and get rid of them, you can try to solve the nation's security problems however you wish, but God's judgement still remains. At first, your father had peace; now he will keep having wars.'"

∾

Jehoshaphat mulled over his new-found knowledge for days. How should he respond? His father had known that he would be finding out this information and had said that he would not listen to any more discussion about it.

How did his father expect him to respond?

How did Yahweh want him to respond?

If he were to take over as king, what should he do about this situation? He could not keep any of these people in prison. God's prophet, God's representative – locked up for more than 20 years! The symbology of it frightened him. The nations around had gods that they set up in temples or carried around on carts, and they showed them respect, but Yahweh was the living God. He was not the servant of Israel – he was its maker, its master. To lock up a messenger of the true king of Israel!

Yet his father was still king.

Jehoshaphat struggled with his thoughts, but was unable to see any clear path to take. He could never do anything like his father had done – at least, he didn't believe he could! – but nor could he demand that his father do something to fix the problem. He found himself in the same position as Gershom: not content with what his father had done, but not willing to rebel against the Lord's anointed. Yet God *had* sent a prophet to oppose what the king had done....

One night he sat in his candlelit bedchamber, meditating. His thoughts struggled backwards and forwards, accusing and then excusing both his father and himself. What he should feel about the targets of his father's anger... – he couldn't decide that either. It had been terrifying to have someone lunging at him with a knife, but the young man's desire for revenge was understandable in the circumstances.

He remembered his father's intention to include him in the royal council as leader of the army. Could it work? His father's attitude and his own response to this incident and its ongoing repercussions could easily become a source of conflict between them. Would they fight over it? And if they did, would he be the next target for his father's anger – thrown into prison with the others, deprived of his birthright as the next king? Would his father do that? He couldn't help remembering the anger in his father's face whenever the subject had been discussed. He had never seen such emotion from his father before, and could not predict how he might respond to opposition on the topic.

Then again, did he have any choice anyway? The king had commanded him to take over the army and join the king's council. The king's word was law.

One of the benefits of being a prince was that he had access to the scrolls of scripture. Jehoshaphat wondered if he could find help in the history of the kingdom, particularly the situation of David and King Saul. He had read before how David, later to become King David, allowed Saul to run the kingdom as he chose while contributing in ways that satisfied the demands of his conscience. He had remained an active servant of the king until Saul drove him away, and was the king's subject until God removed Saul.

This, thought Jehoshaphat, seemed to be the answer to his dilemma. Obey his father's wishes where possible, but obey God's commands first, and let God take care of the outcome. At times, there would be flashpoints of conflict. Some he would be able to avoid through silence, but others he would have to face up to if he were to follow the lead of King David – the leader God had chosen because he was a man after God's own heart.[78]

$$\text{CR}$$

Having made up his mind, Jehoshaphat began to address the responsibilities of his new job. The army was now under his direction; the security of the kingdom in his hands.

As prince, he had been trained for war and was expert in both the use of weapons and the leadership of men. When Jehoshaphat had reached the age of 20, King Asa had given him command of a unit in the army that helped to protect Jerusalem. This had continued for some years until King Asa had declared that it was time for him to learn more about the administration of the kingdom and introduced him into the court. Economics and religion, citizenship and demographics, international affairs and strategic direction were all part of his education. King Asa constantly reminded his son that he himself had never had much training in these things and had had to learn on the job as a young king.

Jehoshaphat *was* well prepared for kingship, if it is possible to be truly prepared for the crushing responsibility of holding the lives of millions in your hands, knowing that your decisions can bring them joy or sadness, success or failure, triumph or disaster.

First he must speak to the commander of the army.

"Gershom," he said to the grizzled soldier, the day after his return

---

[78] 1 Samuel 14:13

from Abiel's Academy, "we need to decide what our titles will be. You have been commander of the army for many years, answerable only to the king. You will now be answerable to me, since it is my father's intention that I should take over some areas – more or less as practice for becoming king. However, you are not being demoted in any way and your service to the nation is just as valuable as ever. In fact, we could even say that you get to try out the new king before anyone else does! And you have the chance to give direction to the next king. You can contribute to the direction of the kingdom for many years!

"However, we don't want confusion in titles. You will remain commander of the army. For the time being, I will be the director of the army. How does that sound to you?"

"That sounds fine, sir. I am happy to serve my lord the king and you as his chosen successor – the next anointed king of Judah."

"We have some operational matters to sort out, too. The reporting of troop movements to our enemies must be stopped. Do you have any idea how we can do this?"

"How much freedom do we have in solving the problem, sir?"

"My father is king. I think you know his opinions and attitudes in this matter."

"Very well. Then I don't believe that we can solve the problem *completely*, but maybe we can transfer the camps that are near the border to different places, so that people who live near the current locations will no longer know when we move the troops."

"Do we know any of the people who may report troop movements?"

"Ah, well, sir, how should I...?"

"I would not be passing on any information to my father or using the information to punish such people. The exception to this would be anyone who was trying to assassinate the king or lead a rebellion."

"Well, in that case, I would say that there are *suspicions* about some people, but no proof."

"Could we institute a policy of misinformation for such people? What I mean is, if we suspect that certain people pass on this sort of information, can we feed them false information? Can we whisper in their ears that troops may be moving from, say, Mizpah to Kiriath Jearim, and move them towards Jericho instead?"

"We could try. Of course, if they discover that they have been misled, they will be sure that they have been discovered. Maybe that would make them more cautious."

"Can we try both of these things? Move some of our troop camps to different places, and also try feeding some misinformation to suspected informers."

"Yes, sir. We'll try it. Moving the camps is probably worthwhile anyway, since it leaves our enemies less sure of what they will find if they invade."

The king's council met soon afterwards, with Jehoshaphat present for the first time. King Asa welcomed them all into the council chamber as they entered. His voice sounded tired and old, and his foot was again supported by a small stool.

"Welcome, my lords. We are meeting today at what should be a happy time for the kingdom. My son Jehoshaphat is here for the first time as a member of the council. This has been my plan for some time. Certain conditions have delayed my plan, but now, certain other things have promoted it. I had been hoping to have solved particular difficulties over loyalties in the kingdom before involving him, but things haven't worked out that way. Instead, my foot has forced me to make the change now."

At that moment, his face contorted and he gasped with pain. The proof of his point was shown graphically to all.

The king waited for the pain to ease, then continued, "I have always controlled the army directly through Gershom here, and I am now passing on this control to Prince Jehoshaphat. I have complete confidence that Jehoshaphat and Gershom together will lead the army of Judah from strength to strength."

"Congratulations, sire, on having a son who can be relied on to take over your position with skill and faith," said Gershom. "May the God of David bless your son as he has blessed you."

Others joined in with this praise of the king's decision and his success throughout his long reign. Kish, the governor of Jerusalem, was fulsome in his praise of the king, but also introduced a subject that dismayed many of the nobles present: "I and several others on this council have served you for many glorious years, my lord. Since Prince Jehoshaphat will be joining us as a senior leader, is it your plan to also refresh the company in other ways? If you would like to replace me with a younger man so that the prince is not one young man alone amongst a group of old men, I would gladly volunteer my resignation. I have been proud to serve you, and would continue to proudly serve your son, but I am happy to serve you both by resigning if that is your preference."

It was a gracious speech and King Asa looked surprised, but touched.

"Old friend," he replied with a smile, "your offer does great honour to me and to my son. As you know, my grandfather Rehoboam gloried in the advice of the young and rejected the wisdom of the old.[79] I have confidence that my son will not make such a mistake. Nevertheless, over time, such decisions will be his to make."

The members of the council may well have been shocked by the suggestion to replace their aged faces with younger ones, but they rose to the challenge nobly. One after another reiterated Kish's offer – some perhaps may even have meant what they said in such eloquent phrases.

Asa looked around at his council with appreciation and hoped that his son would listen to the advice of this collection of wise and godly men as he himself had done so many times.

"My friends," he said, "for the time being, the council will be unchanged aside from the addition of Prince Jehoshaphat. Today he joins us as the director of the army, and his authority will expand as his experience warrants it. To tell the truth, he may have to take over the kingship more quickly than I had planned, since the disease in my foot now seems to be spreading to the other foot. My doctors appear unable to halt the advance of the disease, and the pain keeps increasing. At times, I am finding it hard to concentrate on anything else."

"May your reign continue for many years, my lord," said Ladan, who was the king's best friend and an advisor whose wisdom was legendary throughout the kingdom. Everyone agreed – really, there was no reason why the king should not reign for many more years. After all, he was only 60 years old. King David had lived to the ripe old age of 70,[80] and with all of the recent advances in modern medicine, King Asa could be expected to live several years longer than that.

Yet the obvious suffering of the king hung over the room like a pall, and the confidence of the council that he would soon become the longest-reigning monarch in the history of Israel was shaken.

Nevertheless, their deliberations continued. Urgent plans for the development of roads to enable the swift movement of troops were discussed, along with many other items of importance to the kingdom.

King Asa contributed little. His main concentration was on his diseased foot and the doctor who hovered near it.

The news that the disease was spreading to his other foot was a complete, and most unwelcome, surprise to the council – including his oldest son.

---

[79] 2 Chronicles 10:6-19
[80] 2 Samuel 5:4

Chapter 12

Preparations Begin

Gershom's visit had radically changed Abiel's plans. Now he must not only train his own students, but also prepare a tournament for soldiers and academy students across the entire kingdom. The scope of his responsibilities had broadened enormously.

Such an acknowledgement from the king and the army commander that he was competent to arrange the Great Tournament in a very limited time was pleasant, but he could see that the work required would be enormous! He couldn't help feeling some satisfaction that he had been chosen while Vophsi had been discarded – how he would love to see Vophsi's face when he heard the news – but he did his best to put that unworthy thought out of his mind.

Before Gershom left, Abiel had, of course, invited him to speak to the camp, but the commander had declined the offer, telling Abiel that he was sure it would be most helpful if he let him get on with the work the king had assigned him straight away.

Gershom had also asked whether Abiel had enough staff that he could rely on to train his own students, adding, "You're known to be an exceptional trainer, but you'll be busy with other things, so let me know what extra help you'll need. And I'm sure that you'll need more help in preparing the areas inside and outside the camp for the many competitions, as well as for the spectators who will attend. Don't forget that we always have large crowds for the sword fights."

How could Abiel forget? He had been part of those large crowds on more than one occasion, longing to take his proper place in the combat but forced to be content with watching the victories of men whom he knew he could have defeated. Maybe this time he could watch Ben-hail – if only the young man had recovered sufficiently by then.

Abiel had assured Gershom that he would review his staffing immediately and send any requests with his first report of progress. Little did he know just how much help he would need!

Gershom had then ridden off on his donkey with his attendants, eager to return to Jerusalem and begin dispatching a slew of letters about the Great Tournament to army units and academies across the kingdom. Abiel had stood and watched him go with mixed feelings: excitement quickening his breathing and causing him to take a deep breath as he imagined the triumph of arranging a successful tournament, but also a tinge of disappointment at being deprived of the opportunity to train his own students. Could he still find time to help Ben-hail?

CR

That night, Abiel spoke to his staff about the breathtaking news Gershom had delivered. They all saw that this honour would instantly make their academy, already well-known for its ability to consistently turn out top-quality graduates, the envy of every other academy in the kingdom. Not only so, but Abiel's Academy would become the centre of concentration of all the mightiest men in the army of Judah who yearned for glory in the service of God and the king.

Having spent the afternoon in thought, Abiel had developed the seeds of many plans for the Great Tournament, and he shared them with his subordinates.

While most of the fame and renown would go to the soldiers who achieved victory in the king's competitions, the army by no means overlooked those who worked almost invisibly to arrange a successful tournament. The Great Tournament demanded the coordination of so many diverse groups of men from all over the kingdom, and comprised such a wide range of events, that it was quite similar to a campaign of war. This tournament would be even more demanding than usual to arrange, and if Abiel and his staff could pull it off, it would be remembered for every individual as a glittering star on the horizon of their career.

Abiel had no difficulty in kindling his staff's enthusiasm and excitement, and rumours began to spread within moments of them leaving his presence. Abiel had told them not to give the students any details, but merely to spread the report that there was news to be had, and the men did their best to obey. Before the students unrolled their bedrolls that night, everyone in the camp knew that the early morning assembly would reveal some surprising tidings. "Surprising" was probably the least fulsome word used as the rumours spread – amazing, spectacular, incredible, sensational, wondrous, mind-blowing and breathtaking were all used too – and, of course, almost everyone had suggestions as to what the news might be.

Ben-hail and his friends heard the reports with interest, but didn't succumb to the general excitement.

"It's probably a new agreement with Israel," said Darda. "They say that some of the king's advisors have been suggesting that we make friends with them."

"But what about their idolatry?" asked Kilion. "Surely that would stop such an agreement? But maybe Abiel has been given some important appointment, some new honour. It would be well-deserved." Abiel was still helping Kilion to overcome his tendency to sulk, and Kilion was normally quick to praise his commander.

"I hope it's news about dates for the Great Tournament," said Ben-hail, "but I don't suppose it will be. From some oblique comments Abiel made a few days ago, I think he expects it to be cancelled again this year."

Eliam said nothing; no-one was surprised.

The next morning arrived cold and clear, but the wake-up call was received with far greater warmth than normal.

"Well done, lads," said Abiel, standing next to a flaming torch that gave an impression of warmth without providing any of the real thing. "It's a cold morning, I know, but the news I have to tell you will warm your hearts.

"King Asa, may his reign continue for many years, has announced that the Great Tournament will be held this year – in the third month, just after the Feast of Weeks. This is great news! Every one of you will be included in the selection process for the King's Competitions, and you will all benefit from the concentrated training that you will receive."

Despite his slow recovery from his injuries, Ben-hail had gathered with the rest of the students for the morning assembly as usual, and he received the information with a triumphant smile and a flicker of fire in his eyes that reflected the flame of the torch that flared beside Abiel. Kilion and Darda looked across at him, acknowledging the accuracy of his guess but also wondering sympathetically if he would be fully healed in time for the tournament.

One of the students cheered, and soon all the students were cheering. Their normally serious commander responded with a smile that was almost a grin. "It's great news, isn't it, lads? But there's even more to it than that. Whenever the Great Tournament takes place, the king chooses one of the academies to host the events. This time, the king has chosen our academy, your academy, as the venue for his Great Tournament. This is a great honour for us all. It will also mean that there is a huge amount of work to be done, and many opportunities for those whose personal bent is towards methodical organisation rather than athletic competition or hand-to-hand combat. None of you are cowards or you wouldn't be here, but God gives one skill to one man and another to someone else. In the Great Tournament, you will *all* have opportunities for competition, service and success.

"Yesterday, we began some special training for competitions like those in the Great Tournament. We will continue this process and intensify our commitment to testing and training. We have less than three months to work out who should be entered into each competition and then give them special training to help them do as well as they possibly can. Time is short, and the men against whom you will be competing are the best in the kingdom. We will be testing you all and selecting the best men to represent this academy.

"It is my hope and expectation that many of you will win the right to take part in these competitions against other students and soldiers. King Asa wants to replenish his company of mighty men; to improve and revive that famous group. And I want some of you – in fact, many of you – to perform well in these events and be included in that company. Your king wants to see your success, and your nation needs you to be ready to fight against the enemy. With God at your side and the excellent training of your instructors, each of you should be able to chase a thousand[81] and 30 mighty men rout an army – as they did in the days of King David."

$$\text{\large\calligra CR}$$

Once again, Abiel led his students on a shortened run before returning to the assembly area and finishing the process of selecting fast runners begun on the previous day. After a short time, about 30 students had been identified for further training and testing in running over short distances.

Kilion was in the group: although most outstanding when running longer distances, he was still very fast over short distances, and could outrun every other student in Abiel's Academy. Darda was with him, but Eliam wasn't, and neither was Ben-hail. In fact, Ben-hail wasn't even at the testing area. He was outside their tent, still exercising in an endeavour to recover the full use of his limbs. While his left foot had recovered almost completely, it was still a little stiff, and the army doctor, who examined it regularly on Abiel's orders, still thought that it would be best for Ben-hail to avoid running hard – whether over short or long distances – for at least another two weeks.

As for his right hand, while he could now at last use it for simple things again, he still had no real strength in it, and even trying to use it in ordinary ways caused significant, lasting pain.

---

[81] Joshua 23:10

The King's Armour-bearer

Abiel was deeply concerned about Ben-hail. He had been counting on him to do well in the swordsmanship competition. Things could always go wrong in single combat, but Abiel was confident that, if in good health, his protégé would be the master of any student in any academy, and probably of every soldier in the army. Before the accident, he had even begun to wonder if Ben-hail might be a candidate for the Grand Prize – although that was, perhaps, a grandiose dream. The army doctor's report had not pleased him at all. True, the doctor expected a full recovery, but he warned that it could take up to a year for the injured right hand to return to its full strength and mobility.

Ben-hail, for his part, had found the winter difficult. A young man with great athletic ability, he was used to being able to do what he wanted when he wanted to do it. Learning new things was easy for him, but he had always had a strong preference for using his right hand for anything in which accuracy or strength was required. Learning to use his left hand for those things had tested his determination greatly. On many occasions, he had nearly given up.

There had been the time when he had been tying his sandals. Sandal thongs are easy to tie, but not with only one hand, and particularly not when the one hand was his left hand! On that morning, he was the only one left in the tent because the others were busy with a rock climbing activity such as had been commonly practised in the armies of Israel ever since Prince Jonathan and his armour-bearer had climbed a cliff to attack the Philistines. It was now an ancient story, but one that the army wanted its soldiers equipped to repeat. Ben-hail, however, could not climb with his injured hand and foot, so he was in the tent struggling with his sandal thong. It happened to be the sandal on his left foot, which was still quite painful and could not easily be tilted to a convenient angle. As he concentrated on forming the knot, the pain in his foot gradually grew until it caused his hurrying fingers to slip and the thong to come undone. Each time, he stretched out his foot to ease the pain, muttering in frustration. When the fifth attempt failed, he yanked off his sandal and threw it across the tent with a shout of pain and anger. Exasperated, he decided to do without his sandals until his friends returned, but after a while he tried again, this time with a quiet determination that allowed him to endure the sixth, seventh and eighth failures with relative composure. The ninth attempt was so close to success when the thong suddenly slipped that his patience and endurance were again stretched beyond breaking point. He tore off the sandal and flung it out through the door of the tent, followed closely by his bedroll. It was several minutes before the pain subsided enough even to allow him to crawl out of the tent and retrieve his footwear and bedding. It was ridiculous, he thought. Why would anyone drive themselves to achieve something that was clearly impossible – and also unnecessary? When his friends returned, it would be the work of no more than a moment for one of them to help him tie his sandal thong. Nothing could convince him to go through the pain even one more time to tie that cursed thong! And anyway, if he was foolish enough to try once more, it would only fail yet again at the last moment – success was impossible. He would sit and wait until someone else could tie it!

But the pain and frustration slowly eased and his determination re-asserted itself. Just one more time, he thought to himself, and one more time was all it took. Despite the growing pain as he held his foot in that awkward position, the fingers of his left hand at last managed to tie the thong successfully and he was able to lie back and revel in the joy of success in the face of a difficulty that had seemed insurmountable. From that time on, tying his sandals was never quite so hard. The victory was won.

Many such difficulties tried his patience and determination, but each victory fed his confidence and strengthened his determination to never give up.

When present, his friends helped him as they could, and praised God for his gradual recovery. Ben-hail appreciated their support.

℞

The doctor's two weeks passed, and Abiel called the man again to exam-ine his brightest hope for the Great Tournament. The two weeks had made a big difference, and Ben-hail was now easily able to run for short distances. Longer distances were still not easy, but the pain was much reduced and getting better every day.

Looking at Ben-hail, it was hard to believe that he had been so badly injured that he had been unable to run for several months. He looked stronger and fitter than ever before, and his gentle runs were already making an impression on the instructors. Without any specific training for running, his speed and endurance had improved significantly. Im-provements in his general fitness and physical strength seemed to be be-hind the change, and the instructors at the academy were taking notice.

The doctor gave him a clean bill of health – for running at least. However, he was still not satisfied with the condition of Ben-hail's right hand and forbade him to use it hard until he gave permission. Having given this order, he said that he would return in another two or three weeks and left.

Abiel was disappointed, and looked for ways to minimise his loss. In his mind, the best way to achieve this was to direct Ben-hail's training into areas he would not have explored if he had had the full use of his right hand. He had already been encouraging Ben-hail to use his left hand in activities for which he *always* preferred his right. Abiel's goal was for Ben-hail to become equally proficient with his left and right hands at everything. His proficiency with the right hand had always been noteworthy, but if that proficiency were matched with equal proficiency in the left hand, his versatility would give him a good chance of overcoming all competition. Abiel was also confident that Ben-hail's attempts to increase his strength with left-handed activities had also increased his strength and agility with his right hand. Only time would tell whether Abiel was right.

Abiel also had another thought that he had not mentioned to anyone else. He was hoping that Ben-hail would be able to force Kilion to extend himself in order to maintain his position as the premier runner in the academy. Kilion now beat Abiel consistently. Abiel had secret hopes that Ben-hail would be able to challenge Kilion and possibly even cause another upset to the now-established order.

With the doctor's clearance, Ben-hail was to run the next morning, although Abiel had warned him not to overstretch himself.

Never before had Abiel felt such high hopes for any student at his academy. Ben-hail's skills and determination often occupied the commander's thoughts, and that night he lay awake for some time imagining the success that Ben-hail and his friends could achieve in the Great Tournament and the fame they could bring to Abiel's Academy. He looked forward to the next day's run with excitement.

When morning came and Ben-hail joined the company run, there was a widespread sense of anticipation. Ben-hail was easygoing and popular, but he was also seen as a man to challenge. Kilion was acknowledged as easily the best runner in the company. Nobody cherished serious hopes of defeating him. The lightness of his feet and the ease with which he ran over hill and dale made thoughts of beating him more like dreams. Those with longer memories felt that an opportunity might appear if he could be tricked into sulking, but that was easier said than done. But if Kilion could not be defeated, surely now was the best time to defeat Ben-hail? After all, he hadn't run hard for months! Runners who dreamed of winning a place in the Great Tournament made plans to stay in front of Ben-hail and exclude him from the three places that were available for students from Abiel's Academy.

The pack set off and settled into a slightly quicker pace than normal. Some students hoped that setting an early fast pace would leave Ben-hail behind because of his lack of fitness. They needn't have bothered. By the time the half-way mark was reached, Ben-hail and Kilion were running together easily at the front of the pack, just a few metres[82] behind Abiel. Most mornings, Kilion still allowed Abiel to lead for at least two-thirds of the usual distance, only to ease his way past him up one of the

---

[82] A few yards.

hills, leaving him an increasingly distant second on the return to the camp.

On this occasion, Kilion and Ben-hail exchanged glances and each decided, without speaking, that the other would be able to sustain a faster pace without trouble. Increasing their speed, they soon passed Abiel. He tried to build up his own speed and stay with them, but before long, he was obliged to give up. Forced to continue his own race at his own pace, he gradually lost touch with them.

Though close friends, the two young men were extremely competitive, and neither would give up easily. There was a joy in competition, and the pace gradually increased, although the ragged breathing of both showed the great pressure they were under. Watchers at the camp saw the pair running up the last hill towards the camp and commented to each other that there were no other runners in sight.

"They must have left them behind," said Ziba, the trainer.

"How can Ben-hail do that?" said Hadoram. "He hasn't run hard for months."

"True, so I expect that Kilion will have the better of him in the end," said Ziba, sounding a little disappointed.

"Well, he's not a genuine left-hander," laughed Hadoram, "but he's the next best thing. I say he'll win."

"Not a hope," said Ziba. "Kilion has such a beautiful, fluid running style."

"True, but Ben-hail's style is good enough, and I've never met anyone with such amazing strength and determination."

"Oh well, let's see what happens. I think Kilion is ahead."

"Ben-hail is probably just waiting to pounce. In the last little bit he'll run past him like an ostrich passing a sheep."

"A left-handed ostrich, I suppose," laughed Ziba.

"Of course."

Kilion and Ben-hail were approaching the final section where the hillside became steeper for a time before the incline gradually eased and the flat camp area was reached. It was often in this final test that one runner would falter and the other would seize an easy victory. But which would falter? Cold, hard logic said that Ben-hail *must* fail: he could not win without proper practice, and Kilion's flawless running style must give him an edge. Kilion reached the final climb a metre in front of his rival, his legs moving with strength and grace. Ben-hail not only had to make up the metre, but also had to overcome the confidence of an accustomed winner. Yet no-one had pointed out to him that he had no hope of winning, and he didn't seem to realise it himself! He leapt onto the incline with an energy that would have had the doctor reaching for his bandages, but half of the metre was overcome, and now

Ben-hail's face wore a determined smile. Kilion stole a glance behind, and it was easy to see that his confidence was shaken. The view behind was also dearly bought, because his next step was not placed with his ordinary skill and his sandal slipped slightly. He recovered with typical aplomb, but his advantage had slipped too. Neck and neck now, the two friends struggled up the slowly easing slope, neither giving a hand's-breadth.

Legs pounding and breath burning in their throats, the two ran up onto the level ground, their speed increasing with every step. The sprint to the finish line would decide it, because the two runners were equal. The first tent was the appointed finish line and, in a close finish, the victor was the first to touch the tent.

On some occasions, when students had developed a fierce competition, the race had finished in a tangle of arms and legs as two students lunged for victory and collided mid-stride. Neither Ben-hail nor Kilion would give up, but, seeing that a collision might cost them both dearly, by common consent they sprinted towards opposite ends of the tent that stood across their path.

In the last stride, it looked as if Kilion's delightfully smooth rhythm might still snatch him victory, but the brute strength of Ben-hail's straining legs responded and the two outstretched hands touched the tent simultaneously.

Several instructors were watching closely and had placed themselves in the best possible positions for judging the winner. All agreed that there was nothing to choose between the two, and as the runners eased to a walk, a cheer acknowledged an amazing performance by both runners.

"Who won?" panted Ben-hail.

"I think you did," gasped Kilion, disappointed, but pleased for his friend.

"Oh, no!" said Ziba. "Neither of you won! Or, if you prefer it, both of you did. After almost an hour of running, we couldn't separate you by the thickness of a fingernail."

"Or the thickness of an ostrich's feather," laughed Hadoram, "a left-handed ostrich!"

The two friends patted each other on the back and struggled to get their breath back. It was some minutes before Abiel crested the incline and made his way to the finish line, in a clear third position and still with no-one else in sight. He had run distinctly faster than his normal pace, yet he had been left far behind by the two leaders in their joyous competition.

There was a glad celebration in Ben-hail and Kilion's tent that night. Darda had finished in tenth position, and Eliam about halfway down the pack. Ben-hail had finished his first serious run since his accident, and his tent-mates were all pleased that his injury was behind him.

Although they did not know it, Abiel and some of his instructors were also celebrating that night. Abiel knew that he was still one of the fastest long-distance runners in King Asa's army, yet there were in his academy not one, but *two* runners who could easily defeat him. And for one of them, running was not even his most notable skill! Abiel went to sleep that night with his head filled with dreams of victory in the Great Tournament.

Chapter 13

CO-REGENCY

King Asa's doctors said that it was an incurable disease of the feet. Gradually, they told him, it would worsen, spreading through his better foot as well as the one that was already badly affected.

King Asa called for more doctors. He wanted other opinions. Better opinions. He even called for doctors from foreign countries.

The new doctors examined the king, poking and prodding in various painful ways, but in the end they all agreed with the earlier doctors.

The prognosis? Death, eventually. But only after a lot of suffering, with terrible, terrible pain. The deep-seated pain that already felt as if it was spreading through his bones would do just that – spread through his bones. The ulcers that were spreading on his worse foot would cover the entire foot, then begin on the other foot and finally cover it too. Gradually, they would begin to spread up his legs as well, but a strange feature of this condition was that the ulcers would not travel far up the legs. They never reached even as far as half-way between the ankle and the knee, but the disease made up for its limited spread by the almost unlimited pain it unleashed on the sufferer.

One doctor, however, disagreed with the rest and promised the king hope.

Yes, he said, the disease would spread as the others had described, but he had a treatment which, if applied once the ulcers had covered both feet and begun to spread up the legs – at just that stage – would cause the disease to gradually retreat until the sufferer was cured.

The king, being desperate, listened to this prediction with optimism, ignoring the noisy derision of the other doctors, and named the contrarian medic The Royal Doctor.

Life was becoming more and more difficult for the king. Pain was his constant companion. Jehoshaphat watched sadly, wondering why his father concentrated on doctors rather than on Yahweh, his God.

One day in the middle of the second month, Asa called for Jehoshaphat to visit him in his bedroom. The Royal Doctor was waiting at the door; he warned the prince to be gentle with his father, and not to stay too long.

Jehoshaphat entered the room and found his father lying on the bed with his feet swathed in bandages.

"Good morning, my lord," said Jehoshaphat.

"Greetings, my son," replied the king.

"You wanted me?"

"Yes, my son. The time has come."

"Are you dying, my lord?" asked Jehoshaphat in shock.

It was weak, but King Asa did smile. "No, my son, it is not time for that. My doctor will heal me, but until the healing comes, I am likely to suffer greatly and be unable to rule the kingdom. The time has come for you to rule the kingdom with me – or for me. You will be the face of the kingship. Anyone who needs to see the king will see you. Visitors from other nations; those seeking the king's justice; priests or prophets with messages from Yahweh: all will go to you.

"For the time being, the royal council will meet here in my bedroom. I will still try to be involved. I do not want to abandon my kingdom if I can help it, but I expect to be involved less and less until I begin to recover."

"Will I be able to talk to you about difficult matters? Ask for your advice?"

"Of course! As long as I can give help, I will. I have spoken to Ladan about the best way to manage this and I am taking his advice. He recommends a public coronation with all of the formalities involved in anointing a new king. I will be there to show that this has my approval, so that no-one can ever suggest that you have taken over the kingship by force. Then, after the coronation, you will be king. You will sit on the throne of Judah. You will be the lawgiver and judge. You will be the next king in the line of King David: the next of the sons of David to sit on his throne in the City of David. You are part of a noble line, my son, and one of those whom God has chosen to rule over his people forever."

"It is a difficult task, and a great responsibility," said Jehoshaphat. "I am too young to bear it alone."

"You are probably right, but you are much older than I was. In fact, you are older than King David himself was, so if you seek Yahweh our God, you will rule wisely and well."

Jehoshaphat reached down and hugged his father.

"Oh, and Jehoshaphat," added Asa, "don't forget that you need a bodyguard. And also one special guard who must always be with you whenever anyone else is around. I don't want anything to happen to you like it almost did when that young lunatic tried to assassinate us. That time, my bodyguard was there, but they were distracted. You need one guard who will always be watching you in particular – what used to be called an armour-bearer back in the days of Saul and David."

"The Great Tournament is just a month away, father. It will show us the mighty men we have to choose from. Good, loyal and faithful men who can keep me safe from the assassin's knife."

"Maybe the winner of the Grand Prize could be your new armour-bearer."

"Maybe."

○Ω

When King Asa married Azubah[83] not long after he became king, she was a strikingly beautiful young woman. Many in the kingdom had considered it time for him to marry – after all, what would happen to the line of David if he died as suddenly as his father had? His advisors and nobles had presented many young women as potential marriage partners. All were extremely beautiful to look at, but Azubah, the daughter of Shilhi, an important nobleman, had caught and held his attention because of the spiritual beauty that he saw clearly at their very first meeting. Asa had not wanted a wife who was solely a pretty decoration for his court, nor had he wanted a woman who would marry him just for the important position he could give her. Likewise, Azubah had wanted a husband for whom God would be king, so Asa and Azubah were well satisfied with each other when they agreed to marry.

She was a deeply spiritual woman whose interest in the God of Israel was equal to that of her husband, and their union had been blessed with the king's first son – Jehoshaphat, the heir apparent. When Asa finally decided to share his reign with Jehoshaphat, she was no longer young – how could she be with a 33-year-old son? – but she was still dedicated to the worship of Yahweh, and very pleased with Asa's newly-announced plans for the succession.

When she heard the news, she sent a message to the prince royal, a sadly formal missive that requested Prince Jehoshaphat to attend the queen at his earliest convenience.

The servant ushered Jehoshaphat into Azubah's visiting room and she smiled at him happily. In Judah, nurses have always played an important part in caring for and raising the royal princes, but Azubah had stubbornly insisted on spending plenty of time with her son, doing her best to instil in him the godliness she knew Asa wanted him to learn,

---

[83] Azubah was Jehoshaphat's mother (1 Kings 22:42; 2 Chronicles 20:31). We know nothing else about her, except that her son was a righteous king.

and which was also vital to her. Jehoshaphat had been an apt student, and mother and son had spent many pleasant hours discussing spiritual matters. She was ambitious for her son, and King Asa knew it, but, as he had remarked to Jehoshaphat, she had never tried to interfere in the appointment of the king's heir. Possibly this reticence was part of the reason for her success in positioning her son as heir, but both parents also felt strongly that the oldest son should be king. Furthermore, Jehoshaphat had never done anything scandalous that would cause the king to question his suitability to reign. His godliness was convincingly genuine.

"I am so pleased to see you, my son," she said in her warm contralto. It was a voice that smiled, and Jehoshaphat couldn't help responding.

"You are looking well, mother," he said, and both felt a little awkwardness in the solemn language they now felt obliged to use with each other. When Jehoshaphat had reached adulthood, the structured atmosphere of the palace had forced them into a formality that both had found difficult. Jehoshaphat's subsequent marriage to a woman with no spiritual outlook at all had added to the restraint in their conversation. Neither was content, and both longed for the free and easy conversation of the past, but each felt constrained by their position.

"I am so glad to hear that your father has decided to make you king."

"Not sole king, mother. Father will still be king as well. In many ways, he will still have the final say."

"So I understand, but he is suffering terribly, the poor dear. He won't be able to give much attention to ruling the kingdom. That's why he wants you to take over. He trusts you."

"I think that he also wants to please you, mother. He has always been so pleased that you don't try to boss him around like so many queens do."

"He is the Lord's anointed, not I."

"True. Yet he has always been very thankful that you trained me in the godliness he wanted me to learn. A king hasn't any time to spend with his sons – not even the one who will succeed him."

"No," sighed Azubah. "You are right."

"A king must serve his nation before he serves his family."

"So a queen's nursemaid decides the spiritual future of the kingdom by training the next king?"

Jehoshaphat laughed. "I suppose so, if you put it that way. But *you* were always there teaching me when I was growing up. You didn't leave it up to my nurse."

She nodded and smiled again. "You were much too important to me, my son, and so was the future of God's people." She paused, then looked down with another sigh. "Not all queens feel like that, you know."

"No, I suppose not." Jehoshaphat pressed his lips together and shook his head. He knew that she was referring to Zeruah, his wife, who was quite content to lounge in luxury and rely on nurses to bring up Jehoram, their oldest son.

"Is there anything that I can do about Jehoram, mother?"

"I don't think so."

"Could you talk to Zeruah and encourage her to spend more time with him? After all, he's your grandson so no-one could object to you showing an interest in him."

"I don't think having Zeruah spend more time with him will help, though, do you? She is no more interested in religion than he seems to be."

"But surely he can be changed? Don't people change as they grow up? Can't he be taught righteousness?"

"The priests already do their best to teach him from the law. Even Jehoiada has tried, but he just doesn't seem interested."

"But he's not even ten years old! Surely something can be done?"

"I'm not sure, my son. However, if you want me to, I can try."

"I do want you to try. I can't give up on the child so early."

"Very well. And I'll do my best not to upset Zeruah – but don't be surprised if you get a message from her complaining about my interference!"

They parted then: she, disappointed that her plan to congratulate him had been sidetracked; he, glad that he had enlisted his mother's help in overcoming the worrying problem of his oldest son.

Chapter 14

TRAINING

The precious days passed at Abiel's Academy, as the students in the company displayed and practised their skills. The target range was set up and students took turns throwing spears, slinging stones and shooting arrows.

Eliam's great strength showed in how far he could throw a spear, sling a stone and shoot an arrow, but a great slinger or archer shows his greatness in speed and accuracy. True, the ability to cover long distances with reasonable accuracy can help an army to keep their enemies at bay, but a truly great slinger or archer is an expert marksman. They are the men who can sling at a hair and not miss, or loose arrows with such speed and accuracy that it is more like facing a company of archers than just one!

Eliam was workmanlike when it came to accuracy, but for distance he was outstanding. Since some of the competitions tested distance, he would be ideal for those.

Kilion and Darda were both excellent slingers, with their backgrounds in farming and husbandry, and their skill in archery was improving too.

With uninjured hands, Ben-hail was better than either, but his injured right hand made archery impossible. It also forced him to use his left hand for slinging. His accuracy was still improving, but he found it difficult to maintain proper balance. As for throwing spears, he could not use his right hand, and throwing with his left hand required his left foot to provide impetus for the throw. This had made practice with either hand impossible for months, and it was only as his left foot approached full recovery that he had been able to begin to develop his skill in left-handed spear throwing.

Yes, everything seemed to be working against Ben-hail in his preparation for the competitions. The most frustrating thing of all was the rumour that, this time, King Asa might be awarding the winner of the Grand

Prize not only the usual special prize, but also an important position.

For several years, Ben-hail had secretly cherished the aim of winning the Grand Prize. It was the goal of his life, the basis of his determined pursuit of excellence, and now it was slipping through his fingers by an accident of timing.

Some nights as he lay in bed he almost wept with frustration at lost opportunities, but when the morning dawned, he could always see possibilities again. He would not give up.

Sword fighting was the most prestigious event in the Great Tournament, possibly because it was the only one that involved hand-to-hand conflict. The competition was immediate, dangerous and close up – spectators and competitors alike felt the dangerous importance of the bouts. Each man faced his opponent with nothing but his armour, a shield and a sword to both protect himself and carry the attack to the enemy. Yet it was almost never the weapons or the protective equipment that determined the result; instead, it was the skill with which a contestant used his equipment against his opponent in the unpredictable conditions of conflict. This fact kept the hearts of spectators and officials in their mouths during these contests, and successful swordsmen were greatly respected.

There were few rules in these bouts, and at times they even ended up as wrestling matches if swords were lost or broken. Shields were occasionally used as weapons, and in recent years, some fighters had begun to carry daggers as well. These had proved useful at times; however, they also posed a risk to the swordsman, because, although they were carried in small leather scabbards, some movements could make the dagger cut through the scabbard and cause serious injury.

Abiel had a feel for where most of the students ranked in swordsmanship. While instructors paid periodic attention to other skills, training for swordsmanship continued throughout the year. Students honed their skills by participating in many bouts, and many a student watched countless bouts in the hope of picking up ideas.

As the time of the tournament approached, Abiel often presented display bouts with his best students, and this was a popular afternoon activity, attracting large audiences of students and academy staff alike.

Ben-hail's unusual fighting style was particularly popular to watch. After all, *everybody* used a shield, and the idea of watching a swordsman facing his opponent's naked blade with nothing more than his own blade for protection was mesmerising. Everyone in the audience admired his courage – and his ability – but the thought of fighting without a shield horrified even the bravest of swordsmen.

Training

Yet, for a swordsman with Ben-hail's skill, it actually *was* an advantage. Shields were heavy and awkward. In the jostle, scuffle and scramble of conflict, they often caused a fighter to lose his balance or stumble when his shield knocked against his legs or struck the ground unexpectedly. In such situations, Ben-hail was unencumbered and free to attack with his usual terrifying speed.

Ben-hail also refused to carry a dagger in his bouts. He considered the risk too great and would only have carried a dagger if he could have held it in his hand at all times. Now, though, his injured right hand precluded that possibility.

But while Ben-hail had many friends and admirers among the other students, a few resented his proficiency. One such man was Mattaniah, a senior student whose swordsmanship had been fancied among the other students when Ben-hail joined the academy. A proud and arrogant man, he used his skill to bully others and his tongue as an offensive weapon. Abiel had been looking for an opportunity to expel him from the academy for some time, but so far without success.

Since Ben-hail's altered fighting techniques had gained him such acclaim, Mattaniah's attitude had become even more aggressive. While Abiel himself was not slow to state his opinion that fighting without a shield was utter foolishness – a quick path to the grave, he said – yet he could not disagree with those who watched Ben-hail fighting without one and were quick to point out the advantages if one had sufficient skill.

Mattaniah, however, ridiculed the idea and said that he would have no difficulty showing the advantages of a shield to anyone who ever tried fighting him without one. He showed his contempt for Ben-hail's growing skill by pointedly walking away whenever Ben-hail picked up a sword. As a result, he had never seen Ben-hail's methods of fighting without a shield, which may have been unwise – perhaps some knowledge of what he was facing might have helped him when he decided it was time to put an end to the widespread admiration of Ben-hail's technique.

One afternoon after the army doctor had given Ben-hail the all clear to use his left leg for running, Mattaniah decided it was time to take Ben-hail down a peg or two. Ben-hail was busy showing a younger student how to use his sword to deflect the thrust of an opponent's sword and many students were watching in admiration. However, when Mattaniah joined the crowd, it was clear that he had no intention of watching with a view to learning. He was there solely to challenge Ben-hail and teach him a lesson. That was the plan, and Mattaniah was not afraid to use rudeness to force Ben-hail to fight. He carried his sharpened sword and shield for the purpose, and was already wearing his helmet and breastplate. A small dagger hung from his belt.

"It's all very well to use a staged fight to demonstrate your pet theories," he challenged Ben-hail, "but if you really believed in them, you'd try 'em out against some better swordsmen, not just the bunnies."

"At the moment, Mattaniah, I use them whenever I fight, and whoever I'm fighting. I have no choice – my right hand is injured."

"It's been injured for a long time, hasn't it? Such a pity that it stops you from fighting the best swordsmen."

"What are you trying to say, Mattaniah?" asked Ben-hail wearily. "If you have a point to make, why not come out and say it?"

"Come on Mattaniah," said Kilion, who had been watching Ben-hail's lesson, "you know that Ben-hail injured his hand when he slipped in the river. You know that he can't hold a shield."

"Oh, yes. I'm sure he had a sore hand for a while."

"Meaning that you think I'm faking it now?" asked Ben-hail.

"Well, it *is* taking a long time to recover, isn't it? And I suppose that it's just a coincidence that you can't fight the best swordsmen while this 'injury' heals."

"Meaning yourself, I suppose," said Ben-hail, evenly.

"Of course," said Mattaniah. "If your fighting methods are so good, why won't you fight me?"

"I'm still learning how to fight without a shield," said Ben-hail.

"'Still learning'!" mimicked Mattaniah. "Ha! Why don't you fight me now? Then everyone will see just how much you've learned. And then we'll hear no more about this stupid idea of fighting without a shield!"

"And if I beat you?" asked Ben-hail. "Will we hear no more about this stupid idea of fighting *with* a shield?"

There were nervous laughs from several students in the audience, and Mattaniah's face darkened with anger.

"You cheeky upstart! You think you can beat me?"

"Come on, Mattaniah, just wait a few weeks until Ben-hail has recovered," said Kilion, trying to avoid a fight.

Mattaniah ignored him and thrust his chin forward as he challenged Ben-hail, "You're just too scared to fight me!"

"No. I think I can beat you without a shield."

"You? Defeat me without a shield? Like a baby defeating a lion," sneered Mattaniah.

"Or a shepherd boy defeating a giant?" asked Ben-hail quietly.

"You're no King David!"

"Maybe not, but you're just like Goliath."

"What do you mean by that?" Mattaniah took a step towards Ben-hail and lifted his sword threateningly.

Training

"All talk and no action," said Ben-hail. He gestured with an outspread hand towards Mattaniah and continued, "Sword and spear, shield and helmet, but no heart for the fight."

Mattaniah lifted his sword in fury and rushed at Ben-hail, who was standing at ease with his sword-point resting on the ground. A gasp went around the watching crowd, and Kilion took a step forward to get between Mattaniah and Ben-hail. The man who stood beside him wisely pulled him back, judging that the interference would be more likely to distract Ben-hail than to help him.

Ben-hail reacted immediately: his sword rose quickly and he brought it across his body to the position he had found provided the best protection when he was not holding a shield. There was a smooth expertise in his movements, and it was hard to believe that he had never used a sword in his left hand until just a few months before. Mattaniah's shield was held high and his sword was poised to attack as soon as he was within range of his opponent.

But Ben-hail didn't wait for the attack. He moved his left foot forward and the sword in his left hand began a smooth thrust that would have ended in Mattaniah's chest if the attacker had not brought his shield across to parry the thrust. He tried to stop, but his momentum carried him one step too far. Ben-hail had already seen the moving shield and his supple wrist instantly changed his line of attack. This had become the hallmark of Ben-hail's swordsmanship: his opponents could never be sure that he would complete any move that he began. One of the greatest dangers in sword fighting is over-commitment – a swordsman committing all of his resources to a particular manoeuvre. It can leave a man wide open to swift counter-attacks or sudden thrusts towards exposed parts of his body.

Mattaniah's angry rush had brought him too close and Ben-hail had many options for attack, as long as he could deflect that thrusting sword that threatened his chest. Calmly, smoothly, he engaged Mattaniah's sword and pushed it up and to the right. For an instant, his opponent's entire right side was unprotected, except for the breastplate the man wore. To avoid the breastplate and aim for unprotected flesh would have been simple, but with the effortless speed of an expert, Ben-hail aimed for the breastplate and allowed his blade to strike it firmly.

For friendly bouts, this was a winning stroke, and Ben-hail immediately withdrew his sword, stepped back and stood waiting to see what would happen. He had a suspicion that Mattaniah would not let the bout stop there, humiliated as he had been by such a swift demonstration of Ben-hail's skill.

He was right. Mattaniah ignored the strike on his breastplate and the generous action of his opponent which had saved him from serious injury or death. Blinded by fury and still convinced of his own superiority, he was determined to punish the opponent who stood mockingly before him without a shield.

"A touch on the breastplate," called Kilion. "Victory to Ben-hail."

Mattaniah ignored him, raised his sword once more and prepared to attack. His shield was placed more carefully this time, and it was clear that Mattaniah intended to test Ben-hail's defence with a swift series of thrusts and cuts.

Once again, though, Ben-hail didn't wait for the attack to come. As Mattaniah prepared to launch his assault, his opponent took a sudden step forward and Mattaniah found himself having to make a hurried defence with his shield. Yet it was a defence against a blow that never arrived, because Ben-hail had changed his line of attack again with a lightning twist of the wrist as he moved swiftly forward. Suddenly, Mattaniah found himself facing a blade that sped towards him at a speed he had never encountered before. Desperately, he flung himself backwards, but it was too late as this will-o'-the-wisp opponent changed his line yet again, effortlessly touching Mattaniah's breastplate just out of reach of the shield that now felt so heavy and slow.

Mattaniah's fury had passed. The sudden terror caused by a blade approaching his face had achieved that much, and he slowly lowered his sword and shield. Yet his desire to punish Ben-hail was in no way diminished – indeed, it was stronger than ever after the humiliation he had suffered.

"Satisfied?" asked Ben-hail.

"I suppose you think you've proved that no-one needs a shield?"

"I wasn't trying to prove anything. You attacked me without warning. I was defending myself."

"You were trying to make a fool of me."

"I don't need to do that."

Mattaniah wasn't sure whether Ben-hail was deliberately mocking him or not – his voice and face were impassive. But the audience felt that they knew. Scattered laughter rose, and Mattaniah's fury returned in a flood. Far from teaching this young upstart a lesson, he had been made to look a fool. He knew in his heart that no honest fighter would ever do what he did next, but his anger had driven him beyond all control. Mattaniah reached down to his waist and yanked his dagger from his belt. Ben-hail had turned away and put down his sword, sure that the encounter was over, but a spectator saw the dagger in Mattaniah's hand and shouted, "Look out!" Hastily, Ben-hail turned again and saw his adversary leaping towards him, dagger raised. Mattaniah was too close for Ben-hail to pick up his sword again, and there was little he could do but grab Mattaniah's wrist with his left hand and try to keep the dagger away.

All the fury of Mattaniah's humiliation was bound up in that cowardly attack, and Ben-hail was knocked off his feet as he locked the fingers of his left hand around Mattaniah's wrist and deflected the menacing dagger away from his chest. The two of them fell to the ground with Ben-hail on his back, struggling to force his opponent's hand away. It was quickly made clear that his left hand was stronger than Mattaniah's right hand, and soon he had forced Mattaniah's dagger hand onto the ground where he held it firmly. Almost weeping with anger, Mattaniah reached for the dagger with his left hand and Ben-hail had to quickly grasp that wrist also. But Ben-hail's right hand had not yet recovered its full strength, and he was unable to prevent Mattaniah's hand from inching towards the dagger. The faces of the two men showed the intensity of their struggle, while Ben-hail's also showed some of the pain his effort was costing him. Nevertheless, he was slowly losing the battle; if he didn't do something in a hurry, Mattaniah would reach the dagger and use it.

Desperately, Ben-hail worked to lift his shoulders off the ground without making it easier for Mattaniah to continue his relentless movement toward the dagger. He was sure that he could best his rival if only he could get into the right position. Slowly, he was able to lift his right shoulder until he was able to get more leverage and stop Mattaniah moving his left hand towards the dagger. With increasing confidence, he twisted onto his left shoulder and began to force Mattaniah over onto his back until the positions were reversed and it was Mattaniah who was lying on his back in the dust with Ben-hail sprawled across him, forcing his hands to the ground on either side of him.

"Give up?" he asked.

"Never," said Mattaniah, striving to wrench his hands out of Ben-hail's grasp.

Still holding Mattaniah down, Ben-hail brought up his left foot and quickly kicked at Mattaniah's right hand, which was still holding the dagger. The sandal protected his foot and the dagger was sent spinning as Mattaniah was taken by surprise. With equal speed, Ben-hail let go of his opponent and leapt to his feet, then took two steps and grabbed the dagger.

"Do you give up now?" he asked, standing between Mattaniah and his sword.

Mattaniah looked at him with hatred for a time while his chest rose and fell with the exertion. Finally, grudgingly, he answered, "Yes."

"What's going on here?" came an authoritative voice from beyond the ring of students.

"Mattaniah attacked Ben-hail," answered a student.

"When he wasn't expecting it!" added another.

"Is Ben-hail hurt?" asked Abiel, anxiously. The circle opened and Abiel walked across to where Ben-hail was offering his hand to help Mattaniah stand up.

"No, sir," said Ben-hail. "I'm not hurt."

"What happened?"

"Ask the spectators, sir. I was rather busy at the time and I might not get all the details right."

Kilion disgustedly described how Mattaniah had attacked Ben-hail once without warning, then ignored the touch to the breastplate that signalled the end of the bout and attacked again – and then finally, after he had lost a second time, attacked with a dagger when Ben-hail was turning away.

"Is this true, Mattaniah?" asked Abiel, looking at him with contempt in his eyes.

"He knew I was coming. After all, he sneered and needled me until I did attack. I wish I'd given him what he deserves!"

"So the report is true?"

"It's biased."

"Then come to my tent and you can tell me what did happen. You are on report, and if I find that events are as Kilion described them, appropriate action will be taken. Follow me."

Mattaniah followed Abiel away and Ben-hail bent down to pick up his sword.

"Well done, Ben-hail," said Kilion. "He had it coming to him."

Several others in the audience also congratulated him on his success. Mattaniah had few genuine friends – bullies rarely do.

As Kilion and Ben-hail walked towards their tent, Kilion asked, "How's your right hand? It looked as if it was hurting you at times."

"Yes, it was, but I think it should be alright. I'll have to wait and see."

Chapter 15

A Visit Home

The coronation of King Jehoshaphat was the cause of great celebration throughout the country. A three-day holiday was declared, and only the permanent army and necessary officials were excluded.

Students at Abiel's academy were assembled and given the good news: they had three days of leave. Those who wanted to do so could visit their families – and they were free to go immediately. Ben-hail left the camp shortly after the announcement was made. It was late afternoon as, with his belongings in a bag on his shoulder, he set out at a steady run along the road that passed the camp. He followed the roads west, running without a pause. As the last of the light was fading from the sky, he jogged into Aijalon[84] and hurried to his mother's home. She welcomed him joyfully before he even reached the door.

"Ben-hail, my son! I hoped that I would see you, but I didn't think it would be until the morning. What a blessing." She reached up and put her arms around his neck and kissed him. "You've been running."

"Yes, mother," he panted. "Our leave only started this afternoon." He took the bag off his shoulder and put it down near the door, his breath still coming in short gasps.

"Did you run all the way?"

"Yes."

"Then you must have recovered from your accident. Wonderful!"

"I had to run to get here before dark. I couldn't miss the opportunity to see you again."

"You haven't hurt yourself on any rough roads, I hope."

"No, I'm fine, and most of them have been fixed since winter."

---

[84] Joshua 21:24 tells us that Aijalon was in Dan's tribal area but allocated to the Kohathite family of the Levites. When the tribe of Dan abandoned their tribal allotment, Aijalon was taken over by Judah and later fortified by King Rehoboam (2 Chronicles 11:10).

"I never travel far myself, but I only ever hear complaints about the state of the roads."

"They're alright. I passed one or two work crews as I came, but there wasn't much left for them to do."

"They're probably making sure that the roads won't stop anyone from going to the coronation."

"Do you want to see it, mother?"

"Of course not," she said through tight lips, then changed the subject. "Has spring arrived near Jerusalem?"

"I believe so, but I haven't been there recently."

"Everything is growing wildly here."

"And how are your food stores going, mother? Do you have enough food left to keep you going until this season's crops are ready?"

"I have plenty of food stored, Ben-hail. I still receive your father's share of the tithes, and I can glean in the private fields around the town as well."

"Nobody causes you any trouble when you work?"

"No, never. And anyway, working hard keeps me younger. As you know, there are a few widows around town, and we work together."

He nodded and smiled, "And talk together, I suppose."

She smiled and looked at her son. He was still filling out and looked even bigger and stronger than when she had last seen him. He was a son to be proud of.

Ben-hail looked at her also, noting that she stood straight and tall. He supposed that for her age she was young and attractive, with a ready smile and a willingness to work hard.

"Is Naphish still pestering you?"

"It's not fair to call it pestering, Ben-hail. He is a widower and I am a widow – and he thinks that that means we should get married. I keep trying to tell him as gently as I can that I'm not interested, but he's lonely and would like the companionship of a wife."

"Then why doesn't he find a young girl who *needs* to get married and will marry an older man?"

"Ah, so I'm too old to get married again, am I?" She looked at her son and laughed at his embarrassed expression.

"I wasn't saying that, mother – it's just that if you aren't willing to marry him, then he should find a biddable young girl and marry her. She could give him children and keep him happy."

"Meaning that I couldn't?" She tipped her head back and laughed as Ben-hail looked even more embarrassed. Sobering suddenly, she patted his arm and said, "Don't worry, my son. I don't plan to marry again, even though Naphish keeps reminding me that he wants me to accept his offer. Neither of us is really that old, you know."

He didn't answer, and she laughed again. "Your father and I were both very young when we were married. I was only 18 when you were born. Thirty-nine may seem very old to you, but Naphish doesn't think I'm too old."

Watching him, she knew he wasn't completely convinced, and decided to change the subject. "Anyway, let's get back to catching up on other things. How are your feet now after your accident – and all that running? And, even more importantly, what about your right hand?"

"My feet are both almost back to normal now, mother. The left foot still hurts a bit at times, but it doesn't stop me doing anything I want to do."

"And your hand?"

"My hand is almost completely healed. I can fight and write again. Those are the important things, aren't they?"

"Certainly writing is important. After all, I need to hear how you are. But then, your notes are always too short – and always leave out the parts I want to hear!"

"They don't give us much time for writing, mother," he protested. "Training takes almost all of the available time between sunrise and sunset – and often other times as well. We don't get much sleep."

"I'm sorry, son. I do appreciate your notes – though the last one frightened me. That Mattaniah sounds like a terrible man."

"Oh, he's just arrogant and conceited. It leads him into trouble, too, and then his temper can turn trouble into disaster, both for him and for others. He wants to be a leader, but he'll never be a good one unless he can change those bad habits."

"Now, my son, I know you too well. What you told me didn't sound like the whole story. What really happened? Do I need to write and ask Darda?"

"He wasn't there, mother, so that wouldn't help you."

"Well, you said that Abiel was investigating what had happened, and he wouldn't do that unless it was something important. I'm glad to see you unharmed. I had wondered if you might have been wounded and not told me."

"No, he didn't hurt me at all, and I didn't hurt him either – apart from his pride. He doesn't like the fact that I sometimes fight without a shield, and he thought he could teach me a lesson."

"You fight without a shield?"

"Yes, mother. You know that my right hand was injured, so I couldn't carry anything with it – not even a shield. So I had to fight without one. It wasn't my choice, but Mattaniah didn't like it."

"You do wear a breastplate though, don't you?"

"Yes, normally."

"Were you wearing one then?"

"Ah... no. You see, one of the straps had come off, so I had to remove my breastplate at the end of the previous bout."

"Did Mattaniah know that you didn't have a breastplate on?"

"Probably not, but I don't think it would have made any difference. He was so angry that I'm sure he would have attacked me anyway."

"You didn't mention in your letter that he was angry."

"Didn't I? It doesn't really matter."

"What else didn't you tell me?"

Ben-hail looked a little guilty and asked, "What did I tell you? It was a while ago now."

His mother laughed and said, "So now you want me to tell you what you *did* write so that you will know what to avoid when we talk about it?"

"Of course not, mother! I don't try to hide everything from you. Otherwise I wouldn't send you letters at all."

"Maybe not quite everything, but anything that might worry me."

"Well, I was able to write to you, so it can't have been too bad!"

"It's very hard sometimes: knowing that you might be in danger, but not able to be there."

"I thought you were telling me that I should have faith, mother?" teased Ben-hail.

"Maybe that's why it worries me," she answered, pointedly.

Ben-hail decided that it was time to change the subject. "Did you get the money from the sale of father's share of the town's lands?"

"I ended up coming to an arrangement with your uncle Terah. He's working your father's part of the pastureland around the town, and he's very generous with the share of the crops that he gives me. He says that everything is growing well, and, when you put it all together, I have no problems with getting enough food."

"So you don't have to work there at all?"

"No, I'm left alone to mind my own business. Many in the town know that I have a son who is in one of the king's elite training academies. And I'm not above repeating the reports I hear from army officers who know of your fame there."

"If my 'fame', as you call it, keeps people from causing you trouble, then I'm glad."

"Oh, yes! The name of Ben-hail is on many lips as the next winner of the Grand Prize. I'm proud of my famous son."

"Mother, you know that your son isn't famous – at least, not yet. But never mind that; do you have enough food for me to eat now, or do I need to organise more?"

"When I heard that there was to be a three-day national holiday, I hoped that you would come home, and so I did my best to get enough food to satisfy even *your* appetite."

"Thank you, mother. I do eat quite a lot."

"How are your preparations for the Great Tournament going? How many of the competitions will you win?"

"Oh, mother, mother, mother! You are always so confident. Until the competitions have occurred, I cannot tell you what the results will be. And how can I say that I will win *anything* when there are thousands of men competing?"

"You'll win, my son, you'll win. There is no-one else with your natural ability, nor anyone else who puts in the endless practice you do. Just listen to what everyone around here says when they meet you tomorrow morning. Everyone is proud of the local boy who can outdo all the mighty men from all over the kingdom. And a Levite, no less! You are the greatest hope for the Levites since Benaiah the son of Jehoiada."

"Even by birth he was greater than I, mother. He was a priest, not just a Levite."

"I suppose so, but it wasn't as a priest that he made his greatest contributions. It was his might and his ability as a leader, plus the faith that supported it. Don't forget that, my son." She looked at him with anxious eyes. "You need faith in Yahweh to be a truly mighty man."

"Yes, yes, mother. You have told me so before – many, many times."

"And your father would have too. He also lived that way."

Ben-hail turned away lest his mother hear his muttered response: "... and look where it got him."

ℭ

Next morning, his mother fed him an enormous breakfast and fussed around him like a mother hen. It was a pleasant contrast to the pre-dawn wakeup calls he was used to, and bliss to eat a morning meal without having to do a lot of strenuous exercise first.

After breakfast, his mother overrode his objections and led him out to the well, where many of the women and girls were collecting their water for the day. It was everything Ben-hail most feared. He could cope with long runs, excruciating exercises, dangerous ventures and angry opponents who were doing their best to kill or maim him – but gossiping women and the admiring glances of young girls on the lookout for a husband terrified him!

"Oh, look, it's Ben-hail, the hero!" said Orpah, his mother's friend. "He looks even taller, Elisheba," she said to Ben-hail's mother.

"Yes, he is," she agreed with satisfaction.

Ben-hail compressed his lips and looked plaintively at his mother. His expression begged her to let him escape and hide. She ignored him for a moment, enjoying the admiring looks he was receiving from several young girls. He really was a magnificent figure of a man: tall and solid, with broad shoulders and a lithe, cat-like way of moving that hinted at a strength and speed that few could match. Appearances are not always misleading, and a quick look at Ben-hail's physique would have discouraged most from picking a fight with him.

His appearance also suggested that his growth and development were not yet finished.

But how awkward he looked when surrounded by a group of women! – and that was his current plight.

"Mother, I'm going to see if Peresh is at work yet. Then I'll come home again."

"Very well," said his mother, sounding a little disappointed at the loss of her star exhibit.

Relieved, Ben-hail walked away towards the smithy, hearing one last unwelcome sentence of breathless admiration as he did so: "He's so tall, and those arms could rival Samson's!"

The sound of a hammer pounding on an anvil greeted him as he approached the smithy. Entering the dark, hot room, he found Peresh hard at work shaping the metal point of a goad. With those last words of praise ringing in his ears, Ben-hail couldn't help noticing Peresh's arms and comparing his own with them – unfavourably. A blacksmith must have physical strength, but Peresh stood out even among blacksmiths. This was the man who had inspired Ben-hail's love of physical strength and his desire to develop his own. Eliam had helped him to refine his methods, but Peresh had been the original inspiration who made strength such an honourable goal.

He was a giant of a man, tall and broad, with legs like tree trunks and great hairy arms that looked like the haunches of a lion. His beard was broad and bushy, and his voice echoed out from its depths. Once it had been jet black, but now it was more grey than black, and correspondingly less forbidding.

Everything about Peresh was larger or louder than anyone else.

"Waheb in Suphah, it's Ben!" he roared as he saw Ben-hail.

Ben-hail smiled with delight. No-one else ever called him "Ben", but Peresh never called him anything else.

"I'll just finish about this here goad before it a-gets cold," he said, continuing to pound his hammer on the goad that was quickly losing its cherry-red colour. Each stroke was fluid and powerful, and the shape of the goad could be seen to change with each downward stroke.

After several well-aimed blows, he dipped the goad in the water barrel that stood next to his anvil. It sizzled briefly. Peresh lifted it from the water and carefully examined its shape, then, appearing satisfied, dropped it on his bench.

"What's up wi'e, Ben?" bellowed the powerful voice.

"I've got leave. Three days." He took care to speak loudly, for the blacksmith was increasingly hard of hearing.

"It's well ye're looking, and no mistake."

"Thanks. I've been developing my strength more."

"There's joy in that, me lad. Can ye lift me anvil now?"

The anvil was firmly fastened to the section of tree trunk on which it stood; together, they made a fearsome load.

Ben-hail had heard that challenge before. It was Peresh's measure of a man, and Ben-hail had often heard him express it to men who considered themselves above a simple village blacksmith.

"Ye may be rich, and ye may be wise," Ben-hail had once heard him say to one of the town's judges, "but can ye lift me anvil?"

The judge had tried to brush the challenge aside, but when he visited the market in the following weeks, he was met with less respect than usual and heard a few mocking whispers: "Can ye lift me anvil?"

When those born into a self-satisfied position of importance in the town tried to lord it over him, they met an unexpected challenge. "Ye are what y'do," he would say, "and... can ye lift me anvil?"

No-one ever could. In fact, no-one ever tried. Outside the smithy, many denied that it was possible for even two men to lift that anvil, but they never challenged Peresh to lift it. There were men who said that they had seen him do so, and from time to time, his customers observed that the anvil was within the smithy, so surely it must be Peresh who had moved it.

"Well?" asked Peresh, and for once his voice was quiet. "Can ye lift me anvil, Ben?"

"I don't think so," said Ben-hail. "Should I try?"

"I thinks as ye should."

Ben-hail wondered if he should mention the recent injury to his right hand and his left leg, but it felt like an excuse. Could he lift that massive union of metal and wood? Would even Eliam be able to lift it?

He put his hands under the anvil and placed his feet apart in the best position for lifting. He breathed deeply once or twice and then exerted all of his strength to lift the anvil. He could feel it moving slightly on the tree trunk – he was lifting the anvil alright, but to lift the base as well was beyond him. He relaxed and looked at Peresh, shaking his head.

"Not yet, Ben?"

"I don't know if I'll ever be able to lift that."

"Do ye want to, Ben?"

Of course he did. He had always wanted to lift that impossible load. He remembered times as a child when he had visited the smithy after lessons and wrapped his young arms around the anvil in a futile attempt just to move it. Peresh had laughed at his puny efforts, but had continued to encourage. Ben-hail remembered one particular afternoon a few years earlier when he had given up the attempt with a frustrated, "I can't!"

Peresh had patted him on the shoulder and said, "If ye wants it bad enough, Ben, ye'll do it."

"But how?"

"Ye'll finds a way, Ben. Ye'll finds a way."

"How do you find a way?"

"Build up thy strength, Ben, that be what matters. Lift ye heavy things. Then lift ye heavier things. Ye're the only one who can teach yerself how. If ye don't work at it, t'ain't no-one who's a-goin' t' work at it for ye. 'Member, ye only gets what ye works for, Ben."

Those words had often echoed in his mind over the last winter as he'd fought almost hopelessly to overcome his injuries and struggled to use his left hand with a dexterity that only his right could achieve. His confidence that Peresh was right had kept him going; yet now, despite all his accomplishments, he still could not take that final step. The anvil remained beyond him.

Ben-hail had spent many hours in the smithy as a youth, and his close companionship with Peresh had burgeoned into a desire to be a blacksmith. It had seemed a much more manly pursuit than the work of a Levite, and he would have sought an apprenticeship with Peresh had not his mother put her foot down. Even after that, he might have considered waiting a few years and becoming a blacksmith anyway had not Terah, his father's brother, made it clear that he could not do it. Ben-hail never quite knew what was wrong, but somehow, deep down, he felt that his mother did not approve of Peresh. As far as Ben-hail was concerned, Peresh had taught him the important lessons of life: self-reliance and how to achieve success. Ben-hail had been a willing student, and with his vast natural talents had learned to work hard and achieve amazing results in anything he ever put his hand to.

His mother, however, wanted him to be a true Levite. Having a son who would work in the temple of Yahweh had been his father Raddai's greatest desire, and his mother had remained determined to achieve it. Yahweh had been the centre of Raddai's life, and he could see no better goal for a Levite than to work in the temple of Yahweh from youth to old age. He would not have been averse to his son's development of physical prowess. After all, strength was a great benefit in preparing sacrifices, carrying firewood and handling the tithes. Levites should be perfect physical specimens, giving glory to Yahweh through their physical service.[85]

But Ben-hail had dreams of strength and victory. His dreams of becoming a blacksmith had been only a passing phase, triggered by the companionship of a man who had filled some of his need for a father. But dreams of battles and victory, of mighty men and their amazing deeds, had filled his head from childhood, and quickly returned when blacksmithing was denied him. He loved to read of the achievements of King David and his mighty men – men who could kill an army of enemies at one time. They were an inspiration to him, and his amazing dedication and determination were leading him to a point where emulation might be possible.

He was sure that if he learned and practised, studied the champions' methods and copied their skills, then he too could become a mighty man.

And above all of the other heroes, there was one hero who stood out to him. It wasn't Jashobeam, the man who excelled in might even among the mighty. He had killed 800 men at one time,[86] and Ben-hail marvelled politely along with everyone else, but Jashobeam was not the man. It wasn't Eleazar either, left by his companions to fight an army single-handed. When his companions finally returned, all there was left to do was to collect the spoil from those whom he had slain.[87] Ben-hail yearned to triumph in such a way, yet, still, it was not Eleazar who filled him with a burning desire to succeed. Nor was it Asahel, great Joab's mighty brother, as fleet of foot as a gazelle,[88] or his brother Abishai, responsible for killing 300 enemies with his spear.[89]

Rather, it was Benaiah, the son of Jehoiada,[90] a descendant of Levi[91] and that one of David's mighty men who later became King Solomon's army commander.[92] This was the man who inspired Ben-hail's dedication and lit the torch of his dreams. It was Benaiah, with his gloriously heroic yet pragmatic approach, that drove Ben-hail with a relentless determination to achieve success.

Benaiah was a truly mighty man and Ben-hail was determined to be like him – whatever might stand in his way.

---

[85] There were no physical requirements specified for Levites except for priests (descendants of Aaron) who were to be excluded if they had any physical defect (Leviticus 21:17-23).

[86] The ESV calls him Josheb-basshebeth a Tahchemonite in 2 Samuel 23:8 (which possibly should read Joshebeam, the son of Hachmoni), and a Hachmonite in 1 Chronicles 11:11, where it reports that he killed 300 men. When different records report different numbers, it is often hard to know what is intended. The KJV translates 2 Samuel 23:8 as "that sat in the seat" instead of assuming that a name is intended.

[87] 2 Samuel 23:9-10; 1 Chronicles 11:12-14

[88] 2 Samuel 2:18; 23:24; 1 Chronicles 11:26

[89] 2 Samuel 23:18-19; 1 Chronicles 11:20-21

[90] 2 Samuel 23:20; 1 Chronicles 11:22-24

[91] 1 Chronicles 27:5

[92] 1 Kings 4:4

Chapter 16

THE CORONATION

The sun rode high above the Mount of Olives and poured down the blessing of morning warmth from a cloudless sky. Thousands of happy people lined the roads that skirted the eastern walls of Jerusalem, the massive walls towering above the crowd.

Down in the valley, the Kidron flowed noisily, and the Gihon spring added its own contribution as it forced its way out from under the city. This had been the starting point of Joab's clever incursion into Jebus that had overwhelmed the city's self-confident inhabitants.[93] Though the water shafts were intended to provide access to the spring from within the walls Joab had used them to gain easy and completely unexpected access to the city above. The spring itself had come to represent the right of David's line to rule in Jerusalem. Here at Gihon, Solomon had been crowned king,[94] and here each of his successors in turn had become "Yahweh's anointed" – kings who ruled over Judah on the throne of David.[95]

Above the spring, a platform jutted out from the hillside, constructed especially for the occasion, and now Jehoshaphat was to be crowned king.

At the centre of the platform, King Asa sat upon a grand throne, attended by his bodyguard and the Royal Doctor. His feet rested on a stool to ease the pain, but he grimaced from time to time when the torture became too great.

His oldest son stood behind him, waiting quietly. At the rear of the platform where it met the hillside, Azubah, Asa's queen stood with Jehoshaphat's wife Zeruah. Zeruah's sons were with them, and Jehoram, the oldest, concerning whom Jehoshaphat had sought his mother's help,

---

[93] 2 Samuel 5:6-8; 1 Chronicles 11:6
[94] 1 Kings 1:32-34; 38-40
[95] This is only a guess: there is no mention of where later kings were anointed.

was standing next to his grandmother. He was looking annoyed, pushing her hand from his shoulder. Azubah was grateful that the noise of the crowd masked the sound of his complaints as she tried to shush him. Asa was a proud grandfather at times, but the pain in his feet often rendered him short-tempered and quick to find fault with the children. Jehoram could easily find himself banished from the magnificent event altogether if his grandfather heard his protests.

Asa was fidgeting on his seat, his feet moving incessantly. Although Jehoshaphat stood close by and Ladan was at his elbow, Asa sat alone, wrapped up in his own suffering but still struggling to maintain a regal appearance.

"What is the delay, Ladan?" he asked his old friend once, coming briefly out of his lethargy.

Ladan answered calmly and soothingly, and the querulous voice subsided once more. It was clear that Ladan had been given the most difficult problem of the day: dealing with the ageing king.

King Asa leaned back and consciously tried to forget the pain and clear his face of all expression. He lifted his face to the sky and let the sun warm his skin. Why was his suffering so intense? he wondered. He had been a righteous king – within the limits of his character, at least – and surely he had led the kingdom well? Yet now he was suffering, possibly even more than righteous Job had done. It was not fair, there could be no doubt of that. But at least he lived at a time when medical advances could offer solutions that had not been available to Job. Even so, his suffering was getting worse. Almost every day the area affected by the disease seemed a little larger. And the pain! It was beyond anything he had ever imagined possible, and he had begun to question his ability to cope. At times, even his faith in the Royal Doctor was shaken, and he wondered if he should consult another doctor. Yet what did other doctors have to offer? Nothing but suffering and death. He clenched his teeth and squared his shoulders. He would beat it. He deserved the recovery the Royal Doctor had promised him, and he was sure it would come when the disease had progressed far enough. Then he would be rewarded for his patience. So he told himself.

"My lord," said a voice in his ear, and he shook his head to clear it and return to the present. It was Ladan, with a messenger standing beside him. "The security arrangements have been completed, my lord. The coronation can begin."

"Explain to the crowd what is happening and introduce me. I want to get this over with."

The king's nobles, who surrounded the platform, were all watching their lord sympathetically. Asa's wives stood near, mingling with Jehoshaphat's wives, all of them surrounded by palace guards. Beautiful women, beautiful clothing and beautiful jewellery, but King Asa had eyes for none of it. He must get through the proceedings and then he could withdraw; leave the kingdom in the hands of his son. Oh that it might all be over! that he could settle again in his own bedchamber, lying in the darkness, free to scream when the pain was too much to bear.

"Hurry!" he said to Ladan, and withdrew again into his isolated cocoon of anguish.

Ladan stepped forward and called the crowd to attention. Slowly the silence spread across the valley and lapped up the sides of the Mount of Olives. Formally appointed callers repeated Ladan's words, spreading them towards the corners of the throng. In pockets where the words could not be heard by all, self-appointed callers repeated them to those whose limited hearing robbed them of the sense. The crowd settled down to enjoy the spectacle, and Ladan led them eloquently through the admirable achievements of King Asa. In a long reign, any king will make enemies, and at times King Asa had made many enemies, but this was a time for celebration and the audience were those who could rejoice. Cheers arose as King Asa's victories were recounted, and the tribute would no doubt have continued for a long time had not Ladan cast a quick glance at his master and seen how close he was to total collapse.

Quickly then, he introduced the king and the warm cheers echoed across the valley. King Asa slowly stood, then shuffled towards the front of the platform. Ladan took his arm and said, "Lean on me, my lord."

Asa did so, gathering his strength for the task.

"With the blessing of Yahweh, our God, I have ruled over Judah for 39 years," Asa began. His voice was weak, and the caller Ladan had made sure was close by immediately repeated the words loudly. Asa took the opportunity to breathe deeply before continuing. "Now, I have a disease in my feet. The Royal Doctor will cure me, but it will take time. In the meantime, the pain makes it impossible for me to continue to rule over you." Once more he paused as a spasm of unbearable pain engulfed him. He did his best to regain his composure as it passed. "Now, my son Jehoshaphat will take over the day-to-day administration of the kingdom.

"When my father Abijah died, I became Yahweh's anointed king over Judah. As a descendant of King David, I am not abandoning this responsibility. I will regain my health and return to the duties of kingship, but when I do so, it will be in concert with my son Jehoshaphat. Until then, he will take on the responsibility of ruling this great nation by himself.

"My son is a man of faith. Listen to his guidance. Come to him for judgement. Obey his commands. Honour him as your king."

King Asa gasped as another lightning bolt of pain seared through his feet and he almost collapsed. Faithful Ladan read the situation immediately and signalled to the Royal Doctor. Together, they helped Asa back to his throne, where he hunched his shoulders and hid his face in his hands. Nobody knew that this would be almost the last public appearance of the great King Asa.

Jehoshaphat stood sadly behind his father's throne, gazing at the large crowd that filled the hillside near the Gihon Spring.

Coronations are normally arranged with very little notice – it is the way of an inherited monarchy. In general, a new king is only crowned after the death of the old one, and the death of a king is often unexpected.

Jehoshaphat pondered his good fortune in having his father present at his coronation. Yet he couldn't believe that the Royal Doctor would ever cure his father. If only his father would call on Yahweh for healing!

Ladan smoothed over the unexpected interruption and restored the solemn grandeur of the ceremony with soothing and encouraging words. Skilfully, he blended these with an introduction to his final task, the centrepiece of the formalities. As Jehoshaphat knelt on the platform, Ladan placed the golden crown on his head and gave him a few private words of encouragement. Then he stood beside the new king and raised him from his knees. His arm was under Jehoshaphat's elbow as he announced loudly to the multitude, "Here is your king!"

Then he stepped back.

King Jehoshaphat was welcomed by a cheering crowd on the sides of the valley that shared his name: the Valley of Jehoshaphat. He made a speech dedicating his reign to Yahweh, the God of Israel. All the people cheered, rejoicing in the new king, and the figure of the old king, curled up in his private agony, receded into the background. Choirs sang psalms of praise to Yahweh, and a crown was placed on the new king's head. A new king, welcomed by everyone present – with a right good will.

Here was a king with no enemies – unless, of course, a king can inherit enemies.

Before the ceremony was over, King Asa was quietly hurried away in his palanquin, escaping to his palace; his private chamber; his bed.

The new had taken control, the old had stolen away to hide, and the kingdom moved on.

Presents were distributed with royal liberality to all who attended, and the cheers and singing were heard far away. When finally it was time for Jehoshaphat to return to the palace, choirs from the temple marched before him, singing praises to God and extolling the virtues of a righteous king who would please Yahweh.

Azubah, now the queen mother, was well pleased with the day's events, but her pleasure was tempered by the knowledge that a time would come when her son would also have to pass on the kingship to his son, whether by death or through this sort of unfortunate situation. Then Jehoram would be king, and even at his present tender age, she had little confidence that he would ever make a good king.

Jehoshaphat entered the palace and made his way toward his father's bedchamber. As he entered the antechamber, his father's personal secretary looked up from the desk at which he was sitting.

"Welcome, your majesty."

"I would like to see my father, if that is possible."

The secretary looked doubtful, but agreed to enquire if a visit would be possible. In a short time, he returned, looking a little awkward.

"King Asa," he said hesitantly, "is indisposed. He cannot receive you at present."

Jehoshaphat turned away, uncertain what to do. After a few moments, he walked to the throne room. As usual, guards stood at the doors, but they looked at him in surprise as he approached. They stood aside uncertainly as he opened the door and walked in. The room was deserted, and Jehoshaphat felt a strong sense of dislocation and fragmentation, breakage and dissolution. Something strong had finished and there was nothing ready to replace it. His father was gone. The throne sat vacant and alone in an empty room that had always been so full of people and activity.

Now he must take up the reins and guide the kingdom.

He approached the magnificent throne from which Solomon had reigned and for a moment felt like an impostor. He was no wise man like Solomon, no brave hero like David. Could he join those famous ancestors as God's shepherd of Judah? How could he ever earn respect as a king in such company?

He slowly climbed the steps, flanked on either side by exquisitely carved lions, until at last he reached the top. Here was the seat of kings – and now it was his.

King Jehoshaphat.

King of Judah.

He sat on the throne of his father and felt the responsibility weighing on his shoulders. He smiled to himself and wondered if this concern was a reflection of his age. Would a younger man worry less and feel less of that load on his shoulders?

After all, his father was still available for him to question – but not so available that he could easily interfere. Jehoshaphat would have a free hand, at least as long as his father's poor health continued.

He had no doubt that Ladan and others would carry reports to his father of what was afoot in the kingdom. He made a mental note to make sure that he always told his father whenever there were questions or events that might provoke a nostalgic chinwag between the ageing advisors and his father.

Prayer came naturally to the new king as he sat on his throne, and his apprehension at the enormity of his duty eased a little as he committed the guidance of his reign to God.

He was king, and must lead the nation to Yahweh.

The Great Tournament was fast approaching, and that was important for the morale of the army. Positions as the king's bodyguards and possibly even his armour-bearer would be worthy goals for the mighty men of his kingdom to aspire to.

And there were also some harder decisions to be made. Hanani – what of him? And what of those who had supported Yahweh's prophets against Yahweh's anointed?

He smiled a wry smile: there was a fitting test for a new king's judgement.

As he mused, several servants and advisors had quietly entered the room. They were all men who had served his father faithfully; Jehoshaphat had often met them in the throne room before. Now they had come to serve him, and he must win their trust and respect – or should he replace them with others? But that question could wait.

Suddenly he noticed his former throne, the one his father had placed for him when he had taken control of the army and joined the royal council. At the moment, it wasn't needed – but what if his father recovered soon?

He called the servant who managed the furniture and pointed to the throne.

"Take it away," he said.

Chapter 17

WINE AND SONG

Aijalon was one of the towns Joshua gave to the tribe of Levi when he led the Israelites into the land of Canaan. Levi was a special tribe in Israel because the men of Levi had dedicated themselves to God at a time when the other tribes had chosen to worship a golden calf. Moses returned from meeting with God at the top of Mount Sinai, and was shocked by the idolatry he found in the camp. He had called for support in fighting it and the Levites had answered his call, so God had chosen them as his special tribe, bound to him for the work of worship and teaching.[96] Following the successful invasion of Canaan, most of the tribes were given farming land as a possession, but the Levites were given many towns scattered throughout the land.[97] These towns generally had a "religious" feel to them, and the Levites' knowledge of God's law was put to good use in the local courts. When the kingdom of Israel later split in two, many of the Levites refused to accept King Jeroboam's perverted religion in the north and moved to Judah.[98] As a result, there were many extra Levites crowded into the Levite towns of Judah, and spread through other towns as well.

Some of these Levites wanted to serve Yahweh in the temple in Jerusalem, and they were put on a roster for service.[99] Ben-hail's father had been such a one: eager to serve; disappointed that he could not be a priest, but thankful that he was able to be more closely involved in temple worship than the lay people. Each year, he had spent time in Jerusalem, helping with the tasks that made the worship of God possible for the other tribes: preparing sacrifices, teaching the people the requirements of the law, and working under the direction of the priests to assess cases of disease or mildew. A man of strong faith, he had been excited

---

[96] Exodus 32:19-29; Numbers 3:6-10; Deuteronomy 33:8-10
[97] Joshua 21:1-42
[98] 2 Chronicles 11:13-17
[99] Deuteronomy 18:6

and pleased when King Asa had shown his dedication to Yahweh through his religious reforms.

Yet Levites were not the only inhabitants of Aijalon. There were also men of Judah who liked the religious feel of the town, as well as a few who were not religious at all – in fact, who were malcontents and trouble-makers, and even the occasional petty criminal who enjoyed the absence of criminal competition in what was generally a law-abiding town.

Such a group was sitting near the marketplace on the afternoon after Ben-hail's arrival. As usual, they were drinking wine and admiring their own intelligence.

They had all heard stories about the local boy who was making good in one of the best military academies in the country. According to the rumours, he was expected to win many prizes in the Great Tournament, and possibly even take the Grand Prize.

One of the group – the one with the loudest voice and the slowest brain – was named Carmi. Having no reason to expect that he could ever achieve anything useful himself, he hated to hear anybody else praised for genuine achievements or ability. So he poo-poohed the idea that Ben-hail could possibly deserve such a reputation.

"Can you imagine anyone from this sleepy little town having any outstanding ability?" he asked his friends.

The afternoon sun was warm and the wine sat comfortably in their stomachs, so none of them answered his question. Fortunately, it had been largely rhetorical anyway.

He continued, as he often did, sure that he was captivating his audience with his scintillating wit and humour.

"Can you imagine a Levite being skilful enough to win any competition at all? Most of them aren't even smart enough to tie their sandal-thongs, and I bet Ben-hail's just the same."

His closest crony offered his valuable support: "Yeah, I bet he'd run a mile if he ever saw an enemy."

"Maybe he could run away faster than anyone else and win the prize!"

They all laughed at the joke, and it might have ended harmlessly enough there if Ben-hail hadn't walked past at that moment, going to see his uncle.

"Hey, there's the champion, striding around as if he owns the place."

Ben-hail saw a group of ne'er-do-wells lazing around in the sunshine and paid no attention to them. He knew that such men were normally best ignored and fully intended to do so.

Carmi, however, saw an opportunity to show his wit and take this self-important country hick down a peg or two.

"It's Ben-hail the Champion," he said loudly, "come to impress us with his bravery!"

Ben-hail kept walking; he had not heard the comment at all.

"Don't ignore me, you young fool," shouted Carmi, his face darkening. "You should listen to your betters instead of parading before us as a great warrior."

He finally had Ben-hail's attention, but that young man was wise enough to know that nothing good can come from meeting drunks on their own level. He walked on and had passed out of sight around the corner before they could do any more.

Carmi took some time to respond, which reflected his state of alertness. Then he took a mouthful from his wineskin and asked if anyone had ever seen the like of that before. If anyone had, they didn't seem inclined to acknowledge it. Once more, the matter would probably have lapsed if Carmi's next attempt to take a mouthful of solace hadn't come up dry. His wineskin was empty, and in his drunken disappointment, he fixed on Ben-hail as the cause.

"It's all his fault," he said bitterly, to no-one in particular.

"Is it?" asked one of the group.

"Mmm. He walked around the corner and now I've run out of wine."

None of the company was sober enough to see any flaws in his logic, and he was left to expound on his grievance.

"He thinks he can parade around here and take away our wine," he said.

"Take away our wine?" asked another. "Who's taking our wine?"

"Ben-hail," said Carmi, affronted.

"He can't do that!"

"He's done it!" He turned his wineskin upside down and shook it. Only a few drops came out. "Look!" he said. "No wine left."

"I'll show him what happens to anyone who takes away our wine," said a third, reaching down to his belt and fumbling awkwardly with a small pouch. At length, he pulled out a dagger and held it up for all to see. "This is what we use for him."

"Anyone else got a weapon?" asked Carmi.

Apart from two staffs, there were no other weapons among the group, but they were content that these would be enough to teach Ben-hail a salutary lesson.

It was almost two hours later when Ben-hail returned, and by then, the gang of drinkers was no more alert than they had been, except perhaps for Carmi. His empty wineskin had left him just a little more sober than he liked. The intervening time had heard many befuddled reflections on Ben-hail: his parentage, habits and failings.

Wine and Song

When he rounded the corner, it was Carmi who saw him first – which was not surprising given that he had been watching for him.

"There he is," he said.

"Who?" asked one of his cronies, vaguely.

"Ben-hail. The arrogant show-off."

"The one who doesn't know anything?"

"Yes, that's him." He stood up and shouted at Ben-hail, "Come over here and talk to us."

Ben-hail looked a little uncertain, but finally turned and began to walk towards the waiting group.

As he approached, Carmi tried to make sure that everyone was awake and alert. Some were able to sit up, including the two armed with staffs, who picked them up and held them ready. Only one man failed to respond: the man with the knife, which lay in his lap as he reclined, snoring gently. Carmi slowly picked it up, keeping it carefully out of Ben-hail's sight.

Ben-hail neared the group and, realising that they were mostly well beyond the point of being dangerous, relaxed a little. "What do you want?" he asked, stopping a few metres[100] away.

"You are a consheeted so-off," said Carmi, "ah, a conceited show-off."

"And you are drunk," said Ben-hail in a polite voice.

"You think you're a hero!"

"No I don't. But you're only a hero at drinking wine. You should go home and sleep it off."

"Don't you tell me what to do!"

"I'm not telling you anything that isn't obvious to everyone. You're drunk and you're an embarrassment to the town."

"How dare you talk to me like that!" Carmi was rapidly losing his temper and the knife was ready in his hand. His friends were trying to follow the discussion but finding it heavy going. But they saw Carmi moving his hands and dimly realised what he was holding. The two with staffs clumsily prepared to stand up.

"If your mother and father had said it to you more often, I wouldn't need to now. Are you going home, or do I have to find out where you live and drag you there?" said Ben-hail, pleasantly.

Carmi made an inarticulate growl in his throat and ran unevenly at Ben-hail, swinging up his arm and bringing the knife into view as he ran. His friends did their best to mobilise in support.

From that instant, everything happened very quickly.

Ben-hail took a step towards Carmi and kicked him in the stomach.

---

[100] A few yards.

The drunk's lungs emptied explosively and he suddenly doubled over. Ben-hail then stepped to his right and snatched a threatening staff from its owner. There was little resistance and Ben-hail quickly used his new weapon to strike the last armed man, who was still clumsily rising to his feet. Swinging back again, he dealt more enduringly with Carmi, who fell to the ground, dropping the knife. One of the men tried to turn and run, but Ben-hail thrust the staff between his legs and he tripped and fell. The staff was not Ben-hail's favourite weapon, but he wielded it with astonishing speed and accuracy nevertheless, and soon all of his would-be attackers lay helpless on the ground.

One man had bested seven – although they were not the strongest or brightest seven, nor were they at their best. Nevertheless, the incident was seen by a passing Levite, and before nightfall the story was all over the town.

Ben-hail could not have better announced his bravery and skill had he planned the entire event. His opponents were unpopular trouble-makers and Ben-hail was praised as a model of civic duty.

His mother basked in the praise of her son, but marvelled at the calm way in which he acknowledged the praise without seeming to revel in it.

○ℛ

Ben-hail spent his second day of leave visiting many relatives and friends. It was the day of Jehoshaphat's coronation, but none of the townsfolk seemed to have gone to Jerusalem for the celebration.

Darda's family lived close to Aijalon and he too returned home for the holiday, although not until the morning after Ben-hail's arrival. Family business had taken him first to his maternal grandparents' home, where he had stayed the night.

On the morning after Ben-hail's encounter with Carmi and his gang, Darda visited the market and discovered that his friend was the talk of the town. Delighted with the news, he went to Elisheba's house to congratulate Ben-hail.

Elisheba opened the door at his knock and welcomed him. "Darda, it's good to see you. Have you heard about our hero yet?" she asked as she shepherded him in to the room where Ben-hail sat.

"Oh yes," laughed Darda. "That's why I came to visit. I'm proud to be acquainted with such a great man. Was it really as exciting as I've been told? Seven against one, and all over in a few seconds?"

Ben-hail rolled his eyes. "I suppose that's one way to describe it, but it wouldn't give the true picture. How about 'a minor incident dealing with a bunch of drunks'?"

"I'm glad to hear it! It's not the first time you've had to handle drunks, though, is it? I seem to remember about six years ago you dealt with a couple of drunks who were attacking an old man. They didn't like his singing – or at least, they didn't like the fact that he wouldn't sing the sorts of songs they wanted him to sing."

"Yes, but that was a much more dangerous incident."

"Well, you were only 15 at the time."

"And they did both have knives and weren't too drunk to use them."

Elisheba had been listening to this conversation with a look of growing surprise and concern on her face, and now she interrupted: "What's this about, Ben-hail? I've never heard of any of this before."

"It was a long time ago, mother. I didn't tell you at the time because I knew you would be worried if you knew. And the wounds healed quickly, so it didn't matter."

"The wounds? This is getting worse and worse."

"Just some minor cuts on my hands and arm. Nothing important."

"But didn't you have problems stopping the bleeding for a few days?" asked Darda.

"I suppose so – I'd forgotten that."

"The old man you saved helped you by putting a poultice on the main cut, as I recall."

" 'Saved'?" asked Elisheba. "This really is getting worse and worse. Were those drunks trying to kill the old man?"

Ben-hail tried to wave away the question, but Darda answered, "Yes – they'd already stabbed him once when Ben-hail arrived. He was lucky to survive at all. I arrived a little while later, just as Ben-hail was dealing with the attackers – too late to help. So I got to tie up wounds for the old man and the brave hero. Hey, Ben-hail, you didn't get any fame from that incident, did you?"

"No, thankfully – it was hard enough keeping my mother from noticing the wounds. And since I didn't want her to know at the time, I didn't tell anyone else, and the old man mustn't have told anyone either."

"But what about the men who attacked him?" asked Elisheba.

"When they sobered up, I don't think they wanted anyone to know what they had done," said Darda. "It would have been hard for them to convince the judges that there was no malice on their part, and there were enough witnesses for the judges to convict them. I believe they left town that same day and have never come back."

"And what about the old man?" asked Elisheba.

"I don't know," said Darda. "Do you know, Ben-hail? You spent quite a bit of time with him afterwards when he was treating your wounds."

"I'm not sure where he went," said Ben-hail, dismissively. "He left the town soon afterwards and I've not seen him since."

"All I know about him is that he had a beautiful singing voice," said Darda. "He hadn't been in town for very long, but I heard him singing some psalms in the marketplace two or three days before he was attacked. I've never heard such an amazing voice. He made the songs so beautiful, it was hard to walk away."

Ben-hail made no comment.

"I didn't hear anyone singing like that then," said Elisheba, "but here's an interesting coincidence: an old man arrived in town only a few days ago, and I've heard several people comment on his exquisite singing."

Ben-hail still made no comment, but Darda noticed that his friend's lips were compressed and that he frowned slightly.

∝

On the morning of the third and last day of Ben-hail's leave, he was back at the smithy. Thoughts of the anvil were still bothering him and he was determined to lift it.

Peresh welcomed him in his usual manner and looked at him knowingly.

"'E's come to lift the anvil," he said.

"I've come to try again."

"Try 'e then."

Ben-hail made sure that he was in the best possible position, with his feet on either side of the tree trunk and his arms underneath the horns of the anvil. He strained to lift, taking all of that daunting load on his arms. Once again the anvil lifted, and this time it seemed a little easier, but still the log refused to move. At last, he had to give up.

"Not this time, Ben. 'E can't do it this time."

"No. But I won't give up. I wonder if my friend Eliam could lift it?" Ben-hail shook his head in exasperation. "He probably could."

"Be yer friend stronger than you, Ben?"

"Oh, he's much stronger that I am!"

"Just ye wait. One day it'll be enough t' make a man famous – being stronger-like than you!"

Ben-hail smiled. "I don't think that's likely, Peresh."

"R'member that ye be the one who decides yer fame."

"But what about faith? Everyone else seems to agree that the mightiest men have faith in Yahweh."

"I be what I be, Ben, and I never got no stronger except by work."

"That's what you've always told me, Peresh, and I've always found it to be true."

CR

The hubbub of the market filled Ben-hail's ears as he walked from Peresh's workshop towards his mother's home. Traders offered him fresh produce, fruit and grains, bread and fish. Suddenly, amidst the noise he heard a man singing to the sound of a lyre, and his heart began to beat faster. He recognised that voice!

Ben-hail stopped. Where was the source of that haunting sound? It seemed to come from over near the gate. He walked deliberately past the market stalls, politely acknowledging the thanks and admiration of voluble stall-keepers and customers for his heroics of the previous evening. The drunks often harassed the townsfolk, so their public humiliation was bound to be popular.

Soon Ben-hail could see past the remaining stalls into the hollow under the gate, and then there was no longer any doubt: it was the old man whom he had saved six years earlier. The notes of the lyre rose, sad and sweet, while the clear voice sang the words of a Psalm of David with utter conviction. It was as if the words had been written for the singer, reflecting his sufferings as an honest man in a world of traitors. Ben-hail stopped and listened, now close enough to appreciate the old man's deep absorption in the music as his gnarled fingers caressed the lyre.

> "Lead me, O Lord, in your righteousness
> because of my enemies;
> make your way straight before me.
> For there is no truth in their mouth;
> their inmost self is destruction;
> their throat is an open grave;
> they flatter with their tongue."[101]

Without warning, the mesmerising performance stopped and Ben-hail found himself looking into the singer's eyes. Knowing eyes; eyes that made it clear he had been waiting for Ben-hail.

"Ben-hail. You have come."

"Yes, Nezib. I heard you singing."

"I knew you would." The old man surveyed Ben-hail, seeming pleased with what he saw. "You've grown much since we last met," he said. Then he smiled and continued, "I hear that you have been dealing with drunks again."

"Yes, but these men were not much of a danger to anyone."

---

[101] Psalm 5:8-9

"Were you hurt at all?"

"No. I've learned a lot about combat since I was 15."

There were plenty of people in the gateway, but none of them were paying any particular attention to Ben-hail or the old man. Nevertheless, Ben-hail looked around quickly when the old man asked, "Are you happy fighting for the man who killed your father?"

Nobody seemed to be listening, so Ben-hail replied cautiously, "Why do you ask?"

"I came to Aijalon to see you, Ben-hail. Yesterday, Prince Jehoshaphat was crowned to rule alongside King Asa. Yet we know that King Asa's evil behaviour of more than 20 years has never been rectified. How do you feel? You fight in his army!"

"My father died in King Asa's dungeon. You know that. How do you expect me to feel?"

"Yes, and God's prophet was locked up too. Where is he now?" Nezib looked around quickly, then, confident that no-one was within earshot at that moment, said bitterly, "Asa has brutally mistreated many righteous people like your father. Even today, many families don't know whether their loved ones are alive or dead." The old man's eyes were intense, filled with anger.

"We can't talk about that here," said Ben-hail.

"Very well. Where can we talk?"

"I don't think I want to talk anywhere."

"The king has flouted God's laws time and again. The nobles and priests do nothing. Surely he can't be left to oppress people more righteous than himself. Would your father have approved of doing nothing?"

Ben-hail laughed bitterly. "My father thought he was working for God when he wrote that letter," he said, "and look where it got him."

"Throughout history, God's servants have suffered."

"And surely if he cared for them at all he would look after them!"

"Don't you see that it is man's resistance to God that causes the problems?"

"Look, King Asa acts as if he is leading Judah in the pure worship of Yahweh, but he's just a hypocrite like all the others that fill the temple and support him in his brutality. He uses religion to keep the people under control, nothing else. They all sing psalms – like you do – and make pious comments, but they ignore God's rules whenever the rules go against what they want to do."

"Your father would be shocked at your words!"

"But then again, maybe if he had felt like I do, he would still be alive."

"And now you fight for the man who killed him!"

"I make my own decisions and my own plans. I don't need you to approve of my actions."

The old man looked at him thoughtfully for a few moments and then changed tack.

"Did you hear that there was an attempt to assassinate King Asa recently?"

"Yes, I did. But it failed."

"Uriel was a young man, not much older than you. But he didn't have your training."

"What happened to him?"

"He's locked up in the king's dungeon – as far as we know."

"One man against the king's elite guard. What chance did he have? A sacrificial lamb."

"We distracted the guard. I sat beside the road as the royal party passed by and sang as I have never sung before. Everyone was enthralled, and then Uriel attacked from the other side of the road. It was a perfect opportunity, and for one priceless instant there was no-one between him and either the king or the prince. No-one. If you had been given the same opportunity, you would have succeeded easily!"

"What went wrong?"

"Uriel's stroke was deflected by a breastplate that Prince Jehoshaphat wore under his clothes. Then he couldn't decide what to do before the guard closed in. You would have made the right choice first time."

Ben-hail looked thoughtful and was about to reply when he caught sight of Darda approaching the gate through the marketplace. His friend saw him and came over.

"Nezib, I presume," he said to the old man.

"Yes. How do you know me?"

"I helped to patch up you and Ben-hail a few years ago."

The old man stepped back and looked at him. "When you say that, maybe I do recognise you," he said with a furrowed brow.

"So why did you recognise me and not Darda?" asked Ben-hail.

"I've kept an eye on you, young Ben-hail," answered Nezib. "From a distance, but an eye nevertheless."

"He thought you might be useful," said Darda, shrewdly.

Nezib frowned. "What do you mean?" he asked sharply.

Ben-hail looked at Darda, wondering what he was talking about.

"He's looking for another sacrificial lamb like Uriel," said Darda, unconsciously using the same metaphor as Ben-hail. "From what I hear, there have been quite a few over the years. Nobody else has ever got as close as Uriel though, have they? But you think that Ben-hail could do one step better."

"How do you know about this, Darda?" asked Ben-hail.

"I've heard of Nezib from time to time over the last six years, and I remember what I hear."

"Who are you?" asked Nezib, puzzled.

"A student," said Darda, looking warningly at Ben-hail.

"You mean a Levite studying in the temple – like Ben-hail's father was?" said Nezib. "You are doing a good work then, young man. Do you support the prophets of Yahweh?"

"Yes, I support the prophets of Yahweh, and the worship of Yahweh our God."

"Good. I do not seek to exploit your friend, Darda, but God's work must be done."

The interruption had brought Ben-hail up with a start, and he realised that he needed to consider the subject further before making any commitment to the old man.

The three parted, Darda going to his farm and Ben-hail to his home, while the old man returned to strumming his lyre and continued the words of David's Psalm. As Ben-hail walked away, he recognised the significance of the words:

"Make them bear their guilt, O God;
let them fall by their own counsels;
because of the abundance of their transgressions
cast them out,
for they have rebelled against you.
But let all who take refuge in you rejoice;
let them ever sing for joy,
and spread your protection over them,
that those who love your name may exult in you.
For you bless the righteous, O Lord;
you cover him with favour as with a shield."[102]

ॐ

It was almost time to go, and Ben-hail's uncle had come to say goodbye and to wish him well for the Great Tournament.

"Your father would be proud of you, Ben-hail," he said. "Is it the king who awards the prizes to the winners?"

"Yes, most of the time. But King Asa is not well, so he may not do it this time. Maybe the new king, Jehoshaphat, or one of the nobles will award them."

"But what about the Grand Prize? That prize is the king's favourite,

---

[102] Psalm 5:10-12

isn't it? He likes to acknowledge mighty men who are mighty not just in one field but in all of them. Men like you. If it's so important to him, wouldn't the king give that prize?"

"I hope so. That's one of the reasons why I want to win that prize more than any of the others."

"Surely it's the prize that's important, not who gives it to you?"

"Maybe so, but I've always wanted to meet King Asa. I've always dreamed of him placing the golden sash around my waist and tying it on. Can you imagine that – having the great King Asa tying a sash around your waist? What an opportunity!"

His uncle and his mother saw the glow in his eyes and recognised the joy of picturing the fulfilment of his long-held dream. Little did they know that the success they pictured was not quite what Ben-hail was visualising.

Chapter 18

THE KING'S VISIT

When Ben-hail returned to Abiel's Academy, he found the camp seething with the latest news from Jerusalem. Actually, much of the news wasn't really news at all because rumour had already suggested many of the details; however, this was official confirmation.

Now that Jehoshaphat was king, he wanted to travel more among his people, and for that he needed a bodyguard. Not just one man, but a small unit of superlative soldiers. The recent attempted assassination of his father had shown that enemies could strike even in the heart of the kingdom, and no such attempt could ever be allowed to get so close to success again.

King Jehoshaphat was an excellent soldier and swordsman, but as king he would not have the liberty to concentrate on self-defence. The king must be the face of the kingdom, available to his subjects as much as possible. King Asa had always worked to be available to his people and had spoken to many on friendly terms – at least for the first half of his reign, until the incident with the prophet Hanani. The situation had been more strained since then, but still, many people had been able to meet their king and talk to him briefly.

King Jehoshaphat wanted to continue the tradition and, if possible, extend it even more widely. He wanted any Israelite who desired to meet his king to be able to do so. His advisors said the idea was impossible. Ridiculous! His army commander said it was too dangerous. But King Jehoshaphat was determined.

However, he did compromise by accepting their advice regarding a bodyguard. He agreed to appoint a bodyguard who would always be with him whenever he was in public. Armed guards, experts in the use of sword and spear, and permanently on the alert.

Thus far, the news Abiel announced was nothing but good. However, for students in military academies across the nation, the remainder of the news was disastrous.

The king's plans had prompted some changes to the Great Tournament. In the past, both professional soldiers and amateurs had been able to enter the competitions, though there had been a clear separation between the two. Students in the king's military academies were counted strictly as amateurs, since they had not completed their training.

This year, amateurs were to be excluded from the tournament altogether.

Apparently, the intention was to raise the standard of the competition so that the king's bodyguard could be selected from the best possible candidates – the professional soldiers who won the various competitions.

The students at Abiel's Academy were shocked and upset – particularly those who had cherished hopes of winning one or more of the competitions. Ben-hail was devastated. His hopes, dreams and plans were slipping from his grasp before he had the opportunity even to reach out for them.

Abiel called his students together and explained the situation to them in detail. He did his best to present the information without prejudice, but he, too, was overwhelmingly disappointed. A few observant students noticed the discrepancy between his matter-of-fact words and his discontented expression, but most were too upset for themselves to notice their commander's emotions.

Abiel's selection plans were thrown into turmoil by the news. What purpose was there in selecting students for competitions that were not to take place? But what should they do instead?

Already the camp site was being prepared for the grand occasion, and many of the students were spending much of their time ensuring that the tidiness and presentation of the camp and the competition arrangements would not disappoint the king. How could Abiel prevent his gifted students from giving way to discouragement and frustration? The tournament was intended to help morale, but this decision would be more likely to demoralise his students.

There was, however, one small benefit that he could tell his students about.

Since King Jehoshaphat was still director of the army, he wanted to get a clearer view of the troops he controlled and the new soldiers his training academies were producing. Thus, he intended to visit every major army camp and every military training academy in the kingdom.

This news had arrived with the same courier who bore the news of the changes to the Great Tournament. Written in Gershom's characteristic crisp, blunt style, the letter had also included the surprising announcement that King Jehoshaphat would be visiting Abiel's Academy the very next day.

CR

King Jehoshaphat was eager to ensure that the Great Tournament was successful. As a result, Abiel's Academy was the first military academy he visited.

There was no time for Abiel to get properly worried – in fact, there was not even enough time to get the camp completely tidied up before the king's chariot was seen approaching on the road from Jerusalem, attended by Gershom, some lesser officials and a company of horsemen.

All of the students were gathered on the parade ground wearing their uniforms and armour. Abiel had decided that the entire company would welcome the king with a psalm of praise written by the king's ancestor, King David.[103] The musicians in the camp led the celebration and the remaining students sang the praises with great gusto. It was a wise decision. The king, who had not expected such a welcome, was touched and pleased.

Ben-hail was surprised at how few soldiers attended the king and mentioned it quietly to Darda, who was standing next to him as they waited. As usual, Darda had gleaned more information than most and replied, "I heard that, until the king's bodyguard is appointed, half of King Asa's guards will protect his son Jehoshaphat, while the other half stay with him. For a time, the new king will have less protection than usual, but it is not considered a real security risk."

Ben-hail looked interested, but said nothing. It did not seem to fit with the ideas of security for leaders that Abiel was teaching his students! Still, for the next week, the king would be spending most of his time in the vicinity of many soldiers, so the lack of dedicated guards should not matter.

Abiel received another surprise when Gershom, the commander of the army, introduced him to King Jehoshaphat.

"Who's your best student?" asked Jehoshaphat, before any displays of training or ability had begun.

"In what way, sir? Do you mean the best candidate for the Grand Prize, for combined ability? Or the best potential leader in the group?"

"I suppose that I really want to know both," said Jehoshaphat.

"Well, the most gifted and expert student in practical soldiering is Ben-hail, the son of Raddai. He has great physical strength and amazing speed, and can make a sword move so quickly that it is as if it forms a wall around him. None of my other students can touch him."

"And his skill with a spear or a sling?"

---

[103] David was Jehoshaphat's great-great-great-grandfather (Matthew 1:6-8).

"After our recent concentrated preparation for the Great Tournament and his recovery from a serious accident, he is now at least as good as any of the other students."

Abiel felt that he had to mention the Great Tournament, even though it might cause awkwardness. Jehoshaphat looked at him thoughtfully but made no comment. Instead, he continued his enquiries about Ben-hail.

"Can he beat you in any of these areas of skill?"

"Ah... every one of them, sir," said Abiel in embarrassment.

"But weren't you – aren't you still – known as the best swordsman in Yahweh's army?"

"It's kind of you to say so, sire, but once Ben-hail is in the permanent army, no, I won't be."

"And aren't you the best runner in the army?"

"It's kind of you to say that too, sire, but Ben-hail has a friend who is an amazing runner. Both he and his friend can beat me easily."

"What about strength? Sheer physical strength for lifting heavy loads, pushing or pulling?"

"Ben-hail has another friend who is as strong as an ox. Both of them can easily beat anyone else in the company – except each other! Ben-hail just keeps on getting stronger, and now they are about even."

"Take me to this wonder-man," said the king.

"He is warming up in the field where we practise sword-fighting. I was going to take you there soon."

"Let's go now."

As they walked, the king asked Abiel about his academy. He had heard that Abiel was a man of faith as well as skill, and the religious flavour of his welcome had pleased him. For his own part, Abiel was gratified by the open references to Yahweh in the king's conversation. Having been too young to know much about King Asa when the Ethiopians had invaded, Abiel had only known him as a king who was openly religious, but did not always seem consistent in the application of his religion. Asa was a king you had to be careful of; King Jehoshaphat seemed to be one step better. Abiel was glad.

They approached the sword-fighting field with its many smaller enclosures separated from each other by low fences, obviously set up to allow men to test their mettle with a sword without the fighters getting mixed up in other contests.

Abiel led the king and his guards towards one of the enclosures where the king saw a tall young man with mid-length dark hair and a slightly lighter beard. He was involved in a friendly bout with another young man. Jehoshaphat had enough skill as a swordsman to quickly recognise that Ben-hail was toying with his opponent. It was not being done in a way that was obvious or condescending, but it was clear to highly skilled watchers that every move the man made was anticipated and bested by Ben-hail.

"I see what you mean," said Jehoshaphat to Abiel after a few minutes. "Masterful."

"For a while it was very dangerous to fight against him, because he didn't realise just how good he was and assumed that I would easily be able to defend myself against him. He has this amazing attitude of concentration, and when he drops into it he moves with a speed and accuracy that you wouldn't believe. I have never seen a swordsman like him."

This conversation was carried out in low voices so that no-one else could hear what was being said. Ben-hail finished his bout by effortlessly touching his opponent's breastplate. With the final healing of his injured hand, he had returned to holding the sword in his right hand and using a shield, so his stance and actions were not obviously unusual, although his shield was much smaller than most.

Abiel walked into the enclosure and took the sword and shield from the student who had been fighting Ben-hail. Jehoshaphat stood beside the fence as Abiel brought Ben-hail across and introduced him.

"This is Ben-hail, sire," said Abiel. "You've seen some of his swordsmanship, but you really need to fight against him to fully appreciate it."

"I can imagine that would be quite different."

"Yes – it's instructive, sire. Would you like to?"

"Well..." said Jehoshaphat, considering, then he shook his head. "No. If there was no audience, I might try it, but I don't believe it would be good to have the king made to look foolish by a trainee soldier!"

"Very well, sire. I'll try to demonstrate instead. Let's take a turn, Ben-hail."

"Yes, sir."

For a while, Abiel and Ben-hail fought in a conservative, conventional style. Abiel already felt himself outclassed, but realised that Ben-hail was choosing not to publicly disgrace him. Smiling, he stole an instant to look at King Jehoshaphat, and was satisfied to see that he had a knowing smile on his face.

"Now, Ben-hail, put down your shield," said Abiel.

Ben-hail did so, and Abiel immediately started to attack more vigorously. It was clear that Ben-hail had to work a little harder, but he still had plenty of opportunity to attack while keeping Abiel's blade at bay and being in no obvious danger.

Once again, Abiel glanced at Jehoshaphat and saw a look of growing wonder. He smiled to himself again and said, "Now, Ben-hail, use your sword in your left hand."

Ben-hail swapped hands as requested and Abiel concentrated fiercely on his attempts to score a hit on his opponent's breastplate. It was an inspired passage of sword fighting. Again and again Abiel's blade darted with bewildering speed towards his opponent, but Ben-hail's sword was always there to thrust it away and initiate an incredible counter-attack that had Abiel scrambling to protect himself. He redoubled his efforts to attack, yet defended with a care he had never before needed. It was the performance of a virtuoso, yet Ben-hail weathered the storm with ease. Few lucky enough to be in the audience that day possessed the skill to appreciate the display that was being put on for them, but for those who did, it was something they would never forget. King Jehoshaphat's skill was great enough to allow him to appreciate some of the skill presented, but much of it was beyond him. What he did understand took his breath away. Two swords darted back and forth, probing, defending, attacking and repelling attacks in turn, yet the younger swordsman's mastery of his craft was highlighted most by what he did not do. Swordsmanship must take advantage of every opportunity and press home that opportunity to achieve victory and avoid defeat, yet in this bout, only one sword sought for victory; only one sought to expose any possible weakness in defence. The other was used merely to defend and provide an appearance of aggression that was carefully controlled so that no danger would result. Ben-hail defended in a way which suggested difficulty and attacked with a constraint that never taxed Abiel's defence more than it could manage.

Abiel had never felt such mastery over his own swordsmanship, yet nothing he did seemed to hurry Ben-hail or cause him any difficulty at all. Abiel marvelled at his student's skill and gradually tired until he was forced to drop his point and stop the bout.

Breathing heavily, he looked at King Jehoshaphat and his eyes challenged the king to acknowledge that such swordsmanship was without parallel. The king compressed his lips and smiled a smile of wonder while shaking his head a little.

Abiel gave the sword and shield to another student and led the king to the open area where Kilion and others were practising sprinting.

"I think that I see what you mean," Jehoshaphat said as they walked. "Left hand, right hand, with or without a shield. If a king's bodyguard had such skill with a blade, what possible danger could there be for a king?"

It was a rhetorical question – King Jehoshaphat had no way of knowing that the answer might be important.

❧

King Jehoshaphat left Abiel's academy and moved to the next. He couldn't get Ben-hail out of his mind because he believed that he had never seen a swordsman with such skill. Yet, really, what was the chance that he had met the best swordsman in the nation at the very first academy he had visited? After all, Ben-hail was only a student! It was most likely that something was mixed up somehow, he decided as he prepared for his visit to the next academy.

Two hours later, though, he had no more doubts. The second academy he visited most definitely had competent soldiers, but there was no-one even faintly like Ben-hail! He could still see in his mind's eye the lightness and accuracy of Ben-hail's touch as he caressed the sword into the perfect position for an utterly impossible parry.

And those friends of his, too! One with the strength of an ox and the other with the speed of a horse; yet Ben-hail could equal each of them. It was unbelievable!

Jehoshaphat made a quick decision. In many ways it would make his visits to the other military academies easier – and it would give him more freedom of choice.

He called Gershom over and explained what he intended to do. The commander was happy to agree with his proposal, and his secretary wrote a letter that was immediately dispatched to Abiel. Many more copies of the letter would be sent out later that day.

Jehoshaphat continued to visit training academies and army camps throughout Judah, becoming familiar with the academies and their leaders, as well as the quality of their students. His visits to the army camps showed him the standard of his existing soldiers and allowed him to compare them with the developing skills of the students who were being considered for the permanent army.

He thought back to his original need for increased protection and imagined a would-be assassin facing Ben-hail's startling speed. It would almost be beyond a joke; more like having a child competing with a skilful adult.

The king was content that his decision was correct.

Sitting in the administration tent, Abiel carefully unrolled the letter from Gershom and began to read.

His subordinate, who was working nearby, wondered what had happened when his chief suddenly jumped up and shouted, "Wonderful! Marvellous! Hallelujah!"

There was no time to ask questions, however, because Abiel immediately rolled up the letter again and hurried out of the tent.

The subordinate scratched his head and pulled meditatively at his earlobe. Sometimes understanding his boss was beyond him. Stolidly, he returned to his work while Abiel rushed away to call a general assembly for all students.

"Great news, lads!" he shouted when everyone had gathered. The smile on his face was convincing enough, but the words that followed elicited a spontaneous cheer from the students. "The commander of the army has decided to clarify the ruling about amateurs being excluded from the Great Tournament." Abiel held up the scroll and waved it in front of them before unrolling it theatrically and saying, "Commander Gershom says: 'While amateurs will be excluded from the Great Tournament, students in our military academies are considered to be professionals, since they have already committed themselves to a career in our army.' "

The cheer caught the attention of Abiel's subordinate as he worked away in the administration tent. Once more, he looked up from his work. Frowning, he stroked his beard and pursed his lips. How was he ever to get his work done with these persistent interruptions?

Ben-hail was at least as excited as the rest of the students. He was also thrilled that his right arm had completely recovered. In less than a month, he would face the challenge of his life.

What he did not know was that Abiel was already counting on his contribution to bring Abiel's Academy to the forefront of the new king's mind and make it famous. Abiel had several other names on his private list of men he hoped would perform well in various competitions, but Ben-hail was at the very top, the prime candidate for the Grand Prize and many other prizes. Surely the winner of the Grand Prize would warrant a special position in the king's new bodyguard?

But Abiel was not one to count his victories before they had been won, so he put aside the list and began planning the next day's training of the academy's students. He must take the time to supervise the preparation of the sword-fighting area. It wouldn't do to have his prize student hurt by slipping on a poorly prepared arena!

That night, the academy was buzzing with expectation. Although many had already decided that Ben-hail was unbeatable competition they could not overcome, hope springs eternal in our hearts, and each student harboured some unspoken dream of fame and success. Perhaps Ben-hail would be injured again....

Chapter 19

DUNGEONS AND DARKNESS

I say: Keep the king's command,
because of God's oath to him.
Be not hasty to go from his presence.
Do not take your stand in an evil cause,
for he does whatever he pleases.
For the word of the king is supreme,
and who may say to him,
"What are you doing?"

Ecclesiastes 8:2-4

King Asa's dungeons were unpleasant places. No one who earned entry to their terrible confines ever left as the same man as he had been when he entered. In most cases, he did not leave alive.

Food was provided – sparingly – but light was much more strictly rationed. Solitary confinement, it was called, and solitary it certainly was. King Asa rarely called anyone from his dungeons to answer charges. After all, their very presence in the dungeons proclaimed their guilt. What more was needed?

Dampness, darkness and death were always close to any against whom the king's displeasure had been so thoroughly aroused.

In the early years of King Asa's reign, the dungeons were used with fairness and equity, but then the great inequity came when the king's anger overrode his justice.

Yahweh sent a prophet to the king, a man with a message of criticism. The strength of the message showed the force of God's disapproval, and the prophet delivered it fearlessly. It was an act of courage, but at the same time, Hanani did not expect it to be particularly dangerous. King Asa had shown great faith and godliness throughout his reign until that time, 15 years, and had always responded well to Yahweh's messages.

It was, therefore, a terrible shock to Hanani when the king responded to God's message with vindictive fury and called the chief of his dungeons to lead the prophet away to those cold and horrible depths.

Light departed from his life and only the darkness remained. Surely, thought Hanani, it would only be a short stay, a brief interruption in his life, and soon he would again see the sunshine and enjoy the wind on his face.

Instead, almost twenty-four years later, he still languished in the king's dungeons. Never had the king called him. Never had there been any formal charge or indictment. The days had passed monotonously, indistinguishable from the nights except by the endless round of scanty meals. Over time, jailer had replaced jailer and the men in the nearby cells had all been granted freedom or died, he did not know which. He had outlasted them all.

The damp and dark conditions caused most inmates to succumb to fatal diseases within months, but Hanani lived on without respite.

He asked his jailers for news, but received none. He asked for information about the seasons, but was given none, and the months passed with little variation in his dungeon climate. He asked about the passing of the years, but the duration of his unjust incarceration was only counted – inaccurately – by the faint marks he scratched on his cell wall.

Almost twenty-four years – yet still he held on to life, knowing nothing of the world outside his cell.

His family: what had happened to them? His wife? His son? Surely Yahweh must have provided for them? They wouldn't have been left to beg, would they? Or had they died of starvation without him there to support them?

Hanani didn't know, and had no way of finding out. He also didn't know that he was not the only one who had suffered because of King Asa's unreasoning rage. Tragically, the king for whom righteous obedience to Yahweh was so important had not limited his brutal retribution to just one messenger of Yahweh.

Hanani had friends, and at first, some of these had bravely tried to tell the king that he was being not only unjust, but ungodly. In a further display of passion, King Asa had rounded up the complainers, beaten some, fined others and thrown many into the same dungeon as Hanani.

Yet not all those punished were guilty of the things of which they were accused. One innocent victim – arrested almost two years after Hanani's detention – was a Levite named Raddai, the son of Benaiah, from the town of Aijalon. Someone from that town sent a letter to the king full of bitter criticism and righteous anger. The letter was not signed, but it was delivered at a time when Raddai was in Jerusalem, serving in the temple, and Raddai was known to be a relative and friend of Hanani.

That was all it took. King Asa's dungeons swallowed him up.

Reactions to institutional injustice vary. For most people, however, the response is impotent anger or hatred. Revenge is contemplated, but never pursued. Words alone – many words – condemn the injustice.

Raddai's widow, Elisheba, felt that hatred immediately and spoke of her wish for revenge. Her family and friends quickly hushed her up – after all, there was still a chance that he would be freed soon.

Life went on, but quickly became more complicated for Elisheba. She had already suspected it at the time when Raddai was arrested, but as he lingered in the king's dungeons, she became sure: she was pregnant. She tried to pass on the good news to Raddai, but communication with the king's prisoners was forbidden: no visits, no gifts, no verbal messages, no letters were allowed; no communication at all. Elisheba had to accept that her husband would not hear the good news before the birth.

Widows were normally well cared for in a close-knit community like Aijalon, but the pregnant wife of a prisoner of the king was a different matter. While there had initially been significant support in the town for Hanani, it had been driven underground. Any public support of Hanani would make one an enemy of the king, and that was much too dangerous. Offering help to the wife of such an enemy of the king? Many considered it was much too dangerous.

Elisheba learned swiftly the difficulties of having to support herself. The law allowed widows to glean in the fields, but Elisheba was not a widow: she was the wife of a traitor. Harvest came and went, but many of the fields around the town were closed to her. Life became a daily struggle, and without the support of Raddai's family – bravely given – she would soon have starved.

Winter was setting in when her first and only child was born. She dutifully named her son Ben-hail – Son of Might – the name she and Raddai had chosen when they had prayed for a son.

Once again, there was no way to pass on the news to Raddai. Terah, Raddai's brother, did his best. He went to Jerusalem, but found that anyone who wanted to meet the officials in charge of the king's dungeons had to provide all sorts of personal information that would allow them to be easily tracked down if the king considered it necessary. In trepidation, Terah gave the information – and then waited while it was verified. But when he met one of the officials at last, the man would neither confirm nor deny that any prisoner named Raddai was incarcerated there and said that regulations forbade the passing of messages to prisoners anyway.

The lonely young mother took comfort in the company of her new son – her last connection with her husband.

Then, one morning, about a year later, she heard a knock on her door and scooped up her son before opening the door.

A grim, unsmiling soldier stood outside.

"Are you the wife of Raddai, the son of Benaiah, the enemy of the king?" he asked.

"I am the wife of Raddai, but he is no enemy of the king."

"Raddai is dead," he announced in a grave, flat voice, making no attempt to soften the blow his news must bring.

"Dead?" she gasped, unknowingly tightening her arm around Ben-hail. "How? When?"

"That is all the news I have."

"But what can I do now?"

"There is nothing to do. Judgement has been meted out. May all enemies of the king perish in like manner."

Without waiting for any further answer, the soldier turned and walked away.

Elisheba watched him go, and shook her head numbly. It felt completely unreal. Should such news ever be delivered in this way? The question echoed again in her head, "But what can I do now?"

"Mumma?" said a small, strained voice, and she looked down at her son, sitting on her hip.

Little Ben-hail was looking up at her, worried. Suddenly she realised that she was holding him far too tight.

"Sorry, Ben-hail," she said, relaxing her grip.

"Dadda?" he asked, looking up at her questioningly.

It was almost too much for her. How much did the toddler understand, she wondered? She was constantly being surprised by the things he understood, and she talked to him about his father daily. Every day she hoped that Raddai would return, but now that hope was finally crushed. Should she find a gentle way to explain the cruel situation to him or take the easy option and gradually change the way in which she spoke of Raddai?

At the moment, though, it didn't matter what was best: she couldn't discuss the subject now. She shut the door and turned away. Life must go on – somehow.

"Dadda won't be here today, darling," she said.

Her own words brought home the truth to her – Raddai never would be there again – and with that she dissolved into tears.

Ben-hail sat quietly in her arms as the sobs shook her and the tears ran down her face. Slowly he reached up and touched her face gently with his pudgy little hands. "Wet," he said.

CR

In the years that followed Raddai's death, his only son grew rapidly. Ben-hail was tall and strong for his age, but he was also light-footed and quick. When he played with the other boys of the town, his ability to run, throw and catch stood out, and before long the older boys would often include him in their games.

At times, however, some of the older lads reacted badly to being beaten by a younger, smaller boy. Although he was not an aggressive child, he never backed down when he believed he was right. Fights were sometimes forced upon him, and he quickly learned to defend himself, ably assisted by his phenomenal timing and outstanding reactions. From an early age he became a leader among the boys, mostly because of his extreme physical ability. Whenever teams were selected, everyone wanted to be on the same team as him, but he also led with good judgement and fairness.

When schooling began, his ability to learn quickly stood out too, and his concentration was immediately seen to be outstanding. In short, once he set his mind to learn or do something, he was certain to achieve it.

He was not afraid to talk, but was by no means garrulous, often preferring to watch rather than talk. His glance was clear and open, and he was known to all as an honest, fair lad.

His mother was very proud of him and only wished that Raddai had been able to see his son, with all of the admirable qualities she was sure the boy had inherited from his father.

Yet she was in a quandary. She wanted to be faithful to her husband's memory, but also to his love of God and his law. Raddai had not been a man who hated, and, despite her own feelings, she didn't want to turn his son into one who did.

Many times through Ben-hail's childhood, Elisheba mulled over the direction his upbringing should take. In the night hours, before the tiredness of honest labour drew her into sleep, she wondered how she should present to Ben-hail the father he had never met. Certainly he must learn to admire him, for he was an admirable man. But what of his death? And how should she present the king whose injustice had stolen his father? She knew that sooner or later Ben-hail would hear his father called a traitor – or a martyr. She must tell him the truth, but how much of it?

King Asa continued to rule Judah well, and consistently led the nation in worshipping Yahweh, yet Elisheba hated him as a hypocrite. How could he claim to follow Yahweh and yet imprison Yahweh's prophet? How could he frequent God's temple after having killed an honest servant of the temple like her beloved husband, Raddai?

Yet planting and fostering hatred in a young lad would not do justice to either his father or his God.

This honest, hard-working young woman's pillow heard many troubled sighs as she struggled to faithfully raise her son alone. Life was not easy, but Elisheba was used to that. Her own mother had died giving birth to a younger brother when Elisheba was only seven years old, and seven years later her father had been killed in the amazing battle where Zerah and his million men had been put to flight. While everyone else rejoiced, she had mourned her father. Left an orphan, she had been forced to accept her uncle's grudging offer of protection, and for two years she had lived in her uncle's house with his short-tempered wife. Unwelcome and often mistreated, she had been overjoyed when Raddai had asked her to marry him.

Their happy plans were delayed when King Asa called for all able-bodied men, Raddai included, to help dismantle Ramah, the town King Baasha of Israel had been building into a fortress. Since Raddai was not a farmer, tied to the march of the seasons, he was kept at work for longer than most conscripts, and almost 18 months more had passed before he returned from his faithful service to the king. It was during this time that Hanani had delivered his fateful message to Asa and suffered the full force of the king's indignation. Naturally, Raddai was upset for his relative, who was also a close friend, but he persisted in his prayers that the king would repent of his sin and cruelty.

Raddai and Elisheba were married on a rainy day in the shortest days of winter, yet their union began with great rejoicing. Raddai was determined to bring joy to his young wife and make up for all the suffering she had already endured in her short life. How could he know that in only five months tragedy would strike again for her when he was dragged away to the dungeons and she was left to bear and raise their child alone?

How a king's stubbornness and petty anger could affect the lives of his subjects!

Was her bitterness any surprise?

Ben-hail was ten years old when he came home one afternoon battered, bruised and in tears. Elisheba was stirring their evening stew when she heard the door open and turned around.

"What happened, my dear?" she asked, dropping the spoon and hurrying over to him.

"What is a trait... a traitor?"

"A traitor is a bad man who tries to hurt his country."

"Then my father wasn't a traitor," he said with confidence. "I knew they were lying."

"No, your father was not a traitor. Who said that he was?"

"Jobab, Jehu and Hesed, some of the older boys."

Elisheba knew the boys by sight – they were all 14 or 15 years old. She knew their parents as well, and wasn't surprised by the information. "What happened?" she asked, dabbing gently with a damp cloth at a cut above his eye.

"We were playing a game and my team won... Ow! That hurts."

"I'm being as gentle as I can, son. What happened then?"

"They said I shouldn't be allowed to play because I was just a kid."

"If this is how things end up when you 'play' with them, maybe they're right!"

"But there aren't many fights, mother."

"That's good. Tell me more about how this one started."

"Joshua laughed at them. He said if I'm just a kid, why couldn't their team beat my team? Joshua's the same age as them, but he's much smarter. I always get him on my team if I can. He makes us work well together. Anyway, they didn't say any more then, but after most of the kids had left, they started picking on me. They called me a kid and said I was a cheat. Then Jehu said I'd grow up to be a traitor like my father, so I hit him on the nose."

"But you didn't even know what the word meant!"

"I didn't need to. I could tell he was saying something nasty. And I knew it must be a lie."

"Oh, Ben-hail. I can understand why you were angry, but there were three of them and they're all much bigger than you."

"Well, I couldn't let him say that," he said simply.

"No. I understand." She sat down on a chair and put her face in her hands.

"Why did they say Dad was a traitor?"

Elisheba had her answer prepared, but she wanted the rest of the story first. "I'll tell you soon, but how did you get this?" She touched a darkening bruise beside his eye.

"When I hit Jehu, Jobab hit me. So I hit him. Then Hesed hit me, and I hit him back."

"Too much hitting!" said Elisheba. "And look where it got you. Your father would not have wanted you to do that."

"But he's not here."

"No-o-o-o. But you should still pay attention to what your father would have wanted you to do, because he was a wise man."

"I know. Why did Jehu call him a traitor?"

"A long time ago, before you were born, God sent a prophet to King Asa telling him that he shouldn't have done something he had done. The king was angry and threw the prophet in prison."

"But if God said it, why didn't the king listen?"

"We all do silly things sometimes, don't we?" She looked at him and smiled, adding, "Like fighting three boys who are bigger and stronger than you."

"That wasn't silly. I'd do it again."

"Maybe you're right – anyway, that's what the king did. It was wrong for him to do it. But he *is* the king," she finished bitterly.

"But isn't King Asa a good king?"

"Maybe, but not always."

The conversation went on for some time, and most of Elisheba's carefully-prepared words eluded her. She did her best to explain without rancour, but as she described how Raddai had been unjustly imprisoned and had died in the King's dungeons, she ended with tears and a blunt condemnation of the king's cruelty.

"You hate the king, don't you, mother?" asked Ben-hail.

"Yes," she admitted, then added hastily, "but I'm sure that your father wouldn't want you to, my son." Even to her own ears, it sounded lame.

Ben-hail looked at her for a few moments, then said soberly, "If King Asa was here, I'd hit him on the nose too!"

CR

After that first conversation in which Elisheba had admitted to Ben-hail her hatred of Asa and his cruelty, the subject came up again from time to time, and on each occasion, the worried mother warned her son that he must never, *ever* tell anyone about this. She also reminded him that his father would not want him to hate the king anyway.

The first lesson he learned well. The second he kept in mind for consideration. Over the next four years, his mother told him all she knew about his father's imprisonment and death. Ben-hail devoured every detail, eager to learn all he could about his father. Through those years, he slowly made up his mind, and by the time he was fourteen, he had come to a decision that would control his life for the next several years.

Over this period, Ben-hail developed the same hatred for King Asa as he saw in Elisheba, but he spoke of it to nobody, not even his mother. It festered within him, and also ate away at his faith in Yahweh. How could God allow a king to brutally mistreat his subjects? How could a king who called on Yahweh and claimed to follow his commands ever do what King Asa had done – and was still doing? And how could he himself worship a God who allowed such things? His faithful father had been murdered, leaving his poor innocent mother to suffer alone through all the difficulties of widowhood. If God were just, why would he not visit the king's sins on the king, and on his sons? If God failed to punish such behaviour, how could he be worthy of worship? Hatred grew and blossomed, and Raddai's only son looked for ways to let his hatred bear fruit. He longed for revenge. But he had learned from the reports he heard of repeated failed attacks against the king. He would seek his revenge in absolute secrecy. Never would he admit to anyone that he hated the king. Never would anyone hear that the king was his target – or indeed that he had any target – until an opportunity came to kill the king and so avenge the death of his innocent father.

Ben-hail nursed his hatred and made plans for revenge.

The plans were deep-laid, and very mature for a young lad.

Elisheba had told him that Raddai had wanted a son who would follow in his steps as a Levite, deeply attached to the temple of their fathers, but Raddai wasn't there, and Ben-hail chose instead the path of a more warlike hero: Benaiah, the son of Jehoiada. He had been a mighty man, and Ben-hail longed to be a mighty man also.

Mighty men, he knew, won the trust and confidence of leaders. Even kings met with military heroes. And then he would find an opportunity for revenge. He didn't know exactly how, but he was determined to meet with the king as a hero, and to find an opportunity then. He must avoid the dangers of unwarranted haste. He would have only one attempt and it could not, must not, be allowed to fail.

He had no plans for escape, no thought of trying to lead a rebellion against the house of David. Asa alone was his target. Asa must die as Raddai, his father, had died, and he was ready to pay the penalty for success.

At seventeen, he had volunteered for the army when Israel attacked Judah. His courage and natural ability had drawn his commanders' attention, as he had hoped they would. Unfortunately for him, the emergency passed quickly and he had had to return home for the winter; however, he was recalled when spring returned. Once again, he stood out from the other volunteers, and he was soon offered a place in Abiel's academy. The first steps of his plan were under way. If he had not enjoyed the life of a soldier, not longed to be a mighty man in his own right, then perhaps his secret plans would have faded away as the adolescent plans of many a young man do. But events were following his plans and he saw no reason to change them. A naturally quiet lad, he felt no need to explain his deepest thoughts to his companions. No-one knew that Ben-hail's ambition to gain glory in the Great Tournament, particularly in winning the Grand Prize, was an ambition of revenge.

When King Asa appointed Jehoshaphat as joint king, Ben-hail had feared that the opportunity for revenge was slipping away. The old king might die before he had a chance to pay him back for his injustice. But he wouldn't give up yet. Maybe the new king was a new opportunity. King Asa had hurt him through his father; possibly he could hurt King Asa through his son. His plans had focussed on Asa, but there was no reason why Jehoshaphat shouldn't do just as well.

King Jehoshaphat's visit to the academy had almost given him the chance he wanted. For just a moment, it had appeared that Jehoshaphat might try a short bout with him, and his mind had prepared for the perfect opportunity. He knew that Jehoshaphat was a competent swordsman, but he was sure that he could dispose of him easily – he could probably even make it look like an accident. In that instant, he had glimpsed the possibility of killing both father and son.

How frustrated Ben-hail had felt when Jehoshaphat had decided that pitting the king against a mere trainee soldier who could easily best him was not good for appearances and quietly avoided the situation. But though Ben-hail could almost have cried with disappointment, nothing of this had shown in his face. He would have to be patient and wait for a better opportunity.

Chapter 20

Final Preparations

Only one week remained before the Great Tournament was to begin.

To anyone familiar with Abiel's Academy, the camp and its surrounds were almost unrecognisable. New areas had been set up for competition wherever the terrain allowed it, and a forest of tents had sprung up to provide accommodation for the extra staff.

Abiel was busy. Of course, this is an understatement: he was doing far too much and getting far too little sleep. None of his associates or family members would have expressed any surprise at this; indeed, they would even have predicted that he would take on far too much responsibility for ensuring that the Great Tournament was an event for the king to be proud of – in fact, both kings! And this was exactly what he was doing.

Yet, in addition to his habit of working hard, he also had a gift for organising others that enabled a team under his leadership to achieve more than most would believe possible. Not only so, but his choice of helpers was far more often good than bad. Many extra staff had been sent for him to choose from, and the staff he had selected understood his goals and were helping him to achieve them with minimal need for interference.

The whole camp was like a beehive: movement everywhere – but at least it was ordered movement. Everyone was working towards a shared goal, and a huge amount had been achieved already.

Abiel felt that everything was coming together. Each of the many competitions had a location that suited its nature, and all were carefully prepared. Even the steep cliff that would be used for the climbing competition had been scaled many times by officials, to make sure that the competing climbers would have no unexpected surprises due to falling stones or attacks by unfriendly rock-dwelling creatures.

Judges, marshals and officials from all over the kingdom had been appointed to ensure that the competitions would be fair and the results above question. Long-serving soldiers, experts with bow, sling, sword and spear, would supervise the competitions, keeping a close eye out for any sign of cheating or possible fraud.

Thousands of competitors had entered the tournament, some for just one or two events and others – those seeking the Grand Prize – for every possible event.

There was one entrant whose application was questioned by Abiel's Manager of Athletic Standards. It was his job to make sure that no competitors of doubtful character were welcomed to this, the peak of military competition and honour in Judah. Acknowledged cheats and those of uncertain loyalty were not welcome to the tournament at all. In fact, a nation-wide list was kept, with new entries being added from time to time whenever any of the army's commanders reported shameful behaviour. However, the entrant in question was not on the list. Not yet.

After Mattaniah had lost his temper and attacked Ben-hail in such a dangerous and cowardly way, Abiel had carried out the promised investigation. During this probe, Mattaniah had first tried to brush aside the questions as trivial, and then, when that failed, done his best to blame everything on Ben-hail. When that too failed, he blamed the trainers, the supervisors and even Abiel himself for allowing the situation to get out of hand. Abiel had assessed the evidence impartially and made his judgement, but the heavy workload of preparation for the Great Tournament had delayed him in writing the report that would have seen Mattaniah's name added to the list of unwelcome applicants.

"What should I do, sir?" asked the Manager of Athletic Standards.

Abiel sighed. Leaving work unfinished always caused trouble. If only he had finished the report and submitted it.

His subordinate seemed to read his mind. "If you had submitted the report, it would have caused even more trouble with Vophsi."

Abiel sighed again. It was true: lack of time had not been the only reason for the delay. Somehow, Vophsi had heard of the incident and approached Gershom about the progress of the investigation. Gershom had notified Abiel and asked him to avoid a confrontation with Vophsi if possible – particularly before the Great Tournament began. Vophsi had also followed up his enquiries with a request for Mattaniah to be transferred to Vophsi's own academy immediately. Abiel had raised his eyebrows at that, but a few enquiries of his own had revealed Mattaniah to be a relative of Vophsi. He had sighed over that too, but had finally decided to keep Gershom and Vophsi happy for the time being. He still intended to submit his report about Mattaniah once the Great Tournament was over, but in the meantime, he had signed the form and transferred him to Vophsi's Academy. He was pleased to be rid of him, but it had not occurred to him that Mattaniah would be entered into that most prestigious of all competitions in the Great Tournament, the competition to become the King's Swordsman.

"I suppose that we will have to accept his application," said Abiel. "After all, he is not on the banned list."

"I could write the report for you and send it in to headquarters, sir."

"To be honest, I wouldn't have time to read it. Or even to sign it. And certainly I have no more time now to discuss such a man. Accept his application. Perhaps he will be disqualified early on."

❧

The fact that Abiel's Academy was the venue for the Great Tournament wasn't the only reason the tournament was particularly important to the academy. Two years earlier, the academy had been one of several chosen to use modified methods for training their students, and this tournament would be the first major test of whether those methods were effective. Abiel was convinced that they were, and he was determined that his students should feature strongly among the elite soldiers who would stand before the king to receive awards.

It was Abiel's unimaginative subordinate, in charge of the day to day administration of the camp, who came up with a suggestion that proved surprisingly important. Being responsible for procuring the armour used in the camp, he was in a meeting of marshals, when, just in passing, he observed that it would be much easier to recognise the competitors from the academy if they all wore a coloured patch of material.

No-one paid much attention at the time, but when he later repeated it to Abiel as part of his report, the commander saw a great opportunity.

Each group of a thousand troops, and every military academy, had its own unique flag, and it was common for the flag to be flown whenever the soldiers or students were gathered in a body. The flags were simple – plain colours, words or geometric patterns, since making the likenesses of animals or people was forbidden by Moses' Law.[104] Abiel's own flag was plain red with a hollow black diamond shape on it.

Here was a chance to make the students from Abiel's Academy stand out. Imagine if many of the winners presented to the king wore a red patch of material that announced them to be part of Abiel's Academy! What better way could there be to proclaim the effectiveness of the training methods he was so pleased with?

Suddenly, the subordinate found himself arranging for a supply of small hemmed squares of red-dyed linen, and before the end of the week, each student of the academy was proudly wearing this symbol of his association with the best academy in the country!

---

[104] Exodus 20:4

Nevertheless, for the students at Abiel's Academy, this was a side issue. The main goal of that last week was practice.

Climbers climbed, runners ran and lifters lifted. Archers, slingers and spear-throwers all spent their time trying to improve the way in which they directed their projectiles at a target. Swordsmen concentrated on trying to fine-tune the balance between defence and attack, honing their trained reflexes.

Ben-hail did everything, while his friends did their best to help him. Each wanted – of course! – to win his preferred competition, but they also wanted Ben-hail to win the Grand Prize. Since someone had to win, they argued, it should be Ben-hail.

"After all," said Kilion with a serious expression, "he has the best friends!"

"All of whom want to beat me in their own competitions!" laughed Ben-hail.

"Naturally!" replied Kilion. "It spurs you on to do better."

"That way, when you win, we will become famous as the ones who taught you everything you know," said Darda.

Eliam grunted, and showed Ben-hail again how to place his feet when lifting a wide, heavy object. Eliam was amazingly skilful at lifting and consistently did the best he could to pass on his knowledge to Ben-hail. For his part, Ben-hail noticed the improvement in results as he learned different techniques. He couldn't help wondering if the extra skills he had learned already would allow him to lift Peresh's anvil. He was certain that Eliam would be able to.

Darda gave him hints for refining his slinging action and was pleased for his friend – though a little disappointed for himself – as he saw the swift improvement that resulted. Ben-hail really did find all physical skills disturbingly easy to master.

Together, they all shot hundreds of arrows, concentrating at different times on speed, accuracy or distance. The academy's trainers were also eager to provide extra training to anyone who could help to bring fame to Abiel's Academy. It was a time where everyone, students and staff alike, saw an opportunity to be involved in something outstanding. Nor was this an opportunity for just one man to achieve fame, for, although Ben-hail was the best of all the students in several areas of competition and undoubtedly the best in overall performance, there were many students who were expected to score very well in the competitions. Abiel was quietly confident that his academy would produce unheard-of numbers of winners and runners-up. Despite this, though, he was a little frustrated. He could not be sure that the improved training methods were the reason for the expected success. Had these improved training methods really produced a man with Ben-hail's skill? Or would he have succeeded equally well whatever training regime he had been sub-jected to?

That, however, was a question for another time, because the final inspections by Gershom and the king's nobles were planned for the day before the competition – and that was tomorrow! Had the extra fruit for these visitors been collected?

He hurried away once more.

CR

The day before the tournament began, Ben-hail received a letter. The scroll was delivered by hand, but the man who delivered it refused to wait for Ben-hail to be called.

When the camp servant to whom he entrusted it finally found Ben-hail, the latter was busy climbing quite near the cliff that was to be used in the competition. Darda, who was watching from the bottom, accepted the scroll from the servant.

"A letter for you, Ben-hail," he called.

"What does it say?" asked Ben-hail as he traversed a crack to reach an easier section of rock.

"I'll just open it," said Darda. He broke the seal and unrolled the scroll. In a few moments, he had scanned the scroll – a frown growing on his face as he did so. He looked quickly around, then rolled it up again and shouted, "I think it's best if you read it yourself."

Chapter 21

"LET THE COMPETITION BEGIN"

Everyone attending the Great Tournament was excited, and King Je-hoshaphat was no exception. The competitors had all arrived at Abiel's Academy on the previous evening or in the early morning of what was to be the first day of competition. Unprecedented crowds of spectators were also gathering.

The Great Tournament was about to begin.

The various competitions were meant to test different areas of sol-diering, and were to be held over ten long days. Individual competitions would determine who were the fastest, strongest, most accurate and most skilful of all the soldiers in Judah's army.

Foot races, long and short, were to be run first, and these would begin within the hour. Each academy had selected its best students for each race, and the commanders of thousands had selected the fastest soldiers in the permanent army.

Only permanent soldiers and students attending the military acad-emies could join in the competitions, but that didn't stop thousands of others from coming to watch. Old soldiers came to watch the young men who had taken their place in the army, as well as to meet former col-leagues and discuss old times. Younger men came to appreciate the physical strength and skill of the soldiers, and some would even use this tournament to decide their own commitment to the national army. Wives and children came to watch their husbands and fathers compete, and perhaps some young women came to admire the young soldiers.

Sadly, many of the existing army who were not joining the compe-tition could not come as spectators either. Instead, they had to remain in their camps, ready for emergencies – particularly those in camps near the borders of the land. No army commander could allow too many sol-diers to leave their post when the enemy was in position nearby.

And now, competitors and spectators alike were waiting for the king to begin the proceedings. But who was the king? King Asa had been eager to have the tournament arranged, even at short notice, but was he well enough to attend? Everyone had heard rumours that Asa suffered terribly with the disease in his feet. Some stories had it that the king couldn't walk at all – not even one step – while others had it that his feet had turned black, and that he would be dead before the tournament ended.

Knowledgeable men who had seen King Jehoshaphat arrive on his donkey without his father had drawn their own conclusions.

The proceedings were to begin in a large open area where spectators could recline on the surrounding slopes. A large wooden platform had been constructed for the royal party, while a smaller platform nearby would be used for making announcements to the crowd. The open area was to be the location of the first competition.

Jehoshaphat climbed the stairs to the royal platform wearing a plain, simple crown. Six soldiers were already waiting on the platform, while six more stood around the stairs. Ladan and Gershom had strongly advised the king that he should always have at least six picked soldiers within reach at all times. Jehoshaphat had laughed a little and protested that this was excessive. How, he asked, could he ever convince his hard-working regular soldiers that they were important to him if he wouldn't let them get near him? If soldiers were willing to give their lives for their king, surely their king should be willing to do something for them!

The six soldiers were close, but not so smotheringly close as to be always within reach. Jehoshaphat was content: security was tight.

The king went to the grandest of the thrones on the platform and the crowd hushed for a moment. As he sat down, a cheer began among the soldiers from the camp in which Jehoshaphat had learned first a soldier's skills and then a commander's skills. He turned towards the cheering soldiers and recognised their standard with a smile. He waved, and the king's greeting was sufficient reward for those men. Azubah, the king's mother, climbed the stairs next. Jehoshaphat had suggested that she should attend to be, in part, a representative of her husband, King Asa. The king rose and led her to a smaller throne where a servant helped her to make herself comfortable.[105] She presented a regal picture, smiling as the crowd welcomed her.

Queen Zeruah followed with Jehoshaphat's sons, Jehoram and Azariah, while the youngest, Jehiel, was carried by a nurse. They all sat down, and Jehoshaphat was pleased to present his family to many who had not seen them before.

This decision to present his family was a conscious choice, based on his observation that God had worked with families throughout history

---

[105] Leviticus 19:32; Exodus 20:12

and a royal family should be no different. He wanted the countless other families in the kingdom to see that the king's family was no different from their families, wherever they might live.

He was happy to acknowledge the greatness of the kings who had preceded him, but he felt that in this area they had not been wise. Surely it didn't take great wisdom to know that King Solomon had got it badly wrong: having 1,000 women in his palace could never have been thought wise! Since that time, the kings of Judah had been cutting down, and Jehoshaphat was convinced that this was an important, positive change in the kingdom.

At last, everything was in place and Abiel came and told him that it was time for the tournament to get underway. Jehoshaphat stood and moved to the front of the platform.

Raising his arms, he welcomed the crowd and reminded them of the purpose of the tournament.

"As you know, the Great Tournament has been held every two years for many years. Unfortunately, two years ago, conditions forced us to change the custom. We are now glad to be able to witness it once more. Abiel, known to all as one of the greatest swordsmen this nation has ever seen, has welcomed us all to his academy where we will witness a series of gruelling contests. In taking on the task of arranging this tournament, he has honoured my father, Asa the King, and sacrificed what may be his last opportunity to successfully compete at this level. This is an example of sacrifice and commitment of which we are all proud. This is the standard to which our competitors all aspire.

"In the men who compete this week, we are looking to find mighty men like those from the days of my ancestor, King David: men who defended their nation not only from the ravages of foreign armies, but also from the ravages of foreign gods that will lead us away from Yahweh our God if we let them.

"Do we still have such mighty men today? This is the question our Great Tournament will answer.

"Let the competition begin!"

Jehoshaphat stepped back and sat down, while his rousing words were repeated far and wide so that all could hear.

On the adjacent platform, an announcer stood and began to explain the first competition: a short run of only 135 metres[106]. This was the most popular race of all, because everybody can run 135 metres. Hundreds of men stood waiting for the opportunity to show how fast they were. The sheer number of competitors made the selection process a little more difficult, but the experienced marshals knew just what they were doing.

---

[106] 300 cubits; 150 yards.

Soon, only 50 runners remained – the fastest runners from several larger races. All of these runners would score points towards the Grand Prize, but who would score the most was still to be determined.

Abiel was very pleased to see that Kilion and Ben-hail were both in the remaining group of runners, along with two other runners from his academy. There was no doubt that having to compete with faster runners like Kilion and Ben-hail during training had helped others to achieve better results also.

Two heats were arranged, and the top five runners from each were chosen to run for the final victory. Ten runners left! As they stood in line waiting for the signal to start, Abiel revelled in the success he had already achieved in this competition. Three runners from his camp were among the ten fastest in the entire kingdom! Such results had never been achieved by any academy before, and the marshals were obviously surprised.

Ten runners stood in a line, waiting for the signal to start. Ben-hail and Kilion stood next to each other, and Abiel fully expected that they would be competing for first and second, for although neither was at their best in such short races, they had a blistering turn of speed that nobody else in the heats had been able to match.

Once everyone was ready, the starter dropped a sandal and the race began. Kilion led them away, and within 10 or 15 metres, he and Ben-hail were clearly ahead of the field. Kilion moved at the head of the field with his normal easy grace, making Ben-hail look a little awkward. 40, 50, 60 metres, and it seemed as if Kilion had the race wrapped up. But a student from another academy was starting to reel them in. Within another 15 metres he had caught Ben-hail and was stretching out in pursuit of Kilion. With about 50 metres to go, he had caught Kilion and was starting to edge ahead! Many in the crowd were cheering, but there was silence from Abiel and his students as the leader began to lengthen his stride and stretch out for the finish line. However, short races can be won and lost in short distances, and it was at just that instant that Ben-hail showed his character. He was two or three metres behind the two leading runners when he too lengthened his stride, seeming to fly over the ground. Within moments, he had halved the deficit and was making the pace look easy.

The leading runner wasn't giving up, but he flung a quick glance behind to check where his competitors were. It wasn't exactly a stumble, but there was the slightest hint of unevenness in his stride and immediately Kilion was back in the lead. Ben-hail was still closing the gap, but would he have time to catch either of the leaders? With about 10 metres to go, all three were within half a metre of each other and the whole crowd was shouting. Ben-hail's hopes of victory were slipping away but he refused to give up, and his strength began to tell. Just a metre from the finish line, he hit the front for the first time and won the race from Kilion by the smallest possible margin, with the other student fading quickly to third in the last few paces.

Excited cheers filled the air as the first points of the tournament were decided.

Special awards were given to the winner and the runner-up in each competition, but bonus points were awarded to all those who made it to the last ten competitors.

As the winner and the runner-up were presented to the king, he noticed that each had a bright red patch on his clothing, and recalled that a similar patch had adorned a third competitor in the final. Abiel's Academy had begun well.

The last competition of the day followed: the long distance race. All the runners started together, lithe and fast, away from the starting area and down towards a small river. It was hard for them to find enough space for themselves, and quite a few tripped on the heels of those in front. Ben-hail and Kilion were near the back of the largest group as they reached the river and hurried across it. Up the hill they ran, passing some of the runners as they did so, but still going at an easy pace. As the last of the competitors reached the top of the hill and disappeared from sight, most of the spectators settled down to wait for the leaders to return into view. It was the best part of an hour before any did so, but when they did, it was to present a tame end to a race that many had thought promised so much. Ben-hail seemed to have been worried by the narrowness of his win in the short race, and so had tried harder than ever before. He crested the hill first and it was some time before Kilion appeared, running smoothly as usual but unable to keep up with the cracking pace set by Ben-hail.

Ben-hail sprinted down the hill to finish first and Kilion took an easy second, giving Abiel's academy first and second places in both of the first two competitions. Knowledgeable men looked at each other and wondered just how often they would see those red patches on students who were being presented to the king as winners or runners-up.

It took some time, but more and more runners hurried down the hill to have their finishing positions recorded by the stewards. Once again, each of the first fifty scored points towards the coveted Grand Prize.

With two competitions completed, one man had won the maximum number of points. Some said it was all going to be too easy – Ben-hail was sure to win everything and take the Grand Prize. Others urged caution, stating with confidence that the small, wiry type who made good runners were never any good with anything that required true strength!

Ben-hail was called to the platform once more to receive his prize as winner of the long distance race. After Jehoshaphat had presented him with the prize, he looked at the young man with a friendly smile.

"Tell me about yourself, Ben-hail," said Jehoshaphat.

Ben-hail paused for a moment, and the king would have been shocked if he had been able to read the young man's thoughts. Yet none of those thoughts showed on his face, and the answer when it came was just an ordinary description of life growing up in a Levite town in Judah.

"I come from Aijalon, where my father and mother were married in the eighteenth year of your father's reign. I was born almost a year later and am their only child. My father died before I was born and my mother is a widow. I wanted to work in King Asa's army to support my mother. I suppose that it's your army now, sire."

"Aijalon is a Levite town, isn't it? Are you a Levite?"

"Yes, but I am still too young to work properly as a Levite in the temple."

"Who was your father?"

"Raddai, the son of Benaiah," answered Ben-hail. He was looking down, working to keep the anger he felt from showing. As a result, he didn't notice the arrested look in Jehoshaphat's eyes.

"And your mother?" asked the king.

"Elisheba."

Jehoshaphat nodded and looked as if he was about to say something more, then thought better of it and changed the subject. "When did you start learning to use a sword?"

"When I was about ten, my uncle gave me an old sword that he had found among my grandfather's goods after he died. Because my grandfather's name was Benaiah, I always used to ask for stories about Benaiah the son of Jehoiada, who was a mighty man in King David's time. I wanted to be like him and slowly learned to use a sword. Then, when I finished my religious schooling, I found a use for my hobby in the king's army."

The king listened to his story with interest. Though Ben-hail didn't know it, the repeated mention of his grandfather's name had made the king feel more confident that he knew who this young man was. Both Gershom and Jehoiada had mentioned Raddai and his fate when describing King Asa's injustices after God had rebuked him for his lack of faith. Did this young man know what had happened to his father? Yet he was eager to be a soldier in Judah's army – surely he could not know what the king had done to his father? Jehoshaphat's heart went out to

Ben-hail and he wondered if there was anything he could do for him. He was not willing to openly attempt to undo all the damage that his father had caused with righteous people – at least, not while his father was alive – but perhaps he could help some of those who had suffered most unfairly, or their surviving families. He would have to talk to Jehoiada about that. At the moment, however, it wouldn't help to tell the lad that he knew his situation.

"I appreciate your dedication to the defence of the kingdom, Ben-hail. As king, I rely on people like you and your loyalty to the house of David. As a Levite, you know how important the worship of Yahweh is for our nation, and it is also very important for me personally as king."

Ben-hail walked away from the king with mixed feelings. It was easy to plan to execute people when you knew them only by name. Somehow, though, the idea of cold-blooded killing seemed harder when you knew a little more about someone, and found characteristics that you liked. King Jehoshaphat had appeared genuinely interested in Ben-hail, even sympathetic – but maybe it was all just a pretence, the sort of performance that a king needed to display to keep his subjects happy. That must be it; after all, King Asa had shown his true attitude in how he had treated Ben-hail's father.

Chapter 22

THE KING'S SWORDSMAN

Ben-hail was fit from an early age. Even before his accident, his fitness stood out amongst the other students.

However, his accident and subsequent recovery had changed things, and by the time the Great Tournament began, he was much fitter than he had ever been before.

Confronted by the possibility that he might not fully recover, he had attempted to mitigate the damage to his plans by striving to overcome what he had always thought of as a fundamental limitation. By nature, he was right-handed, so the skills of his left hand had not kept pace with those of his favoured right hand. As with most people, he only used his left hand when two hands were required for an activity, and it really was a bit of a handicap.

His accident had forced him to change his attitude – but no! it hadn't *forced* the change. Ben-hail had been unwilling to accept the other alternatives and tentatively, doubtfully, took up the challenge of training his left hand instead.

The results were as amazing as they were unexpected.

At the end of the first day of the Great Tournament, Ben-hail decided to do one last cliff climb in preparation for the climbing competition that would begin the next morning. He climbed quickly and smoothly, then sat down at the top of the cliff. The sun was setting over the mountains of Moab and he admired the intricate tracery that edged the clouds with gold. If King Jehoshaphat had seen the sight, he would have been quick to ascribe praise to the creator who oversees the endless rolling of the days, but Ben-hail had no such habit.

Coincidentally, though, his right hand and his left foot had each given a slight twinge as he pulled himself up over the cliff-edge, and it caused him to think back over the months since he had injured both as the result of a simple misjudgement during a morning run.

He held up his left hand and examined it. It looked no different from how it had looked on that morning, but how altered it was! That hand could now write – neatly. It could wield a sword and turn aside the most dangerous attack of a skilled swordsman with finesse and strength. Weights he could not have lifted – even with his right hand – he could now lift easily with either hand.

Eliam and Abiel had challenged him to increase his fitness in many different areas. He had taken up that challenge, and the results in all areas of physical performance, from running and climbing to archery, had truly shocked him.

What would his father think of him if only he had lived and could see him now? For a moment he looked again at the sunset, and suddenly he imagined his father sitting beside him, drinking in the beauty of the moment and sharing his awe of the creator with his son. Ben-hail shook his head to rid himself of the picture, but the softened feeling of closeness to his father remained. Had his father been right about Yahweh? How would he have wanted his only son to react to his imprisonment and death? Once more, Ben-hail shook his head and did his best to re-direct his thoughts to the Great Tournament.

If he did well in other events over the next few days, he would be close to King Jehoshaphat again. Perhaps an opportunity could arise. The question of what his father would think of that rose unbidden in his mind, but he pushed it aside and returned to the camp.

ෙ

Competitions progressed in the Great Tournament. Ben-hail did not win everything – in fact, he didn't even win most of the competitions – but he did score points in *every competition*, something that no-one, student or permanent soldier, had ever achieved before.

Abiel was busier than ever during the tournament, but he still took the time to observe his students' results and weigh their achievements. As a teacher, he wanted them to succeed; as the leader of the academy, he *needed* them to succeed. Yet as a trainer committed to new methods of training, he also wanted clear proof that those methods were making a difference. The results Ben-hail and his fellow students were achieving satisfied all of these aspects.

Even if he removed Ben-hail from the analysis, his students were still over-represented among the top 50 in each competition. He acknowledged that his academy might be a preferred place to send better students and tried to make allowance for that possibility in his assessment. After all, based on the number of men in the army and the number of military academies in Judah, he might reasonably expect a student from his academy to appear in the top 50 in *only one or two of the competitions.* Yet as competition followed competition, students from Abiel's Academy were among the top 50 competitors in every one, standing there proudly with their red scrap of material. That scrap of material became a symbol of irresistible success, a thorn in the side of the academies whose students consistently missed out on positions in the top 50.

Yet that was not all – and Abiel was very pleased to see this. The students of the other academies which had been applying the new training methods were also showing up in the top 50 much more often than those from any of the other academies.

Abiel felt vindicated. He had been convinced that the methods worked, with their concentration on improving fitness and refining skills, but it was pleasing to see the evidence in results. At the same time, he knew from conversations with the commanders of the other selected academies that, while they had all applied the methods to some extent, none had thrown themselves into it as wholeheartedly as Abiel had.

And then there was Ben-hail.

He was no ordinary student, and since his personal concentration on fitness had increased, the observable differences between him and ordinary students had burgeoned. Abiel was now certain that fitness was fundamental to success, even for gifted athletes like Ben-hail.

Eliam had won both of the weight lifting competitions, with Ben-hail coming a close second in one and third in the other behind a true giant who had won the lifting competitions four years ago and had clearly expected to win them again easily this time. Abiel smiled to himself, thinking that this soldier was the perfect example of the difference between the old training methods and the new. The man was enormous and naturally extremely strong, but he carried around too much of his own weight and was not outstandingly fit like Eliam.

Eliam also performed particularly well in the competitions in which distance was the prime goal. Whether throwing a spear, shooting an arrow or slinging a stone, he could achieve distances that no-one else could. If that had been the only measure of success, he would have won them all. But there was still a requirement for accuracy even in the competitions that focused on distance: the spear, arrow or stone must strike a target at the selected distance. As the distance was steadily increased in each competition, men who missed the target with all of their allowed attempts were eliminated. Normally this was because they could not reach the target, but Eliam was just as likely to send the projectile well beyond the target as to have it fall short. Fine control was not his gift, although as Abiel watched the distance slinging competition, he saw some problems with technique that he believed Eliam could overcome with more dedicated training. True to the man, Abiel was disappointed with himself that he had not seen these possibilities before the competition began. If only he'd had more time to spend with his students in those last few weeks!

Even so, Eliam was runner-up in the distance spear-throwing competition and placed in the top ten for both archery and slinging. Ben-hail scraped into the top 50 in each of these, but using weapons to fight from a great distance was not where his ability stood out most clearly.

Other competitions concentrated on accuracy and speed, and Kilion and Darda performed very well in these, particularly using the sling. It was an astonishing experience to watch the top competitors shooting at the target and never missing. There really did seem to be men who could emulate the great slingers in the ancient army of Benjamin who were known to be able to sling at a hair and not miss.[107]

Ben-hail watched the final competition for accuracy among the top ten slingers with Hadoram, the left-handed instructor from Abiel's Academy.

"Look at all of those left-handers," rejoiced Hadoram.

"Intriguing, isn't it?"

"Most virtuoso slingers have always been left-handed."

"What do you mean?"

"Everyone remembers that there were 700 slingers from Benjamin who could hit a hair if they wanted to, but what most people ignore is that they were all left-handed." He smiled and continued, "Yet that's really the most important point!"

"If I could shoot like these men, I wouldn't care whether I did it with my left hand or my right. It's amazing." Once his right hand had recovered completely, Ben-hail had reverted to using it when slinging.

"Maybe if you had kept using the sling in your left hand, you would have been up there with the best by now," Hadoram teased Ben-hail.

"I doubt it. But maybe I should go back to practising with my left hand again anyway."

Abiel's Academy was well represented in the final – Kilion and Darda were both included, and so was Jeberechiah, another student from the academy. Five of the ten contestants were left-handed.

On the last day of competition for the first week, before the Sabbath rest day, King Asa made an admirable effort, travelling from Jerusalem to Abiel's Academy to watch the spear-throwing competitions. This was more to show support for his soldiers than through any personal desire

---

[107] Judges 20:16

to attend, and by the time he arrived, his face was grey with pain. He had to wait in his palanquin for some time before he had recovered enough to move from it.

Jehoshaphat was there to meet him when he at last alighted, and was visibly upset at his father's condition. Azubah had returned with her husband, riding on her own donkey, unwilling to leave him to the sole care of the Royal Doctor, in whom she secretly had little confidence. Asa appreciated her solicitude, although he would never have told her so.

Ben-hail was passing by and saw the commotion. When he realised who was in the palanquin, he was surprised, and even felt some sympathy for the old man's obvious suffering. However, he quickly caught himself and reminded himself sternly that the old man was not suffering as much as his own father had.

Shortly afterwards, he received an even greater surprise which took his mind off the king altogether. He was standing near the entrance to the competition area, and saw his own mother walking towards him.

"Ben-hail!" she called, a broad smile on her face.

"Mother," he said, looking bewildered.

"You don't look pleased to see me," she teased. "Nor Naphish," she added, with a smile at the man who stood beside her.

For the first time, Ben-hail noticed that she had someone with her, and the fact left him more confused than ever.

Naphish was a tall, pleasant-looking man in his early forties. A widower, he had been trying to convince Ben-hail's mother Elisheba to marry him for several years.

"The Lord be with you," said Naphish.

"The Lord keep you," answered Ben-hail, automatically.

Naphish chuckled and said, "Your mother and I got married yesterday. We decided not to invite you because it would have meant either dragging you away from the tournament or us having to wait to get married. I'd already waited so long trying to convince Elisheba to marry me that when she finally agreed, I wasn't willing to wait any longer. I'm sorry if you would have liked to be there, but I thought it was the best choice to make."

"Oh, that's all right. I'm sorry, but it's a big surprise."

Darda saw the couple with his friend and came over to greet them. "Naphish and Elisheba," he said. "I guess Naphish has finally engineered the marriage he was looking for."

"You're right," said Naphish. "You're young Darda, aren't you? How did you know that I wanted it? Has everyone been talking about it?"

"Don't worry," said Ben-hail, "Darda remembers anything he ever hears or sees – and he sees a lot more of what is going on than most people."

Darda turned to congratulate Elisheba, and Naphish took Ben-hail by the arm and led him a few paces away.

"Elisheba wanted to come and see you competing, and I thought it was best to avoid the sword fighting if we could. That meant it had to be today."

"Thank you. I'm sure that's best, sir," said Ben-hail.

"You don't need to call me 'sir'," said Naphish. "Your mother and I will be living in my house from now on, and you are welcome at any time. I'm your step-father, but I'm not trying to displace your father. His house is now yours, so if you want to keep away from me when you visit Aijalon, that's fine. However, if you want us to, we will look after the house when you are away.

"Your father was a few years older than me, Ben-hail, but I admired him greatly. He was such a good example to everyone. A man of faith, a good teacher of the law, a helpful worker around the town, and a faithful servant of the king. You have much to live up to. How are the competitions going?"

Ben-hail wasn't quite sure how to respond to this long but concise statement. In the end, it was easiest to just answer the final question, so he said, "Well."

By then Darda had finished giving Elisheba his congratulations, and the pair strolled over in time to hear Naphish's question and Ben-hail's reply.

" 'Well' doesn't really do justice to how Ben-hail is going in the competitions," said Darda. "Already, there is nobody who could beat him for the Grand Prize even if he withdrew from all of the remaining competitions. And we haven't even started the sword fighting yet!"

"You're not doing so badly yourself, Darda," said Ben-hail. "You've already scored more points than anyone from the academy did at the last Great Tournament."

"I suppose we're all doing 'well', then. Ah, here comes the giant."

Naphish was tall, but he had to look up at Eliam as he approached. "Whew! He *is* a giant," he said.

"Yes," said Darda, laughing, "it's bad enough just having Ben-hail and Eliam, but with you here as well, I feel like an insect. Eliam will be coming to say that we need to go to the checking area for the spear throwing comps."

Eliam nodded. Ben-hail introduced his mother and brand new step-father, but as usual, Eliam had little to say.

"Once the tournament is over, Ben-hail," said Naphish, "you should bring your friends to see us in Aijalon. That way we could catch up on all the news and maybe discuss the future. Elisheba would like to discuss the past a little too, but that will depend on you."

"I'll talk to them about it later, and mention it to Kilion, too," said Ben-hail.

Naphish looked at Eliam again. "I'd like to see you again – it's good to feel like a midget every so often! You look as if you could lift old Peresh's anvil. By yourself," he added, with a meaningful look at Elisheba that puzzled Ben-hail.

Darda, Ben-hail and Eliam made their way to the marshalling area, while Naphish and Elisheba found a place on the crowded slopes where they could sit and watch.

The spot they had chosen was opposite the royal platform, and they watched uncomfortably as Asa struggled to climb the steps. Jehoshaphat was on his right, while a servant helped on the left. Asa kept his face down, but even so, a little of the agony on his face could be seen at times as he drove his diseased feet to walk. Azubah stayed close behind like an attentive mother hen, paying no attention to anything but her husband. Behind her came the Royal Doctor, looking rather glum.

Finally, King Asa reached the platform and then his throne, onto which he collapsed and withdrew into a private world of agony. It was some minutes before the pain eased a little and he could look up again, struggling to smile at the crowd.

Some in the crowd ignored the king completely, while others looked away almost in embarrassment that a man's private suffering should be so publicly on show. Many, however, watched with silent sympathy, and the noise of the crowd only returned to normal when Asa finally managed that wan smile. Some even cheered.

"Why did he come?" asked Elisheba. "Why not stay in Jerusalem with this Royal Doctor we hear so much about?"

"I can't be sure," replied Naphish, "but maybe he came so that everyone can see his support for the tournament and the men involved. If you like, Elisheba, I think he is showing honour to men like Ben-hail. Men who have helped to keep his kingdom safe."

Elisheba gazed at Naphish without expression for a few moments, then looked back at King Asa and said softly, "The poor old man."

❧

Perhaps Ben-hail was inspired by his mother's presence in the audience, but whatever the reason, his accuracy and speed that day were phenomenal.

The two competitions involved throwing the spear at a target from a short distance. One demanded accuracy and the other speed, and only a stroke of ill-luck stopped Ben-hail from winning both. The speed competition he won comfortably, but in the other, his last throw let him down. Eleven spears from his previous throws were already clustered around the centre of the target and his last throw was heading inexorably to join the others when it hit three other spears that were closely grouped together, their points almost touching, and bounced off. Thus, only eleven spears were counted in Ben-hail's score, and one seasoned soldier was able to better it with his twelfth spear. The few soldiers present from the winning soldier's camp erupted in cheers, and Ben-hail went and congratulated him with a rueful smile.

King Asa defied the terrible pain in his feet to present the awards to the three men – two prizes to Ben-hail, and one each to the others. The marshals brought them to the royal platform where Asa sat on a throne, with Jehoshaphat standing by his side to help if necessary. Azubah also sat nearby looking concerned, but avoided interfering in any way.

A marshal loudly announced the awards to the watching crowd as King Asa presented them, then indicated to the recipients that they should remain near him. Once the noise of cheering had quieted, King Asa spoke quietly and privately to the three.

"Men, you are a great encouragement to me. God chose Abraham as his friend and blessed his descendants, making them a great multitude in Egypt. He led our ancestors into this land and has blessed us although we've not always served him well. King David was a mighty man and his mighty men are still famous today. But Solomon the Wise lost his way in his old age and began to serve other gods with his many wives, so God punished our nation and my family by splitting the nation in two. Yet God kept the kingdom of Judah – two tribes with David's sons to reign over them. I'm sorry that I am so weak when I talk to you as king and congratulate you. My son Jehoshaphat is now king and he will lead the kingdom with genuine strength of faith, just as King David did so long ago. He needs men like you and the winners of the other competitions to help, not only with physical strength and skill, but with a faith that encourages the whole nation. Perhaps I would have been a better king if I'd collected more such men around me and listened to them. I'm sure that my son Jehoshaphat will do so."

All three men were affected by his words, and King Asa put his hand on the shoulder of each in turn. Then he signalled to Ben-hail to remain and Jehoshaphat led the other two men away. Asa and Ben-hail were left alone.

"Ben-hail, I hear not only that you have achieved amazing things in the competitions so far, but also that the area in which you have the greatest skill is yet to come. Unfortunately, I am too sick to be present for the sword-fighting competition and so will not be able to personally congratulate the winner as The King's Swordsman. My son will do that, and I hope that he will be able to have The King's Swordsman as his armour-bearer and his friend, a man who can protect him in all situations so that he can concentrate on leading the nation towards Yahweh our God. From what I hear of you, I hope that you will achieve this distinction; if so, please care for my son and help him to watch over our nation."

☙

The Sabbath was over and the new week signalled a new stage of the Great Tournament. The remaining days of competition would determine who would be The King's Swordsman.

With so many men eager to earn the title, the early stages of the competition had to eliminate large numbers of men as quickly as possible. Bouts were arranged between two groups of about 50 men each, armed with blunt swords and equipped with armour and shields. When the signal was given, the mock battle between the two groups was on. Marshals surrounded the melee, and immediately excluded anyone who received a touch on their breastplate or helmet from an opponent's sword. Once about half of the men in the bout had been expelled, the bout was stopped and the next mass bout began. Unfortunately, this method of quick selection, though necessary, sometimes resulted in the exit of a skilled swordsman due to some unexpected trick or accident.

In many cases, a number of the men on one side came from the same academy or army company, so these often worked together.

In Ben-hail's first bout, he was one of about 15 students from Abiel's Academy, while the remaining men in his group of 50 were soldiers from three army companies. As everyone was preparing for the bout, Ben-hail noticed Mattaniah standing with the opposing group. For a moment, their eyes locked, then Mattaniah looked away quickly.

Darda was standing next to Ben-hail and noticed the direction of his friend's gaze. He said quietly, "He didn't want you to see him. Be careful of Mattaniah, and anyone he's standing near. I wouldn't be surprised if they try to gang up on you."

Darda was right. As soon as the bout began, Ben-hail saw Mattaniah and a few others moving around the boundary of the area in which the bouts were held. He guessed that they were probably trying to circle around and attack him from behind. By so doing, they had abandoned the men on their side whom they were meant to be helping, leaving them outnumbered by Ben-hail and his companions. Ben-hail quickly moved forward, having decided that attack was the best method of defence. Choosing a group of opposing soldiers, he ran towards them with his sword at the ready. Some of the soldiers, recognising him as a student, moved confidently towards him, but several of their companions recognised him as the man who had won so many competitions and called out a warning. Nevertheless, Ben-hail was able to engage one of the overconfident soldiers and easily slipped his own sword past the outstretched sword to touch the man's breastplate. Without wasting a moment, he turned to another man and thrust his blunt sword towards him. When the expected defence came, he withdrew his sword a little before moving his foot across and thrusting low and hard. Once again the defender brought his shield down and began to counter-attack, swinging his sword towards Ben-hail's helmet. Calmly, Ben-hail lifted his own shield defensively, then stopped his thrust, realigned his sword with an elegant twist of the wrist, and thrust quickly once more, gently touching his opponent's breastplate.

Two dealt with, he thought, and still Mattaniah and his men were working their way around behind him. With amazing speed he dealt with another three men, touching two on the breastplate and one on the helmet.

Five out, and Darda had dealt with two more. The field in front of them now looked empty; it was time to face Mattaniah and his helpers.

The chagrin on Mattaniah's face when Ben-hail and Darda turned together to face him was almost laughable. He had clearly been counting on that cowardly attack from behind to give him a chance of eliminating Ben-hail from the competition.

Nevertheless, with four on his side and only two opposing them, Mattaniah smiled confidently as he approached.

"Given up the fancy tricks, hey, Ben-hail?" he called. "Using a shield again, I see."

"Maybe, but I see that you haven't give up your trick of attacking from behind," said Ben-hail grimly.

Mattaniah's face contorted with anger and he ran towards Ben-hail with his sword swinging. It was a foolish attack that left him unprotected and would have earned him death in battle. Ben-hail was about to take the easy opportunity to touch the man's breastplate with his sword when the chief marshal signalled that the bout was over. Ben-hail and his companions had touched the breastplates or helmets of 20 of their opponents, while five on their side had been touched themselves.

As Ben-hail expected, Mattaniah was too angry to stop at the signal, but one of his helpers grabbed his sword arm and eventually calmed him down enough to stop.

"I'll kill you next time," growled Mattaniah. "If you make it through."

"Well, you've made it through this time – without doing anything," said Ben-hail.

Two of Mattaniah's companions took an arm each and dragged him away, still struggling.

Quickly the number of competitors was whittled down until the thousands had been reduced to hundreds and it was time to begin bouts between individuals. Opponents were selected at random and the winner of each match progressed to the next round.

Each bout ended when one of the competitors touched his sword on the breastplate or helmet of his opponent, and many of the early bouts finished quickly.

Unfortunately for Abiel, Ben-hail met Beker, another student from Abiel's Academy, and the one for whom Abiel had the greatest hopes after Ben-hail, in an early round. The marshal controlling the bout commiserated with Beker afterwards, saying that he had never seen a better swordsman lose so easily in such an early round despite demonstrating such great skill.

After that, all of Ben-hail's bouts attracted large audiences. He progressed through the rounds with little difficulty, although he met some fancied swordsmen. None, however, could pierce the metal web he seemed to weave around himself. Abiel watched many bouts and was finally convinced that he would still be able to better any of the swordsmen he watched with the exception of Ben-hail. His respect for Ben-hail's swordsmanship continued to increase: his skill seemed to be improving with every bout, and none of his opponents appeared even to hurry him.

Mattaniah also progressed through the competition. When he kept his anger under control, he really was a good swordsman! He too attracted large audiences and won most of his bouts quickly, often having won them before the fighting even began by his intimidating attitude. Vophsi was often there to watch.

One by one Ben-hail's friends were eliminated, until only Darda remained. Though a skilful swordsman, he often seemed to be able to beat swordsmen with even more skill simply by out-thinking them. Darda tried to work out who he would face in coming rounds and then watched them at work. Thus when he met them in combat, he was more familiar with their style than they were with his, which enabled him to predict their moves with great success.

At last, there were only eight men left in the competition. Darda and Ben-hail were both included and were glad that they had not drawn each other as opponents. Darda, however, had drawn Mattaniah.

A large crowd came to watch the bout and Vophsi was there too, looking serious and aloof as usual.

The bout began with each man feeling out the other's defences. Mattaniah had tried his normal trick of sneering at his opponent beforehand, and continued to talk disparagingly as the bout began.

Darda didn't say a word, but gradually stepped up the tempo of the bout. Faster and faster he danced forward and stepped back, and Mattaniah was obviously finding it annoying. He began to overreach himself a little and make some basic mistakes, but never quite enough for Darda to pierce his defences.

Feeling that success was within reach, Darda tried to move even faster, but slipped a little as he drove forward and only just managed to recover and protect himself with his shield.

At once, Mattaniah leapt forward to attack, lifting his sword to take a swing at Darda's helmet. Darda ducked, Mattaniah missed and Darda's return thrust missed also – just barely.

For a few moments, the two combatants stood facing each other, breathing hard. Darda was preparing for another lunge, when suddenly a voice from behind shouted, "Look out!"

Darda turned and looked around, and as he did so, Mattaniah moved smoothly forward and the end of his sword clanged against Darda's breastplate.

Darda was bewildered. What had happened? What was the warning about?

"Mattaniah wins," said the marshal, doubtfully. "But who distracted Darda?"

"It doesn't matter," said Vophsi. "The crowd is not required to be silent. Crowd noise is allowed."

"Yes, but that wasn't crowd noise," said a man in the crowd. "That was cheating!"

Vophsi flushed and his expression hardened. "Crowd noise is allowed. Confirm the victory, marshal."

"I confirm. Mattaniah wins, but..." he stopped and said no more as Vophsi glared at him.

❧

There was plenty of discussion in the breaks between bouts after that. Some argued that the rules were the rules and that Mattaniah's victory was within the rules. Others scoffed and said that if such disgraceful behaviour was within the rules, then people like Mattaniah must have written the rules and they needed to be changed.

Someone from Abiel's Academy quietly suggested that this wasn't the first time Mattaniah had shown himself a cheat, and described his attacks on Ben-hail. The story spread quickly and it wasn't long before Mattaniah heard it. As might be expected, he didn't like the story, and promptly found the man he suspected of telling it and attacked him. It would have gone badly for the man had not Eliam been nearby.

"Leave him alone," said Eliam in a verbose moment.

Mattaniah ignored him until Eliam took his arm and twisted it up behind his back.

"Leave him alone," Eliam repeated.

Mattaniah was not easily convinced, but after an unpleasant scene, he eventually accepted that Eliam was able to physically enforce his demands.

Some other students from Vophsi's Academy were nearby and a nasty situation might have arisen had not King Jehoshaphat and his guard passed by just then.

"What's going on?" asked the king.

No-one seemed inclined to explain the situation, least of all Mattaniah, and, after waiting in vain for an answer, the king looked at him and frowned. "You're Mattaniah aren't you? I understand that you just won a bout in doubtful circumstances. At the moment, the result will stand, but be careful. Don't forget that, in the end, the king chooses The King's Swordsman!"

Three more bouts decided who would contest the semi-finals. As everyone expected, Ben-hail won through, his bout a perfect picture of supreme skill.

The semi-finals had different requirements from the earlier bouts: to win, a swordsman needed to touch his opponent's breastplate or helmet not just once but five times. No competitor could win by a single stroke of luck.

At the drawing of lots, Ben-hail and Mattaniah found themselves in different semi-finals. This situation disappointed many who would have liked to see Ben-hail take on Mattaniah and teach him a lesson, ensuring that he would not reach the final.

Mattaniah, however, was pleased and cocky. With three of his cronies, he looked around and found his semi-final opponent, then began to sneer at him while pointing out his own abilities and achievements. However, by this time, Eliam had appointed himself Mattaniah's watchman, and once more he outdid himself in garrulousness.

"Stop it."

Mattaniah turned angrily, ready to abuse the interfering troublemaker. But when he saw who it was, he blustered and grumbled, but left the man alone.

Despite Eliam's help, though, the man had already been overawed by Mattaniah's speech and Mattaniah won the semi-final easily, without the need to resort to the sort of trick he had played on Darda.

Ben-hail was approaching his dream, the pinnacle of the plans he had worked on for years in utter secrecy. If he could win just two more bouts, he would be acclaimed The King's Swordsman, and that would open many doors for him.

Two more bouts.

He must not fail.

The second semi-final started cautiously. Ben-hail wanted to avoid over-confidence and the movements were slow on both sides. Gradually, though, the contestants began to move more freely, and Ben-hail's skill showed at once. Slowly he began to push his opponent back, and soon they were moving backwards around the area, one in desperate, hurried defence and the other with a smooth, relaxed attack that threatened to overwhelm his opponent's defence at any moment. Suddenly there was a clash and the marshal recorded the first score in Ben-hail's favour. After that, the bout was over very quickly as Ben-hail touched his opponent every few seconds until the fifth touch was noted and the bout concluded.

$$\text{CR}$$

The last competition of the Great Tournament was underway.

Again, five touches of the opponent's armour would decide the result, and thousands were watching. An enclosure stood in front of the royal platform and within the enclosure, Ben-hail and Mattaniah had begun their dance of opportunity. The winner would take everything: fame, glory, patronage and wealth. A small error could lose it all.

Mattaniah had a debt of hatred to pay and aimed to injure Ben-hail if he possibly could. The swords used in this bout were less blunt than those used in the earlier bouts, and Mattaniah was hoping to use the sharpness of the edge to repay Ben-hail for his humiliating defeat and forced transfer from Abiel's Academy.

In contrast, Ben-hail had little interest in his opponent. Teaching Mattaniah a lesson would not be unwelcome, but it was victory that was important. More important than anything else.

And at the moment, he must concentrate on the contest.

Two men circling slowly, looking for an opportunity.

A feint, a tentative push, a withdrawal.

Then, in an instant, Ben-hail was on the attack. As quick as lightning and as smooth as a striking snake his sword flicked out, his foot reached forward and the flick became a terrifying lunge.

Mattaniah was a little slow to move and his shield was not completely ready when Ben-hail's sword struck it with force. Almost as if it was looking to find a way through, the sword twisted and turned, then slipped off the face of the shield. Finally, Mattaniah began to move, his body convulsing in a desperate attempt to avoid the lunging sword. Too late. The first score was Ben-hail's as his sword slid across Mattaniah's breastplate. Mattaniah's widening eyes showed shock and fear.

The frenzied movement settled down, and once more the two men circled slowly, looking for an opportunity.

Another explosion of activity; another scoring thrust for Ben-hail.

This time, Mattaniah's fear had a portion of anger in it, and when next the crowd saw frenetic action, his anger slowed his reactions and drove him to seek retribution. Once, twice, Ben-hail touched first his breastplate and then his helmet, before stepping back so swiftly that Mattaniah had the sense of grasping at a cloud.

Only one more strike and Ben-hail would be The King's Swordsman.

Mattaniah did his best to regain his calm and douse his temper, knowing that if he didn't, that terrible sword would be back again and he would lose everything he wanted.

Carefully. Slowly. Watching...

"Duck!" The shout came from behind Ben-hail, but he ignored it, concentrating on his opponent more than ever.

Mattaniah had seemed to be gathering himself to attack, but he held back when he saw that Ben-hail had not been distracted. Instead, he suddenly stepped back, dropped his sword and tugged at his belt. Ben-hail saw his hand come free, but he could not see what it held until Mattaniah pulled it back above his shoulder and threw the dagger at Ben-hail.

He was too close and the move came as too much of a surprise for Ben-hail to dodge that spinning dagger. It hit his right hand and immediately blood gushed. Pain filled his hand and arm, but he couldn't stop yet. Mattaniah had bent down to reclaim his sword, and it wasn't hard to guess what he would do next.

Ben-hail dropped his shield and swapped his sword into his left hand, and he was back to the last time Mattaniah had attacked him: no shield and his sword in his left hand. He had bested him then, but that time he hadn't had a bleeding hand. Mattaniah began his attack and Ben-hail parried his first thrust easily, with perfect timing. He needed to slow Mattaniah down so that he could get used to the pain in his right hand. He thrust forward, but carefully, and Mattaniah stopped his headlong rush. Now was the time, while Mattaniah was within reach.

He feinted with a high thrust, but with no intention of following through. As Mattaniah moved his shield upwards, Ben-hail turned his wrist and thrust towards the bottom of the breastplate. Mattaniah's hopeless attempt to realign his shield did nothing to stop the thrust. The sword struck his breastplate and the contest was over.

Cheers erupted from the watching crowd and someone began the chant, "Ben-hail! Ben-hail! Ben-hail!"

A broad grin spread across the young man's face and he just stood there, drinking in the applause and feeling the hesitancy of an unimaginable joy. This was what it felt like to win everything you wanted – but what came next?

The marshal came across and took Ben-hail's hand, wrapped it quickly in a cloth to staunch the bleeding and then held it up. "Ben-hail, the victor!" he shouted, and the cheering surged again.

On the royal platform, King Jehoshaphat stood up with a smile and beckoned to Ben-hail and the marshal, and the pair began to walk towards the platform.

At that instant, Vophsi rose from where he had been sitting opposite Ben-hail. Despite his disappointment at Mattaniah's failure, he had a look of malicious triumph on his face as he raised his arms above his head and curled his hands into fists.

"Don't let him near the king," shouted Vophsi. "He's a traitor! He's planning to kill the king!"

Chapter 23

VOPHSI'S REVENGE

The marshal leading Ben-hail to the king immediately stopped and barred Ben-hail's way.

"We'd better stop," he said apologetically. "Just in case."

Gershom stepped forward from his position near the royal platform, placing himself directly between Ben-hail and the king. Abiel had been close by, cheering the success of his protégé, and now moved to stand beside Ben-hail.

"Do you know anything about this?" he asked Ben-hail quietly.

"No, sir," answered Ben-hail.

Vophsi strolled across to meet Gershom and spoke to him calmly. Abiel waited a few moments and then walked over to join them. For a few minutes, there was an intense discussion in which all three men looked angry at times. Around them, the crowd stood or sat waiting as they chose, some silently, others shouting, but it was obvious that the majority of the crowd supported Ben-hail. As the pause lengthened, some even returned to chanting his name, which clearly irritated Vophsi.

Finally, Gershom held up his hand for silence and made an announcement.

"Fellow countrymen, I'm sorry for the delay, but we have to settle a question or two from Commander Vophsi before we present the final awards of the tournament. We should be able to complete this within the hour, so I hope that you can all wait that long for the final celebrations."

Gershom told his staff what was required for the unexpected investigation, then approached Jehoshaphat for his confirmation or further instructions. Vophsi tried to take advantage of his seniority and suggested to Abiel that he would provide a guard of students to make sure that the king was kept safe, but Abiel observed tartly that they were in an army academy, so there was no shortage of guards and other loyal soldiers who could guarantee the king's safety!

Jehoshaphat confirmed Gershom's plans but indicated that he also wanted to be present to listen. Gershom dispatched an officer to tell Abiel that his administration tent would be required and that he and Ben-hail should wait there. He also recommended that Ben-hail have a friend with him who could be trusted to give him good advice if necessary. Since Vophsi claimed that he had some evidence to provide, a few reliable witnesses would be useful. Abiel immediately sent for Darda, having gradually become aware of his quick mind and how good a man he was to have on hand in a tense situation.

As soon as Darda arrived, Abiel led the way to the large administration tent, from which his staff had cleared away the ordinary furniture, replacing it with several seats.

Jehoshaphat soon arrived with Gershom and Vophsi and was led into the tent.

"You'll be organising this, Gershom. I'll just listen," said Jehoshaphat, and sat down.

"Very well," said Gershom. "Vophsi, tell us more about your accusations."

"I can't tell you the details with *him* here," said Vophsi, gesturing at Ben-hail.

"Why not? Surely facts are facts."

"It involves others who have a right to remain anonymous."

"If we are talking about treachery and plots to assassinate the king, *no-one* has a right to remain anonymous," said Gershom, bluntly. "Everyone has a responsibility to report any such threats."

"Who needs to remain hidden? And why?" asked Jehoshaphat, unable to keep quiet.

"If I name them, my witnesses may be in danger from this traitor! If he knows who has reported him, he will get his own back."

"If this hearing finds anyone to be a traitor, I can assure you that he won't be going around taking revenge!" said Gershom.

"What is your evidence, Vophsi?" asked Jehoshaphat. "You have accused a man of being a traitor. I assume that you can back it up with evidence."

"Of course, your majesty! This man, Ben-hail, is a traitor and the son of a traitor!"

"Under our law, no man is ever to be put to death for the actions of his father,"[108] said Jehoshaphat. "What evidence do you have that Ben-hail himself is a traitor?"

"There is a faithful servant of the king who spoke to Ben-hail recently in Aijalon," said Vophsi. "Ben-hail admitted to this man that his

---

[108] Deuteronomy 24:16; 2 Kings 14:6

father had been a traitor, writing a letter condemning the king. He then called the king a hypocrite and discussed the recent assassination attempt on your majesty and why it had failed."

"Sire, may I ask some questions?" interrupted Darda.

"Who are you?"

"I am Darda, a friend of Ben-hail's. I was with Ben-hail when we both talked to this so-called 'faithful servant of the king'. Nezib is his name – yes, I thought you might have heard of him," he interrupted himself as Jehoshaphat and Gershom started and Vophsi looked worried.

"Yes, I have heard of Nezib," said Gershom, grimly, turning to look at Vophsi. " 'Faithful servant of the king,' hey?"

"Nezib has used several young men to try to assassinate King Asa," continued Darda. "The most recent was a young man called Uriel, who tried to kill you as well, sire. Nezib tried to convince Ben-hail to be his next dupe, but Ben-hail refused even to discuss it. Nezib then sent him a letter here at the academy in which he tried to convince him to meet him for further discussions, threatening to report him as a traitor if he didn't cooperate."

The eyes of everyone in the tent were fixed on Darda as he made these revelations, so nobody noticed the confused look on Ben-hail's face, which he quickly did his best to hide.

"I have the letter here," said Darda. "Ben-hail let me have a look at it, which is hardly the sort of behaviour you would expect from a secretive, plotting traitor, is it? Would you like to read the letter yourself, your majesty?" Darda pulled a folded scroll out of his cloak and offered it to Jehoshaphat, who took it and unfolded it.

He scanned the writing and a look of amazement spread across his face. "Is this letter really from Nezib?" he asked.

"Yes," said Darda. "Apparently he delivered the note but refused to wait to see Ben-hail. Instead, his letter demanded that Ben-hail meet him near here on the Sabbath just past. He threatened that if Ben-hail didn't turn up, he would report information to a senior commander of the army who would have Ben-hail convicted as a traitor. We all know now who that senior commander was."

Jehoshaphat looked up with excitement in his eyes. "You've explained the present situation very well, Darda," he said, and the excitement was in his voice too, "but I think you have also stumbled on another important fact: I recognise this writing!" He showed it to Gershom, pointing out some characteristic flourishes and letter forms that combined to produce an unusual writing style.

"Whose is it, sir?" asked Gershom.

"I'll need to confirm it by examining a letter stored in the records in Jerusalem, but I am almost completely sure this letter was written by the same hand that wrote a treasonable letter to the king many years ago. If I weren't so sure, I wouldn't mention this detail, Ben-hail, but if Nezib wrote this, I believe he also wrote the unsigned letter that was blamed on Raddai, your father."

His audience sat in stunned silence for a few moments.

Vophsi then stood and said, "Excuse me, my lord, I must go and, ah, cover my feet."[109] He turned and began to walk towards the tent entrance, but Darda swiftly blocked his way.

"Yes, stop him," said Jehoshaphat, wearily. "He's probably a traitor, but I don't want to jump to conclusions yet. Jumping to conclusions has already caused enough suffering in this whole sorry tale."

"But what has Vophsi to do with this?" asked Gershom.

"The king received a treasonous, but unsigned, letter, and naturally tried to find out who had written it. My father appointed an army captain to investigate the situation, and the man reported back that there was no doubt that Raddai, the son of Benaiah, had written the letter. That army captain was Vophsi."

"But if the letter was written by Nezib, why would Vophsi have said that it was written by Raddai?" asked Gershom.

"Vophsi?"

"None of it's true," said Vophsi defiantly. "Raddai wrote that letter. He was angry with what the king had done to Hanani. Many people were."

"If I may interrupt, sir," said Darda, "given Vophsi's recent behaviour with Mattaniah, I wouldn't be surprised if Nezib is related to Vophsi."

Vophsi suddenly looked defeated and his shoulders slumped. Darda's analysis was convincing – everyone listening felt sure it was correct, explaining as it did Vophsi's actions past and present.

Jehoshaphat nodded and said, "That seems like a good theory to start with. Vophsi, you will be detained and examined on suspicion of treason. Gershom, have him taken to Jerusalem under guard."

ℭℛ

"People of Judah, the competition for the King's Swordsman has been decided. One man has progressed through the competition almost without effort, and such skill with a sword may never have been seen before. He was even able to finish the last bout with no shield and using only his left hand! You will all be glad to hear that the doctors are confident that his injured right hand will recover quickly."

---

[109] 1 Samuel 24:3 (KJV)

A cheer erupted from the crowd as Jehoshaphat stood on the royal platform and gave them the news they had been waiting for.

"For the first time ever," continued the king, "a student has won this competition. Ben-hail, the son of Raddai, the son of Benaiah, is the King's Swordsman."

"Ben-hail! Ben-hail! Ben-hail!" chanted the crowd as Ben-hail stepped forward and knelt before the king to receive his award.

Jehoshaphat presented the winner's golden cup to Ben-hail, then put his hand under Ben-hail's elbow and lifted him up to stand by his side.

"Commander Vophsi's charges against Ben-hail have been dismissed, and Vophsi himself is now under investigation for the very treachery of which he accused Ben-hail. Moses gave us a law that rewards false witnesses with the punishment they tried to have inflicted on the brother they lied about.[110] The judges will enquire diligently, and if Vophsi's claims are proved false, he will be punished appropriately."

Scattered cheers arose: Vophsi was not a popular commander.

"Command of Vophsi's Academy will be temporarily assumed by Abiel, the outstanding commander who has arranged this exceptional tournament with so little notice and who was also the trainer of the King's Swordsman. If anyone has genuine evidence regarding Vophsi's behaviour, please pass it on to Abiel, who will ensure that it is included in the investigation."

"Ben-hail is the King's Swordsman. Who came second?" called a voice from the crowd.

Jehoshaphat answered, "Normally we would present an award to the runner-up, but in this competition, the runner-up, Mattaniah, has repeatedly disgraced himself. As a result, there will be no second place awarded."

Mattaniah, listening in the crowd, resented this humiliation strongly, but for once was reluctant to draw attention to himself.

"We have one more award to present at the conclusion of this Great Tournament. The Grand Prize is given to the man with the widest range of skills in the tournament. Points are given to all who finish in the top 50 in each competition, with bonus points being given to the top ten and even more to the runner-up and the winner. The points earned by each man are added up and the man with the most points wins the Grand Prize. For the first time ever, a man has won points in every competition, as well as winning seven competitions by himself and coming second in three more.

"Congratulations to Ben-hail, the winner of the Grand Prize!"

---

[110] Deuteronomy 19:16-21

Once again the crowd cheered and chanted while Ben-hail knelt before the king, who praised him as the greatest soldier in the army. King Jehoshaphat could not have guessed the confusion his words caused in the mind of this young man who, though he had dreamed of this success for several years, had worked towards it as part of a goal that he was no longer quite as sure about as he had been.

Chapter 24

ANSWERS IN AIJALON

Ben-hail, Darda and Eliam made their way to Aijalon two weeks later. Kilion was invited but could not refuse the demands of his family, who planned to celebrate his success in the Great Tournament.

At the conclusion of the Great Tournament, all four of the friends had been offered places in King Jehoshaphat's special forces, and Abiel had given them a special dispensation to graduate from the academy immediately.

As they left the academy early in the morning, Abiel spoke to them seriously: "Lads, you have done well in your training. But don't forget that the training we have given you is just a start. In the next few years, you will meet many soldiers with far more practical experience than you have. Weigh their advice carefully. Never consider yourself above learning from others. You four have been blessed with remarkable abilities, and ability often turns to pride if you don't remember that it is Yahweh who gave you those abilities. I hope that you will become truly mighty men in the service of Yahweh and his anointed king."

The clear summer day grew hotter as they joined the road from Jerusalem and made their way out of the hill country into the Shephelah.[111] The broad Valley of Aijalon opened up before them, with fortified Aijalon perched on a hill, shimmering in the heat. From the valley, they made their way up to the gates and passed through into the city.

"Where are we going first?" asked Darda. "Your house or your step-father's house?"

"I know that my mother and step-father are expecting us this morning, but it's probably best to drop off our luggage, such as it is, at my house first. They're not far apart anyway."

As they walked through the market area near the gate, Ben-hail couldn't help thinking how many things had changed since he had last

---

[111] The lowlands. A band of rolling hills between the coastal plain and the hill country.

seen Aijalon: his mother's marriage, his victories in the Great Tournament and his unfolding career. And what of his secret thoughts and plans? He was no longer quite sure how he felt about the two kings of Judah. Asa was still the man whose cruelty had caused his father's death in captivity, but the king's part in the heinous crime was not quite as great as he had believed.

For the time being then, his old plans were on hold. He would wait. King Jehoshaphat had ordered a review of Raddai's case and a thorough investigation of the work of Nezib and Vophsi – and he seemed to be pursuing it in good faith. Where it would lead, Ben-hail did not know. It wasn't hard to see just how difficult – maybe even dangerous – it could be for Jehoshaphat to reopen the old sore of Hanani's criticism of King Asa.

Once again, he asked himself the question: Why was King Jehoshaphat doing this? Was it out of kindness towards him, Ben-hail, or was it driven by a strong desire to right a long-standing wrong? Either reason seemed admirable, but one was personally more important to him.

What would his father or the prophet Hanani have thought of the turn of events? He was fairly sure that both of them would have seen the hand of God in it, but Ben-hail was not open to such thoughts. Religion, said his old habits of thinking, was just a tool for exercising control. Rulers used it to oppress their people, paying just enough lip-service to it to convince their superstitious subjects that they genuinely believed it themselves. His loss had made him fertile ground for such thoughts and Peresh had schooled him well in it.

The three friends walked to Ben-hail's home where they left their packs and walked towards Naphish's house. Their route took them past Peresh's workshop, and as they passed, the giant blacksmith came out carrying a new plough.

"Ben!" he roared, "Ye's back home! W'friends, too."

"Yes," Ben-hail replied, smiling. "You know Darda, of course, and this is Eliam, who I told you about – he's much stronger than I am."

"Giant-like, too!" said the blacksmith, as he put down the ploughshare.

Ben-hail spoke in a reasonable imitation of Peresh's booming voice: " 'But can ye...' "

"... lift me anvil?" finished Peresh, laughing.

Ben-hail's friends were already aware of Peresh's anvil, so the immediate challenge was not unexpected. Ben-hail led the way into the darkened smithy, ducking under the doorway himself, and laughing as he watched Eliam bend low to clear it. The stifling heat in the smithy was even greater than the growing heat of the morning outside, and the dark room seemed crowded with large bodies.

Peresh crossed to the enormous anvil and removed the tools that lay upon it.

"Ah, me anvil," he said fondly, flapping at it with a linen cloth to remove any dust and grit. Then he turned to Eliam. "Can ye lift me anvil?"

Eliam grunted and took his stand in front of the anvil. His legs were well spaced and he wrapped his enormous arms around the horns of the anvil. Ben-hail watched in envy as he methodically but confidently settled himself, then breathed deeply and lifted. The anvil rose, and the attached log rose with it. Eliam held it up for a few moments, then gently set it down where it had been.

Ben-hail and Darda erupted in applause, but Peresh's mouth fell open and he shook his head in disbelief.

"How could 'e lif' dat?" he muttered. "Just one man!"

Eliam smiled briefly and stepped back, avoiding any display of self-importance or achievement. Then he smiled again and looked quizzically at Ben-hail.

"I suppose so," said Ben-hail, and stepped toward the anvil. He had observed Eliam's placement of his feet and arms carefully and now copied it as best he could. For some reason, he felt that this was an important moment in his life. He did his best to relax and settle his feet and arms comfortably. Then he began to lift. Surprisingly easily, he lifted the anvil until it separated a little from the log it was mounted on, but then the log soaked up all of his momentum and stopped him completely. He knew that he must quickly take the strain and move on to lift the impossible. Every muscle was tense, but nothing seemed to help. He was dashing himself against a rock, breaking himself in failure. As he slid towards despair, he remembered some of the words of advice Eliam had given him. Eliam's words were few and far between, but those he spoke were worth listening to. "Lift through," he had said, and it had taken Ben-hail time to understand what he meant.

The pith of Eliam's maxim was that a lifter must lift as if he is about to succeed. Never lift as if the load is immoveable; and don't try to simply raise the point of contact where your hands or arms touch the load. Instead, picture lifting through the contact point, up into the centre of the weight. Then lift it.

Carefully, Ben-hail lowered the anvil.

There was silence. Peresh was stroking his beard, and Darda wondered for a moment if he saw a fleeting gleam of pleasure in his eyes. Was Peresh pleased that Ben-hail had failed?

Ben-hail wasn't finished, however. He remained in front of the anvil, moving his feet and arms a little to make sure he was best placed to lift. Once it was clear that he was going to try again, Eliam's deep voice said, "Lift through."

A quick smile of acknowledgement, and then Ben-hail did lift through. The anvil lifted and he felt the extra load of the log as he kept lifting. This time, it was just a part of the process. Anvil and log rose together, and once more, Ben-hail had achieved his goal. He stood and felt the vast load, yet felt too his control over it. He recognised the victory of technique over raw, unguided strength; then, gently, he lowered the anvil and set it back in its place.

Darda exploded with cheers and even Eliam was gushing: "Well done," he said, and smiled.

Quickly studying Peresh, Darda saw a little chagrin in his face, although it was quickly hidden as Ben-hail turned and said simply, "Eliam can lift your anvil, Peresh – and so can I."

"Waheb in Suphah, Ben," said Peresh, and the older man was shaking his head as if he couldn't believe the evidence of his eyes. "Waheb in Suphah," he repeated. "How did ye do it, Ben? There's nobody as has ever done it before!"

"But what about you?" laughed Ben-hail. "You've done it too, so that's three!"

"Ah... yes... three. Hmm."

After that, he fell silent, and Ben-hail's smile slowly faded away. Something didn't seem quite right, but he wasn't sure what.

The three friends left soon afterwards, but the parting was a little awkward. Peresh almost appeared to be in shock, and there was none of the celebration Ben-hail had expected.

⅏

Ben-hail's joy at lifting the anvil had reasserted itself by the time the friends arrived at Naphish and Elisheba's house. He knocked on their door and was greeted by his step-father with a big smile – and surprised by a hug to match.

"Ben-hail! Welcome. It's good to see you. Your mother is inside preparing some food for you." He stepped out of the doorway to greet the others as Ben-hail went inside. "Greetings, Darda and Eliam. Welcome to our home. We were very pleased to hear the rest of the news from the Great Tournament. From the results of past Great Tournaments, it seems to me that your achievements – and Kilion's as well – deserve to be legendary, but will probably be forgotten quite quickly."

Eliam smiled his slow smile, but made no comment.

"Never mind! We'll be famous anyway," said Darda. "We know Ben-hail!"

"True. And you'll get to know our king, Jehoshaphat, too. I think he'll end up more famous even than Ben-hail."

"Naphish, you are known as a wise man," said Darda, abruptly changing the subject. "What do you know about Peresh the blacksmith?"

"Your question is a little too vague for me, Darda."

"Can he lift that anvil of his?"

"He might have been able to in the past, but I'm sure that he can't now."

"How do you know?"

"He has a brother, another very strong man who also works as a blacksmith, who visits from time to time. Two years ago, he was passing through Aijalon – arrived late one afternoon and left very early the next morning. I happened to walk past well after sunset, when the streets were empty. The smithy was dark except for a red glow from the embers in the forge. I heard them talking together and could just see the silhouette of two men – Peresh and his brother – carrying the anvil. Obviously Peresh had decided it was time to move it again, as he has occasionally over the years. The next morning, people noticed that the anvil had moved and asked Peresh about it. He refused to say whether he had moved it by himself or not. Nobody seemed to know that his brother had visited."

"Interesting. We stopped in on our way here and Eliam and Ben-hail each lifted his anvil. Peresh looked as if he couldn't believe his eyes, and what he said suggested to me that he has never been able to lift it himself."

"I'm not surprised, but I've never known for sure. He's a good blacksmith, but... Anyway, I'm glad you were able to lift it, Eliam. I'm sure Ben-hail will pay more attention to what you say because of that."

"But how can Ben-hail pay attention when Eliam never says anything?" asked Darda, laughing.

Ben-hail found them all laughing when he came out with Elisheba to invite them in. It was a very happy group that stepped out of the hot sun into the cool darkness of the stone house.

Congratulations flowed freely from both Naphish and Elisheba, and the young men were glad to relax and share a little food and drink after their long morning's walk.

Ben-hail and his friends spent a relaxed week in Aijalon – or mostly so. Their peace was interrupted by a civic reception in which the town honoured the town's greatest ever hero – Ben-hail, the King's Swordsman and winner of the Grand Prize. Darda was also celebrated as a local boy who'd made good, and welcomed as a winner of honours in the Great Tournament along with Eliam.

The friends took the opportunity to help Darda's family with some work around their farm and also spent plenty of time with Naphish and Elisheba. Mother and son spent many hours alone, discussing Raddai: his tragic death, his goals, his aims and beliefs. Ben-hail had an opportunity to think, although at the moment, the extra time was merely accumulating extra questions. How would his father have responded to King Asa's anger, misjudgement and mistakes? His father, who had earned respect from so many people, had apparently been willing to accept the king as God's anointed even when his behaviour had included cruel mistreatment of a messenger of Yahweh. His father had believed that Yahweh was ultimately in control and that misrule by kings would be judged – and terminated if necessary – by God alone.[112] After all, it was said that Yahweh had sent a prophet to tell Jeroboam that he was to become king after the death of Solomon as a result of Solomon's sins.[113]

Was Yahweh really the true God of Israel? If so, shouldn't Ben-hail worship him as his father had done? Could he act as the avenger of blood, killing King Asa as a murderer?[114] Or was the king the ultimate judge in Judah, the final arbiter who answered only to Yahweh?

And did Ben-hail believe in Yahweh as a god who deserved worship anyway?

Darda watched him carefully, and Ben-hail would have been shocked if he had realised how much his friend saw of his thoughts and questions. For Darda, there was no doubt that Yahweh had chosen Israel as his people, led them out of Egypt, given them the land of Canaan and cared for them since that time. However, he knew that his friend had doubts, driven, he was sure, by the tragic situation of his father – a father he had never known.

Elisheba could not abandon her hatred of King Asa either. The very idea felt like a rejection of her first husband, a complete erasure of his memory. Her marriage to Naphish had only strengthened that conviction. Yet the recent news that King Jehoshaphat had re-opened Raddai's case, arriving when she was in a gentler mood following her marriage, had softened her determination.

A week after the friends' arrival, an unexpected cavalcade approached Aijalon from the direction of the capital. The leaders of the town and its military garrison had been warned beforehand, but the rest

---

[112] For example, Saul (1 Samuel 9:15-17; 10:1; 15:1-3, 17-29). David was anointed to replace Saul, but refused to kill him himself, leaving that up to God (1 Samuel 26:8-11).
[113] 1 Kings 11:29-38
[114] Numbers 35:16-21

of the populace only gradually became aware that royalty was visiting.

By the time Queen Azubah's attendants entered the gate, the walls were lined with interested onlookers and the city elders were standing by to welcome her and her brother, who attended her.

Another civic reception ensued and the visitors were welcomed with pomp. Once the reception was over, Azubah and a few attendants left the rest of their party and were led to Naphish and Elisheba's home.

Naphish and Elisheba met her at the door, dressed in their best clothes, having been warned a short time earlier of the great honour they were being accorded. Elisheba had hurriedly cleaned the house and done her best to ready it for royalty, but in the end had thrown up her hands and turned her mind instead to providing a meal that might make up in quantity what it lacked in exotic quality. At the last minute, Naphish had taken over that task and hurried her into changing her clothes instead, ready to welcome the visitor.

"Why is she coming?" she asked Naphish breathlessly as she worked.

"It will be to do with Raddai's imprisonment and death," he said; then, seeing her doubtful, even fearful, reaction, he laid his hand on her arm and added, "but don't worry: it can only be good news."

Azubah greeted them warmly and asked if she could enter their home. She was not, she said, quite as young as they and would appreciate the opportunity to sit down.

Naphish invited her in and offered her a chair, then, sensing that she would like to talk to Elisheba alone, offered to leave them. She smiled and thanked him, and he left.

"Now, my dear," said Azubah, "I've come to tell you how sorry I am about the terrible misunderstanding that led to your first husband's death. From what I have been told, Raddai was a good man, a good Levite, and a good husband."

"Yes, my lady," said Elisheba, a little overwhelmed by this introduction, "he was all of those things."

"But it wasn't only a misunderstanding, it was an injustice. Though your husband was a faithful subject of Judah, he died under punishment that I would prefer nobody ever to suffer."

"I don't know what to say, my lady. Raddai was faithful and I still believe that he would have forgiven those who brought about his death." She chose her words carefully, remembering that Azubah's gracious words were intended to give comfort where they could, but would never go so far as to directly criticise her husband, the king.

"My son continues to pursue the investigation into what went wrong, and what part traitors may have played in this. He is confident now that Vophsi and Nezib are both traitors. Apparently Vophsi has long used his position and the location of his academy to provide our enemies with information about troop movements and armaments. He's done rather well out of it until now, too. Now, retribution will come to him – the sort of retribution that we women won't want to know about."

The two women continued to talk; Azubah leading the conversation, but doing her best to answer Elisheba's unspoken questions and soothe her years of suffering.

Elisheba was surprised at how gently the queen treated her, and the sympathy she expressed for the hardships of a mother working without the support of a father. Azubah also conveyed her son Jehoshaphat's admiration for Ben-hail, and his satisfaction that the King's Swordsman would be a bodyguard without peer.

Noting a sudden flicker of concern in Elisheba's eyes at that, Azubah made a mental note to remind Jehoshaphat again that he needed to make certain of Ben-hail's loyalty before allowing him to be armed in the king's presence. A man whose father had died unjustly under the king's punishment had good reason to question his loyalty; however, she knew Jehoshaphat was confident that the clearing of Raddai's name would be sufficient to repair the damage.

After a lengthy conversation, the queen partook briefly of the offered feast, then took her leave, content that she had achieved several of her goals. Justice was closer to being done, and a suffering wife and mother had received some of the sympathy she deserved. It was also a pleasing thought that the risk to the kingdom from rebels and traitors had probably been reduced by her son's attention to this injustice.

The two women parted in friendship and understanding.

Chapter 25

THE BOOK OF THE LAW

"Your majesty," said Jehoiada the priest, "when you were younger, I showed you the Book of the Law of Yahweh."

Jehoiada had requested an interview with the king and Jehoshaphat had granted his request.

"Yes, you did. And I read quite a lot of it, too."

"I don't know whether you remember, but God included a few instructions particularly for kings. If you will allow me to mention it, sire, now that you are king, they will apply to you."

Jehoiada was convinced that a king would rule better if he paid attention to *one specific command* given by Moses, and he was determined to tell Jehoshaphat so early in his reign.

"Now that you mention it, I do remember you showing me those rules when I was much younger, Jehoiada." Jehoshaphat laughed and continued, "I must admit, though, what I remember most was that Solomon the Wise seemed to *break* them all."

"You're right, and it's easy to see that now," said Jehoiada earnestly, "but I wonder if he saw it at the time? I'm sure that if he had obeyed the rule I'm about to read to you, he would have done better. This, my lord, is one of Moses' rules specifically for the king:

"And when he sits on the throne of his kingdom, he shall write for himself in a book a copy of this law, approved by the Levitical priests."[115]

"Ah, yes... I do recall reading that. But how am I meant to find time to do it? Could I get a scribe to write it for me? I never seem to have enough time to do all the work I already need to do as king."

"If you consider the words, my lord, I think you'll have to conclude that God meant you to do the writing yourself. 'Write for *himself*' are the words."

---

[115] Deuteronomy 17:18

"I suppose so, but how can I do it? There's no time. I'm already so busy I don't have enough time to sleep. There are some advantages in being poor, you know: many of the poor in my kingdom can't afford oil for lights or candles, so they can only work during daylight. I can have candles and lights everywhere, so I never have time to sleep!"

"True, sire. Many benefits have corresponding problems. Can you remember what else the king is to do with that Book of the Law, my lord?"

"He had to read it, didn't he?"

"Yes, my lord. Moses wrote:

"And it shall be with him, and he shall read in it all the days of his life, that he may learn to fear the Lord his God by keeping all the words of this law and these statutes, and doing them, that his heart may not be lifted up above his brothers, and that he may not turn aside from the commandment, either to the right hand or to the left, so that he may continue long in his kingdom, he and his children, in Israel."[116]

" 'All the days of his life.' Does that mean the king must have a habit of reading God's law as long as he lives – you know, just every so often – or that he should read it *every day?*" In those last two words Jehoshaphat's voice was filled almost with horror, and Jehoiada did his best not to smile. The old man was hopeful that in Jehoshaphat Judah was blessed with a king whose godliness could stand out in history. Nevertheless, the job would never be easy.

"You may like to get a second opinion, sire, but I believe that it means you should read it every day, and that that should be your habit all the days of your life. The longest Psalm – by your ancestor, King David – says, 'Oh, how I love your law! It is my meditation all the day.'[117] Obviously King David must have had that law and read it every day."

"I suppose you're right – but still, how do I fit it in with all of the other things I have to do? If only being a king was all sitting on thrones and feasting! It would be much easier."

"With respect, my lord, if that's all being a king meant, we wouldn't need one."

"True, true."

"I brought you a scroll of the Book of the Law for you to copy, if you want to, sire."

"If I want to? Is that how you view it, Jehoiada?"

"No, my lord – but it is not for me to give you orders. God commands you and me alike."

---

[116] Deuteronomy 17:19-20
[117] Psalm 119:97. The Bible does not say who wrote this Psalm, but King David seems a likely candidate.

"And somehow I need to find enough time in my day to obey God's commands. I'm afraid that it might have to wait until I'm more used to being king, though. Maybe things will get easier as I become more familiar with them. I'll see."

By the time Ben-hail and his three friends arrived in Jerusalem, the investigation into Raddai's imprisonment was over, and for Ben-hail, the news couldn't have been better.

Raddai was completely exonerated. Nezib, the old singer, had been tracked down and admitted to writing the original letter. He argued that it was an expression of justifiable, righteous anger at the wrongful imprisonment of Hanani – for which justice had never been served. Had that been all Nezib was guilty of, Jehoshaphat might have quietly freed him, but wider investigations had quickly turned up plenty of evidence that he had recently been involved in many activities against the king that were far more aggressive than just sending letters. When they questioned Uriel, the failed assassin – still languishing in the king's dungeons – the young man admitted that Nezib had been the mastermind of the plot, including the clever ploy to distract the king's guards with his singing. While Nezib's actions might originally have sprung from a godly base, they had long since branched out into other, far less innocent areas, including earning money by helping Vophsi report troop numbers and movements to Israel and other aggressive neighbours.

Jehoshaphat had both men executed for treason.

King Asa heard of the investigation and its results, and was convinced that, yes, Raddai's treatment had been unjust. He was willing to leave any restitution in his son's hands. Jehoshaphat suspected that his father would have gladly thrown Nezib into the dungeons on the basis of the letter alone, so, in a sense, he was pleased to have evidence of worse wrongdoing.

Hanani the prophet, meanwhile, remained in prison – but very few realised that he was still alive.

Gershom, the commander of the army, felt that Jehoshaphat's exoneration of Raddai had reduced the danger of attack from one quarter at least; nevertheless, he was pleased at the opportunity provided by the Great Tournament to refresh the king's special corps with younger blood, especially now that there were two kings to protect. Several competition-winning soldiers had joined Jehoshaphat's bodyguard immediately after the tournament, and were already protecting the king. A number of older soldiers in King Asa's bodyguard felt a strong loyalty to the old king and wanted to continue to attend him whenever he left his room, although this was becoming increasingly rare. Asa's diseased feet continued to worsen and were quickly approaching the condition the Royal Doctor had said they must reach before he could begin his special treatment that would reverse the progress of the disease. Other doctors ridiculed his suggestions, but the king clung to his promises rather than face the unwelcome prognosis presented by a slew of other medics. The time of judgement was almost upon them: the time when the Royal Doctor would either earn his preferential treatment, or warrant the ridicule of his peers.

Ben-hail, Darda, Eliam and Kilion were all to join the king's special forces, and when they arrived in the capital, they were welcomed by Oded, the head of those forces.

"You've made an impressive start, men," he said, "but now comes the real test. With us, you won't just be protecting the border of the kingdom – you'll be protecting its heart. In Ephraim, kings are betrayed, killed and replaced often. Just imagine having a king who lasted only seven days![118] Here in Judah, our kings are descendants of David: God's true anointed king. We've never had a king assassinated, and our third king is still alive. Do you know how many kings they've had in Ephraim?"

"Seven – or eight," answered Darda; "depending on whether you count Tibni when he was sort of king at the same time as Omri."[119]

"Yes, well done," said Oded, looking impressed. "You're Darda, aren't you?"

Darda nodded and Oded continued.

"So even if we ignore Tibni, they're already up to their seventh king – and from four different families! Here in Judah, we stay faithful. We stick to Yahweh, and his anointed king. And it's up to you lads to make sure that no crazy maniac is ever given the slightest opportunity to attack our king. Earlier this year, there was an attempt that could have succeeded if we hadn't had some good luck. I won't go into details: the guards, your new comrades, were extremely embarrassed by it all, and it's one of the reasons why we've been looking for new, gifted soldiers, like you, to join the forces. But ability alone isn't enough. We'll be training you to recognise dangers and demanding that when you are on the job, you concentrate like you've never concentrated before. All the time.

"You'll be part of the king's special forces in the city:[120] the Guardsmen Executioners[121] and the Couriers.[122] Over time, you may rise in the

---

[118] Zimri reigned for seven days (1 Kings 16:15-20).

[119] 1 Kings 16:21-22

[120] In David's time, it appears that his special forces were the Cherethites, the Pelethites and the mighty men (2 Samuel 20:7).

[121] A combination of two possible meanings of the name "Cherethites".

[122] A possible meaning of the name "Pelethites".

ranks, and perhaps even to become one of their senior leaders."[123]

Oded consulted the list he was carrying and said, "Ben-hail, the King's Swordsman, and now also to be the King's Armour-bearer, is joining the Guardsmen Executioners. And yes," he added, looking them over grimly, "sometimes, they do have to be executioners. When Solomon had some enemies to dispose of, he used the chief of the Guardsmen Executioners himself to do the job – my predecessor from many years ago. Do you know who that was?"

"Benaiah, the son of Jehoiada,"[124] said Ben-hail immediately.

"Yes! Right again. You lads really do know your stuff."

Winning Benaiah's exalted position had been one of Ben-hail's boyhood dreams, before his desire for revenge had led him towards more subversive ideas. Now, that goal was reviving, thanks to Jehoshaphat's review of his father's case.

ℛ

Before Ben-hail arrived in Jerusalem, Jehoshaphat had consulted with Gershom and Jehoiada about him. He observed that a king's armour-bearer must be completely trustworthy and asked them to keep an eye out for any indication that Ben-hail's loyalty might be compromised. But he also reminded them of the unjust treatment of Ben-hail's father, despite his faithful service and godliness, and explained that, as a result, he did not want to exclude Ben-hail from service unless there was clear evidence that his loyalty was suspect.

Jehoiada had suggested that, in view of his family background as a Levite, Ben-hail should spend time with the temple gatekeepers as well and learn a little of their responsibilities. That would give Jehoiada an opportunity to get to know him better. Gershom agreed, and Ben-hail was introduced to the priest shortly after his arrival.

"You are Raddai's son," said Jehoiada when they met. "You look quite a lot like him."

"Yes, sir."

"Your father was a righteous man – and a hard worker. It was a tragedy that he should have died because of the false witness of a traitor."

"Yes, sir. I am glad that the truth finally came out."

"It normally does, Ben-hail. I'm always amazed how often God helps us to catch evil people."

"Well, in this case, if I hadn't saved Nezib a few years ago when he was attacked by some troublemakers in Aijalon, he wouldn't have been alive to get caught for what he did!"

---

[123] A possible meaning of the name "Carites" (2 Kings 11:4, 19).
[124] 2 Samuel 8:18; 20:23; 1 Chronicles 18:17

"Did you really?"

"Yes, I did. It's just an interesting coincidence."

"I don't believe much in coincidences. God orders events as he wishes, and he helps people who behave in a godly way. After all, helping to protect an old man is the sort of work God wants his people to do."

"I don't know, sir," said Ben-hail in an expressionless voice. Jehoiada watched him shrewdly.

"Maybe you're wondering why your father died as he did. I didn't know him well, but I do know that he was an enthusiastic and reliable worker in the temple. He was always eager to help people in their worship, and he had an excellent knowledge of the law." Jehoiada looked at Ben-hail in sympathy. "It really is unfortunate that you couldn't have met him. You would have admired him. However, you can still try to be like him if you want to."

"I don't know about that either. I've spent many years feeling sort of confused about my dad."

"Well, at least now you can be sure that no-one will be suggesting your father was a traitor, so that's good."

"It is. And my mother will be so happy too. I think my dad would've been glad that I will be able to help keep King Jehoshaphat safe."

"I'm sure that he would, although he might also have liked you to work in the temple as a Levite – as he did himself."

"Yes, my mother says that he would have liked that. Maybe sometime I can do something like that: do God's work and keep everybody happy."

"Oh, I wouldn't be so sure about that, young man! We just got news that Elijah the prophet is being called a traitor in Israel because he delivered a message from God to King Ahab."

"How's that?"

"Apparently Elijah announced to the king that there won't be any rain in Israel until he says so."

"So how does that make him a traitor?"

"Israel is a funny place. King Ahab has a foreign queen called Jezebel. She's from Sidon and she hates Yahweh. She's been trying to kill off all of his prophets for a few years now. If anyone follows Yahweh, she declares him a traitor."

"Do Elijah's prophecies ever come true?"

"They do – but we'll have to wait and see about this one. It's big."

"Would a drought in Israel affect us here in Judah?"

"I'm afraid we'll have to wait and see."

The friends spent three months in training, learning the basic work of both the Guardsmen Executioners and the Couriers, in preparation for their specific assignments. The Couriers were the king's messenger service, carrying the necessary messages from the capital to the forces spread throughout the kingdom. Donkeys were used whenever possible, but many messages were carried by runners, particularly at times when the roads were crowded or degraded due to winter weather. Being a superb runner, Kilion was to join the Couriers, and they would have liked to claim Ben-hail too, but his appointment as the King's Armour-bearer was already decided. It was during the time spent learning the methods of and reasons for carrying messages that Darda's particularly unusual ability came to light – an ability that the chief of the Couriers couldn't quite decide whether to consider a blessing or a danger.

Early in the training, before they had been taught about keeping a scroll dry in wet weather, Darda was given a message and instructed to carry it to the quartermaster at a camp in the south of Judah. As he ran, though, the first rain of the season fell and, despite his care, the scroll became damp, the ink spreading and smudging. By the time he arrived, it was unreadable.

Fortunately, it was not a sealed scroll, and Darda was able to tell the quartermaster exactly what the message had been – word for word. The official pursed his lips and looked at him thoughtfully. He rinsed off the ink, then dried the scroll and wrote a new message. This he sealed and packed in a leather pouch to protect it from any rain that might fall.

When Darda handed the pouch to the chief of the Couriers, he took out the scroll, broke the seal and read the message.

"Hmm," he said. "So you can remember what you read?"

"Yes, sir."

"That is good and bad. Normally, a messenger does not need to know the message. In fact, most of our messages are sealed to make sure that they are not tampered with. Your message wasn't sealed, and it wasn't even rolled up when I gave it to you, so there is nothing wrong with what you did. But I need to know: how well can you do this trick?"

"I remember whatever I read, sir."

"Everything?"

"I think so."

"For how long?"

"I don't think I have forgotten anything recent, sir."

"And what about things that you hear?"

"I remember them too."

"So can you remember what your mother said to you when you were... say, three years old?"

"No, sir, not everything. I remember some things from then, but my continuous memory starts when I was about seven years old."

"And you remember everything that anyone has ever said to you since then?"

"Yes, sir, I believe so."

"And what about the things you have said?"

"Yes, sir."

"And what you have read?"

"Yes. That's easier, sir."

"Phew! Well, you could make a very valuable messenger at times. We had intended that you and Eliam would join the Guardsmen Executioners along with Ben-hail, but now I see that you should join the Couriers instead. When you do, Darda, make sure you don't read the messages you carry – unless you are told to do so."

"Very good, sir."

CR

As Ben-hail's training progressed, Gershom and Jehoiada became more and more convinced that he was no traitor, and they reported their conviction to King Jehoshaphat.

The complete exoneration of his father had certainly helped to overcome his doubts, and so many Levites and temple gatekeepers had shared fond memories of his father that it was a happier, more open and relaxed young man who was finally ready to begin his daily work for King Jehoshaphat.

Four armed soldiers always stood behind Jehoshaphat's throne, and it had been arranged for Ben-hail and his teacher to join them for a week to allow Ben-hail to learn the protocols of the throne room and how his new master would want him to act in different situations.

So it happened that he was standing behind the king with the other guards when Jehoiada, having plucked up his courage and requested another audience with the king, spoke to him a second time about the Book of the Law.

"I've noticed that you haven't given me back the Book of the Law, my lord. If you don't mind me asking, how have you gone with copying it?"

"I haven't copied it yet. I started, but writing is so slow and the Book of the Law is a big book. But I've been reading the scroll you gave me every day, so that's what Moses would have wanted anyway."

"How many times have you read it, sire?"

"You're really asking questions, aren't you? Checking up on me! Are you the royal supervisor? If you…"

Jehoiada fell on his knees and said quickly, "My lord, I am neither your conscience nor your master. I am your humble servant. You are king, and you must choose your own path. But I am also a humble servant of Yahweh, one of his priests, and as such it is my responsibility to try to help you."

Jehoshaphat breathed deeply, and then sighed.

"You're right, Jehoiada. Well, I have not yet finished reading the Book of the Law, and that's probably the point you are making – on God's behalf. If I can't finish reading a scroll in more than three months, then I need to commit more time to reading it. And maybe if I do so, I won't react as I started to. Oh, Solomon was right about the difficulties of being king over the people of God. It takes more wisdom than I feel I have."

"If you walk humbly with God, you will always be a good king, my lord."

"Can I ask you a question, Jehoiada?"

"Of course, sire."

"Were you afraid of me when you asked your first question just now?"

"Yes."

"Were you afraid that I might react very badly, maybe even imprison you?"

"Yes, sire."

King Jehoshaphat sighed again, then said, "Thank you."

Chapter 26

New Directions

"Your belt looks splendid, Ben-hail," said Jehoshaphat.

"Thank you, sir," responded his armour-bearer.

The newly woven belt had been presented by Gershom to Ben-hail that morning in recognition of his victory as The King's Swordsman. Prepared by the royal weaver, its golden threads spelled out his name and his achievements in the Great Tournament on a background of purple.

"I hope that you can add more victories to the list in future."

"Thank you, sir. I hope that I can help to keep you safe as your kingdom grows ever greater."

By that time, the king knew Ben-hail well enough to be confident that such words were a pledge of loyalty he could fully rely on. Gershom and Jehoiada had each reported separately that Ben-hail was known for his honesty and that he would keep silence in preference to making a commitment he was not willing to keep.

King Jehoshaphat smiled and replied, "Thank you, Ben-hail."

℧

Ben-hail was settling in to his changed life. He revelled in the admiration and respect accorded him as the King's Swordsman and a trusted guard of the king.

A king's bodyguard sees much of both the internal workings of the kingdom and the attitudes of its king. Ben-hail quickly developed a great respect for King Jehoshaphat as a dedicated, hard-working ruler. King Asa had prepared his son well to lead the kingdom, and Judah was reaping the reward. Before long, Ben-hail also became convinced that the king's religion was not a pretence, and this helped him to reconsider his own inherited profession as a Levite.

He enjoyed King Jehoshaphat's friendly attitude – although at first he wondered if it was prompted only by a feeling of guilt. Perhaps it was, but whatever the reason, Jehoshaphat was engagingly open with his new armour-bearer, and the two soon found shared enjoyment in their conversation. Both men were forward-thinking – able to see a goal and work towards it with determination – and each saw attitudes to be admired and learned from in the other. Before long, they were often seen in conversation whenever breaks in the timetable of the royal court or delays in the roster of judgements permitted.

Ben-hail was intrigued by the variety of questions King Jehoshaphat was asked, and sometimes he found it hard to see the reasoning behind the answers the king and his advisors gave. When Jehoshaphat observed that he was genuinely interested, he began to explain some of his decisions to Ben-hail. He found the young man a ready learner, and after a time the two began to play a game. Ben-hail would listen to the questions and all of the background information presented to the king and decide what his own answers would be. After each decision had been presented to the supplicant, the king would often ask him whether he had come to the same conclusion. At first, the answer was often a confused, "No", but over time he grew able to predict the outcome more accurately as he better understood the basis of the decisions.

"What did you think of that case, Ben-hail?" Jehoshaphat asked one day after the elders of Ramah sent a delegation asking permission to build a new high place in the centre of their town. "How would you have responded?"

"Well, sir, I must admit that I would have acceded to their request. Their argument that this was a cultural matter, not a religious one, seemed convincing to me."

"But they didn't even believe it themselves!" laughed Jehoshaphat. "Otherwise, they wouldn't have been asking for permission at all! I have not forbidden them from building cultural or practical items, perhaps a stone bench for the citizens to relax on, or a shelter for tired travellers. But, no, this was a high place. A place for worship. Perhaps it would even have started off being used for the worship of Yahweh."

"Then what was wrong with that?"

"You are a Levite, Ben-hail. Where does God say that we should worship him?"

"In the temple."

"Yes, in Jerusalem. And we are not to build altars in other places."

"Oh. Yes, I suppose I do remember that rule, now that you mention it."

"They were trying me out, Ben-hail. Testing me to see if I would let them work around my restrictions on high places. And if I had let them, I would suddenly be overrun with requests to build 'cultural' items on high places everywhere."

"I guess so."

"At least they feel that they have to ask," said Jehoshaphat. "That's encouraging."

Over time, Ben-hail noticed that the cases Jehoshaphat chose to explain seemed to all have aspects related to the Law of Moses, and he was surprised to find that he still remembered many of the matters of law that had been taught him as he grew up in Aijalon – despite his resistance at the time to his father's calling.

Jehoshaphat's interest in the law was contagious, and Ben-hail soon found himself eagerly trying to learn more of the law he had once despised. The king even began, tongue in cheek, to call Ben-hail his Armed Advisor, which dismayed Ben-hail for a time; overall, though, he enjoyed the opportunity to see how a king rules.

Nevertheless, he missed the open air and the hard physical work of training. His mornings no longer began with early morning runs in the hills surrounding Abiel's Academy, and he found that he missed them. Physical activity had always been a major part of his life, and he soon began to feel that he was losing his edge as day followed day of inactivity.

Yet how could he complain when the king treated him with such kindness?

Coincidentally, it was Abiel who brought the matter out into the open and also suggested a solution.

Jehoshaphat had been very pleased with the masterful way in which Abiel had arranged the Great Tournament, and impressed with the amazingly high concentration of successful competitors his academy had produced. In consultation with Gershom, Jehoshaphat had called Abiel to Jerusalem for an audience.

Ben-hail was standing behind the king as usual when he heard the guard at the door announce Abiel's name. Had he not been well-schooled in maintaining an expressionless face, he would have looked at Jehoshaphat in surprise.

Abiel entered the room, looking lithe and fit as usual, and Ben-hail couldn't help wondering whether he looked so fit himself after his months of enforced inactivity – and how he would fare in a bout with his old instructor now.

"Abiel, welcome to Jerusalem," said Jehoshaphat.

"Thank you, your majesty," responded Abiel.

"I called you here because I want to have a quick review of the Great Tournament, its arrangements, and any further acknowledgements or rewards that should arise from it. You will know already that Vophsi and Nezib were executed for their treason, and you have been successfully running both your training academy and Vophsi's ever since."

"Thank you, sire."

"The results in the Great Tournament from students of your academy were outstanding. You are obviously an exceptional commander."

"Thank you again, sire. I do my best. However, I am sure that other academies would also achieve great results if they applied the training regime we agreed to trial. The other academies which applied *some* of those methods also achieved much better and more consistent results than many expected."

"Are you saying that yours was the only academy that really gave the new methods a fair trial?"

"I wouldn't put it that way, my lord, but I know that all of the other commanders who were asked to apply those methods were a little concerned that they might not be completely successful, and therefore they tried to use a mixture of old and new. Their improved results show that these new methods can help, even if we only use some of them. The results from my academy show that a wide application of methods that aim to improve both skill and fitness will have a great effect."

"So, my armour-bearer here is just the product of a good training regime?"

Abiel smiled. "No, sir," he said. "He has God-given talents that have been honed by good training. In fact, over the last few months before the Great Tournament, he took the methods we were using and extended them even further. He became fitter than anyone else in the camp and concentrated on developing his skills more than anyone else did. Ben-hail is the greatest example of the success of the methods, but you saw that many other students from our academy were also successful beyond expectations."

"That's true."

"Imagine an entire army trained in the same way, my lord! None of our enemies could stand before us. When we direct our efforts towards developing God's gifts, the results are amazing."

"Yet surely the greatest victories in the past have occurred when individual heroes have triumphed. Isn't that true?"

"Yes, you are right, sire. Your ancestor David and his mighty men showed that. Even your father, King Asa, won a battle through his faith. Nevertheless, he also had a massive army, though we were badly outnumbered. Yet when the king acknowledged God's contribution to the battle, his success was guaranteed."

"And I suppose that David was an expert with the sling before ever he met Goliath. So we need to provide the best we can, then leave the rest up to Yahweh, our God."

"And keeping our army fit and skilful is part of doing the best we can."

"The whole army?"

"Yes. It's fine to start with the academies, but the whole army needs to stay fit and maintain their skill. It's no use having them standing around getting slow and fat."

"Like Ben-hail here?" asked Jehoshaphat, jokingly.

Abiel smiled, but answered seriously, "He's not exactly fat, my lord, but, at the same time, he doesn't look as fit as he did six months ago."

"Hmm. I was intending to appoint you as chief over all of our military academies, but now I'm having second thoughts."

"You don't approve of my suggestions, sir?"

"On the contrary, Abiel. I'm now wondering if I need you supervising the training of the entire army!" He turned and looked at his armour-bearer. "What do you think, Ben-hail?"

"I have been trained by Abiel and know that his methods work, sire," said Ben-hail. "And he is right about my fitness now."

"So my bodyguards need more exercise too?"

"Yes, sire. At least, I know that I do."

"Then how will they ever have time to work as bodyguards?"

"Maybe Abiel has some ideas about that, sire."

"Do you, Abiel?" asked Jehoshaphat.

"Yes, sire. The trainers and tutors in my academy have time allocated so that they can do their own personal training as well as their work of teaching the students. As a result, they have more physical training in the academy than they ever did as soldiers, and most of them appreciate it. Most believe that it allows them to do their work better. After all, there is little use selecting experts to protect you if they lose their skill and fitness before the threat strikes."

The discussion continued, and Jehoshaphat was convinced by Abiel's words. In the end, it was arranged that Abiel was to take over the training of the Couriers and Guardsmen Executioners for two months as a trial, while he trained their officers in his methods. After that, he would take over as head of the military academies across the kingdom, but continue to have a wider input on training for Jehoshaphat's army.

The result of this interview was that Ben-hail was once again able to enjoy the effects of training and to further refine his martial skills – a process he revelled in. The time spent in physical activity removed the frustration he had been feeling at all the time spent standing around. Extra men were added to the king's bodyguard to protect the king during the hours his existing bodyguard spent in training.

However, the changes to his life were not over.

A few months later, Jehoshaphat suggested that Ben-hail should spend time becoming more familiar with the law of Yahweh and the work of a Levite. Although he felt it was too early to spell it out, the king had a plan for his armour-bearer, should the kingdom remain peaceful. From that time on, Ben-hail's time was split three ways, and he found his life following a path he could never have imagined.

Guarding the king grew more and more enjoyable as Jehoshaphat continued to include him in conversations about the kingdom and the law. Slowly, haltingly, a small seed of faith began to sprout in the young man whose anger and bitterness had frozen it out for so long.

Outside Judah, conditions were changing.

The drought predicted by the prophet Elijah struck with a vengeance in the north. As Elijah had promised, the rains failed and the crops blew away in the dust. Water became more and more scarce, and people and animals alike began to suffer.

Israel's old king Omri died. He had already passed over the kingship to his son Ahab some years earlier, and Ahab was rapidly building a name for himself as the most idolatrous of all the kings of Israel.

He took many wives for himself, but one stood out from the rest as the hand that truly guided the kingdom – and its king. Her name was Jezebel, and she was the daughter of Ethbaal, the king of the Sidonians.[125] Perhaps the match had been intended as a smart diplomatic move, but when Jezebel arrived in the capital, she quickly bewitched her husband and carved out for herself a position of great power in the kingdom. Ahab was not naturally as bad as she, but he was very open to being egged on. Jezebel took every opportunity to egg him on, leading him into more and more idolatry. She also grasped every opportunity to blame any problem in the kingdom on the followers of Yahweh. The drought seemed the perfect chance, and she seized on it with enthusiasm. Elijah was a prophet, so she mercilessly slaughtered every prophet of Yahweh that she could find. Perhaps she was looking for Elijah – but if so, she didn't find him. Ahab did nothing to stop this, although there were rumours that some of his servants were using inside information to whisk prophets into hiding when they heard of planned arrests. Did the news come from Ahab?

Jezebel, meanwhile, was building up her own collection of idolatrous prophets – hundreds and hundreds of them – all living on the king's silver.

As conditions changed, Judah also ceased to be the target of attacks from her neighbours. Traitors like Vophsi were no longer providing useful intelligence, and Jehoshaphat's actions had placated much of the anger of the enemies within.

---

[125] 1 Kings 16:31

In Judah, King Asa was declining. The disease in his feet was still worsening and the Royal Doctor's revolutionary "cure" had done nothing to stay its progress or reduce the king's suffering.

His fellow medics reminded anyone who would listen that they had all predicted this and that the erstwhile Royal Doctor was nothing but a charlatan. However, their triumph won them no favour from a king who wanted healing, not haughty reminders.

Jehoshaphat watched sadly and did his best to provide doctors who could comfort his father. Nothing worked.

King Asa had little to do with the running of the kingdom now, yet Jehoshaphat still felt somewhat constrained. Soon, the reign of the great King Asa would come to an end and new opportunities would arise. In the meantime, why look for confrontation or upset an old man unnecessarily?

"Honour your father and mother," said the law.[126]

Hanani the prophet remained in prison.

---

[126] Exodus 20:12; Deuteronomy 5:16

Chapter 27

ALL THE CITIES OF JUDAH

"Miriam is quite pretty, isn't she?" said Jehoshaphat to Ben-hail, one morning.

"If you say so, sire," replied Ben-hail, awkwardly. The other guards standing with him behind the king's throne tried to hide their smiles.

"Why, what would you say instead?"

"I have never seen anyone more lovely, my lord."

"Would you like to marry her?"

"Of course! Who wouldn't? But she is from a noble family, and I'm not."

"I am told that she loves you and would be happy to marry you."

"Really?"

"Yes. A king can ask many questions that others would not dare! When I noticed her looking at you throughout the feast last night, I asked her father about her. He told me that she is 'a sorry case' who has had eyes for no-one but the king's armour-bearer for many months."

"I... I... don't...," stammered Ben-hail.

Jehoshaphat laughed and asked once more, "So, would you like to marry her?"

"Yes," said Ben-hail.

"I'm sure that the two of you will be very happy together if you keep your admiration for each other alive. You should go and speak to her father this evening. Arrange it now, then you can concentrate on preparing for the Great Tournament without the uncertainty."

○ʀ

Almost two years had passed since Ben-hail won the title of King's Swordsman, and once again it was time for the Great Tournament. After Abiel's outstanding success two years earlier, he had again been given the task of managing the Great Tournament.

If possible, every aspect of the tournament was even better this time. It was acclaimed by spectators and competitors alike, although this time Abiel's old academy claimed far fewer victories. Yet Abiel considered even that a success, because it reflected the fact that now *all* of the king's academies were concentrating on developing their students' fitness and skills. The same training methods were slowly spreading through the army too, and the results were amazing. Throughout the tournament, spectators never stopped commenting on the endurance of the runners, the skill of the archers, the strength of the climbers and the frightening speed of the swordsmen. Judah's army was quickly becoming a formidable enemy.

Nevertheless, Ben-hail still stood out from all the other competitors, despite their improved skills. For a second time, he won the Grand Prize, and this time the monetary reward for winning the prize was much greater, reflecting Jehoshaphat's wish to improve both the standard and size of his army.

Ben-hail was presented to the nation as a perfect example of a soldier in the king's new army, and watching him inspired many young men to join the army themselves. Ben-hail had been surprised by his fame after the last Great Tournament, but this time he found that he could not walk anywhere without hearing his name on the lips of perfect strangers, often in the form of awed whispers from young boys who looked up at him in open admiration. It was embarrassing.

As the tournament progressed, he won competition after competition, until finally it was time for his favourite event: the sword-fighting. Since the king had adopted Abiel's suggestions about training, Ben-hail had been able to spend much more time concentrating on developing his skills with the sword, and he was satisfied that he had improved again.

In practice, he often fought without a shield, and at times carried a dagger instead, setting himself the challenge of touching his opponent's breastplate with his dagger rather than his sword. For him, it was the ultimate challenge of skill and speed, moving so far inside his opponent's guard without ever being touched by the man's defence. It demanded not only perfect timing, but also the ability to change his line of attack instantaneously.

Very occasionally – and it was easiest when fighting without either shield or dagger – he would unexpectedly swap his sword into his left hand if he sensed a valuable opportunity. During the final of the sword-fighting in the Great Tournament, this tactic allowed him to make the first touch on his opponent's breastplate early in the fight. All of the watching experts – except Abiel – had shaken their heads when they saw that the defending champion was not carrying a shield in the final. Despite his acknowledged skill, they considered it far too risky. Nevertheless, that first touch unsettled his opponent so that the man moved tentatively, giving Ben-hail several easy opportunities to touch his breastplate. Ben-hail took those opportunities masterfully, and in a remarkably short time, the bout was over and the crowds were again chanting Ben-hail's name. For the second time, Jehoshaphat congratulated him on the royal platform as the King's Swordsman, but this time he greeted him as a familiar associate – even a friend.

Ben-hail married the lovely Miriam shortly afterwards, her noble father, Nethanel, having given them his blessing – well pleased to have such a famous soldier as his son-in-law.

The king's armour-bearer was popular with the people, and his influence in the king's court was growing too. Although not yet rich, he had been well rewarded for his success in two Great Tournaments. He was able to look back on the poverty of his childhood almost as a fading memory. Yet he never forgot what poverty was like, nor the situation that had caused it. Though devoted to King Jehoshaphat, and able to feel some sympathy for King Asa in his suffering, he could not altogether banish the picture of his innocent father dying in Asa's dungeon.

He remained a cautious young man in his social dealings: easy to get on with, but not so easy to get to know well. Yet for those who got to know him well, the time spent was worth the effort, for he was strongly loyal and never forgot a friend.

His three former tent-mates were each achieving their own success in Jehoshaphat's army, and had again performed well in the Great Tournament. Eliam's strength was still unequalled, while Kilion's speed and endurance in running had only been eclipsed by Ben-hail. Darda had shown his skill with a sword, but once again, had lost his semi-final, this time to the man whom Ben-hail had so easily bested in the final. Most agreed that Darda would have performed much better in the final had he reached it, but he laughed at such suggestions, acknowledging that his opponent had beaten him fair and square, and that it wouldn't have mattered anyway – he could never have beaten Ben-hail!

Darda had also been recognised as a trustworthy messenger who could be relied on to deliver wise advice as well as a timely message. There was even talk of his being made an aide to Ladan, Jehoshaphat's wisest but ageing advisor, who needed younger legs to do some of his work. Ladan always kept an eye open for young men who might have the potential to become royal advisors, and Darda had caught his attention.

 endCR

As the first rains of autumn came to Jerusalem, the great king Asa died. He had held fast to his faith in Yahweh to the very end, worshipping him fervently – which was why it seemed so strange to his friends and family that he looked only to doctors for help in curing his diseased feet.

Yet the doctors could not cure him, and his death brought an end to a record-breaking rule of 41 years – the longest reign of any king of Israel or Judah. The people came together to mourn his death, and a massive bonfire was lit in his honour.[127] His reign would be remembered by posterity as a peaceful and righteous rule. Mostly.

Several events happened close on the heels of Asa's death. One was a shock to everybody.

Raddai had already been completely exonerated, but now Ben-hail and his mother received money from King Jehoshaphat that was equivalent to the amount that hard-working Raddai might have been expected to earn in the years since his arrest, had he not been falsely accused by traitors.

This was a pleasant surprise to any who cared, but it was not a shock.

A few days later, however, an event occurred that astonished almost everybody in the kingdom.

That morning, King Jehoshaphat and his armour-bearer went to the king's dungeon. They were guided by the prison supervisor and a guard to a cell on the lowest level, far from the autumn sunlight that shone in the streets above. The dank darkness was unpleasant; the smell intense.

"Open the door," Jehoshaphat instructed the guard who led them.

"Excuse me, sir," said the guard, looking first at his supervisor and then at the king, "there is a standing order for us to be on our guard at this cell, so if the King's Swordsman can make sure he is ready, I will open the door."

Ben-hail eased his short sword from its sheath, then stood beside the king as the guard worked the large key in the lock.

"Good morning, Hanani," called the guard through the door.

Ben-hail glanced in shock at the king, who met his enquiring look with a small smile. "Yes, Ben-hail," he said, "it is Hanani the prophet."

"Still alive, sire?"

"Still alive. And now about to be freed."

The guard opened the door, confirmed that Ben-hail was ready with his sword and stepped into the cell. "No food for you this morning, Hanani. We've got news instead. The king is here to see you."

"King Asa?" asked a shaky voice.

"No, King Jehoshaphat," said the guard.

"My father died four days ago," said Jehoshaphat, stepping into the doorway.

---

[127] 2 Chronicles 16:14

"My lord," said Ben-hail quickly, moving to stand close behind the king. "The guard said to be careful, sir!"

"He said it was an order; he didn't say that it was necessary. I don't believe it is."

"Please, sir."

"Oh, very well. Why is it that *kings* can never have freedom?" Jehoshaphat stepped back, then spoke to the guard. "Bring Hanani the prophet out here."

The guard led out an old man with thin grey hair and a long grey beard. His clothes were ragged and filthy, and he wore no sandals. His eyes were screwed up, seeming to find even the dim light of the torches in the passageway unpleasantly bright.

"I'm sorry, your majesty," said the prison supervisor. "We could have cleaned him up if you had let us know you were coming."

"You are Hanani?" asked the king, looking him up and down.

"Yes," quavered the old man.

"In the name of King Asa, my father, I am setting you free."[128]

"Free? Free to go home?"

"Yes. You are free to go home, but you may like to spend a little time in Jerusalem first, getting used to freedom again."

"But where could I stay?"

"You will stay in one of the chambers in the temple. The Levites there will give you plenty of food and new clothes."

"Thank you, sire."

"All that I ask of you, Hanani, is that you make no effort to spread any criticism or anger against my father. Instead, take this gift of freedom as a last gift from him. Will you do that?"

"I have no more messages from God about King Asa, my lord, so I will have nothing to say about him or against him."

"Good. Ben-hail the son of Raddai will take you to Amariah, the chief priest, who will arrange everything for you. He is expecting you."

"Raddai? My relative, Raddai the Levite?"

"Yes," replied Ben-hail.

"You are his son?"

"Yes."

"How is he?"

"He is dead. He died..." Ben-hail paused and looked helplessly at Jehoshaphat.

---

[128] While this presents a long-awaited pleasant ending for the prophet Hanani, the Bible says nothing about him after he was locked up by King Asa (2 Chronicles 16:7-10).

"...in prison," said Jehoshaphat. "Traitors – false witnesses – reported that he was unfaithful to the king. He has since been publicly declared innocent."

"Poor Raddai. And his young wife... what was her name? Eli-...?"

"Elisheba," finished Ben-hail. "My mother is well, and has recently remarried. The queen mother has also treated her very kindly."

Ben-hail led Hanani into the temple to Amariah the chief priest, before hurrying back to the palace. He would have liked to stay with Hanani, but he felt his responsibility to guard the king very keenly and was anxious to return to him as soon as possible, even though he knew that Jehoshaphat saw no reason to worry about his safety in Jerusalem.

In the days that followed, several others who had suffered from Asa's anger also received aid from the new king.

In all of these generous actions, King Jehoshaphat implied strongly that they represented the dying wishes of his father. The news spread, and it all added a little extra shine to the memory of a righteous king who had not always been able to live up to his own ideals.

☙

"Ben-hail," said Jehoshaphat eighteen months later as he relaxed in his private antechamber next to the throne room, "you'll be interested to hear that Elijah the prophet was seen in the south of Judah three days ago, down near Beersheba. You know how we heard last week about the amazing events that ended the drought in Israel, with fire falling from heaven and slaughtering hundreds of Jezebel's prophets?"[129]

"Yes, it sounded amazing. Maybe even incredible."

"Are you going back to doubting again, Ben-hail?"

"No, sire, but fire coming from heaven hasn't happened for hundreds of years, has it? Why would it happen now?"

"Elijah is a very special prophet. How many prophets can call for a drought like he did? Three and a half years it lasted![130] I'm very glad it didn't affect us much – and that's pretty amazing too! No rain in Israel; no rain in Tyre and Sidon; but plenty of rain in Judah. I find it convincing."

"Yes, sire. I agree."

"But it seems that some of the details of Elijah's victory on Mount Carmel were a bit mixed up. It wasn't the fire that killed Jezebel's prophets: the fire just destroyed the sacrifice and the altar. No, it was the people who were there watching. Yet Ahab didn't stop it at all. Maybe there is hope for him yet."

---

[129] 1 Kings 18:20-46
[130] Luke 4:25; James 5:17

"Yes, sire," smiled Ben-hail. He had heard Jehoshaphat's optimistic hopes about people before. "But why was Elijah in Judah?"

"According to his servant,[131] Jezebel sent him a message threatening to kill him.[132] So Elijah ran away.[133] Apparently he's gone south, somewhere. I hope he's safe. If he wanted to come and live in Judah, he would be welcome."

"A prophet can be an awkward person to have around, sire," said Ben-hail drily, thinking of Hanani and his unwelcome message.

Jehoshaphat looked at him and pursed his lips. "Perhaps you are right. Nevertheless, I think that now is the right time to begin something that I have wanted to do for some time. Elijah has won some sort of victory over Jezebel and her idols, and shown Yahweh to be powerful. It seems the perfect opportunity.

"I want to send teachers throughout Judah. Priests and Levites who can teach God's law, as well as some nobles and advisors to show that the project has my full support.

"The group we are about to meet includes your father-in-law, Nethanel, as well Obadiah, Zechariah and Micaiah, nobles whom you will have seen before in my court and at feasts. They are men who genuinely love Yahweh and his law, and they are just the sort of men I want to lead the task of teaching Judah about God. I want them to travel through all the cities of Judah with some priests and Levites to teach the people.

"I've already spoken to Amariah and Jehoiada, and they have helped me choose the priests and Levites who will do the best possible job. Of course, it won't be a quick job. In fact, it may take a year to travel around all the major towns and some of the villages. I want you to go with them. I don't anticipate any problems with bystanders, but if you are there, no-one will attack my teachers – and some of those thousands of admirers you have may be more willing to listen if they see you there supporting the work, too!"

"But who will look after you, sire?" asked Ben-hail in a concerned voice.

Jehoshaphat laughed. "You don't need to worry about me, Ben-hail. You're my armour-bearer, not my nursemaid. I needed you as my armour-bearer when we visited the cities my father took from Israel, and I'll need you if we ever have to go to war, but your skills are not essential when I'm safe in my own palace. For now, you will be more useful travelling with my teachers."

---

[131] 1 Kings 19:3
[132] 1 Kings 19:1-2
[133] 1 Kings 19:3

"Very well, sire," said Ben-hail, before asking, "And sire, when will we be leaving?"

"In a few weeks, once a small detachment of soldiers has been chosen and the priests and Levites have organised donkeys and carts to carry the scrolls and so on. Why do you ask?"

"Miriam is expecting our baby to be born any day now, and I would like to be with her if possible."

"Ah, yes, I had forgotten. A future King's Swordsman like his father! Good. Well, I doubt that the party will leave for a few weeks, and if the baby still isn't born by then, perhaps you can wait a week or two before joining them. Many of the towns are quite close to Jerusalem, so you should be able to spend the Sabbath here often."

"Thank you, my lord."

Chapter 28

BLESSINGS AND CURSES

"Welcome home, dear," said Miriam.

"You are a sight for tired eyes," answered Ben-hail, smiling down at her before kissing her.

"Is this the end of the travelling teaching?"

"For the moment, yes – though the king hopes to spread the work into Israel as well."

Miriam laughed, "What, teaching Queen Jezebel to worship Yahweh?"

"I'm sure the king will have that at the back of his mind, but first he wants to see what he can do with King Ahab."

"Dadda!" said a voice from the doorway, and a toddler ran into the room, sounding and looking much older than his tender age of one year.

"Jamin, you are such a big boy!" said Ben-hail as he crossed the room, picked up his son and tossed him into the air.

Miriam gasped as he caught the child and said, "Oh, Ben-hail, I should be used to you doing that by now, but it still gives me a shock every time!"

"I've never dropped him yet, my dear. And look, he wants me to do it again." The toddler's face was wreathed in smiles.

"So it seems," Miriam replied, shaking her head and looking away as the grinning child was again thrown skywards and caught deftly, giggling.

The couple walked together into the main room of their elegant home, happily discussing the king's hopes of converting the king of Israel and his chief wife, while Ben-hail indulged their son's love of tumbling. Two servants were preparing the table for the evening meal and Ben-hail greeted each by name.

Ben-hail was still the king's armour-bearer and maintained his fitness, skill and interest in military matters, but Jehoshaphat had long since recognised that his ability extended well beyond these areas. Not only had he included him in the company chosen to travel around Judah teaching the law, he had even appointed him its leader after the original leader, Nethanel, Miriam's father, had been forced to return to Jerusalem to care for his ailing wife.

In that assignment, Ben-hail had shown himself capable of enthusiastically promoting the king's goals in cities, towns and villages across the country. He was also able to maintain the momentum of the project without getting bogged down in particular places, even when the populace begged the teachers to stay longer.

Jehoshaphat had been very pleased to hear that Ben-hail was taking the opportunity to read the Book of the Law himself and become familiar with it. Ben-hail's heritage as a Levite was asserting itself and his relatives were overjoyed to see him walking in the footsteps of his father – and also of Benaiah the son of Jehoiada, that mighty man of faith.

King Jehoshaphat had applied and extended his father's laws that required the removal of idols and Asherah poles, as well as the destruction of the high places where they were worshipped. Under those laws, Ben-hail and his men had reported many idolatrous objects to the king. Ben-hail also reported to the king that there seemed to be a very clear correlation between the amount of idolatry in a town and the flouting of other laws, both religious and civil. Drunks, prostitutes, thieves, blackmailers and other lawbreakers were all much more common in towns with idolatrous high places. Whenever King Jehoshaphat heard of such a town, he summoned the town's elders to Jerusalem for consultations and directed his clean-up teams to visit – with army support.

Yet the king's standards in the towns his father had taken from Israel were more lax. Those towns were permitted to keep their high places for the time being, despite the idolatry and lawlessness that went on there. In this he was again continuing his father's policies, doing his best to avoid alienating the Israelites who lived there and who still identified more with Israel than with Judah.

Ben-hail had enjoyed both the responsibility of leading the group and the opportunity to learn more about God's law. He felt confident that his contribution had been valuable and knew that his basis for making decisions was slowly changing. His father, he thought, would have been pleased.

Yet now the king had called him back to Jerusalem on an important matter. He was to find out the details the next day, but in the meantime, he revelled in his time with Miriam and Jamin. He was enjoying being a father, and having Jamin greet him as he had was a delight.

"Thinking?" asked Miriam.

"Yes, but we should start our meal. Will Jamin eat anything with us?"

"Oh yes, he's always eager to eat any food he can get those teeth of his into."

They began the meal and Miriam reported Jamin's doings in the few days since Ben-hail had last visited, at which time the king had told him to wrap up the teaching expedition immediately and return to Jerusalem for a new assignment.

Little Jamin was growing swiftly, and adding new words to his vocabulary almost every day. Ben-hail ate and relaxed, enjoying the experience his own father had never known. Miriam recognised the look on his face and laid her hand sympathetically on his arm.

"We are very blessed, aren't we?" remarked Miriam. "You know, I hadn't thought about it like this before, but when my father visited yesterday, he mentioned that kings miss out just as your father did. Apparently King Asa saw very little of Jehoshaphat as he was growing up, and now Jehoshaphat hardly ever sees his sons. Imagine that: five sons, and another one on the way, and he rarely meets them. From what I hear, he never gets to sit with them like you're doing now."

"Kings are very busy and most of the training is left up to the mother. The whole kingdom relies on the king for leadership, judgement and so on – and in this case, I don't think that Zeruah wants him to have too much influence over the boys anyway."

"No," said Miriam. "She's not very religious herself, and whatever interest she does have leans far away from Yahweh. I hear that she gives their sons more training about Baal than Yahweh. And she indulges them far too much, particularly Jehoram."

"We all know that Jehoshaphat likes to believe the best about everyone. He thinks that evil people just need more encouragement and support to become good."

"My father says that Jehoshaphat married Zeruah because he was sorry for her, not because he loved her. He says her father was cruel and overbearing, and treated Zeruah more as a display object than a daughter. And since she was particularly good at looking hard-done-by and in need of care, Jehoshaphat was completely deceived. Perhaps I shouldn't criticise the queen, but she's well known for enjoying luxury and indolence."

"Yes, it's a bit frightening really. Jehoram seems to be a mix of his mother and her father, and he's meant to be our next king! Still, he's only ten years old – maybe he'll improve as he grows up."

"You're as optimistic as the king!" said Miriam, smiling.

"King Ahab has sent another letter, your majesty," said Ladan.

"Another letter? That sounds promising."

"Yes, sire. In your original letter, you suggested that Judah and Israel could begin a process aimed at achieving a lasting peace between our two nations. As you know, in his first reply, King Ahab said he would review the idea and hoped to come up with some specific suggestions. Well, this latest letter says he is eager to start the process immediately."

"As you know, Ladan, this matter is important to me. At present we have what you might call a peace by default. We don't want a war with them, and it appears that they don't want one with us either. However, there's very little positive interaction between our nations. I would like to change this and I'm pleased that Ahab may be willing to take steps too."

King Jehoshaphat was sitting in a conference room near the Hall of Judgement with Ladan and several other senior advisors, attended by his armour-bearer and his bodyguard. Peace with Israel was a sensitive matter and the discussions were not for public consumption. Ben-hail was pleased to see that Darda was seated by Ladan's side as his aide.

"King Ahab suggests that we could arrange a series of meetings between his representatives and yours to explore common ground," said Ladan. "Overall, sir, he seems quite keen to move from the current unofficial truce towards a more harmonious relationship with us."

"Good, good. You know that my long-term goal is to unify the two kingdoms again with a son of David as king, but this may take some time. It may not happen in my days. After all, the schism between the two tribes of Judah and Israel's ten has existed for more than 60 years."

"Yes, sire, but remember that the separation began at God's instigation."

"True, but that doesn't mean he intends it to remain forever."

"Agreed," said Ladan.

"Are there any other thoughts about King Ahab's suggestion? I feel that it has merit. In fact, I am eager to pursue a productive peace with Israel."

The king's advisors looked at each other. For some of the older men, the idea of a negotiated peace with Israel was completely unwelcome: Israel had been Judah's enemy all their lives and had been responsible for many atrocities committed against Judah.

"For much of the time since the creation of Judah," said an advisor, "we have been militarily weaker than Israel, but now, sire, you could call on an army of more than a million men to attack Israel. You are in a position of power, sire."

"I don't want to attack them. I want to achieve peace and a national reconciliation."

"Yes, sire. And it is a noble desire, but Israel is full of idolaters...."

"I want religious unity too. The people of Israel are welcome in Yahweh's temple here in Jerusalem. I want them all to learn about the God of Abraham, Isaac and Jacob."

"But we don't want them to bring their idolatry here, sire. King Ahab is bad enough, but Queen Jezebel is even worse."

"So I understand. However, I believe that the power of Yahweh can easily overcome Jezebel and her foolish, foreign ideas. After all, didn't Elijah show Yahweh's power just a year and a half ago? He called down fire from heaven and burned up an offering that had been completely soaked in water, and the altar as well."

Jehoshaphat had made his position very clear. He was king. Advisors were appointed to advise, but in the end, the king must make his own decisions.

Darda showed his growing wisdom by keeping silent. Nevertheless, he did lean across to whisper in Ladan's ear, making a suggestion but leaving it up to Ladan to decide whether to discuss it with the king or not.

After some moments of thought, Ladan leant forward and said to the king, "Following your long-term plan, sire, you have been building up many of the cities in Judah. To convince Ahab that none of this militarisation is aimed at him, it might be worthwhile beginning work on some of those towns in the south that you had planned to leave until later. Towns in the west near the Philistines, and in the east near the Arabians."

"Yes," nodded Jehoshaphat. "That would be a sign of good faith, wouldn't it? Of course, we still control various towns in Ephraim that my father conquered, and I don't intend to give them back, whatever happens. However, we won't do anything there that could be considered threatening. Thank you, Ladan, that is good advice."

"You remember that I introduced young Darda here to you, sire? I understand he's a good friend of your armour-bearer. Well, it was Darda's suggestion."

"Good. I intended Ben-hail to have a part in the negotiations. Wise young Darda can join him."

Jehoshaphat's reign flourished and his fame spread through all the surrounding countries. Neighbouring rulers came to visit him as they had come to visit his ancestor King Solomon. He built fortresses and store cities throughout Judah, and soon he had an army that dwarfed the army his father had had when Zerah the Ethiopian attacked. Judah now had a mobile army of well over a million men, and that didn't include the armed men who were spread through all the cities of Judah, ready to defend against any foe.

Judah was a small kingdom, but its power was becoming immense. King Jehoshaphat was completely convinced that this was the work of Yahweh, the God of Judah, and finally, his armour-bearer agreed.

Ironically, at a time when Judah had possibly its greatest ever swordsman, there was no battle in which his mettle – or his faith – could be tested. Peace reigned in Judah; peace spread beyond its borders in every direction.

The Great Tournaments continued to be held every two years – except for the one after the death of King Asa that had been cancelled in honour of his great achievements, while Jehoshaphat concentrated on recruiting more soldiers.

Ben-hail won victory after victory. At each tournament, he won another Grand Prize and was named once more the King's Swordsman.

Six months after King Jehoshaphat finally forged a peace agreement with King Ahab of Israel, Ben-hail won his third embroidered belt.

A year later, a stubborn man named Hiel of Bethel defied the ancient curse of Joshua and began to rebuild the ruins of Jericho, which had lain for hundreds of years as a stark reminder of God's overwhelming power. He devoted four years to the task, during which time Ben-hail won his fourth and fifth embroidered belts – but Hiel's oldest son Abiram died as he laid the foundations and his youngest son Segub died as he set up the gates, just as the curse had promised.[134]

By this time, Jehoshaphat had seven sons and his oldest son Jehoram had reached the age of 17 – a respectable age for a prince to be married.

Then it was that King Jehoshaphat of Judah and King Ahab of Israel, eager for peace, made a tragic agreement that changed the nation of Judah forever and very nearly brought about its destruction within a generation.

Athaliah was a beautiful young woman – as long as the definition of beauty didn't consider her character. She was a daughter of King Ahab, and she had caused so much trouble in the royal palace that even Jezebel was eager to get rid of her. Jezebel had clearly shown her own brutal nature in killing many prophets of Yahweh and other faithful innocents, but Athaliah seemed to have the capacity to be even worse.

In spite of the rumours, King Jehoshaphat agreed to let Jehoram his son marry Athaliah.[135]

Not weighed down with the burden of a kingdom on his shoulders,

---

[134] 1 Kings 16:34
[135] 2 Chronicles 18:1 in the ESV says that Jehoshaphat made a marriage alliance with Ahab. The KJV and some other translations are more obscure.

Ben-hail was able to build a family that satisfied the king's ideals for families. He was happily married, and he and Miriam had been blessed with two sons and two daughters who knew their father well and admired him more than words could express. They also felt his guiding hand in their lives and learned to value the Law of Yahweh as the king wanted his people to.

Chapter 29

AHAB'S WARS

The wedding was over and Jehoshaphat was already regretting his part in arranging it.[136] He watched King Ahab, sitting at a sumptuously appointed table in his royal robes, eying the newly-married couple with absent-minded benevolence. He must be drunk, thought Jehoshaphat. He had arrived in Jerusalem the day before, bringing his daughter, Athaliah, to solemnise a marriage that brought the royal houses of Israel and Judah together for the first time. The girl's mother was with him too, a beautiful, languorous young woman whose name Jehoshaphat couldn't even remember. It was hard to believe that she was old enough to be the mother of the voluptuous bride, whose revealing robes and painted eyes had shocked many of the nobles of Judah attending the wedding. This was no shy, quiet, retiring bride, thought Jehoshaphat irritably, but a brazen exhibitionist! He glanced at his wife Zeruah and was not surprised to see lurking admiration in her eyes. Trouble would come from this, he was sure, and it would probably spread like a plague through the nobility, and then through the whole nation if he didn't put a stop to it straight away. That would be tomorrow's job.

He looked back at Jehoram, who stood next to his bride, his face unnaturally flushed. He had probably been drinking all day, thought Jehoshaphat, and he hadn't taken his eyes off his bride since she entered the room. The lust in his eyes must be obvious to all! What a son; what a pair. Oh, *why* had he agreed to the marriage? Of course, he had hoped that she would be a good, quiet girl – what a foolish hope for a girl with a father like Ahab and who had grown up in a palace where Jezebel reigned supreme!

And his new daughter-in-law's decisive, determined, self-assured movements didn't look like the dutiful demeanour of the biddable young woman he had hoped for, either. As for her voice... while not exactly *unpleasant*, there was a harshness about it, a note of inflexibility – as if the

---

[136] 2 Kings 8:18 reports the marriage, but does not comment on Jehoshaphat's feelings.

voice had never been used for words of compromise or accommodation.

Yet, perhaps all of this was out of character. She was young. It must be due to nervousness. He must not condemn her too quickly. Surely the atmosphere of Jerusalem, the presence of the temple of Yahweh, and the attitudes of the nation would have a positive effect on her.

CR

"I'm slowing down, my dear," said Ben-hail to Miriam.

"Are you really? I haven't noticed it!"

"Well, I don't have to be very fast when I play with the children. True, Jamin seems quick for his age, but he's only eight years old. No, it's when I meet alert, fit young soldiers that I start to feel slower. Not slow yet, but slower."

"But you won the Grand Prize again just last week. And you're King's Swordsman again – you've added another belt to your collection. That's seven now. Nobody else has ever won so many."

"But during the final, Darda scored a hit against me. That's the first time anyone has scored against me in the final."

"You know that I can't stand watching your bouts, darling. I don't like swords – particularly when people are waving them around near you!"

"They don't just *wave them around*, my love," laughed Ben-hail. "They know what they're doing with a sword."

"Yes, and that's even worse! Anyway, people often tell me that your speed with a sword is incredible. 'Incomparable', dear old Ladan said just last week. And remember, it was Darda you were fighting. He's not only very good with a sword, he's extremely clever as well. If anyone could work out how to touch you, he could."

"I suppose that's true. But even so, I still think I'm slowing down."

"Well, you're not as young as you were when we met – in fact, you've matured into quite a nice man, really," teased Miriam. "But when little Jemima slipped and fell off the step last night, you had taken two steps and caught her, then thrown her up in the air and caught her again before I could even gasp! So if *you* are slow, my dear, I'm not sure what *I* am!"

"You are a perfect wife, darling. By contrast, I saw Athaliah with Prince Jehoram today. They're still acting like a carefree couple with no responsibilities. There was no sign of Ahaziah, their son, and Athaliah is still dressing as if she's trying to seduce every man in Jerusalem."

"Maybe the delightful couple will ask Jehoshaphat to appoint you chief nurserymaid to look after Ahaziah and catch him when *he* falls off steps!"

"No!" said Ben-hail. His face took on a determined look as he continued, "I will never work for Jehoram. Never."

For those who see the hand of God in the events of the world, the contrasting fortunes of Judah and Israel clearly showed God's blessings and curses.

Jehoshaphat followed God and Judah prospered. The army grew ever greater until the number of men at arms exceeded 1,160,000.[137] Judah's neighbours sought peace and offered tribute.[138]

However, in Israel, Ahab and Jezebel served Baal and Israel withered. Confidence failed, and the numbers willing to fight in Ahab's army plummeted. After all, who wants to fight in an army when they have no faith in either their leader or his religion? Ben-hadad, king of Syria, threatened Israel, marching to Samaria with 32 other kings in support, and Ahab tried appeasement.[139] But Ben-hadad would not be appeased, demanding abject submission instead. The elders of Israel advised resistance and the king at last agreed to refuse Ben-hadad's increasing demands – which was exactly what Ben-hadad wanted.

However, in his arrogance, the Syrian king made a foolish mistake. He sent a message to Ahab: "The gods do so to me, and more also, if the dust of Samaria will be enough for handfuls for all the people who follow me."

Occasionally, Ahab did actually admit that Yahweh was the God of Israel, and listen to his words. At this time of terror, God sent a prophet who told Ahab, "Yahweh says, 'Have you seen all this great multitude? Behold, I will deliver it into your hand today. Then you will know that I am Yahweh.' "

The prophet also told him to begin the battle and who should lead the attack.

And it worked: Israel's tiny army defeated Syria.

The prophet then warned that Ben-hadad would rebuild his army and return. Next year Ahab must be ready again.[140]

King Jehoshaphat of Judah rejoiced when he heard the news of Ahab's victory. Surely, he thought, King Ahab would now abandon Jezebel's gods and follow the God who had given him victory! Should he grasp the opportunity to support Ahab and steer him towards righteousness? Should he offer help before the next conflict came? After all, he

---

[137] 2 Chronicles 17:12-19
[138] 2 Chronicles 17:10-11
[139] The incident is described in 1 Kings 20:1-21.
[140] 1 Kings 20:22

didn't want an emboldened Syria on his doorstep, however large his own army was. However, his advisors suggested that he wait. Peace with Israel was one thing, but wholehearted support of their idolatrous king was quite another. Ahab was known as a dedicated worshipper of Baal, and you couldn't blame it *all* on Jezebel!

Grudgingly, Jehoshaphat agreed to wait, and in the following spring, Ben-hadad attacked again as prophesied. If possible, the army he faced was even smaller than it had been the previous year, reduced by deserters who knew that an angry Ben-hadad would be more determined than ever.

Yet Ben-hadad still had not learned his lesson. He said foolish things against Yahweh and God sent another prophet to Ahab who said, "Yahweh says, 'Because the Syrians have said, "Yahweh is a god of the hills, but he is not a god of the valleys," therefore I will deliver this great multitude into your hand, and you shall know that I am Yahweh.'"[141]

Even with people like Ahab, God tries many times.

Once again, Ahab was given victory, and his tiny army killed 100,000 Syrians in the battle.[142] But in the aftermath, Ahab let Ben-hadad and his surviving army leave in peace, and Yahweh was angry. Another prophet was dispatched to tell Ahab that, since he had allowed Ben-hadad to live and freed his army, he, Ahab, would die instead of Ben-hadad, and the army of Israel would die in battle instead of the Syrians.

Ahab went home to his palace and sulked.

Jehoshaphat heard news of the victory and would have sent a message to Ahab had not he and all Judah been busy arranging the biggest and best tournament of all. *This* Great Tournament would live up to its name like no other. It would be a time of great celebration and thanks to God.

He would congratulate Ahab later.

The three years of peace that followed Ahab's second victory over Syria[143] saw two more Great Tournaments in Judah. In the first, Ben-hail entered fewer competitions, and it was clear to everyone that the average skill level was the highest it had ever been. He still won the Grand Prize for overall success, but two young soldiers in their early twenties were not far behind. Ben-hail had already decided that this would be his last serious attempt to win the Grand Prize. He still maintained a remarkable fitness and the outstanding level of skill that had delivered him success

---

[141] 1 Kings 20:23-28
[142] The incident is described in 1 Kings 20:26-43.
[143] 1 Kings 22:1

over many years, but at 36 years old, the achievements that had come so easily for more than 15 years were becoming hard work.

Darda had decided that he was too old to enter the sword fighting competition this time, so Ben-hail met a young, enthusiastic swordsman in the final whose speed of movement closely matched his own. Indeed, his breastplate had been touched an unprecedented three times before his vast experience allowed him make the fifth touch on his opponent's breastplate and bring the bout to an end.

Two months after that Great Tournament came news that cooled any hope Jehoshaphat might have harboured for King Ahab's rehabilitation. As reports had it, Ahab tried to buy a vineyard near his palace so that he could turn it into a vegetable garden. The owner, a man named Naboth, refused to sell the vineyard because it was his family's inheritance which God's law would not allow him to sell. King Ahab went home and sulked, and that was when Jezebel picked up the case. According to the reports – and they seemed to be established facts that nobody denied – Jezebel arranged for Naboth to be set up by false witnesses on a charge of blasphemy. He and his sons were then stoned and Ahab claimed the vineyard as his own.[144]

Jehoshaphat was disgusted by such evil behaviour and, for more than two years, made no more attempts to build any friendship with Ahab. In fact, it was only a fairly frosty peace that remained between the brother-nations by the time the next Great Tournament took place and Ben-hail was named the King's Swordsman for an astonishing ninth time. By this time, Jehoshaphat was fifty years old and no longer making any effort to maintain his own swordsmanship. He had reigned for fifteen peaceful years and the demands on his time never seemed to ease or allow any opportunity for practice. If war ever did come, he rationalised, there were enough soldiers to ensure that he was not needed in the forefront of the battle. Maintaining his skill *just in case* didn't seem worth the effort – particularly when the task had become almost impossible.

Over the three years of peace, the warning of future punishment delivered by God's prophet gradually receded from Ahab's mind. Nevertheless, when Ben-hadad again began to make threatening moves towards Israel, King Ahab hurriedly dispatched a messenger to Jehoshaphat.

King Jehoshaphat was sitting on his royal throne when Darda introduced Ahab's messenger. The letter was delivered and Jehoshaphat broke the seals and unfolded the parchment. After the normal flowery introductions with wishes for Jehoshaphat's long life and so on, the king of Israel got straight to the point. Would King Jehoshaphat, he wrote, be able to come to Samaria on a state visit?[145]

---

[144] 1 Kings 21:1-29; 2 Kings 9:26
[145] Jehoshaphat went to Samaria to visit Ahab (1 Kings 22:2 and 2 Chronicles 18:2) so Ahab

"Interesting," said Jehoshaphat.

The invitation included details about dates, arrangements, expectations and so on. As an invitation from one king to another, it was really quite friendly, and King Jehoshaphat, incurably optimistic as always, wondered if the king of Israel might be opening his mind to the worship of Yahweh. Of course, with Queen Jezebel around, he would need some help. King Jehoshaphat had always been convinced that if Jezebel was dead and gone, King Ahab might have a chance to worship God properly. Maybe he was beginning to assert his authority as king, instead of letting his wife incessantly lead him into evil.

Yes, perhaps this was an opportunity to support Ahab in turning to Yahweh. After all, if *he*, Jehoshaphat, didn't try to help Ahab, who would? The whole nation of Israel worshipped the golden calves and all the other gods of the nations around, so surely he should grasp any opportunity to put in a good word for the worship of Yahweh – whatever some of those priests and other advisors might say. This was an opportunity to talk to Ahab and maybe change his attitude toward Yahweh. And if he could do that, perhaps he could help to save the whole nation of Israel!

"Ben-hail," he said, "I think that we are going to Samaria."

"Yes, sir."

൙

It was strange to be visiting another country, thought Jehoshaphat. There was no army to call on, just his bodyguard who were travelling with him. Judah and Israel had been at war for much of the 75 years since the division between the two kingdoms. Yet here was an opportunity to strengthen bilateral ties and he felt compelled to grasp it. If he could broaden their peaceful interaction then merging the kingdoms again might not be completely impossible – given time. Imagine that, one nation under one king again! Of course, it would have to be a king from the house of David, and that might take a few generations to arrange; the kings of Israel probably wouldn't want to give up their rule immediately. First things first, anyway – and for now, the first thing was to show King Ahab that worshipping Yahweh was the only way to run a kingdom successfully.

King Jehoshaphat had enhanced his bodyguard for the trip. Twenty men was adequate when he had an entire army at his beck and call, but too few when visiting a foreign kingdom, even when they were mighty men with strength, skill and faith. Thus, another 180 men were added to the group, and 200 soldiers accompanied King Jehoshaphat when he

---

probably invited him.

left Jerusalem and travelled north along the highway. Fifty nobles and advisors were also making the journey to provide support and help.

A large contingent of Israelite soldiers was waiting for them at the border, and for a few moments, Jehoshaphat wondered if it were all a plot to assassinate him and conquer Judah. However, the doubts soon passed and he rode confidently up with his men to meet the important officials who were waiting.

"King Jehoshaphat of Judah," announced his herald to the officials as the party stopped. "King Ahab has invited us to Samaria for a conference and bilateral negotiations. The king's bodyguard will remain in attendance throughout the visit as agreed. We seek permission to pass."

The flowery discussions continued, with representatives speaking for other representatives, the formal air seeming to stifle any genuine friendliness. Nevertheless, as agreement had already been negotiated, the delay was only a display of "due process" that soon passed.

As the king waited, he couldn't help comparing his own party with the soldiers sent to meet them. His enlarged bodyguard was dressed in fine uniforms and an ensign displayed the king's coat of arms. They moved with speed and precision and looked well equipped to provide complete security for the king.

Ahab's soldiers, on the other hand, though in much greater numbers, did not instil the same feeling of confidence and competence. Jehoshaphat was glad that the soldiers of Judah were on his side. Their skill, particularly when led by his twenty mighty men, couldn't help but give him confidence. And then there was Ben-hail, who stood at his shoulder looking as fit and strong as ever.

They crossed the border and Ahab's army led the way towards Samaria, tactfully avoiding surrounding the king's party, and thus leaving their rear still, at least symbolically, with nothing between them and the army of Judah.

It wasn't long before the walls of Samaria came in sight, and soon they passed through its massive gates. Nobody could say what the correct protocol should be, since no such meeting between the kings of Judah and Israel had ever happened before. King Ahab was eager to make his visitor welcome and met him in an open square near the gate where a platform had been erected with thrones for himself and King Jehoshaphat.[146] As long as the weather behaved itself, this would allow the citizens of Samaria and visitors from all over Israel to see King Jehoshaphat, his nobles and his famous bodyguard.

This meeting of kings was historic, and goodwill was obvious on both sides.

---

[146] 1 Kings 22:10; 2 Chronicles 18:9

"King Jehoshaphat," said Ahab, "welcome to Samaria and to the kingdom of Israel. We are glad to have you in our kingdom and particularly in our capital."

"King Ahab," said Jehoshaphat, "I greet you in the name of Yahweh, the God of Israel, with greetings from the priests who serve daily in the temple of Yahweh."

"Ah, very well," said Ahab, looking around, possibly to confirm that Jezebel was not present to object to these references to Yahweh as the God of Israel.

"I also bring greetings from Jehoram, your son-in-law, and your daughter Athaliah. They would have liked to come, but are occupied and could not do so."

The fact was that Jehoshaphat had made sure they were occupied and could not come. He had no desire for them to have any contact with either the kingdom of Israel or its king. Not only so, but Jezebel was a powerful character, and Athaliah was bad enough without encouragement! That marriage alliance with Ahab had been a bad piece of misjudgement, he knew, but nothing could be done about it now. He had hoped that Athaliah could be converted to the worship of Yahweh and learn righteousness. The king made a mental note to be careful to avoid that sort of foolish optimism in future. Sadly, Jehoram was not interested in Yahweh himself and was very happy to have a wife for whom righteousness held no attraction whatsoever. Together, they would happily drag each other down to a standard of behaviour equal to the worst found in the northern kingdom. Jehoshaphat worried about it from time to time, concerned about the effect on the kingdom if Jehoram became king without first learning to love righteousness.

"Never mind," said Ahab. "I understand that royalty can often be required to serve the nation instead of choosing their own ways. It can be very difficult, can't it? I find I need to make sure that I have time to myself in my garden; fortunately, I can leave the running of the kingdom to my officials or in the excellent hands of my wife."

"My son Jehoram would agree with you there, I believe."

"Oh, it's the only way to stay sane, I'm firmly convinced – and my wife is as efficient as she is beautiful."

"I don't ever have much time for rest and relaxation except for during Sabbaths and the national feasts. But even then, there are calls on me as king that I can't really hand over to others."

"Sabbaths? Oh dear. I can't imagine my lovely wife taking to Sabbaths very kindly. Aren't they meant to be a day of rest and holiness? Sometimes I think the kingdom really would be a better place if we did that, but it's so limiting, and Jezebel's prophets think more highly of happiness than holiness." Ahab laughed – in truth, it was almost a giggle – and continued, "And their idea of happiness is more and more self-indulgence and immorality. Still, I suppose it's each to his own. Live and let live, I say. We can't force the worship of Yahweh on people who don't want it, can we? Imagine if they forced us to worship their gods: we wouldn't like that, now, would we?"

"In Jerusalem I encourage everyone to keep the Sabbath. I've no doubt that some people ignore my wishes, but I do demand that the city present the outward appearance required by the worship of Yahweh so that people who do want to worship him can do so without trouble. After all, Yahweh is the God of Israel, and the entire nation promised to serve him and to teach their children and descendants to do the same."

"Oh, this all sounds a bit too serious for me, Jehoshaphat. I don't want to be tied down by commitments that my father made. I like freedom – the chance to choose my own path."

"Do your prophets have anything to say about that?"

"Ah, well, there you have a question, and the answer might surprise you. In general, the prophets we have around here are prophets of Baal and Asherah. And even the prophets of Yahweh can be quite accommodating, you know. As far as they are concerned, I can do whatever I want, as long as I make the right offerings and donations to their temples."

King Ahab stepped away to talk to an advisor and King Jehoshaphat shook his head. The conversation wasn't going at all as he had hoped, and he was feeling quite out of place in Samaria. His dedication to Yahweh had always kept him away from the high places where worship did not follow the regulations of God's law. Yet the high places in Judah were nothing compared with what Ahab was presenting to him. King Ahab led a kingdom that had left the law of Moses far behind. Instead, they focussed on the worship of other gods and the satisfaction of every sort of vice.

Looking around the square, Jehoshaphat saw several Asherah poles and idols in front of which worshippers could be seen bowing and scraping. Some of the idols were representations of women in various states of undress, and some of the drunken worshippers who cavorted before them matched them. "What have I done in coming here?" Jehoshaphat asked himself. "It seems at least as bad as the stories I've heard of the cities of Moab and Ammon or the Arameans and Philistines."

The king's armour-bearer, standing immediately behind him as usual, could clearly read his master's thoughts, for he said quietly, "I thought Yahweh told us to destroy this sort of worship, my lord."

"You're right, Ben-hail."

"Is there really any chance of changing their worship so that they worship Yahweh?"

"I don't know. I hope so, but even the people here who say that they are worshipping Yahweh mix it up with all sorts of other religious practices."

"It seems to me the same as joining an army and then fighting for the other side, sir."

"Yes," said Jehoshaphat, smiling; "we wouldn't want anyone to think of anything like that, would we?"

Ben-hail paused for a while, looking thoughtful. "Ah, well, yes sir. You're right. That's just about what I was doing, wasn't it? Then maybe there is a chance of changing people, sire. After all, you managed to change me."

"We'll have to do our best."

"I must say that this feels like being in a completely different country."

"True. And one of the reasons is that Israel has welcomed lots of people from other countries who have brought their own horrible habits here."

"Like the queen, you mean?"

"Well, yes, I suppose so."

At this point, Ahab strolled back towards them and said, "Can we go to my palace now? I have some questions for you and then I hope to make some plans."

"Yes, we can do that. Where can my bodyguard go?"

"I've organised a barracks for them. It's all been cleaned and the priests have blessed it, so there shouldn't be any diseases hanging around. I don't suppose your soldiers will mind the pictures on the walls. After all, soldiers are an earthy lot, I find, whether you try to make them religious or not."

Jehoshaphat called his commander and gave instructions. Most of the soldiers and his advisors would go to the barracks. Jehoshaphat hoped that it wasn't too bad. He would check with them later, and if something had to be done, he would tell them to use as much whitewash as necessary. Ahab's soldiers might not be pleased when they found out, but at least God would be.

Ahab led the way to his palace and Jehoshaphat followed with a few soldiers and his senior advisors. As they entered the palace, Jehoshaphat saw a woman waiting for them with a golden tiara on her head and her face painted with too much makeup. Her dress was of a foreign cut that could never have been described as modest, and her attendants were attired in much the same way. He guessed that this was Queen Jezebel, and this was confirmed when Ahab beckoned to her to follow as they walked into the king's throne room. Jezebel entered after them and Ahab called her to join him on the dais.

Jehoshaphat was invited to sit upon a throne that seemed to be carefully adorned to give a certain measure of honour to visitors who sat upon it, but not too much.

Ahab turned to Jezebel and said, "King Jehoshaphat, this is my queen, Jezebel, the daughter of Ethbaal. She was a princess before she became my queen, and she is famous for her dress sense."

"Queen Jezebel," said Jehoshaphat, graciously, "how long have you enjoyed the opportunity of living in Yahweh's land?"

Jezebel glared at him and Jehoshaphat was glad that he was not one of her husband's subjects. He had heard stories of her brutal methods of disposing of those who tried to serve the God of Israel, and the look in her eye suggested that he would have fared no better than they if she had been able to have her way. He smiled broadly at her and considered needling her further, but decided not to. He wouldn't put it past her to take out her anger on some faithful servant of Yahweh, so it was best to let her alone.

"Jehoshaphat, I have a feast being prepared for you and your men. Even now, my men are killing sheep and oxen that will be cooked to perfection and seasoned with the best spices of Israel and other lands. This evening, you will eat with me and those who sit at my table, and we shall discuss important matters for our two kingdoms."

"King Ahab, I am assuming that the food will all be prepared in accordance with the laws of our God. The meat will be properly drained of blood, won't it?"

"Why, I suppose so, if that is important to you."

"Of course it is. This is what separates us, the sons of Israel, from the nations around us. We follow the laws of Yahweh, while the other nations do what they want and eat whatever disgusting, unclean things they choose."

Jezebel's eyes flashed, but she said nothing. Ahab noticed her irritation and quickly came up with a reason for her to leave the room before her anger got the better of her.

Once she had gone, he responded, "I suppose you are right that Yahweh has required those things of us. But we don't tend to worry too much about them here in Israel. Religion can cause so much trouble, so we try to avoid the difficulties. If people have a conscience about how they eat, we don't worry too much, but they have to realise that they may upset others with their restrictions. In Tyre and Sidon they have few concerns about how food is prepared, or even what food is eaten. Seafood forbidden by Moses' law is very popular there, and most of the time it doesn't cause major problems. And draining the blood from animals is not done at all, unless the blood is being collected for use in certain sorts of delicacies that need it. It seems very wasteful to drain it all out on the ground."

"You can make your own choices, O king, but in Judah, we will follow in the ways of Yahweh our God, eating the food he has blessed and preparing it in the way he has commanded."

"Very well. But it's a pity, all the same."

Jehoshaphat did not respond immediately. Once again, he felt isolated and alone. Surely a king of Israel should understand that God's laws were not just given to stop his people from feasting! He had promised Israel the health and happiness they had not been able to find in Egypt – but it depended on them keeping his laws.

After a lengthy silence, though, Jehoshaphat decided that he must reply, and said, "I am sure that God's laws keep us away from things that make us sick – like the seafood you were referring to. God wants us to be healthy and he knows how to keep us that way."

"Well, you don't need to worry. We will do what you demand," said Ahab, a little irritation sounding in his voice.

"Thank you."

"Now let's talk about international issues. Are you having problems with any of your neighbours?"

"No, not really. The Edomites are our servants. The Moabites and Ammonites are keeping quiet. Even the Philistines are paying us tribute, which, historically, is very unusual. All around we have peace, and the prophets tell me that it is because the kingdom serves Yahweh. We don't serve him perfectly, but we try. What about you in Israel?"

"We are having trouble with the Syrians.[147] You don't have to worry about them much because we're stuck here in the middle, but let me tell you, they are dangerous and difficult neighbours."

"Has it occurred to you that you would have better success if you did your best to serve Yahweh instead of the gods of Jezebel?"

"Oh, come on. God doesn't just give us blessings or curses depending on how good we are! I've got you with this one, Jehoshaphat. I've heard about Job. He was a righteous man – the most righteous man there was, some say – but he suffered terribly; you know, lost all of his money and his family, got horrible boils, and had all sorts of disasters happen to him. So forget that idea."

"I think you should find out a bit more about God rather than just latching on to one story that was trying to teach us a lesson. God does bless righteous people. And God does punish evil people. However, you are right that it's not always as simple as that. Sometimes there are delays

---

[147] 1 Kings 22:3 may suggest that Ahab initiated the trouble.

in both the rewards and the punishments. Do you know the end of Job's story?"

"The end was when he lost everything, wasn't it?"

"No, not by a long way. Didn't you know that Job got better? All of his boils went away and he ended up twice as rich as he had been in the beginning."[148]

"Oh," said Ahab, sounding rather disappointed. "Nobody's ever told me that."

"Well, it's true. Why don't you come to Jerusalem and I can show you the scriptures about Job. And while you are there, you can worship in the temple of Yahweh. You would be welcome there, and your kingdom could benefit greatly. Some of your people already come to the temple regularly, and some have even come to live in Judah so that they can worship Yahweh more freely. Just think what sort of a message it would send if the king himself were to come."

Ahab thought, and the look on his face showed that he didn't like the pictures his thoughts conjured up. Jehoshaphat had no difficulty seeing Jezebel in Ahab's thoughts, and understood that Ahab was too afraid to stand against his wife in such a thing.

"Look, how about we talk about this later? At the moment, I want to talk about the Syrians. I'm sure that they're going to attack me soon and I'd really appreciate some help in fighting them. You've got a massive army now, and you could wipe them out easily. Surely that would be the best way to show our neighbours that Yahweh is a great God! Perhaps you could even convince Jezebel!"

---

[148] Job 42:10-16

Chapter 30

LISTENING TO GOD

"Do you think poor Micaiah will ever be freed?" asked Ben-hail as he walked close behind Jehoshaphat to the king's chariot.

"I don't know," replied Jehoshaphat. "It might depend on what happens today."

"But if Micaiah is a true prophet, Ahab won't ever return in peace, will he? So how will he be freed?"

"That will be up to the new king," said Jehoshaphat as he climbed into his chariot.

"I suppose so." Ben-hail paused and then said, "I'm worried about the battle today, sire."

"Why?"

"Because if King Ahab does get killed, the Israelite army will probably run away, and we don't have many of our soldiers here to protect your majesty. We're a long way from home, here on the east of the Jordan."

"I didn't want to pull out completely after saying that we would join him in the battle. It was quite a clever move to talk to me about Ramoth-gilead. He obviously knew it would be easier to convince me if we were trying to take a Levite city, and a city of refuge. Maybe I should have told Ahab to wait until more of our army could join us."

"Well, you did say that he should ask a prophet of Yahweh first."

"Yes, but when Micaiah gave such mixed messages and King Ahab was obviously willing to listen to his other prophets.... Well, anyway, I thought it would be best if we went along as worshippers of God."

"It looks as if King Ahab is ready to leave camp. Have you got all your armour on properly, sir?"

"Yes, Ben-hail. You insisted on helping me, remember – and I know what I need, anyway. You're meant to be my armour-bearer, not my nursemaid!"

"Sorry, sire."

Ben-hail mounted his horse and followed King Jehoshaphat's chariot closely as the driver picked his way through the crowd to where King Ahab was climbing into his chariot.

"We're almost ready to go and join the infantry, now," called Ahab. "Then, once everyone's ready, we'll start the battle. The Syrians have camped near the city, just off the Kings' Highway. It should be a good day."

"Have you thought any more about Micaiah's warning?" asked Jehoshaphat.

"Not really," replied Ahab. "After all, he's never said anything good about me and I'm still alive, so I ignore him."

"If it's a message from Yahweh, ignoring it won't stop it from coming true."

"Maybe not. Actually, I was wondering if I should disguise myself a bit so that they won't recognise me. Perhaps wear an ordinary helmet instead of this golden one, and put on a plain robe over these ones. That should do it."

"Wearing a disguise won't keep God's word from coming true, either."

"Look, why don't you stop going on about it?" asked Ahab irritably. "After all, I'm the one in danger – *you* don't need to worry about it! You just wear your royal robes as usual. I'm sure the disguise will keep me safe."

"Very well," said Jehoshaphat, slowly. But he shook his head as Ahab strode away to organise his disguise.

An hour later, Ahab's chariot was driven out of camp, closely followed by that of his son Ahaziah and surrounded by many others. Accompanied by Jehoshaphat and his 250 men in chariots and on horseback, they joined the infantry, already congregated on a flat area near the road. Unlike Ahab, Jehoshaphat was dressed in his royal robes – to all appearances the leader of the entire army.

The Syrians stood between Ahab's army and the city, and they were a fearsome sight. As Jehoshaphat surveyed the opposing armies, it was clear that the army of Israel was outnumbered. Had he been more of a pragmatist and less a man of faith, he would have been looking for a way out. Some of his men were more dubious, but courageous enough to rely on his judgement. Ahab's army, however, was full of confidence. Had they not defeated the Syrians on two previous occasions with only a few men? And was not their army much larger this time? Not only so, but the superstitious made much of the presence of Jehoshaphat, a king who had success wherever he turned and had never lost a battle. Ahab's army also contained some true worshippers of Yahweh, and these rejoiced that Jehoshaphat was with them as they fought to regain possession of God's land.

Ben-hadad's army was ready this time around. In fact, Ahab's army was almost caught off guard when their eyes were drawn to the arrival of their king just as Ben-hadad's army began to advance. Trumpets blasted and Ben-hadad's chariots approached Ahab's unprotected infantry. Israel's chariots had to hurry around the infantry's flank to intercept the Syrian chariots that were gradually building to a gallop. Archers from both sides filled the air with arrows that rose gracefully into the air then swooped down on their targets. In the middle of Israel's massed chariots, Ahab was galloping unrecognised into the fray as they moved to intercept the Syrian column, while Jehoshaphat's ornate chariot was close to the rear.

Although Jehoshaphat did not know it, Ben-hadad had given his chariot captains one simple command: go for the king of Israel![149] Thus, as Jehoshaphat's driver rounded the outer flank of the Israelite army and charged towards the attacking army's centre, many of the approaching Syrian chariots began to turn towards him. Through the rising clouds of dust, Ben-hail saw the move and urged his horse on so that he was between the king and the enemy. Others of the king's mighty men saw the danger also and valiantly tried to protect the king, but it was clear that he would have little cover when the chariots of the two armies met.

Ben-hail's horse was a magnificent beast, a gift from Jehoshaphat after his victory in the last Great Tournament, and he rode it as if it were an extension of himself. Twenty other mighty men rode behind him in a wedge, spears held low, to meet the Syrian chariots. Several chariots tried to avoid the oncoming threat and became entangled with each other. Quickly, Ben-hail swung to his left to attack two chariots whose wheels were locked together. His unexpected appearance between them gave no chance for defence, and in moments he swung around again. His companions had veered to the right and Ben-hail was alone until more chariots appeared through the dust. With sword and spear, Ben-hail wreaked havoc on the enemy, but still he was being pushed back, and now Jehoshaphat's chariot was right behind him.

Suddenly four Syrian chariots drove straight at him, determined to get past him and strike the man they believed to be the king of Israel.

Skilfully, Ben-hail guided his horse into the attack, and a chariot driver tumbled from his chariot. But there was too much to do and too little time to do it. He realised in despair that he could not protect the king! He was swinging his horse around desperately to meet the remaining chariots when he heard a shout from King Jehoshaphat.

"Yahweh of armies, save me!"[150]

---

[149] 2 Chronicles 18:30
[150] Jehoshaphat's words are not reported in 2 Chronicles 18:31.

There was no lightning bolt, nor fire from heaven, but Yahweh's answer was immediate. Despite the blinding dust and the deafening noise of battle, calls were heard from several of the Syrian chariot commanders, "Withdraw! Withdraw! That's not Ahab! Withdraw!"

And that was that. The chariots withdrew, regrouping before hunting elsewhere for the king of Israel, and Jehoshaphat was never again in great danger that day. Although the battle went badly for Israel and even the mighty men of Judah had little success, Jehoshaphat and his men were always kept away from the worst of the battle.

❧

Israel tasted utter defeat that day, and many of its soldiers were killed. As the sun set, those who remained alive fled, melting away into the gathering gloom.

Jehoshaphat had also lost many men, and those who survived were forced to fight fiercely to ensure his safe escape. The group hurried southward along the road, glad of the moonlight as darkness fell, and soon caught up with a large contingent of retreating soldiers led by Ahaziah.

"Where is your father?" asked Jehoshaphat.

"My father is dead," answered Ahaziah. "He was hit by a random arrow that somehow found its way through a joint in his armour."[151]

"I'm sad for you," said Jehoshaphat, placing a sympathetic hand on the young man's shoulder. "So he is dead, then, just as Yahweh said."

"Yes. Bad luck, wasn't it?"

"No, not luck. This was Yahweh's work. Can't you see that?"

"I guess people like Micaiah will gloat. Mother will be furious."

"Make sure you don't let her kill him! He is an honest and true prophet of Yahweh. Now that you are king, you should free him."[152]

❧

It was a subdued group of weary soldiers that rode with King Jehoshaphat through the Benjamin Gate into Jerusalem before making their way to the gate of the palace. A man stood there, obviously waiting for them, and moved to meet them as he saw the king approaching. Ben-hail quickly slid off his horse, ready to protect the king if necessary. As he did so, he noted that the man looked slightly familiar.

"What do you want?" Ben-hail asked the man. "The king is tired."

---

[151] 2 Chronicles 18:33
[152] We don't know what happened to Micaiah after he was sent to prison to await the safe return of Ahab which never came (2 Chronicles 18:25-27).

"I have a message for the king that cannot wait, Ben-hail."

"Let him speak," said Jehoshaphat, stopping his chariot.

"Should you help the wicked and love those who hate the Lord?" cried the man. "Because of this, wrath has gone out against you from the Lord."[153]

Ben-hail began to reach for his sword, then stopped. Suddenly he recognised the man as Jehu, the son of Hanani the prophet. He briefly closed his eyes, struck with a sudden fear that history might be about to repeat itself. Would the son of Asa treat the son of Hanani as Asa had treated Hanani?

He need not have worried. Jehoshaphat raised his hand to still his guards. He, too, had recognised Jehu, and Ben-hail guessed that he had been gripped by the same feeling, one almost of irony.

"Jehu, is this... this... condemnation of me the judgement of Yahweh?"

"Yes, but there is more," answered Jehu. "God said, 'Nevertheless, some good is found in you, for you destroyed the Asherahs out of the land, and have set your heart to seek God.' "[154]

Ben-hail saw the mixed sorrow and pleasure on Jehoshaphat's face and felt sorry for him. Yet he also felt proud of this king who could take such blunt criticism without an angry response.

"I had hoped to convince King Ahab to repent and turn to God, but all I did was help him when God had promised to destroy him."

"Don't forget that Yahweh also saved you in the battle, sire," said Ben-hail. "That proves he hasn't rejected you."

"You're right, Ben-hail."

"Sire, God has told you what he likes about your work," said Jehu. "Can you concentrate on doing those things, knowing that he approves?"

"I'll think about it tomorrow," said Jehoshaphat. "At the moment, I'm exhausted."

ରଛ

"Listen to me, men. As your king, I've been travelling around Judah, visiting all the fortified cities and appointing judges who can judge wisely and apply the Law of Yahweh correctly. You have all been chosen as judges for this city and the surrounding towns and villages. Any questions?"

Six older men stood around Jehoshaphat, men carefully chosen from the local area.

---

[153] 2 Chronicles 19:2
[154] 2 Chronicles 19:3

"What happens to the existing judges?" asked one of the men.

"From right now, you replace the previous judges. Some of you were already judges, while others are newly appointed. You six, working together, will now be the judges who sit in the gates and settle disputes."

Another of the newly chosen judges asked, "What happens to the old judges who don't have jobs anymore?"

"I want to change the emphasis of judgement in the kingdom so that it is based clearly on the Law of Yahweh. Some judges have been taking bribes – perverting justice for money. Others have favoured their friends. Still others have made wrong judgements through ignorance. You must be careful in what you do – you're not judging for man but for the Lord. He is with you in giving judgement."[155]

"Do we have authority to pronounce judgement in religious matters?" asked a third man.

"All matters are religious matters: we are one nation under God's law. What exactly do you mean?"

"I mean arguments about the placing of Asherah poles, the sale price of images of Baal, that sort of thing."

"No such idolatry is to be tolerated. Asherah poles have no place in any city in Judah. Images of Baal must not be manufactured or sold. I assume that you all know my armour-bearer, Ben-hail." Everyone nodded. "He is a Levite and knows God's law well." He turned and spoke to Ben-hail. "Remind these men what Moses told us in the law about loving Yahweh and rejecting idolatry."

"Yes, sire," answered Ben-hail. "God said: 'Hear, O Israel: The Lord our God, the Lord is one. You shall love the Lord your God with all your heart and with all your soul and with all your might',[156] and he concluded that section with, 'take care lest you forget the Lord, who brought you out of the land of Egypt, out of the house of slavery. It is the Lord your God you shall fear. Him you shall serve and by his name you shall swear. You shall not go after other gods, the gods of the peoples who are around you, for the Lord your God in your midst is a jealous God, lest the anger of the Lord your God be kindled against you, and he destroy you from off the face of the earth.' "[157]

"Thanks, Ben-hail." Jehoshaphat turned back to the judges and continued, "If you need help in learning more about the law, send to Jerusalem and ask for it. There are many priests and Levites like Ben-hail who are expert in the law and will be happy to come and help you. After all, it would be no laughing matter if my soldiers understood more of the law than my judges!"

---

[155] 2 Chronicles 19:6
[156] Deuteronomy 6:4-5
[157] Deuteronomy 6:12-15

The comment was made jokingly, but the judges took the hint. They must not only know the law, but apply it – even when that meant a significant change to the established order.

"Any support you need for the enforcement of your judgement is available from the troops here or in Jerusalem if necessary. Now then, let the fear of the Lord be upon you. Be careful what you do, for there is no injustice with the Lord our God, or partiality or taking bribes."[158]

Back in Jerusalem, Jehoshaphat appointed additional judges to handle the more difficult cases from all over the kingdom. These were leading priests and Levites or senior members of non-Levite families who could be relied on to give wise judgement for God. He also acknowledged that some circumstances demanded a distinction between civil and religious matters, and appointed Amariah, the chief priest, to be over religious matters and the governor of the house of Judah to be over civil matters.

Jehu's warnings and encouragement had not fallen on deaf ears. Jehoshaphat avoided the pitfall into which his father had fallen and responded to God's admonition, doing his best to extend the worship of Yahweh and the rule of his law in the kingdom of Judah.

"Deal courageously," the king told the judges of Jerusalem, "and may the Lord be with the upright!"[159]

---

[158] 2 Chronicles 19:7
[159] 2 Chronicles 19:11

Chapter 31

SONGS OF VICTORY

Once again it was spring in Judah. The rains had come to an end, and new growth was appearing everywhere. Farmers all over the kingdom were hard at work. Few expected any trouble – why should they with a righteous king sitting on the throne of David, and the nation prospering under God's hand?

True, the Moabites had rebelled against Israel after the death of King Ahab, but by themselves, they were not powerful enough to cause Judah any trouble. None of the part-time soldiers who fought in Judah's army were on duty – they had all been released to perform their daily work or tend their farms.

It came, therefore, as a very nasty surprise when messengers came running from Engedi. They spoke to the guards at the gate, who promptly took the messengers to their captain. He didn't need to hear much of their news to convince him it was news the king needed to hear, so he ran with them to Oded, chief of the Guardsmen Executioners and the Couriers.

Within moments, Oded had sent one message to the chief of the army and another to the king's secretary to request an urgent meeting with the king.

Oded hurried into the throne room as soon as his name was called.

"Something urgent, Oded?" asked Jehoshaphat, with eyebrows lifted.

"Yes, sire. A huge army is within our borders, marching north beside the Salt Sea. Reports say they are at Engedi. Naturally, we are trying to confirm those reports, but I am confident they are correct and felt the king should know immediately."

"Engedi? Why, that's less than two days' march away! How did they get past our border guards?"

"We don't know yet, sire."

"Very well, it doesn't matter now." Jehoshaphat turned and said in a strained voice, "Secretary, call my council immediately."

The reports were officially confirmed within hours, and there were even some estimates of the size of the attacking army. It appeared that Moab had used the quiet of winter to build a confederacy against Judah with the Ammonites, Edom and possibly some Arabian tribes. They had planned a lightning attack that would strike at the very heart of the kingdom before Judah's large and powerful army could be fully mobilised.

The danger was real, and Jehoshaphat was alarmed. Remembering his father's example when faced with the attack by Zerah the Ethiopian and his million men, he set himself to seek Yahweh. Geographically, Judah was small, so when the king proclaimed a fast throughout all Judah, sending mounted riders carrying the message post-haste, everyone heard the news remarkably quickly. All who could were urged to hurry to the temple in Jerusalem, where they would seek help from Yahweh together. And they came in their droves from every city of Judah.

Meanwhile, the king's scouts had reported that, for some reason, the attackers had camped at Engedi! Unexpectedly, Judah had been given the gift of time, and Jehoshaphat saw it as an answer to prayer. Army units were gathering quickly in Jerusalem, and with just a little more time, perhaps the danger could be averted.

"How do you feel now, Ben-hail?" asked Jehoshaphat the next morning, after the chief of the army had reported the number of troops available and expected over the next few days. "Do we wait for more troops or advance to meet the enemy now?"

"You called the people for fasting and prayer, my lord. Thousands have come and the offerings have been prepared."

"So you think I need to talk to the people?"

"The decision is yours, sire," said Ben-hail earnestly, "but the faithful have answered your call. They will welcome a time of prayer and worship."

"I agree." Jehoshaphat drummed his fingers on the arm of his throne for a few moments, then smiled wryly and said, "You know, Ben-hail, you are not the man you were when you first became my armour-bearer."

"No, sir. And it is you who has caused most of the change, both in me and in many of those who have now crowded into Jerusalem."

"Thank you, Ben-hail. My ancestor David started off looking after sheep with four legs, but he said that a king was a shepherd too. And leading my people is my duty from God."

Entering the temple with Ben-hail at his shoulder, Jehoshaphat was encouraged by the large number of people waiting for him, many standing, kneeling or bending in prayer. Suddenly the fear and loneliness that had overwhelmed him when he had first heard of the invasion abated.

He stood among the crowds of his people from Jerusalem and all corners of Judah, those who had hurried to respond to his call. Looking around at the crowd, he saw people young and old, men, women and children, their faces displaying a wide range of emotions. Some showed wide-eyed fear, while others revealed a confidence that helped to strengthen his own faith. All were awaiting his words, to strengthen the weak and support the strong.

He held up his arms and the crowd fell silent. As the early morning sun shone and countless birds flew overhead in a glorious cloudless sky, he gathered his thoughts and prayed aloud, "O Lord, God of our fathers, are you not God in heaven? You rule over all the kingdoms of the nations. In your hand are power and might, so that none is able to withstand you.

"Did you not, our God, drive out the inhabitants of this land before your people Israel, and give it forever to the descendants of Abraham your friend? And we have lived in it and built for you a sanctuary for your name, saying, 'If disaster comes upon us, the sword, judgment, or pestilence, or famine, we will stand before this house and before you – for your name is in this house – and cry out to you in our affliction, and you will hear and save.'

"And now behold, the men of Ammon and Moab and Mount Seir, whom you would not let Israel invade when they came from the land of Egypt, and whom they avoided and did not destroy – behold, they reward us by coming to drive us out of your possession, which you have given us to inherit. O our God, will you not execute judgment on them? For we are powerless against this great horde that is coming against us. We do not know what to do, but our eyes are on you."[160]

Jehoshaphat finished his prayer, his voice echoing through the temple court before dying away. For a few moments, there was silence, then a powerful voice spoke from the middle of the crowd.

"Listen, all Judah and inhabitants of Jerusalem and King Jehoshaphat: Thus says the Lord to you, 'Do not be afraid and do not be dismayed at this great horde, for the battle is not yours but God's. Tomorrow go down against them. Behold, they will come up by the ascent of Ziz. You will find them at the end of the valley, east of the wilderness of Jeruel. You will not need to fight in this battle. Stand firm, hold your position, and see the salvation of the Lord on your behalf, O Judah and Jerusalem.' Do not be afraid and do not be dismayed. Tomorrow go out against them, and the Lord will be with you."[161]

---

[160] 2 Chronicles 20:6-12
[161] 2 Chronicles 20:15-17

"My lord, O king," said Ben-hail, leaning forward excitedly to murmur to Jehoshaphat, "it's my cousin, Jahaziel! I know he's a good man, but I never knew he was a prophet!"[162]

Jehoshaphat was overcome, and the righteous of Judah saw their king bow down before God with his face to the ground. Ben-hail didn't hesitate for a moment, even to consider his king's security – instead, he followed his king in kneeling. Soon, all those in the temple court knelt together in worship before the Lord.

CR

A wise king has many advisors, but sometimes he listens to none of them. That day, many nobles and leaders sought to advise the king, but to no avail. Of course, there were no strident arguments – after all, everyone knew that the king would always be guided by his belief in Yahweh and nothing could change that – but there were gentle attempts to make him see reason! By all means, keep the available army units near Jerusalem until it was time to attack, but to leave them behind and send unarmed, untrained men marching towards an invading horde? It just didn't make sense. Couldn't some of the units from the south march towards Engedi or the Ascent of Ziz?

But Jehoshaphat would not listen. Army units would be allowed to come with him, he said, but only under strict conditions.

The king spent the afternoon in the temple, listening to Levite choirs praising God.

Then he went to bed in good time so that he would be ready to leave early in the morning. After all, they had a long way to travel before they could witness the salvation God had planned for them.

Everyone with faith and enthusiasm rose early in the morning and hurried south towards the wilderness of Tekoa. As they left Jerusalem, Jehoshaphat stood at the gate and encouraged them.

"Believe in the Lord your God," he said, "and you will be established; believe his prophets, and you will succeed."[163]

Once a large throng had departed, King Jehoshaphat and his attendants mounted their horses and hurried after them. Past Bethlehem they rode, finally taking their places opposite Tekoa, with a deep valley between them and the city.

As the crowds on foot arrived, Jehoshaphat consulted with the people and the Levites, choosing singers who could sing to the Lord and

---

[162] This relationship is made up. 2 Chronicles 20:14 tells us that Jahaziel was a Levite of the sons of Asaph, the son of Zechariah, son of Benaiah, son of Jeiel, son of Mattaniah.
[163] 2 Chronicles 20:20

praise him with Psalms and songs. One song the king wanted in particular was so well-known that everyone present would be able to sing
along with the choir as they sang:

"Give thanks to the Lord,
for his steadfast love endures forever."[164]

The army units attending the king – those which had agreed not to
attack except at the king's command – marched behind the singers,
some of them joining in using their shields as drums.

Jehoshaphat led the way, riding along the line of hills high above
the valley towards the old, unattended watchtower that stood above the
wilderness of Jeruel, where the rough-scoured earth fell away rapidly
toward the Salt Sea. After some distance, the path across the hills began
to descend and the narrow valley they were skirting began to widen.

Suddenly, as they passed the lonely watchtower, the voices of the
leading singers began to falter and fall silent. Those behind pressed forward to see, and as more and more saw what lay before them, silence
spread through the astonished crowd.

Lifeless corpses were scattered across the wilderness below. In ones
and twos and larger groups, seemingly endless piles of unmoving clothing filled every crevice and covered every hillock. Thousands of swords
and spears lay where their owners had dropped them, while the hilts of
others protruded from the bodies spread so carelessly around. Brightly-
feathered arrow shafts, embedded in the chests of fallen soldiers, pointed
coldly to the sky. Spears seemed almost to sprout from the wretched
carcases that lay crumpled and silent in the afternoon sunlight.

Nothing moved.

The singers of Judah stood for a time and marvelled at the sight,
while the soldiers behind them still craned their necks to gain a clear
view.

Finally, some of the watchers began to cheer, and soon the whole
company was cheering and shouting.

King Jehoshaphat surveyed the sight in wonder. It was a victory
like none he had ever known. God had delivered them just as he had
promised, without them having to lift a hand in battle. Joy welled up
inside him. He grinned, raised his arms above his head and shouted,
"Hallelujah! Praise the Lord!"

CԐ

Over the next few days, the background to the victory became clearer.
Apparently, as the attackers had made their way up through the wilderness, something had caused the Moabites and Ammonites to attack the

---

[164] 2 Chronicles 20:21

men of Edom, completely wiping them out. Perhaps the groups had followed different valleys as they climbed, and then, meeting each other unexpectedly, had each believed they were fighting the men of Judah. Whatever the cause, once the Moabites and Ammonites had destroyed the men of Edom, they had set on each other until few survived to flee to their homes.

But Jehoshaphat needed no details of the cause. To him, they didn't matter. What mattered was that God had defeated the enemy just as he had promised.

Three days it took to collect the spoil left behind. Goods, clothing and precious things, weapons, food and animals. Each day, the people made their way down through that deep wilderness valley, collecting the spoil and carrying it back up the valley ready to be transported to Jerusalem. Instead of being a time of sudden terror, this unexpected attack had become a time of rejoicing. So many words of praise and blessing filled the mouths of the gatherers that once the work was done, a special celebration was held in the valley, and it was named the Valley of Beracah.[165]

As the people marched back to Jerusalem, songs of joy and praise filled the air once more. Even those who had been doubtful just a few days earlier had to acknowledge God's care and were eager to praise King Jehoshaphat for his faith.

Since the days of Moses, the people of Israel have always kept careful records, and Jehoshaphat's historian recorded these events in great detail. However, his record praised the king a little too much for the king's taste, so he demanded that the extravagant language be tempered and redirected to the praise of God, who had done it all. The historian was a little disappointed – he felt that he had excelled himself in the original prose – but the king must be obeyed.

In the end, he wrote a more balanced piece that satisfied Jehoshaphat:

"Then they returned, every man of Judah and Jerusalem, and Jehoshaphat at their head, returning to Jerusalem with joy, for the Lord had made them rejoice over their enemies. They came to Jerusalem with harps and lyres and trumpets, to the house of the Lord. And the fear of God came on all the kingdoms of the countries when they heard that the Lord had fought against the enemies of Israel. So the realm of Jehoshaphat was quiet, for his God gave him rest all around."[166]

---

[165] Beracah means "blessing" (2 Chronicles 20:25-26).
[166] 2 Chronicles 20:27-30

Chapter 32

BAD COMPANY

"You saw the work of Yahweh yourself, Jehoram," said Jehoshaphat in frustration. "You were there – I made sure you were! You know that God had said we wouldn't have to do any fighting, and we didn't. He did it all."

"It looked to me as if the Moabites and the rest of them did the fighting. They were the ones who killed each other."

"Come on, son, surely you can't claim that it all just happened by chance?"

"Well, why not? After all, if it was a god that did it, couldn't it just as easily have been Baal? Look, if you want to worship Yahweh, that's your choice, but don't expect me to. Solomon the Wise worshipped other gods, didn't he?"

"Yes, and that's why the kingdom was divided!"

"So they say, anyway – though it seems a bit unreasonable to split the kingdom in Rehoboam's time if it was Solomon who did the wrong! But you've got to admit that the kingdom of Israel has been more powerful than Judah for most of the time since the division – and they worship other gods."

The king and his son were standing on the roof of the palace, and Jehoshaphat was experiencing the same irritation he felt every time they discussed religion. Jehoram always avoided answering simple questions and could be relied on to introduce irrelevant side-issues or steer the conversation into areas where he felt more comfortable. Jehoshaphat could not understand how his son was so incapable of basic logic or reasoning! He remembered having had the same feelings about Jehoram as a young lad, but he was sure that seven years of marriage to Athaliah had made things even worse.

Nevertheless, he had called Jehoram to give him some news and mustn't get distracted.

"Jehoram," he said, "I have invited your brother-in-law, King Ahaziah, to visit. It's been a while since his father died and I was wondering if we could help him at all." He didn't mention that his main aim was to convince the young king to turn to Yahweh and lead Israel back to him, using the irrefutable evidence of God's miraculous defeat of the Moabites, Ammonites and Edomites.

❦

"Welcome to the kingdom of Judah, King Ahaziah, and to Jerusalem, the city chosen by Yahweh, the God of Abraham." As Jehoshaphat spoke, he was standing before two thrones in the crowded square between the Benjamin Gate and the temple. Curious onlookers watched as Ahaziah's guards eyed Jehoshaphat's soldiers suspiciously.

"...And here are Prince Jehoram and Princess Athaliah," continued Jehoshaphat, smiling. "They've been looking forward to your visit." It was true: Jehoram had spoken more to his father in the last few days than he had done for years.

The young King Ahaziah smiled at his host – a polite smile – and stepped forward. It was a formal moment, a fleeting opportunity for the visiting monarch to make a favourable impression on Judah's residents.

"Thanks for the gracious invitation, O king." That was spoken loudly for their audience, but then he lowered his voice and ignored the crowd. "Congratulations on your victory over the Moabite hordes. First they rebel against me, then they attack you! I'm glad you were able to put them in their place."

"It wasn't us who did that, it was Yahweh," said Jehoshaphat, seizing the welcome opportunity. "He sent a prophet who told us we'd have no need of an army – we could just march down towards them and see what Yahweh would do. So we marched down into the wilderness and found dead bodies scattered everywhere. It was true: we didn't need to do anything except collect the spoil."

"A-ha. That's nice." Ahaziah turned to his sister Athaliah. "It's good to see you, sis, and you too, Jehoram."

"How's Jezebel your mother?" asked Jehoram. "She's a forceful personality."[167]

"Yes, and full of progressive ideas too," added Athaliah.

"How much do you let her rule the kingdom for you?" asked Jehoshaphat, thinking attack might be the best form of defence against this trio.

This assault stopped the collective admiration for a moment at least, as Ahaziah answered, "She's my mother, not my queen! *I* rule the

---

[167] Taken with 1 Kings 21:25, 1 Kings 22:52 suggests that Jezebel was Ahaziah's mother.

kingdom."

"Good," said Jehoshaphat, drily. "And I hope that *you* can lead the kingdom in wisdom."

"Oh, wisdom..." replied Ahaziah, relaxing again. "My advisors tell me about wisdom and I listen when I want to. But religion is more entertaining – even exciting – the way my mother organises it."

"So religion isn't part of ruling the kingdom?"

Ahaziah's reply was almost haughty. "I worship Baal, and I have appointed my mother as Israel's spiritual leader."

"Were you there when Elijah called down Yahweh's fire from heaven to burn up an offering – and the altar?"

"Oh, that's a nice fairy story! But no, I wasn't there. My mother says it was all a carefully staged performance. I suppose that's why Elijah ran away afterwards: he knew he'd been caught out!"

"But your mother *wasn't even there*!" Jehoshaphat spoke slowly but forcefully, trying to keep his anger under control. "Your father said it was genuine, and he *was* there. Look, I don't want to upset you, young Ahaziah, but Elijah's servant told us exactly why his master ran away: your mother promised to kill him! She sent him a message telling him so." Jehoshaphat stopped and held up his hands, trying to calm the situation a little. "Anyway, I wasn't there on Mount Carmel, but I *was* down near Tekoa last month when Yahweh showed that he can not only predict the future, but control it as well. I *saw* how he defeated the Moabites, the Ammonites and the Edomites. And now I've got a deputy ruling Edom for me. That shows the irresistible power of Yahweh!"

"Well, if you want to talk about gods protecting us, then it's clear Baal has protected me from the Syrians," said Ahaziah. "We lost that battle last year, but Syria hasn't taken over the kingdom."

"That sounds convincing," agreed Jehoram – and to Jehoshaphat's amazement, he appeared to be sincere. How much had Ahaziah paid Syria? wondered Jehoshaphat. Perhaps it was best to change the subject again.

"Let's sit down and talk about your future plans," said Jehoshaphat.

"Yes, good idea. I hear that you plan to build some trading ships."

Jehoshaphat and Ahaziah sat on the thrones, while seats were placed off to one side for Jehoram and Athaliah – who had made it clear that they were not interested in discussing matters of state. Nevertheless, they were still visible to the crowd, and Jehoshaphat noticed that Athaliah was flaunting her charms as usual. What would the woman do once he was no longer around to stop her, he wondered.

"Yes," said Jehoshaphat to Ahaziah, "I have already begun building some ships down in Ezion Geber. I plan to send expert crews to bring back gold and exotic goods that we can trade."

"I'd like to join you. The truth is, I need to refill my treasuries. I had to satisfy the king of Syria, and my mother is a little extravagant in her dedication to religion."

"What sort of involvement were you thinking of?"

"Well, perhaps we could share the cost of building and then provide joint crews and share the profits."

"Hmm. I'd need to think about it and discuss it with my advisors. It might work for building the ships, but as for the crews.... Look, I'll get back to you about it."

"You heard King Ahaziah's request, Ben-hail," said Jehoshaphat, "and my advisors' suggestions. What does my Armed Advisor say? Should I let Ahaziah's sailors man the trading ships we're building?"

"No, sir. God wasn't pleased when we helped King Ahab fight the Syrians, and I'm sure he wouldn't want us to join with Ahaziah's sailors either. A trading journey to Africa takes years, doesn't it? Imagine how much trouble his sailors would cause in that time!"

"Yes," sighed Jehoshaphat, "I'm sure you're right. But I'm still torn. How can he learn to worship Yahweh unless someone convinces him to? And if I don't do it, who will?"

"Maybe nobody can, sire. You tried to change his father but God still killed him. Perhaps Yahweh feels the same about Ahaziah. Maybe he's a hopeless case."

"Perhaps, but..." Jehoshaphat sighed. "Ah, well. I'll tell him that his sailors can't man the ships. He won't like it, but at least he'll be able to share the cost of building them – and take his share of the profits when the men return!"

Ben-hail wanted to tell the king his doubts about the compromise, but he was merely a bodyguard, so he bit his lip.

"That meeting didn't go at all as I expected," said Jehoshaphat to Ben-hail after Ahaziah left to prepare for the banquet. "I thought he just wanted an investment opportunity with these ships, but instead he was eager to provide shipbuilders. Still, I guess those extra skills they've learned from the Phoenicians will be useful."

"Yes, sire," said Ben-hail doubtfully, but Jehoshaphat had already moved on and didn't notice.

"It's obvious that Ahaziah has absolutely no idea about running a kingdom! It's just a bit of a game to him. I wonder how much he leaves to Jezebel? You know, I'm afraid Jehoram would be no better – and *he'd* leave the decisions to Athaliah, which would be just as bad. Perhaps I should get him to start taking over some parts of my job sometime."

Once again, the preoccupied Jehoshaphat didn't notice Ben-hail's look of horror – hurriedly hidden.

$$\text{CR}$$

"It keeps getting worse, Ben-hail. I wish I'd never invited Ahaziah for that visit. He spent most of his time cosying up to Jehoram and Athaliah, and the rest nagging me to let him help build those cursed ships. And now Eliezer[168] says that Yahweh will destroy what we've built!"

"Why not tell Ahaziah you're terminating the agreement? Give him back his money and pay him for his men's work."

"No, I can't break an agreement like that."

"Very well, sire."

"Anyway, Eliezer didn't give me that option. He just said, 'Because you have joined with Ahaziah, the Lord will destroy what you have made.' I don't see any way out."

"At least you didn't let his sailors join ours on the ships."

"True – although I'm sure he'll have another go at changing my mind on that before the ships leave."

"Yes, my lord, I'm sure you're right."

"I suppose we'll just have to wait and see what happens."

"Yes, sire."

$$\text{CR}$$

"Yes, my dear. It happened today," sighed Ben-hail.

"What jobs will he be taking over for the king?" asked Miriam.

"He'll start by looking after the king's household: supplies, provisions, maintenance, refurbishments and so on. Pretty well everything to do with the palace. He's more interested in those things than anything else the king would let him touch."

"I do hope the king won't let him try interfering in religion!"

"Oh, definitely not," Ben-hail reassured her. "At least, not while he's alive!"

"That's a scary thought."

"Isn't it?"

"And the idea of having Athaliah involved too is even more frightening!"

---

[168] Eliezer the son of Dodavahu of Mareshah was a prophet (2 Chronicles 20:35-37).

"Much more – but there's no doubt she'll be involved once Jehoram is truly made king."

"Supervising him, I expect," said Miriam.

"Yes. The king is so disappointed with his son, but there doesn't seem to be anything he can do about it. Aren't we blessed with our oldest son Jamin? He's only fifteen years old, but so mature, cooperative and helpful."

"Yes, a son to be proud of. Like his father. And I'd like to point out that the others are growing up well too."

"I know," laughed Ben-hail. "I wasn't trying to suggest that they weren't. You know, I really respect the king for his work as our king, but I'm sorry for him as a father who doesn't have time for his family."

"What a quandary to be in," said Miriam. "I'm so glad you've been able to spend time with us most of the time."

"I never had a father myself, so I haven't always known how to be one. You know you often had to remind me that I needed to guide my children."

"You've always been a quick learner, so it didn't take much."

"We've been blessed with four wonderful children, and you're the one who has guided them most of the time. They're a pleasure to have around – mostly!"

"I think life is easier for an armour-bearer than for a king," said Miriam contentedly, then looked thoughtful. "At least while there's peace most of the time."

"True. On a different subject, there was another report from Ezion Geber today. The king's ships are progressing well. No problems yet."

"Just wait."

℣

"Bad news, sire. Your ships in Ezion Geber: there was a terrible storm...."

The messenger had interrupted the king's council where Jehoshaphat sat surrounded by his advisors, his son Jehoram and other senior leaders of the kingdom.

"Yes, yes, yes," said Jehoshaphat, sighing. "I expected it."

"Expected it, my lord the king?"

"Yes. Yahweh's prophet told me the ships would be destroyed."

"And bad weather isn't unusual at this time of year," said Jehoram.

Jehoshaphat looked at his son for a few moments but said nothing. Then, turning to the messenger, he asked, "How did it happen?"

"All of the ships were anchored firmly with many anchors. They were also moored to the jetties, but the wind was incredible and the waves were huge. Many of the ropes broke and several anchors slipped."

"Excuse me, sire," said Darda, now one of Jehoshaphat's senior advisors. "May I ask a question?"

"Go ahead," said Jehoshaphat.

"When did this happen?" Darda asked the messenger.

"Two days ago, sir."

"My lord, O king," said Darda to Jehoshaphat, "do you remember what happened on that day last year?"

"No, I... wait, yes, I do know." A look of awe spread across the king's face. "Does God care about anniversaries, Darda?"

"I don't know in this particular case, sire. But we do know that our Passover feast celebrates an anniversary."

"Last year at this very time I was rejoicing and thanking God for saving us from the invading horde of Moabites, Ammonites and Edomites. This year, God has punished me for my joint venture with the king of Israel. Yahweh has judged him bad company. He wants me to keep away from Ahab's evil house."

Jehoram pursed his lips, clearly unhappy with this description of his brother-in-law and his wife's family, but kept silent.

Chapter 33

THE KING'S FRIEND

"I've been the king's armour-bearer for *20 years* now, Miriam."

"You didn't expect that when you first planned to become the King's Swordsman, did you?" Miriam smiled as she spoke. She knew all about Ben-hail's original plan to assassinate King Asa, although they never spoke openly about it.

"No, but I'm wondering if it's time to retire. I'm getting a bit old to be the one who keeps the king safe whatever happens."

"But you've only just won the tournament again. You're still the King's Swordsman! Ten times, and still undefeated in any bout! They call you a freak. But I'd have to say that if you are, you're the most delightful freak ever!"

"Oh, Miriam, my love, don't try to convince me that I'm wrong. I've already told you that I only just won a few of the bouts this time and the final really was touch and go. I was utterly exhausted by the end. It felt like there was a hornet buzzing around in front of me, moving too quickly for me to swat, and waiting patiently for a chance to sting."

"You still won, my dear," she reminded him.

"I know – but only just. I don't know if I could ever get past the first few rounds again, let alone win. No, Miriam, it's time to stop. Time to let the king know that I'm not going to compete any more. And maybe time to stop being the king's armour-bearer too. I've been wondering if I should work as a Levite for a few years, or maybe join Abiel in training young soldiers."

"Talk to the king, then you'll know what he thinks."

"Oh no!" groaned Jehoshaphat. "Here we go again."

The king's secretary had just read out a polite but terse message from King Joram of Israel.[169] He then gave the scroll to Jehoshaphat, who quickly scanned it.

"He says the king of Moab has rebelled." Jehoshaphat frowned. "But it's not as if that's news! It happened when his brother Ahaziah became king after Ahab was killed, and that must be about... what, *two years ago!* Yet now he asks us to help him and requests an immediate answer because he's mobilising his army. Really? How come it's suddenly so urgent?"

Jehoshaphat pursed his lips and stroked his beard. Dealing with the kings of Israel was always a problem, but he mustn't forget his long-term goal: peace and the ultimate re-unification of the two nations.

"I suppose it's another opportunity to help them, and to see if we can convince our brothers in Israel to serve Yahweh instead of Baal. But I don't want to get things wrong again! Secretary, arrange a council meeting for me early this afternoon."

"Yes, sire."

The secretary left the room and Jehoshaphat turned to Ben-hail. "I suppose King Joram needs the tribute money Moab used to pay Ahab. Could Israel defeat Moab? Should I help him?"

"I... ah, my lord, your army commanders know the strength of Moab better than I, and I'm sure the chief priest can give you better advice about helping Ahab's family again."

"I value your advice, Ben-hail. I was teasing when I first started calling you my Armed Advisor, but I haven't been teasing for years. You give me useful advice. Perhaps I need you to learn more about our army. You've been my armour-bearer because of your unparalleled skill with weapons, but now you tell me you're getting too old to be my armour-bearer. Hmm, I haven't used your leadership ability nearly as much as I could have."

"Sire, I think we should be able to march immediately with enough of an army to defeat Moab, as long as Israel's modest army is with us and we can take the units from Edom as well. But surely the biggest question is whether Yahweh will want us to cooperate with Joram, king of Israel."

"Can any prophets answer that question?"

"We can ask the priests and Levites, sir, but most of the prophets seem to be in Israel."

"True. So how do I decide, then? God killed Ahab because of his evil.[170] Then he killed Ahaziah because he ignored Yahweh and asked Baal-zebub the god of Ekron for answers."[171]

---

[169] Ahab's second son to rule Israel had the same name as Jehoshaphat's oldest son and the Bible calls each of them both 'Joram' and 'Jehoram'. This story distinguishes between the two by using 'Jehoram' for Jehoshaphat's son, and 'Joram' for Ahab's son.
[170] 1 Kings 21:17-29; 22:6-28; 2 Chronicles 18:5-27
[171] 2 Kings 1:2-8, 17

Jehoshaphat paused for a moment, looking uncertain. The evidence seemed to suggest that he should avoid any further involvement with Ahab's family. Yet that flew in the face of his conviction that even hardened sinners could be converted by the power of Yahweh if only they were given enough chances. Even Jezebel? he wondered. Grudgingly he had to admit that probably nothing could ever change Jezebel – so maybe Joram was a lost cause too... "But we know that Joram isn't as bad as Ahaziah, or their parents either. After all, he tore down the pillar of Baal that his father made."[172]

"True, but it's not as if he worships Yahweh as he ought, my lord," argued Ben-hail.

"No, but he's already chosen to be different from the others. How can we expect him to keep changing if we refuse to have anything to do with him?"

"Are there any prophets we could ask, sire? I believe that Elijah the prophet said *all* of Ahab's family would be annihilated."[173]

"Yes, but I heard that Elijah has disappeared – gone up to heaven in a whirlwind, or some such."

"A Levite friend of mine said that Elijah's disciple Elisha has taken over his work. There are reports of his miracles everywhere. Perhaps we could send and ask him."

"But that's the nub of the problem. Joram wants an answer now! Will you come with me as my armour-bearer one last time, Ben-hail?"

"Of course, my lord."

ℭℛ

" 'I am as you are, my people as your people, my horses as your horses.' Unfortunately, those words I sent to Joram may prove quite true if we all die of thirst." Jehoshaphat's voice was hoarse and his lips were dry and cracked.

The statement sought no reply and none was expected, but Ben-hail nevertheless answered in a confident voice, "I think we can trust God to look after us, sire. He always has."

Jehoshaphat did his best to smile, truly finding it encouraging when others promoted faith in God themselves instead of always leaving it to him as king.

"Seven days without water," he said. "We knew there wouldn't be much water around, but normally we'd find at least *some* here at this time of year. Uh-oh – it looks as if Joram is coming. We certainly won't get any call from *him* to trust Yahweh!"

---

[172] 2 Kings 3:2-3
[173] 1 Kings 21:20-29

"You said he wasn't so bad, sire."

"No, not compared with Jezebel! But that doesn't mean he's good."

Joram rode up with his armour-bearer and close attendants. He swung his horse around and stopped nearby. "Disaster!" he called out to Jehoshaphat. "Yahweh has called these three kings to give them into the hand of Moab."

"If you're going to blame Yahweh," said Jehoshaphat, "let's at least see if there's a prophet here through whom we can ask his help."

Joram looked enquiringly at his attendants and one of them said, "Elisha the son of Shaphat is here, who poured water on the hands of Elijah."

"I wish we had some of that," laughed Joram, but his throat was dry, and his voice cracked.

Jehoshaphat ignored the comment and said, "The word of Yahweh is with him. Let's go and see him."

Jehoshaphat sent a messenger to call the king of Edom, and together they rode with Joram to see Elisha.

"Why should I talk to you?" the prophet said to Joram. "Go and talk to your parents' prophets."

"No. This is Yahweh's work, not Baal's. Yahweh has brought these three kings together to give us into the hand of Moab."

"I stand before Yahweh of armies, the living God, and if it weren't for Jehoshaphat, king of Judah, I wouldn't even talk to you, Joram. However, bring me a musician."

"A musician? Why?"

"Don't ask questions," said Jehoshaphat. "Just do it."

An army always has musicians, and it didn't take long to find one who was itching to come and play before such an exalted audience. As he took up his position and saw the large crowd gathering, his eyes lit up – although he was disappointed when they made it clear that he was not to sing. Nevertheless, half a performance is better than none, so he sat down and began to strum.

The man truly did have a gift, and the sullen crowd would have enjoyed the music had they not been so thirsty. Elisha sat engrossed until suddenly he stood up and held out his hand towards the musician, signalling to him to stop.

"Thus says Yahweh," called Elisha in a loud voice. He gestured up and down the valley in which the army was stopped as he continued, " 'I will make this dry stream-bed full of pools. You will not see wind or rain, but that stream-bed will be filled with water, so that you shall drink, you, your livestock, and your animals.' "

"Now that would be an amazing miracle," said Joram, and Jehoshaphat couldn't be sure whether he was impressed or merely sarcastic.

"This is a small thing in the sight of Yahweh," continued Elisha. "He will also give the Moabites into your hand, and you shall attack all their best cities, fell every good tree, stop up all springs of water and ruin every good piece of land with stones."

"Praise the Lord," said Jehoshaphat.

Joram looked at him, but didn't respond.

His message complete, Elisha pointedly turned his back on Joram and walked away.

"Thank you, Elisha," called out Jehoshaphat. "Thank you for your guidance and your blessing from Yahweh our God."

A nod of acknowledgement to Jehoshaphat, and then the prophet disappeared in the crowd. The musician looked disappointed: his chance to perform was slipping away.

"Well, there you go!" said Joram, shaking his head. "I suppose he expects us to just keep waiting patiently for a drink! Another night of thirst. And what do we do if this water doesn't come?"

"It will come," said Jehoshaphat, confidently. "So why don't you move your men up out of the way a bit? Otherwise they might get drowned, and then they wouldn't be able to help us cut down the trees or toss rocks on all the good land."

ℭℛ

When the army of Judah returned to Jerusalem, they did so with mixed emotions. The water had come on cue and the battle was won – just as Elisha predicted. Moab was punished, their cities pillaged and destroyed, the trees cut down and the land spread with stones. Yet at the very end, the king of Edom, vassal to Jehoshaphat and ruling under the control of a deputy, had lost his son – captured and offered as an idolatrous sacrifice by the Moabites on the wall of Kir-hareseth.[174] The invasion ended in confusion, as the attackers withdrew leaving the Moabites to lick their national wounds.

ℭℛ

"Ben-hail, you have been completely trustworthy as my armour-bearer, and also as my companion and unofficial advisor, over many years. But I want to ask you a private question while I'm sure no-one can hear. Can I?"

"Yes, my lord, of course."

"I have never forgotten our first meeting. I visited Abiel's Academy

---

[174] 2 Kings 3:26-27 does not make it completely clear whose son was killed and by whom. When taken in conjunction with Amos 2:1, this is one possible explanation.

and he had you demonstrate your prowess with the sword. Then he suggested that I should take a turn against you with a sword to really understand how great your skill was. Do you remember that?"

"Yes, sire," said Ben-hail, cautiously, "I do."

"If I had taken up his suggestion, would you have killed me?"

"Oh, my lord, please don't suggest it! I..., I.... Yes, I would have tried to do so." Ben-hail fell on his knees before Jehoshaphat and looked up at the king. "I have been so very thankful so many times since then that you didn't give me the opportunity!"

"You hid it completely at the time, and you've never mentioned it since. I was a little cautious with you at the start, just in case you knew about our treatment of your father and were looking for vengeance. But you quickly convinced me that you were loyal, and after that I didn't worry anymore. It was not until I saw how you toyed with various swordsmen much better than I had ever been, to become the King's Swordsman for the second time, that it suddenly occurred to me that you might have thought to kill me that day."

Ben-hail looked down at the floor and said with difficulty, "My lord, O king, I was wrong. *All* of my plans at that time were wrong. You showed great mercy to me, and through your example you made my life worth living. Without you as my king, my life would have been completely different – terribly different. You changed everything. Please forgive me."

"Stand up, Ben-hail. I forgive you. You and several others had been treated very badly. I was glad to be able to help."

"Sire, your ancestor, the great King David, said that a king must be a shepherd of God's people. I was a lost sheep and you looked after me. You suspected what I was like, but you thought you could change me. And you did, sire."

"I didn't change you. You changed yourself – with God's help."

"With *your* help mostly, my lord. I doubted God and *you* showed me he was real. I doubted kings and you showed me that a king can serve his people by serving Yahweh."

Jehoshaphat laughed. "You're presenting me as a paragon. But you know how often God has sent prophets to correct me."

"Yes, my lord, I do – but I also know that whenever God has sent his prophets to you, you have listened. And you've asked for the words of prophets many times so that you could follow Yahweh's leadership."

"I suppose that's true. If only I could convince my son Jehoram to do the same! I've done my best, but he's already hardened in evil, and Athaliah is no help. When I am gone, where will they lead the kingdom?"

"Surely God will stop them from destroying the kingdom, sire? After all, he promised King David a son, the Messiah, who will reign *forever* in righteousness."

"You're right, but Yahweh also warned that there would be consequences if David's descendants didn't serve him. I can't tell the future, but I hope that God will keep Jehoram from doing too much damage. I made him joint king with me in the hope that he could get into the habit of ruling in a way that I was happy with, but I don't think it's working. He longs to throw off all restraint, and I fear that he will do so as soon as he can. I fear for my kingdom."

"I'm sure that God will send the Messiah soon. You will be his ancestor, my lord, another righteous king in the line of David – a king whom I admire. I have been glad to serve you and I hope to keep serving you for many years. But I am getting too old to work properly as your armour-bearer. You need a dedicated young man who can look after you better. But I will continue to serve you and Yahweh your God in whatever way you want me to."

"Ben-hail, you have been loyal and faithful in everything. Not only are you the king's armour-bearer, you are also the king's friend. I've been mulling over this problem since you first mentioned it, and I believe I have the solution that will be best for everyone. It's a solution I believe you used to dream about, too – when you weren't thinking of assassinating me! Oded is looking to retire: will you take over command of the Guardsmen Executioners and the Couriers?"

"Yes, sir!"

About the author

Mark Morgan was born in Australia during 1963; the youngest son of Peter and Meryl Morgan. Deeply involved in religion all of his life, he has worked as a lay preacher, Sunday School teacher and missionary – trying to balance the many demands of spiritual life with those of family and paid employment.

After graduating, he worked in engineering for several years before concentrating on software development. Happily married and blessed with eight children, he has spent many years reading the Bible and learning to teach its lessons.

Writing Bible-based novels now fills much of his time.

Free Download

Paul in Snippets

A 109-page PDF novelette by Mark Morgan.

The life of Paul painted from the Acts of the Apostles.

Get your free copy of *Paul in Snippets* when you sign up for the Bible Tales mailing list. As well as the eBook, you will receive a weekly email newsletter with micro tales, informative articles and special offers.

Visit **https://www.BibleTales.online/free-pins**

Bible Tales Online

Other books are available from Bible Tales Online.

Terror on Every Side!
THE LIFE OF JEREMIAH by Mark Morgan

From a family of priests in the peaceful reign of good King Josiah, came a young man Jeremiah, bringing words from God to his people. It was no message for the faint-hearted, either. It was a message of *Terror on Every Side!*

Volume 1 – Early Days
Volume 2 – As Good As It Gets
Volume 3 – Darkness Falling
Volume 4 – The Darkness Deepens
Volume 5 – No Remedy

Available in hardcover, paperback, eBook and audio-book.

Volume 6 – That Broken Reed, recounting Jeremiah's time in Egypt, is planned for Q2/Q3 2022.

Micro-tales

Collections of short stories about Bible characters or events, available in paperback, eBook and audiobook.

Fiction Favours the Facts
Fiction Favours the Facts – Book 2
Fiction Favours the Facts – Book 3
by Mark Morgan and others

Other novels

***Joseph, Rachel's son* by Mark Morgan**

Bible Tales Online continues to publish books.
To find the list of currently available books, visit

https://www.BibleTales.online/books

Bible
Tales
www.BibleTales.online